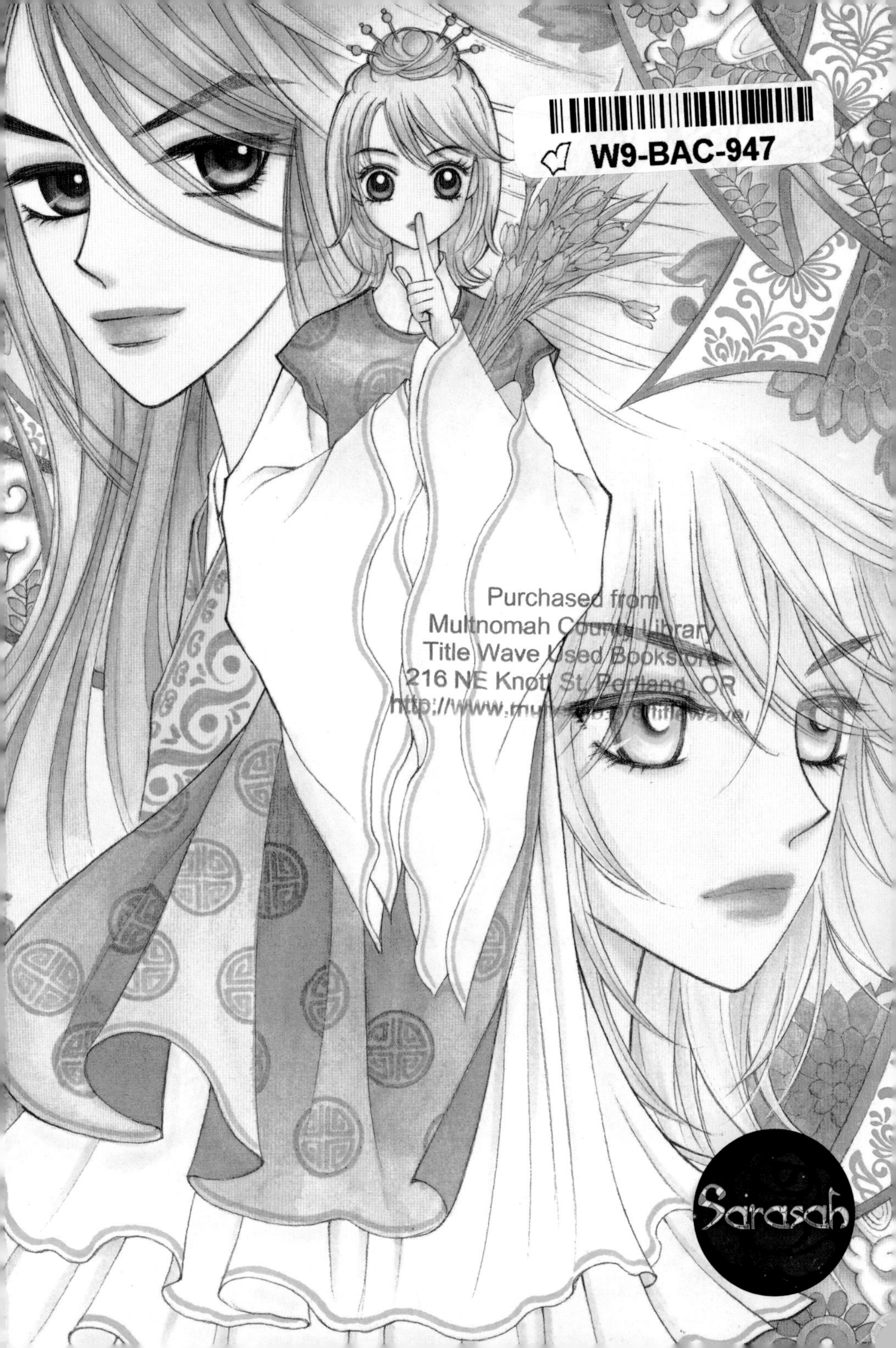
Sarasah

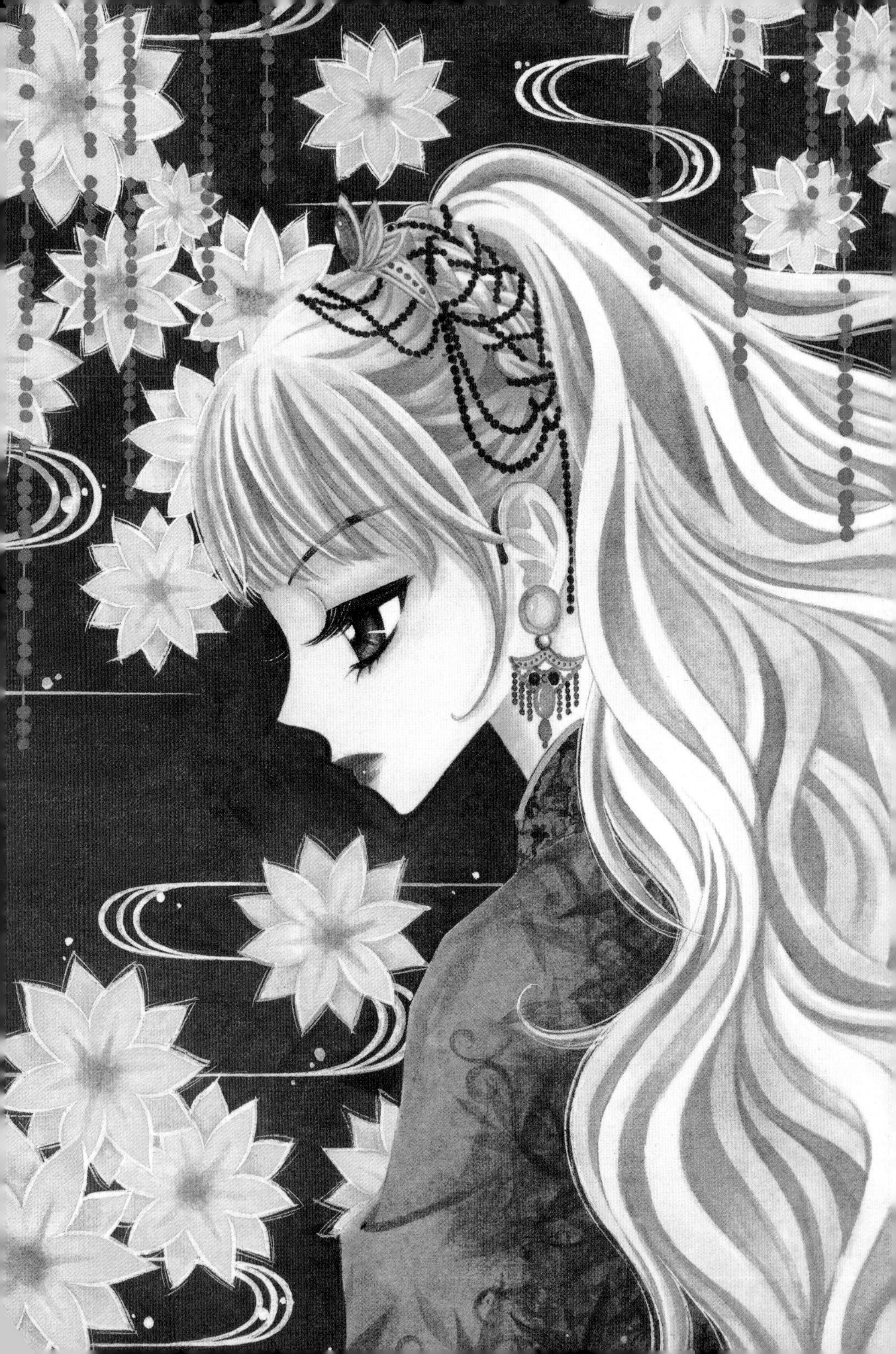

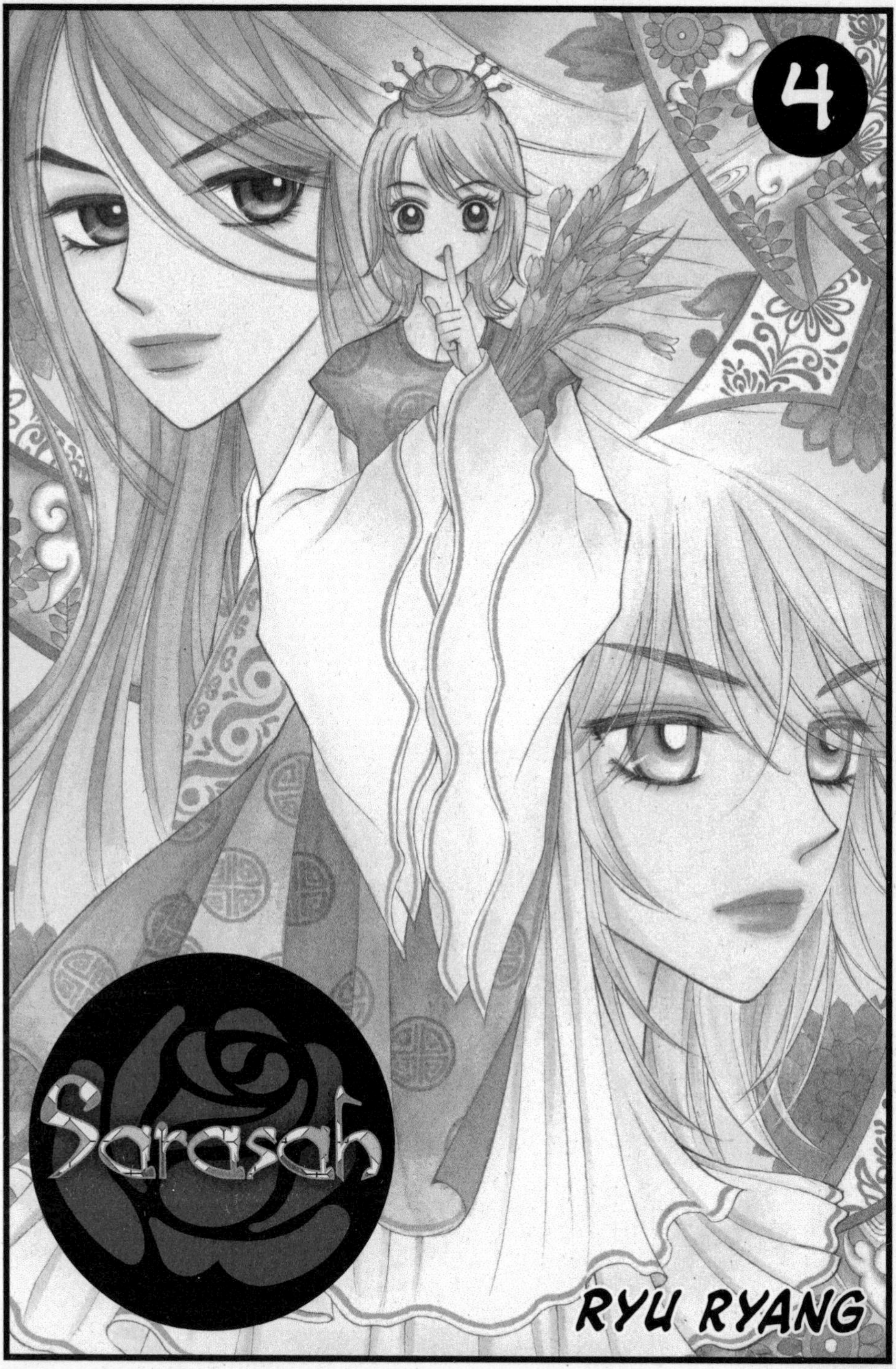
4
Sarasah
RYU RYANG

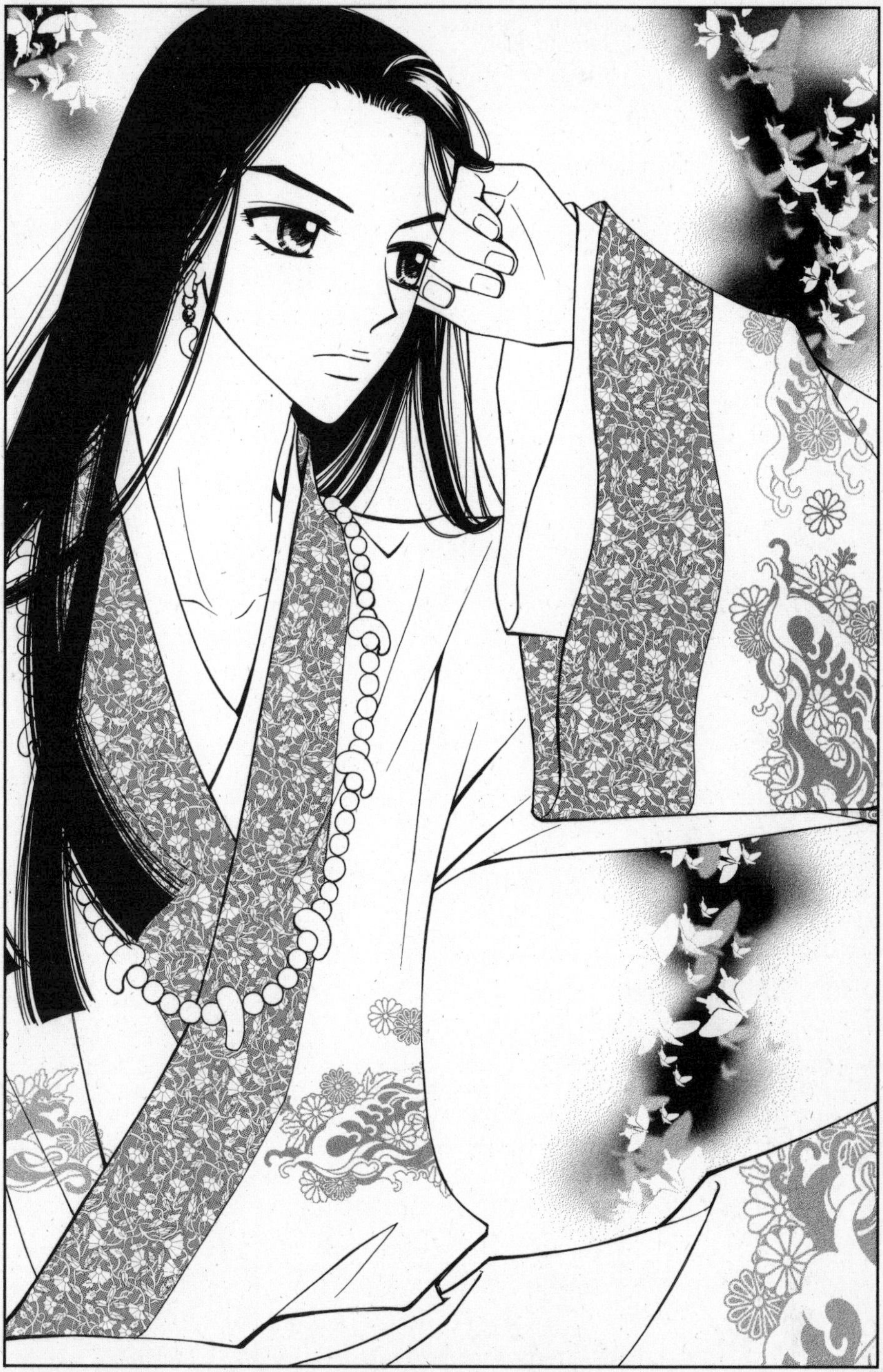

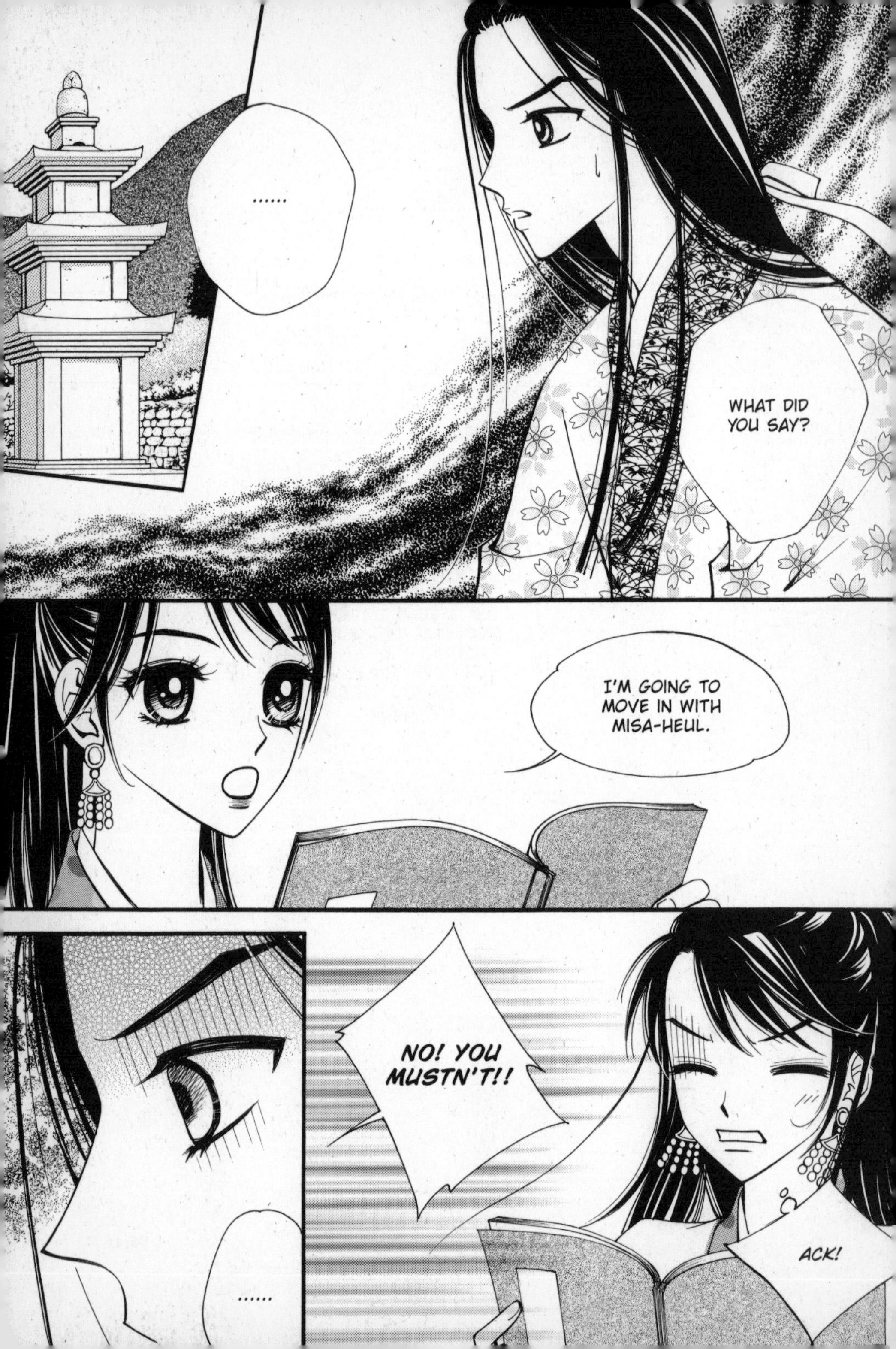
......
WHAT DID YOU SAY?
I'M GOING TO MOVE IN WITH MISA-HEUL.
......
NO! YOU MUSTN'T!!
ACK!

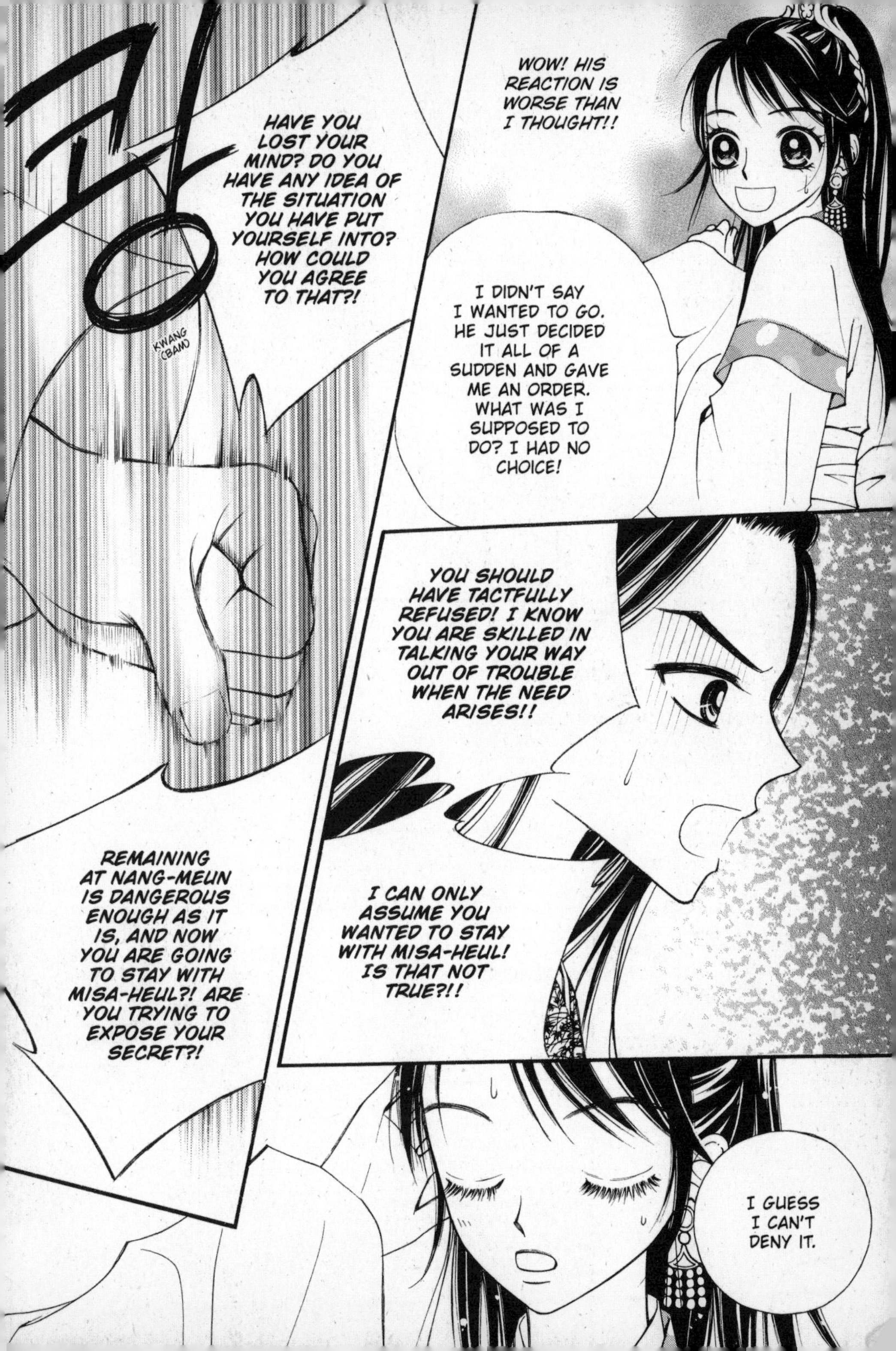
HAVE YOU LOST YOUR MIND? DO YOU HAVE ANY IDEA OF THE SITUATION YOU HAVE PUT YOURSELF INTO? HOW COULD YOU AGREE TO THAT?!
KWANG (BAM)
REMAINING AT NANG-MEUN IS DANGEROUS ENOUGH AS IT IS, AND NOW YOU ARE GOING TO STAY WITH MISA-HEUL?! ARE YOU TRYING TO EXPOSE YOUR SECRET?!
WOW! HIS REACTION IS WORSE THAN I THOUGHT!!
I DIDN'T SAY I WANTED TO GO. HE JUST DECIDED IT ALL OF A SUDDEN AND GAVE ME AN ORDER. WHAT WAS I SUPPOSED TO DO? I HAD NO CHOICE!
YOU SHOULD HAVE TACTFULLY REFUSED! I KNOW YOU ARE SKILLED IN TALKING YOUR WAY OUT OF TROUBLE WHEN THE NEED ARISES!!
I CAN ONLY ASSUME YOU WANTED TO STAY WITH MISA-HEUL! IS THAT NOT TRUE?!!
I GUESS I CAN'T DENY IT.

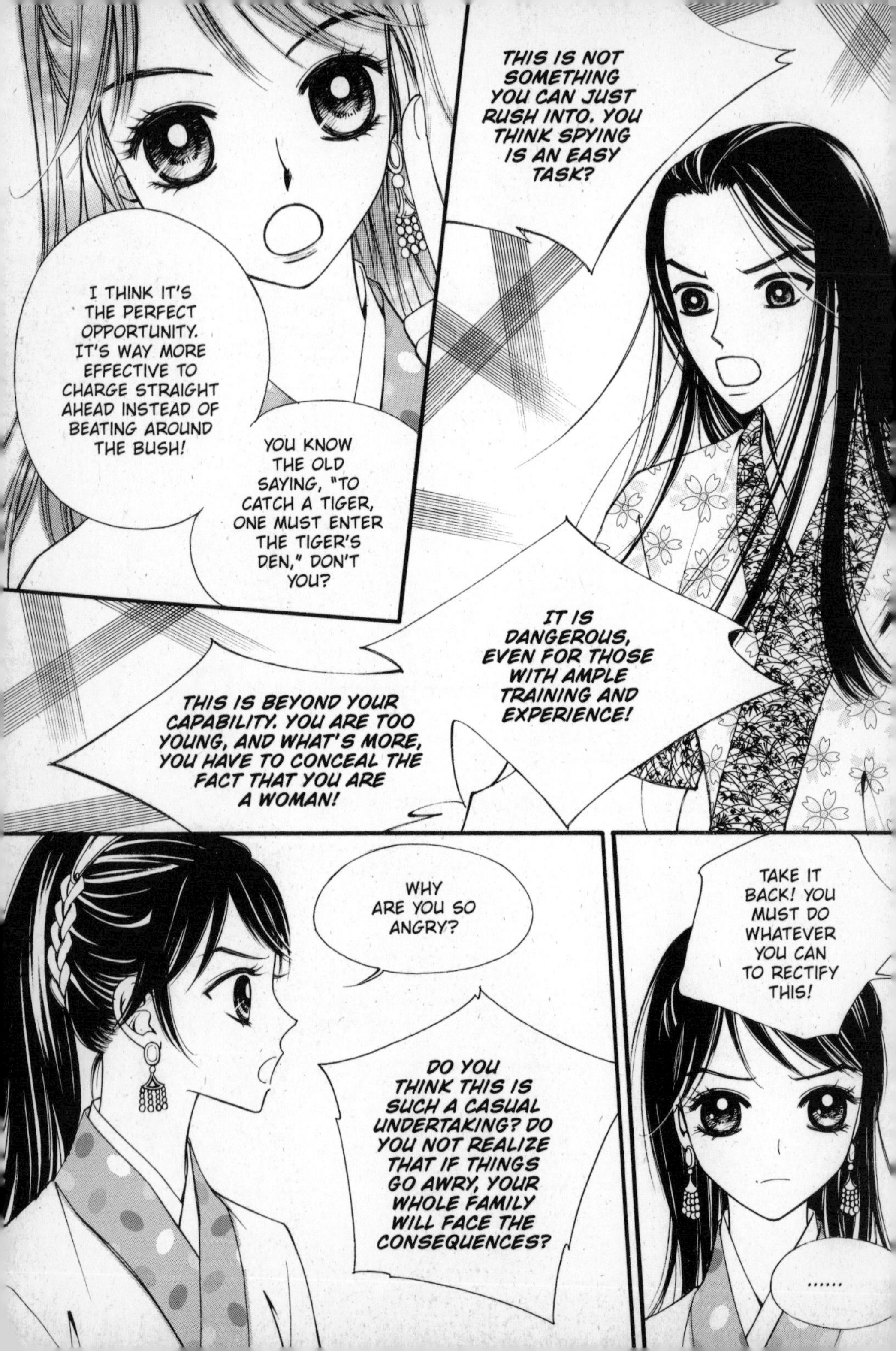

I THINK IT'S THE PERFECT OPPORTUNITY. IT'S WAY MORE EFFECTIVE TO CHARGE STRAIGHT AHEAD INSTEAD OF BEATING AROUND THE BUSH!
YOU KNOW THE OLD SAYING, "TO CATCH A TIGER, ONE MUST ENTER THE TIGER'S DEN," DON'T YOU?
THIS IS NOT SOMETHING YOU CAN JUST RUSH INTO. YOU THINK SPYING IS AN EASY TASK?
IT IS DANGEROUS, EVEN FOR THOSE WITH AMPLE TRAINING AND EXPERIENCE!
THIS IS BEYOND YOUR CAPABILITY. YOU ARE TOO YOUNG, AND WHAT'S MORE, YOU HAVE TO CONCEAL THE FACT THAT YOU ARE A WOMAN!
WHY ARE YOU SO ANGRY?
DO YOU THINK THIS IS SUCH A CASUAL UNDERTAKING? DO YOU NOT REALIZE THAT IF THINGS GO AWRY, YOUR WHOLE FAMILY WILL FACE THE CONSEQUENCES?
TAKE IT BACK! YOU MUST DO WHATEVER YOU CAN TO RECTIFY THIS!
......

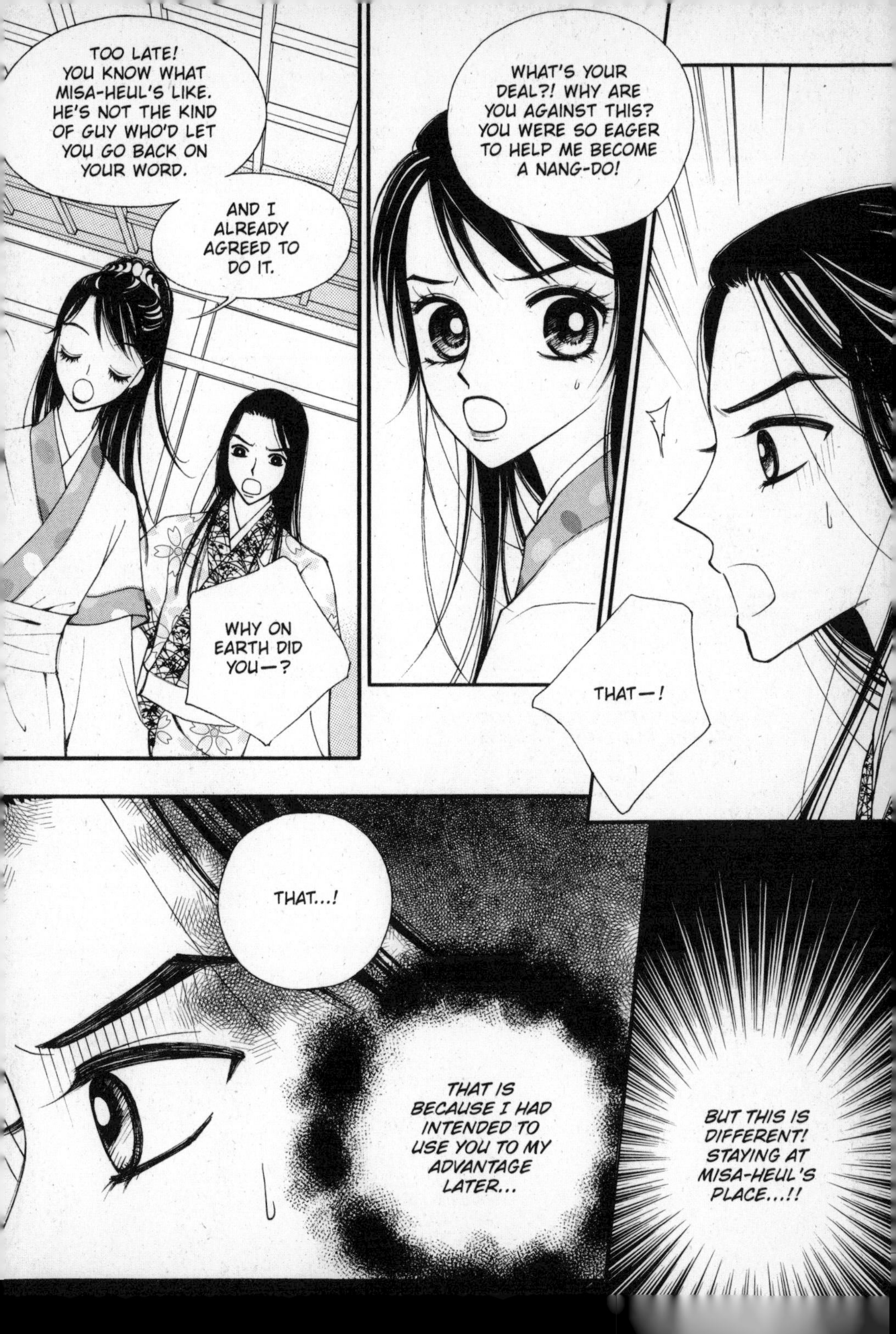
TOO LATE! YOU KNOW WHAT MISA-HEUL'S LIKE. HE'S NOT THE KIND OF GUY WHO'D LET YOU GO BACK ON YOUR WORD.
AND I ALREADY AGREED TO DO IT.
WHY ON EARTH DID YOU—?
WHAT'S YOUR DEAL?! WHY ARE YOU AGAINST THIS? YOU WERE SO EAGER TO HELP ME BECOME A NANG-DO!
THAT—!
THAT...!
THAT IS BECAUSE I HAD INTENDED TO USE YOU TO MY ADVANTAGE LATER...
BUT THIS IS DIFFERENT! STAYING AT MISA-HEUL'S PLACE...!!

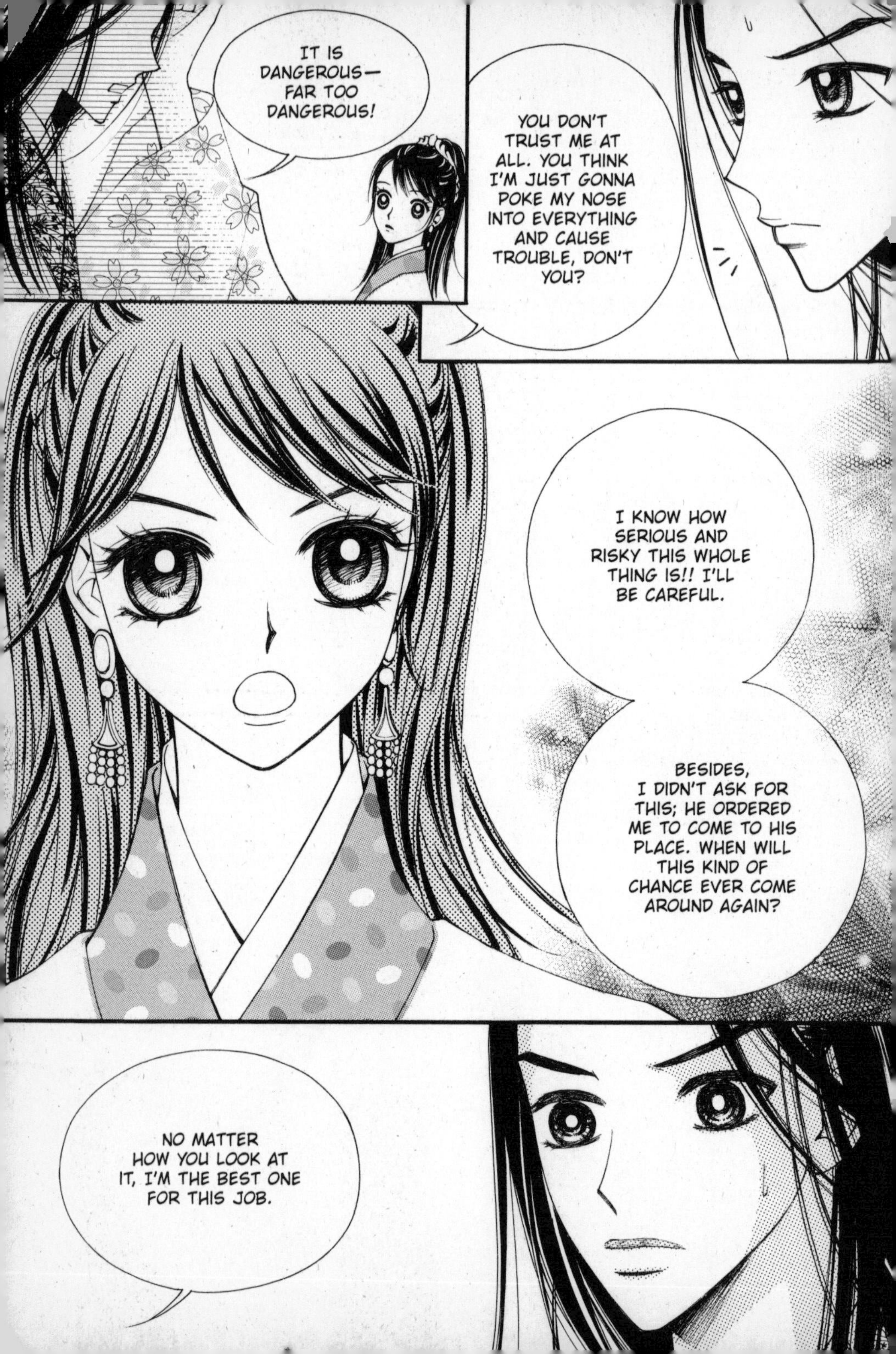
IT IS DANGEROUS—FAR TOO DANGEROUS!
YOU DON'T TRUST ME AT ALL. YOU THINK I'M JUST GONNA POKE MY NOSE INTO EVERYTHING AND CAUSE TROUBLE, DON'T YOU?
I KNOW HOW SERIOUS AND RISKY THIS WHOLE THING IS!! I'LL BE CAREFUL.
BESIDES, I DIDN'T ASK FOR THIS; HE ORDERED ME TO COME TO HIS PLACE. WHEN WILL THIS KIND OF CHANCE EVER COME AROUND AGAIN?
NO MATTER HOW YOU LOOK AT IT, I'M THE BEST ONE FOR THIS JOB.

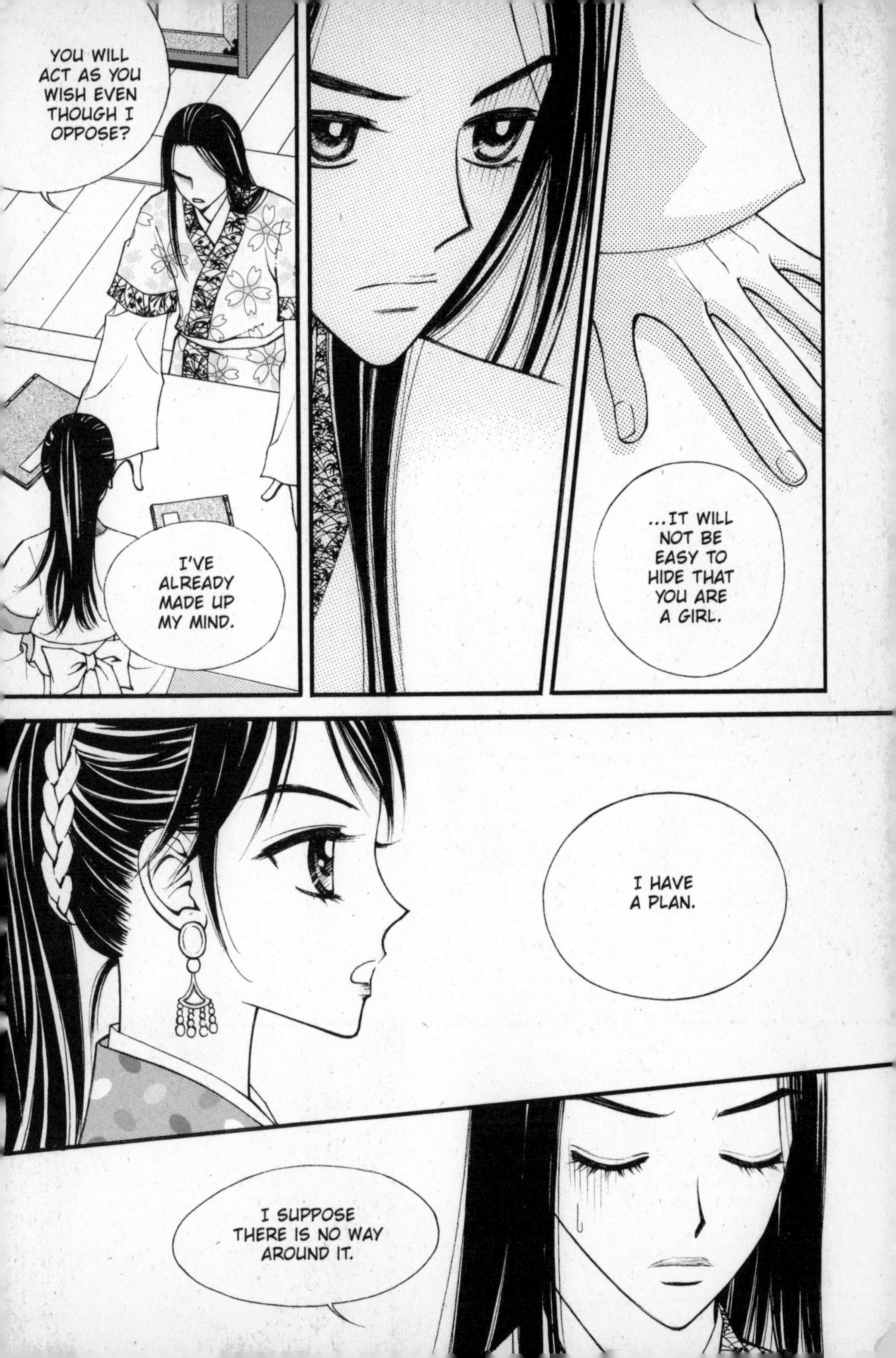
YOU WILL ACT AS YOU WISH EVEN THOUGH I OPPOSE?
I'VE ALREADY MADE UP MY MIND.
...IT WILL NOT BE EASY TO HIDE THAT YOU ARE A GIRL.
I HAVE A PLAN.
I SUPPOSE THERE IS NO WAY AROUND IT.

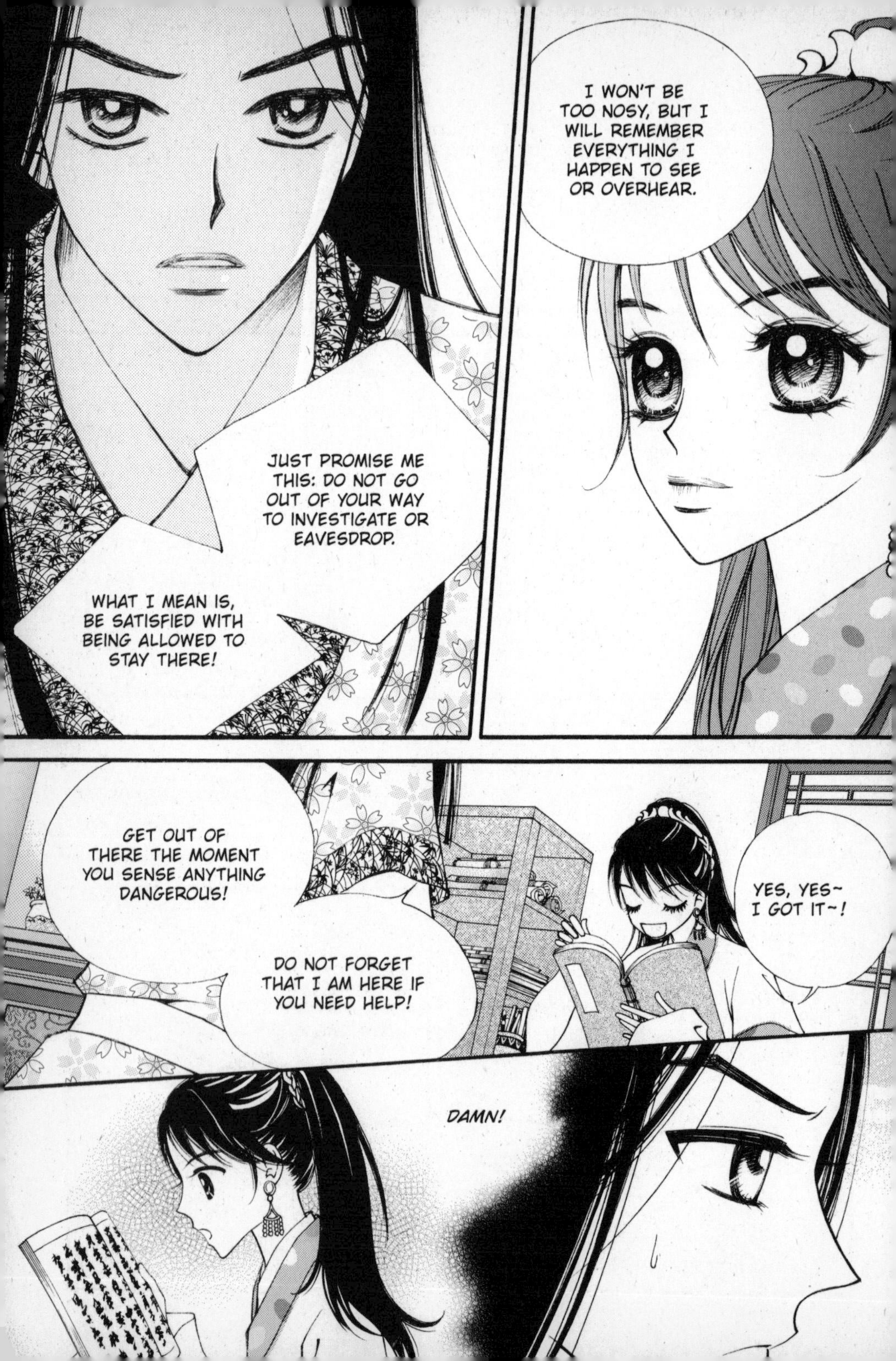
JUST PROMISE ME THIS: DO NOT GO OUT OF YOUR WAY TO INVESTIGATE OR EAVESDROP.
WHAT I MEAN IS, BE SATISFIED WITH BEING ALLOWED TO STAY THERE!
I WON'T BE TOO NOSY, BUT I WILL REMEMBER EVERYTHING I HAPPEN TO SEE OR OVERHEAR.
GET OUT OF THERE THE MOMENT YOU SENSE ANYTHING DANGEROUS!
DO NOT FORGET THAT I AM HERE IF YOU NEED HELP!
YES, YES~ I GOT IT~!
DAMN!

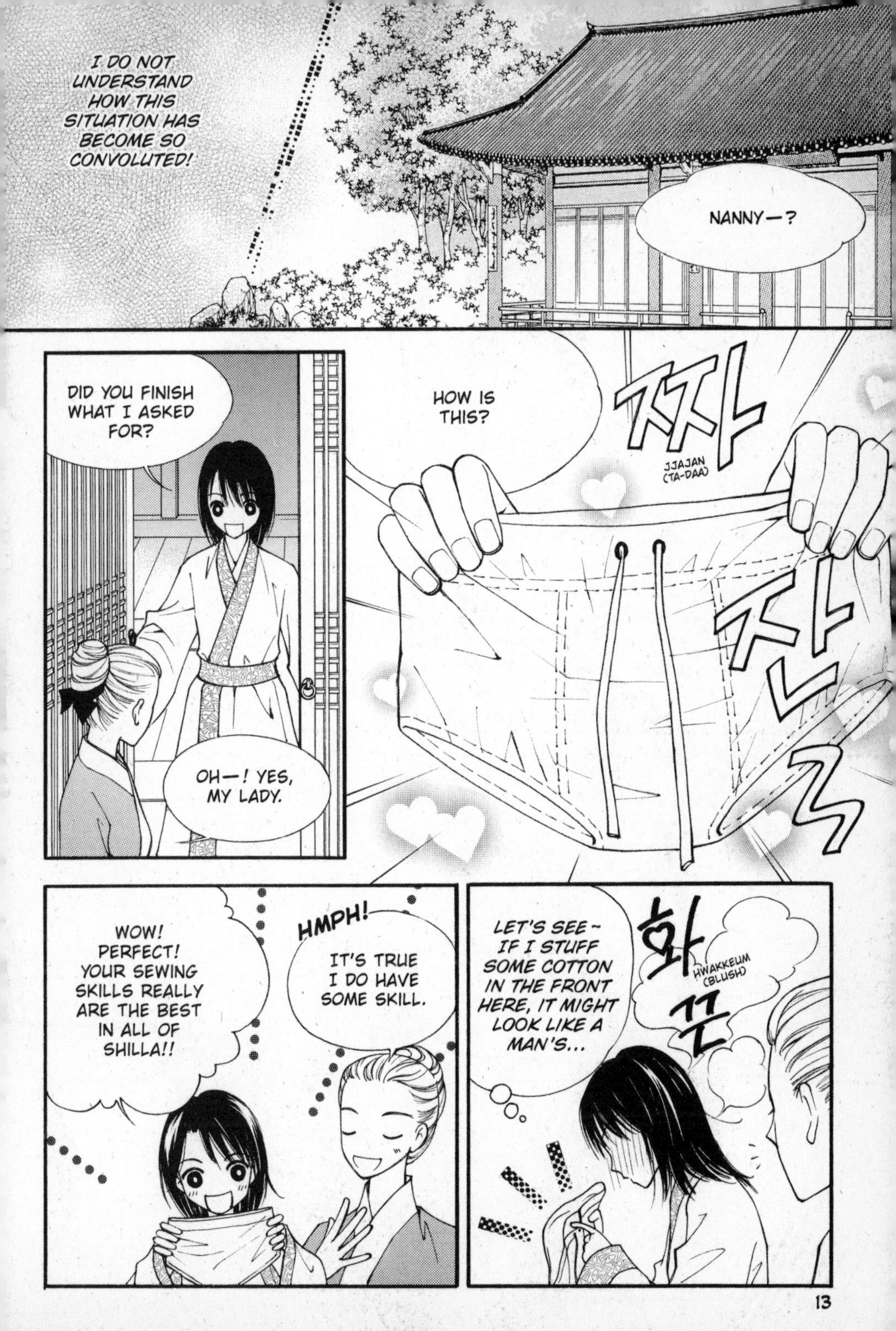
I DO NOT UNDERSTAND HOW THIS SITUATION HAS BECOME SO CONVOLUTED!
NANNY—?
DID YOU FINISH WHAT I ASKED FOR?
OH—! YES, MY LADY.
HOW IS THIS?
짜잔
JJAJAN (TA-DAA)
WOW! PERFECT! YOUR SEWING SKILLS REALLY ARE THE BEST IN ALL OF SHILLA!!
HMPH!
IT'S TRUE I DO HAVE SOME SKILL.
LET'S SEE~ IF I STUFF SOME COTTON IN THE FRONT HERE, IT MIGHT LOOK LIKE A MAN'S...
화끈
HWAKKEUM (BLUSH)

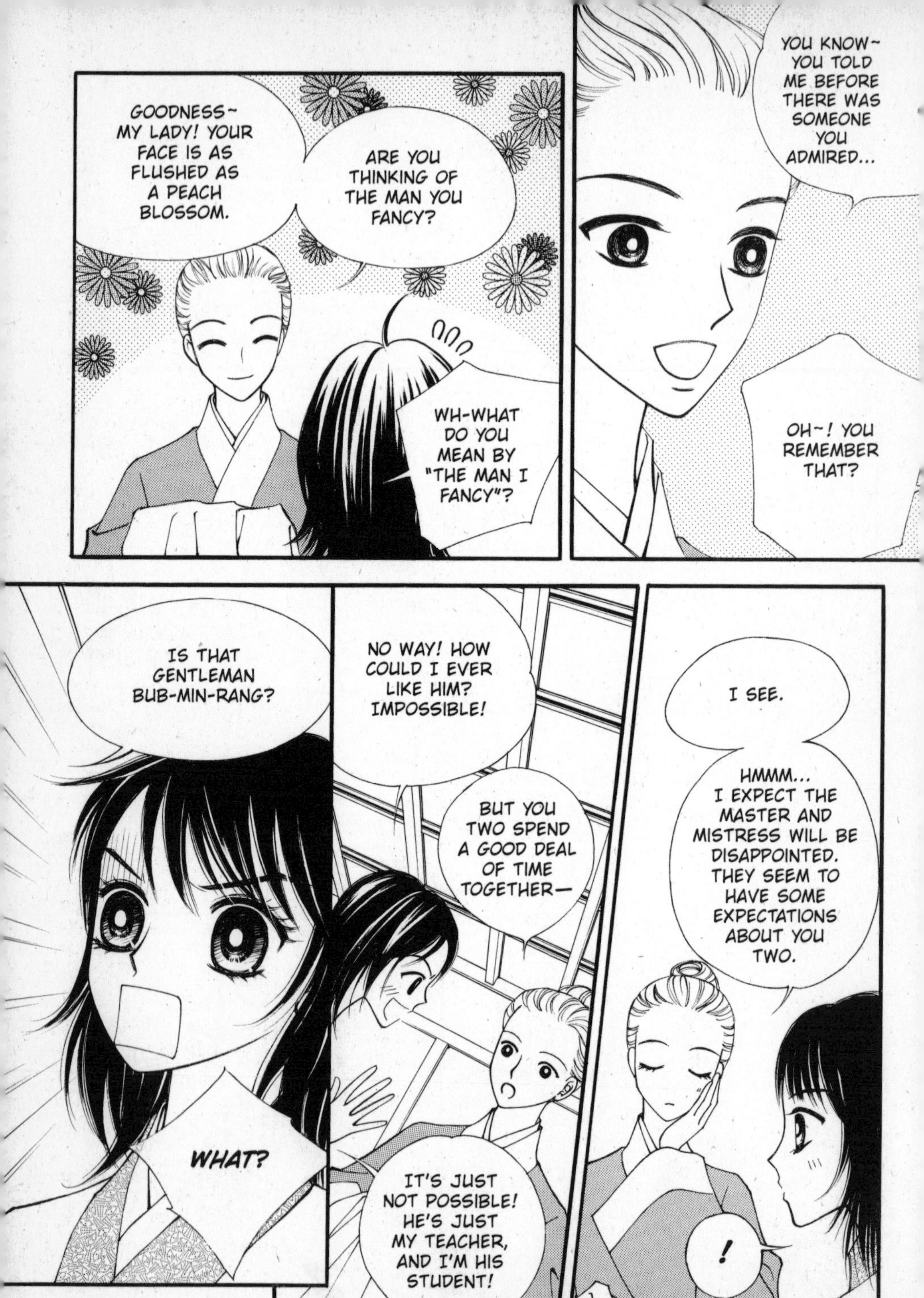
GOODNESS~ MY LADY! YOUR FACE IS AS FLUSHED AS A PEACH BLOSSOM.
ARE YOU THINKING OF THE MAN YOU FANCY?
WH-WHAT DO YOU MEAN BY "THE MAN I FANCY"?
YOU KNOW~ YOU TOLD ME BEFORE THERE WAS SOMEONE YOU ADMIRED...
OH~! YOU REMEMBER THAT?
IS THAT GENTLEMAN BUB-MIN-RANG?
WHAT?
NO WAY! HOW COULD I EVER LIKE HIM? IMPOSSIBLE!
BUT YOU TWO SPEND A GOOD DEAL OF TIME TOGETHER—
IT'S JUST NOT POSSIBLE! HE'S JUST MY TEACHER, AND I'M HIS STUDENT!
I SEE.
HMMM... I EXPECT THE MASTER AND MISTRESS WILL BE DISAPPOINTED. THEY SEEM TO HAVE SOME EXPECTATIONS ABOUT YOU TWO.
!

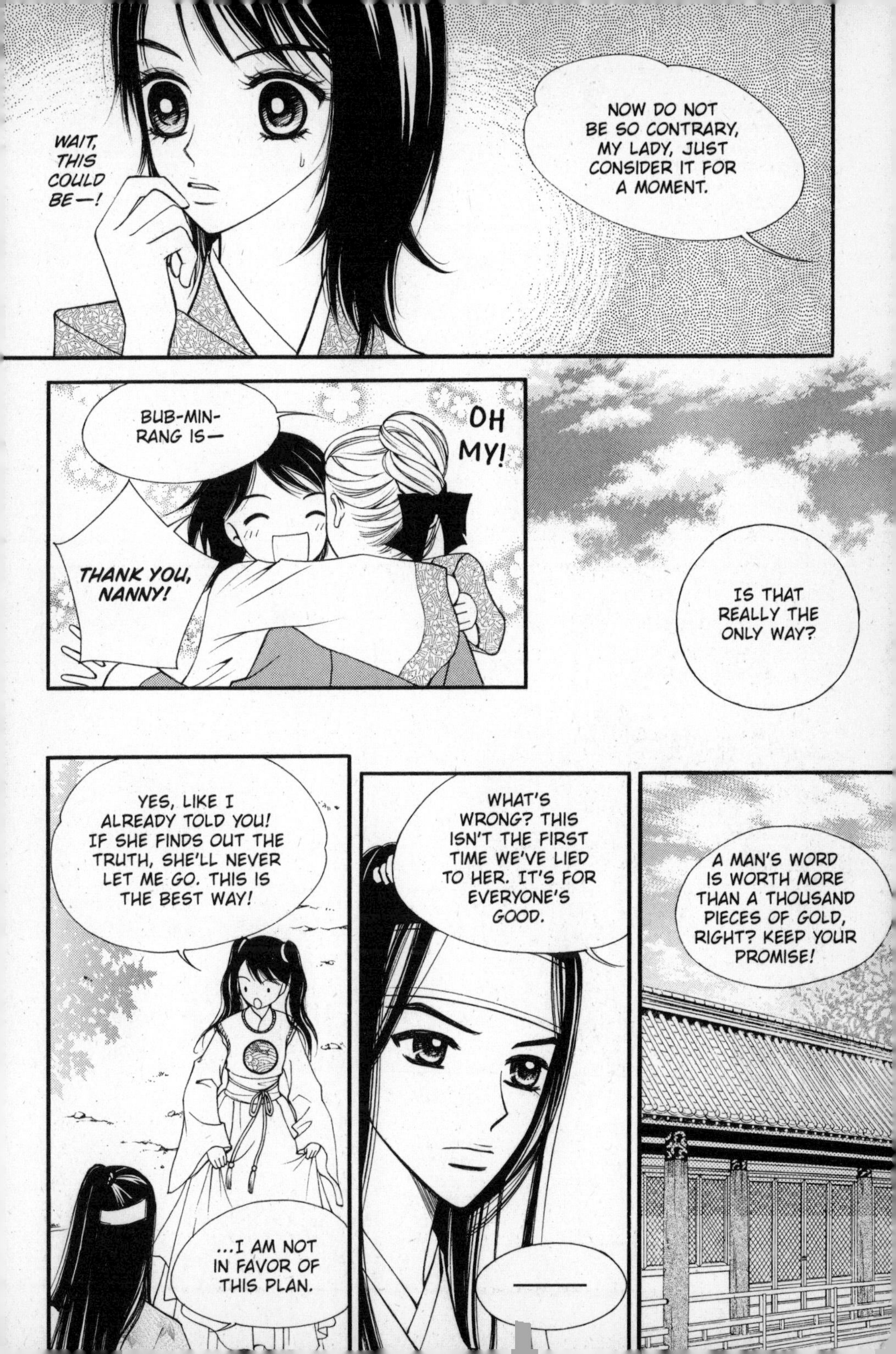
WAIT, THIS COULD BE—!
NOW DO NOT BE SO CONTRARY, MY LADY, JUST CONSIDER IT FOR A MOMENT.
BUB-MIN-RANG IS—
OH MY!
THANK YOU, NANNY!
IS THAT REALLY THE ONLY WAY?
YES, LIKE I ALREADY TOLD YOU! IF SHE FINDS OUT THE TRUTH, SHE'LL NEVER LET ME GO. THIS IS THE BEST WAY!
...I AM NOT IN FAVOR OF THIS PLAN.
WHAT'S WRONG? THIS ISN'T THE FIRST TIME WE'VE LIED TO HER. IT'S FOR EVERYONE'S GOOD.
——
A MAN'S WORD IS WORTH MORE THAN A THOUSAND PIECES OF GOLD, RIGHT? KEEP YOUR PROMISE!

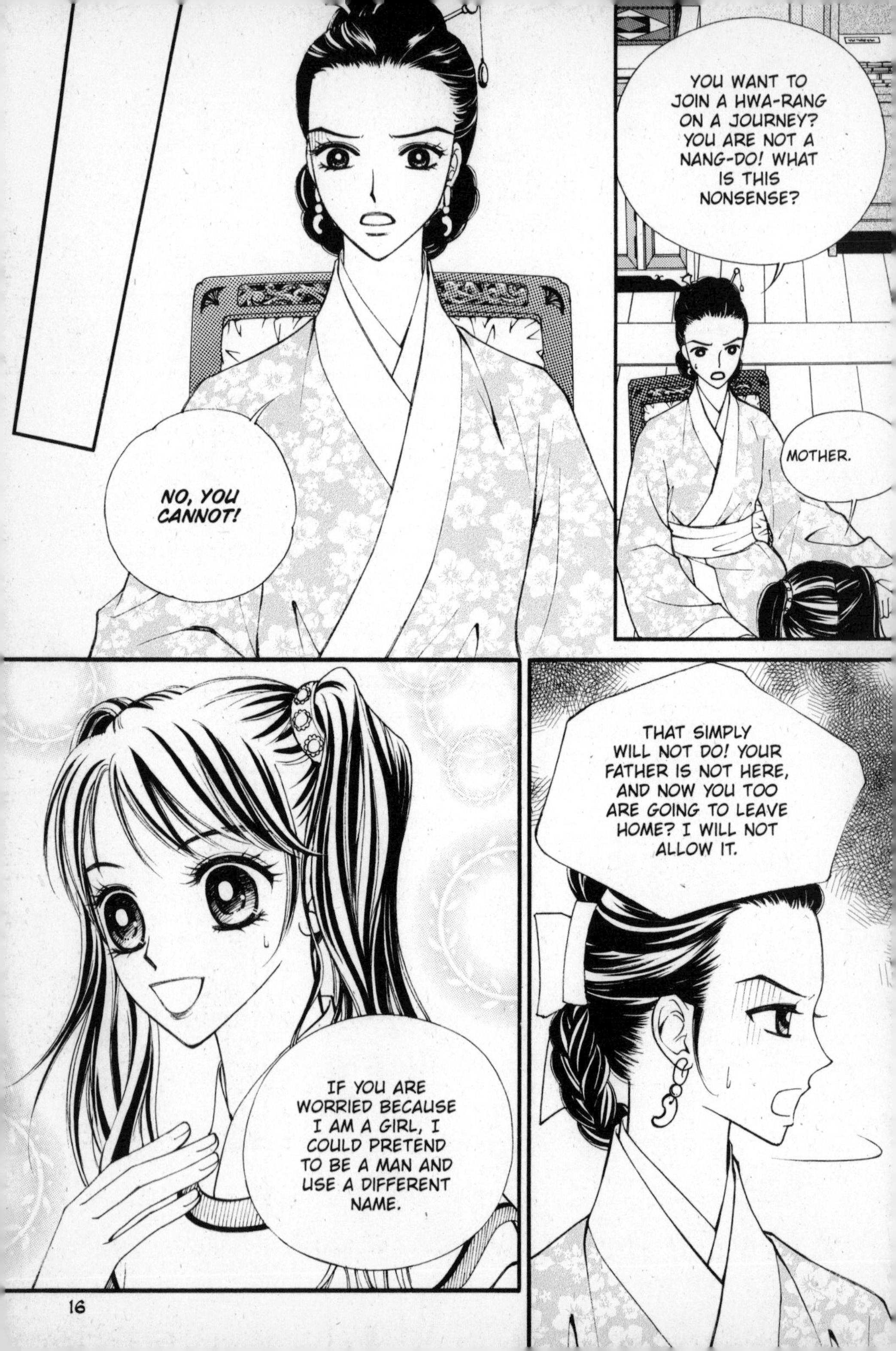
NO, YOU CANNOT!
YOU WANT TO JOIN A HWA-RANG ON A JOURNEY? YOU ARE NOT A NANG-DO! WHAT IS THIS NONSENSE?
MOTHER.
IF YOU ARE WORRIED BECAUSE I AM A GIRL, I COULD PRETEND TO BE A MAN AND USE A DIFFERENT NAME.
THAT SIMPLY WILL NOT DO! YOUR FATHER IS NOT HERE, AND NOW YOU TOO ARE GOING TO LEAVE HOME? I WILL NOT ALLOW IT.

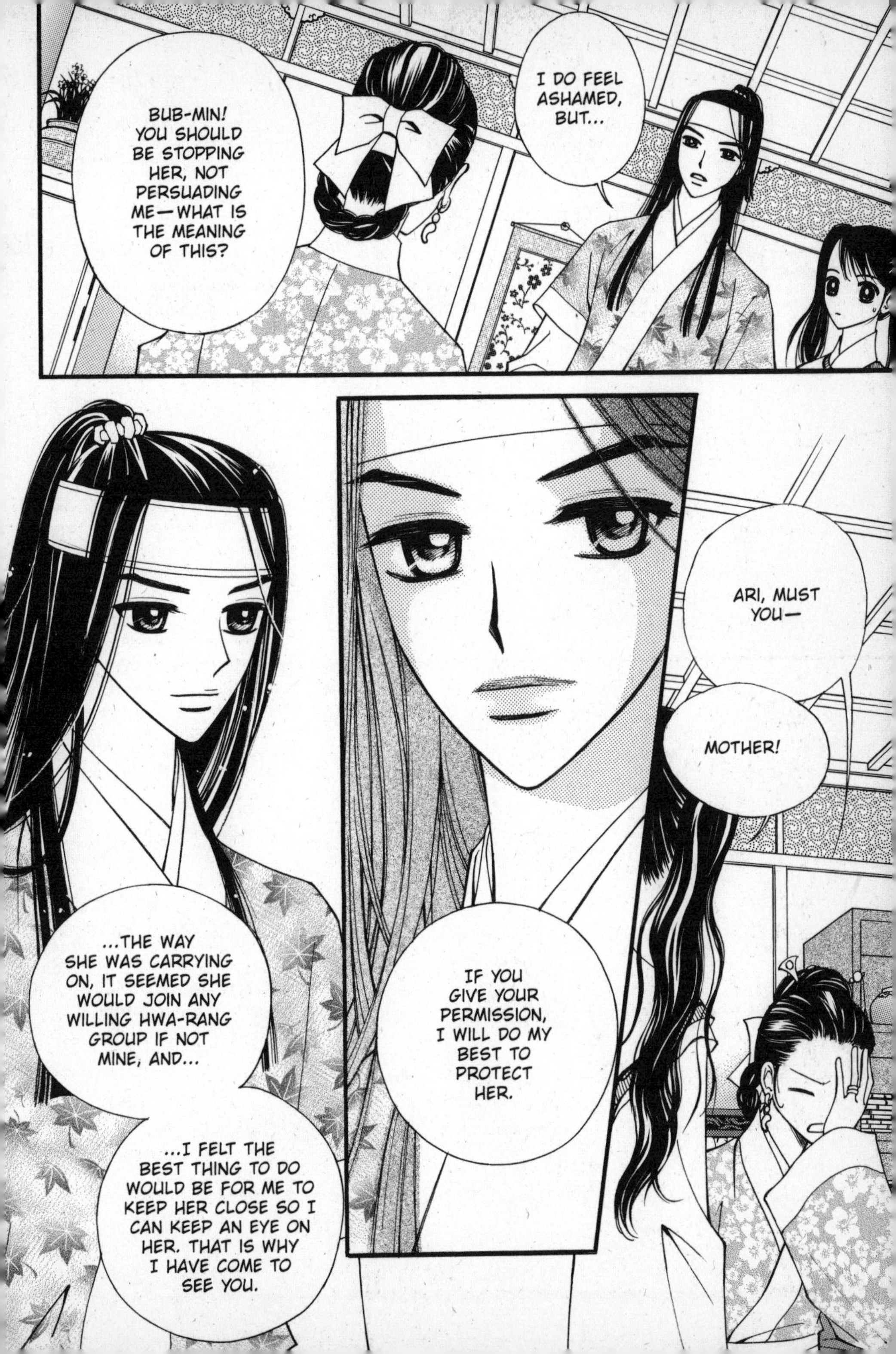
BUB-MIN! YOU SHOULD BE STOPPING HER, NOT PERSUADING ME—WHAT IS THE MEANING OF THIS?
I DO FEEL ASHAMED, BUT...
...THE WAY SHE WAS CARRYING ON, IT SEEMED SHE WOULD JOIN ANY WILLING HWA-RANG GROUP IF NOT MINE, AND...
...I FELT THE BEST THING TO DO WOULD BE FOR ME TO KEEP HER CLOSE SO I CAN KEEP AN EYE ON HER. THAT IS WHY I HAVE COME TO SEE YOU.
IF YOU GIVE YOUR PERMISSION, I WILL DO MY BEST TO PROTECT HER.
ARI, MUST YOU—
MOTHER!

I AM ALREADY FIFTEEN. I KNOW THAT I MUST MARRY SOON...

...MARRY?

DO YOU HAVE SOMEONE IN MIND?

......

...BUT BEFORE I DO, I WANT TO SEE MORE OF THE WORLD AND BROADEN MY PERSPECTIVE.

BUB-MIN-RANG, COULD YOU EXCUSE US A MOMENT?

!

OF COURSE. THERE IS MUCH FOR YOU TO DISCUSS.

THANK YOU.

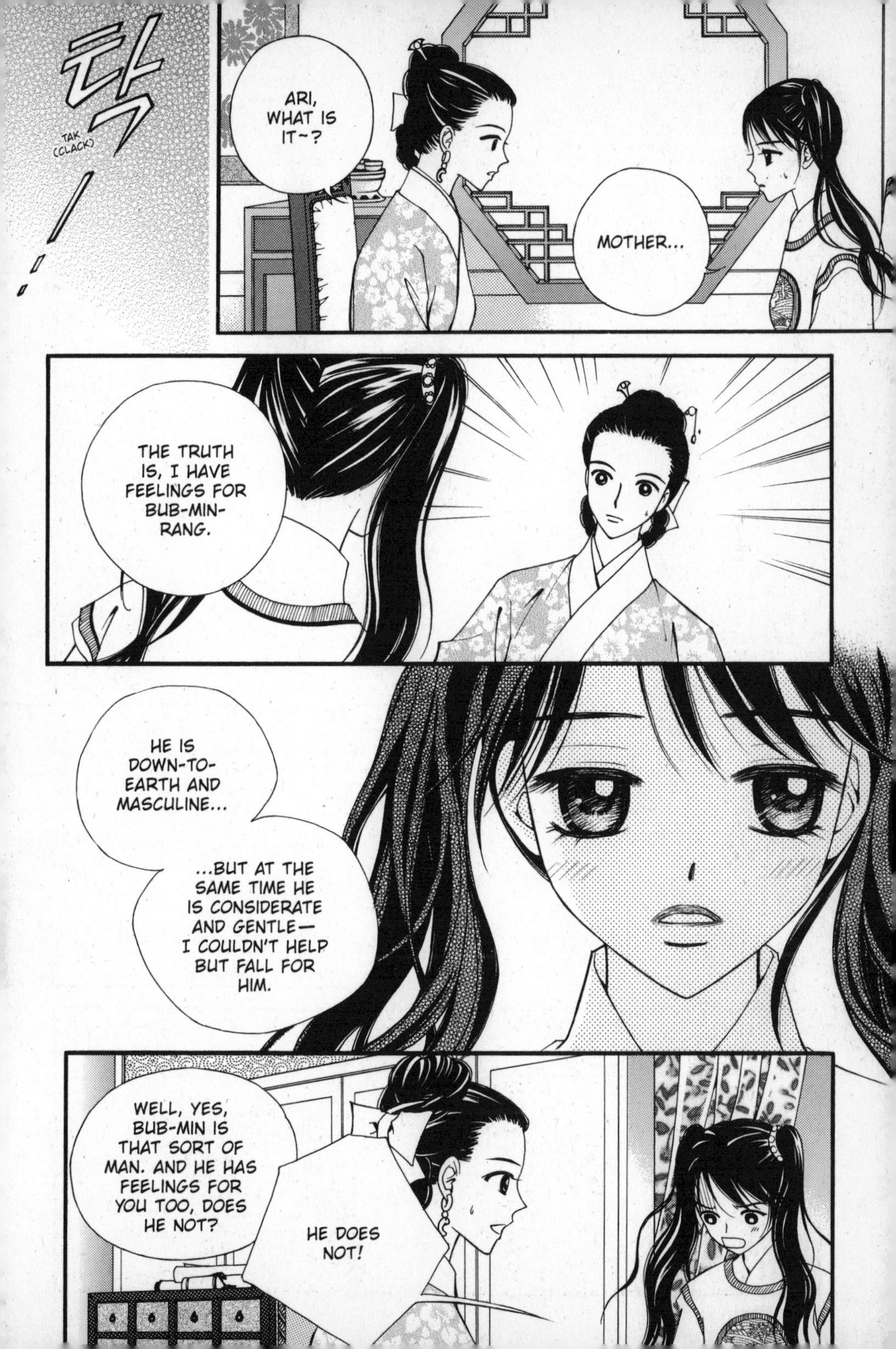
탁
TAK (CLACK)
ARI, WHAT IS IT~?
MOTHER...
THE TRUTH IS, I HAVE FEELINGS FOR BUB-MIN-RANG.
HE IS DOWN-TO-EARTH AND MASCULINE...
...BUT AT THE SAME TIME HE IS CONSIDERATE AND GENTLE— I COULDN'T HELP BUT FALL FOR HIM.
WELL, YES, BUB-MIN IS THAT SORT OF MAN. AND HE HAS FEELINGS FOR YOU TOO, DOES HE NOT?
HE DOES NOT!

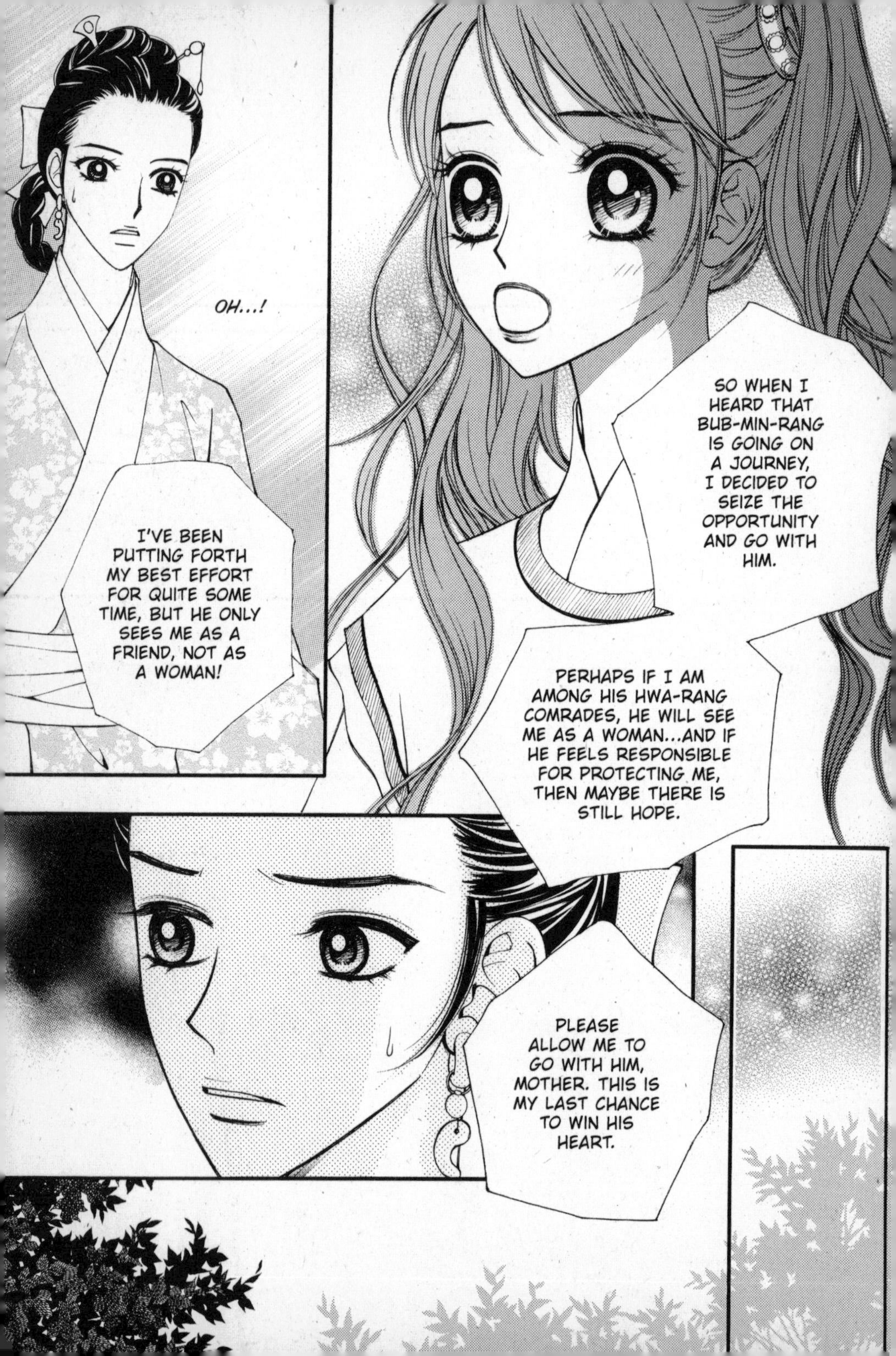
OH...!
I'VE BEEN PUTTING FORTH MY BEST EFFORT FOR QUITE SOME TIME, BUT HE ONLY SEES ME AS A FRIEND, NOT AS A WOMAN!
SO WHEN I HEARD THAT BUB-MIN-RANG IS GOING ON A JOURNEY, I DECIDED TO SEIZE THE OPPORTUNITY AND GO WITH HIM.
PERHAPS IF I AM AMONG HIS HWA-RANG COMRADES, HE WILL SEE ME AS A WOMAN...AND IF HE FEELS RESPONSIBLE FOR PROTECTING ME, THEN MAYBE THERE IS STILL HOPE.
PLEASE ALLOW ME TO GO WITH HIM, MOTHER. THIS IS MY LAST CHANCE TO WIN HIS HEART.

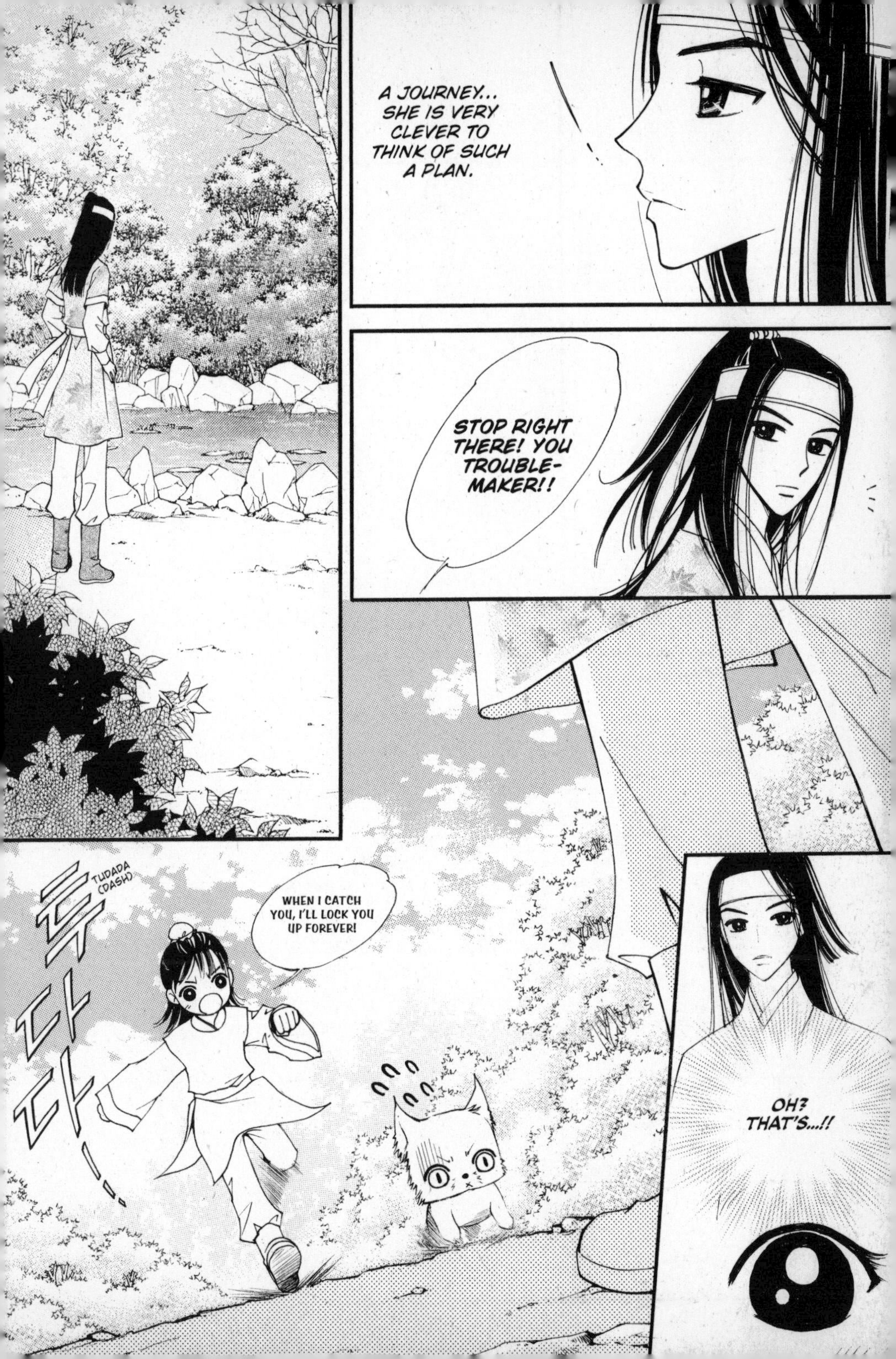
A JOURNEY... SHE IS VERY CLEVER TO THINK OF SUCH A PLAN.
STOP RIGHT THERE! YOU TROUBLE-MAKER!!
TUDADA (DASH)
WHEN I CATCH YOU, I'LL LOCK YOU UP FOREVER!
OH? THAT'S...!!

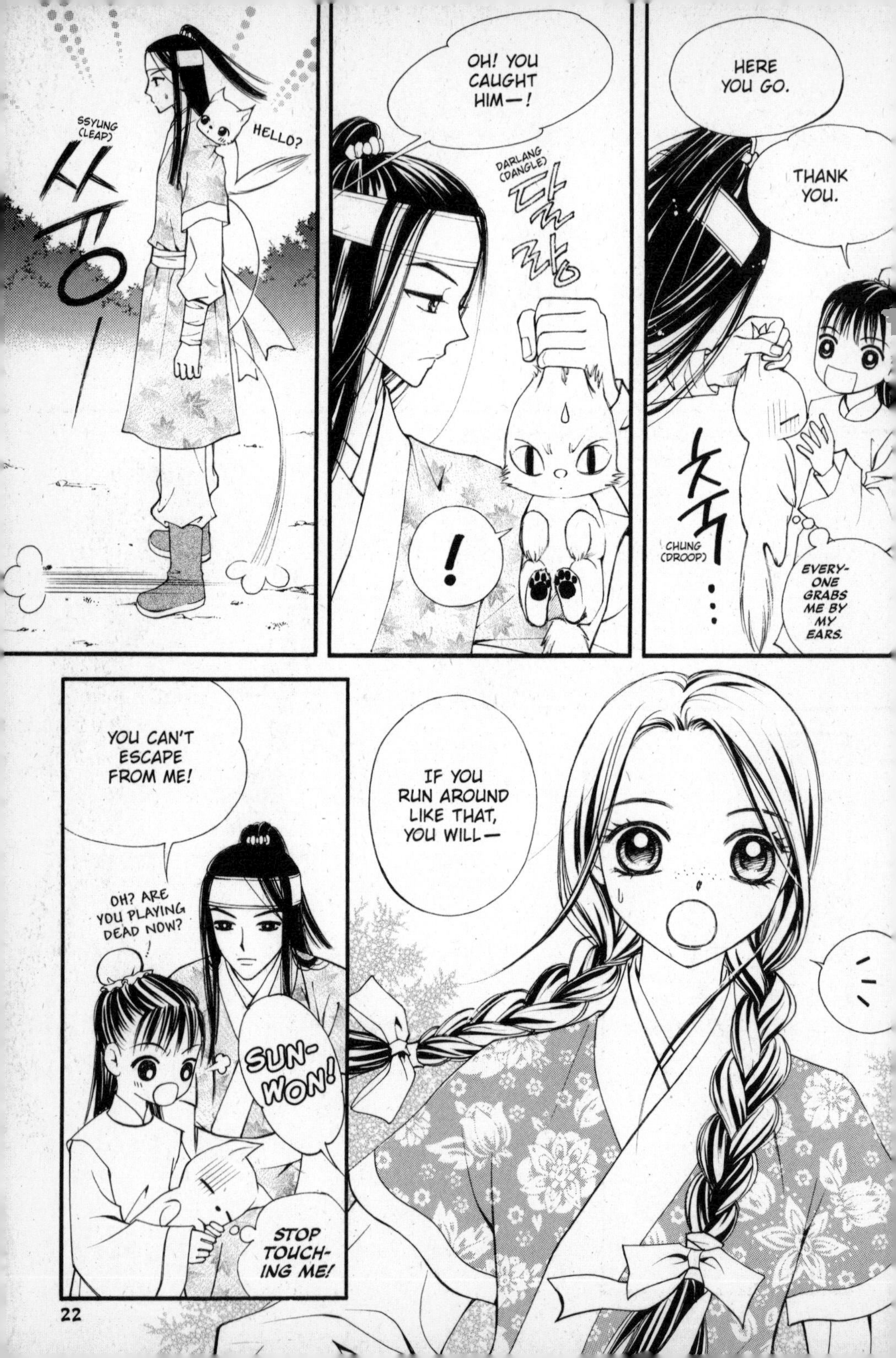
SSYUNG (LEAP)
HELLO?
OH! YOU CAUGHT HIM—!
DARLANG (DANGLE)
!
HERE YOU GO.
THANK YOU.
CHUNG (DROOP)
...
EVERY-ONE GRABS ME BY MY EARS.
YOU CAN'T ESCAPE FROM ME!
OH? ARE YOU PLAYING DEAD NOW?
SUN-WON!
STOP TOUCH-ING ME!
IF YOU RUN AROUND LIKE THAT, YOU WILL—
!

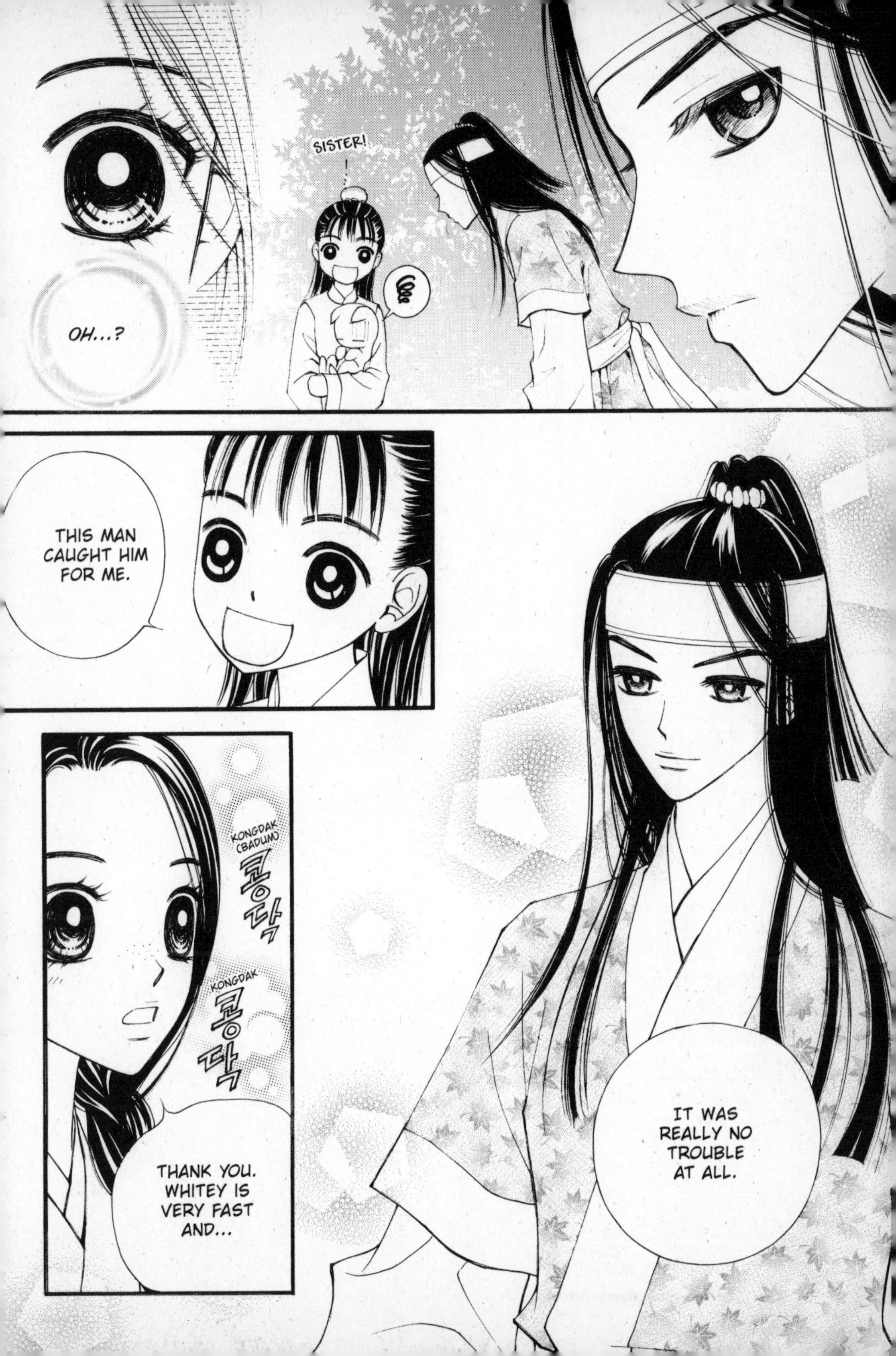
SISTER!
OH...?
THIS MAN CAUGHT HIM FOR ME.
KONGDAK (BADUM)
콩닥
KONGDAK
콩닥
THANK YOU. WHITEY IS VERY FAST AND...
IT WAS REALLY NO TROUBLE AT ALL.

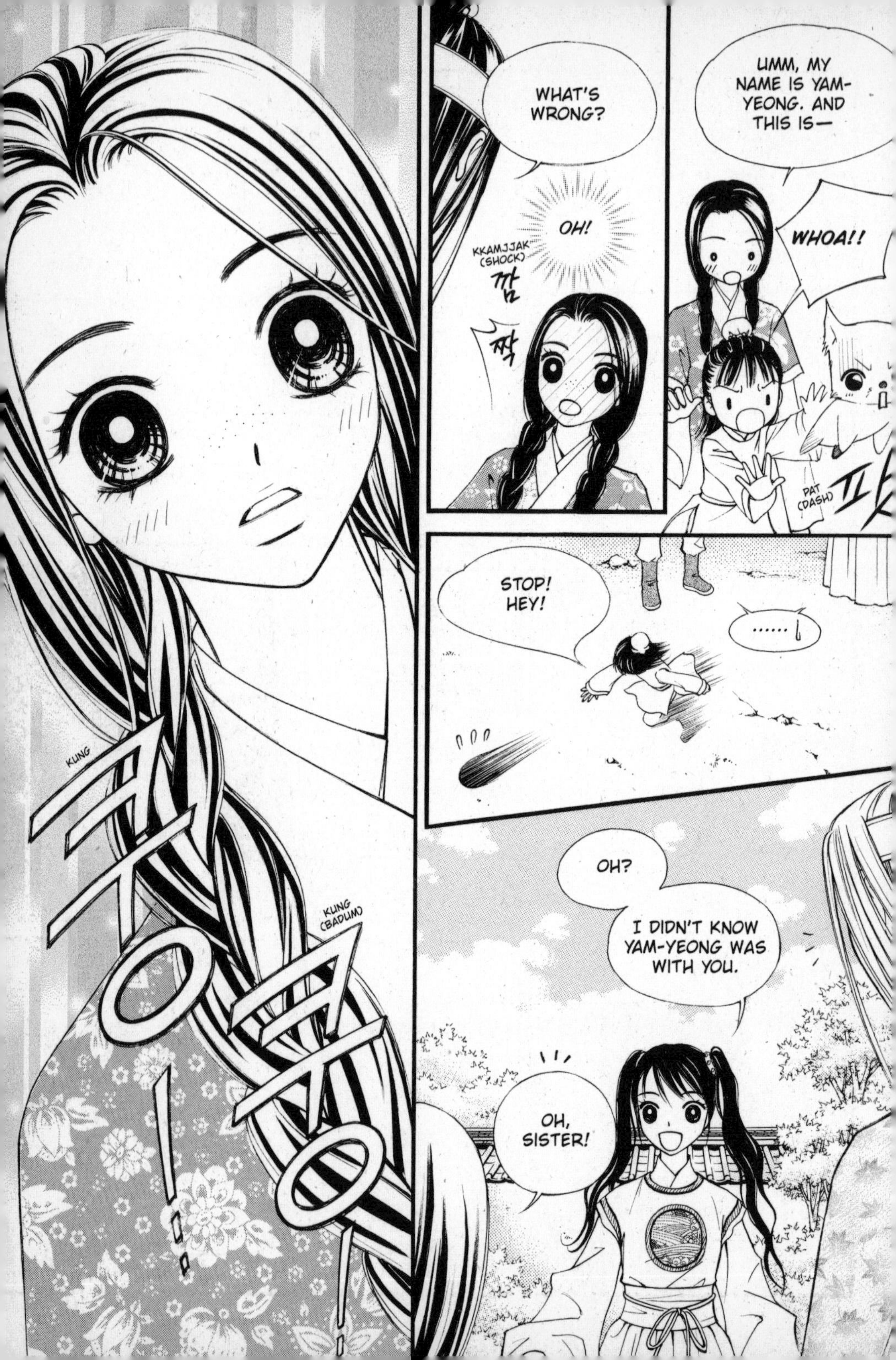

KUNG
KUNG (BADUM)
WHAT'S WRONG?
OH!
KKAMJJAK (SHOCK)
깜짝
UMM, MY NAME IS YAM-YEONG. AND THIS IS—
WHOA!!
PAT (DASH)
STOP! HEY!
……
OH?
I DIDN'T KNOW YAM-YEONG WAS WITH YOU.
OH, SISTER!

YOU TWO HAVEN'T MET BEFORE, HAVE YOU? THIS IS MY SECOND YOUNGEST SISTER, YAM-YEONG.

YAM-YEONG, THIS IS BUB-MIN-RANG.

IT IS A PLEASURE TO MEET YOU.

HE IS AN ACQUAINTANCE OF MY SISTER...

COULD YOU EXCUSE US FOR A SECOND? WE HAVE TO DISCUSS SOMETHING.

SO, HOW DID IT GO?

I THINK SHE'S GONNA LET ME GO! I HAVE A GOOD FEELING ABOUT IT!

IS THAT SO?

I SEE... SO SHE REALLY DOES INTEND TO STAY WITH HIM.

PLEASE DO NOT FORGET WHAT I TOLD YOU! NEVER—

GEEZ~ I SAID I GOT IT.

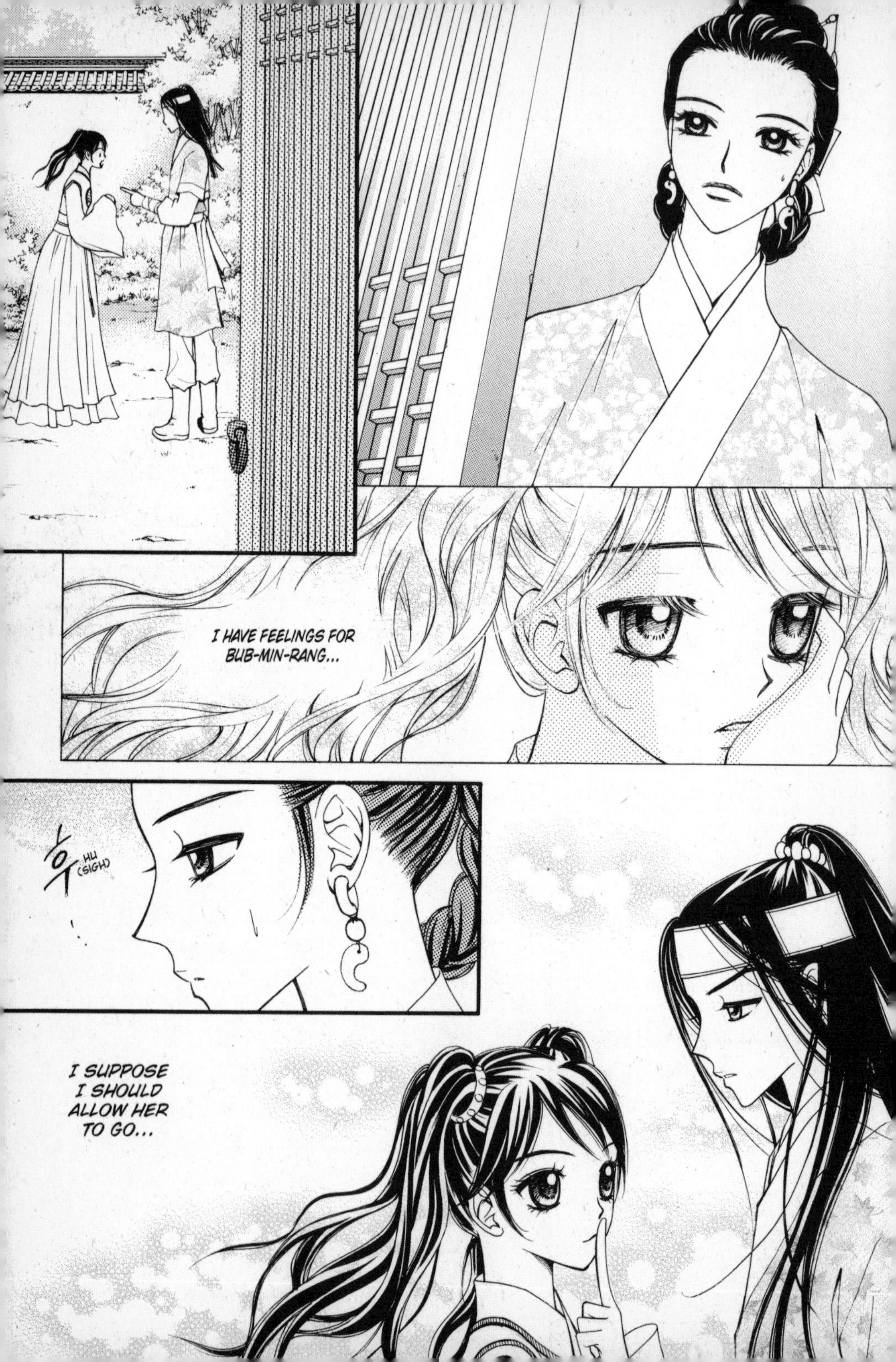
I HAVE FEELINGS FOR BUB-MIN-RANG...
후
HU (SIGH)
I SUPPOSE I SHOULD ALLOW HER TO GO...

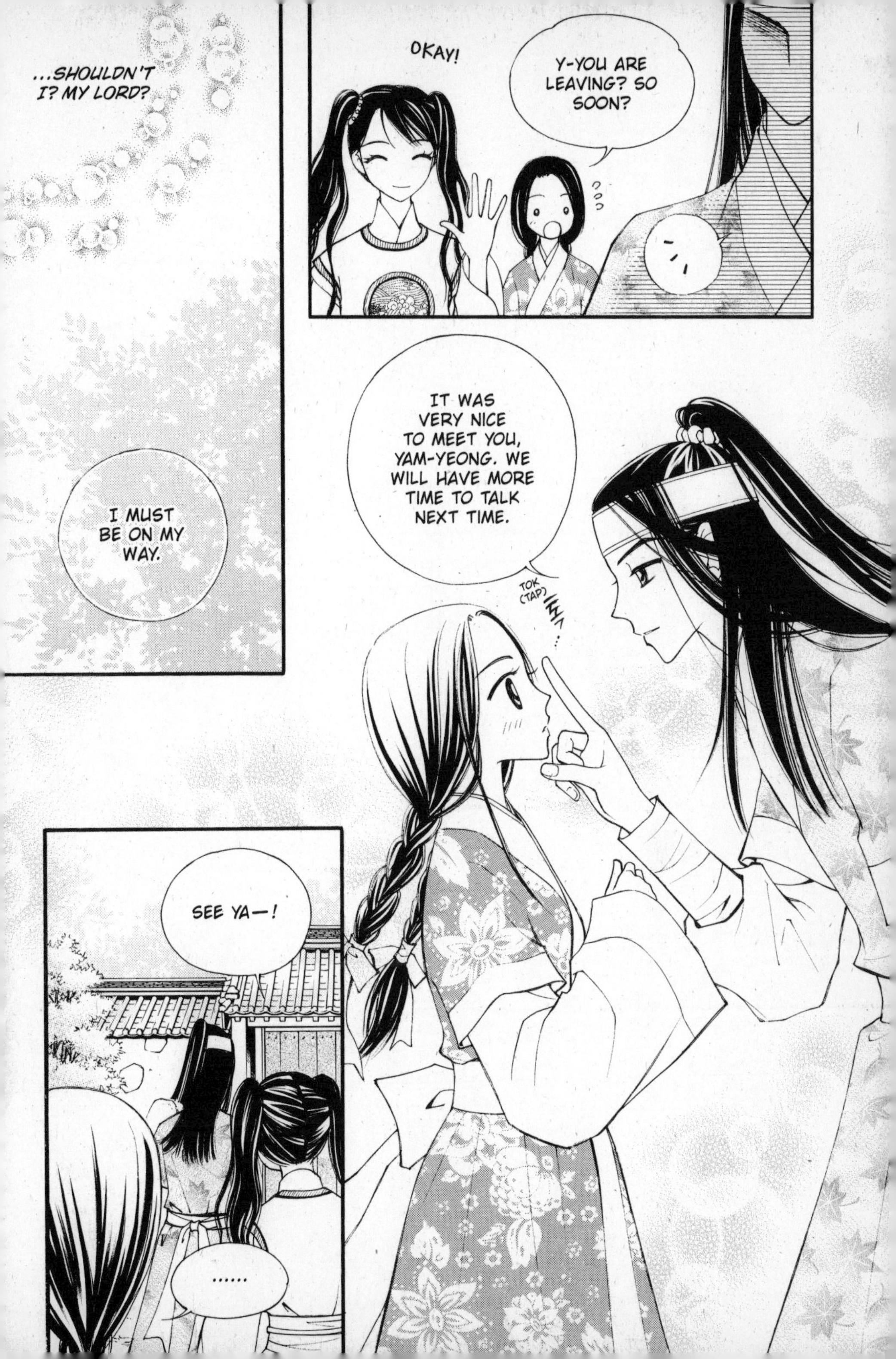
...SHOULDN'T I? MY LORD?
OKAY!
Y-YOU ARE LEAVING? SO SOON?
I MUST BE ON MY WAY.
IT WAS VERY NICE TO MEET YOU, YAM-YEONG. WE WILL HAVE MORE TIME TO TALK NEXT TIME.
TOK (TAP)
SEE YA—!
......

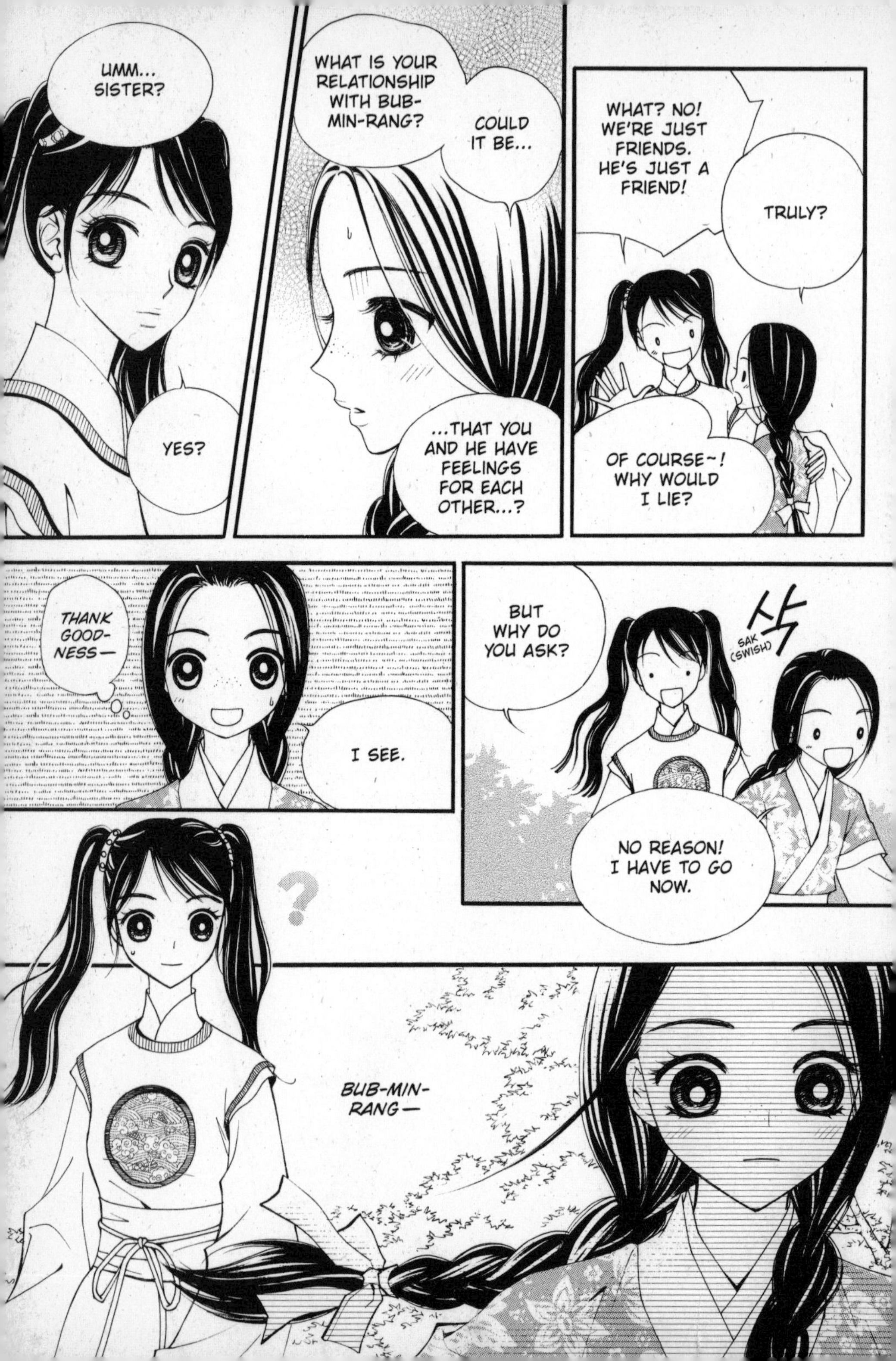
UMM... SISTER?
YES?
WHAT IS YOUR RELATIONSHIP WITH BUB-MIN-RANG?
COULD IT BE...
...THAT YOU AND HE HAVE FEELINGS FOR EACH OTHER...?
WHAT? NO! WE'RE JUST FRIENDS. HE'S JUST A FRIEND!
TRULY?
OF COURSE~! WHY WOULD I LIE?
THANK GOOD-NESS—
I SEE.
BUT WHY DO YOU ASK?
SAK (SWISH)
NO REASON! I HAVE TO GO NOW.
BUB-MIN-RANG—

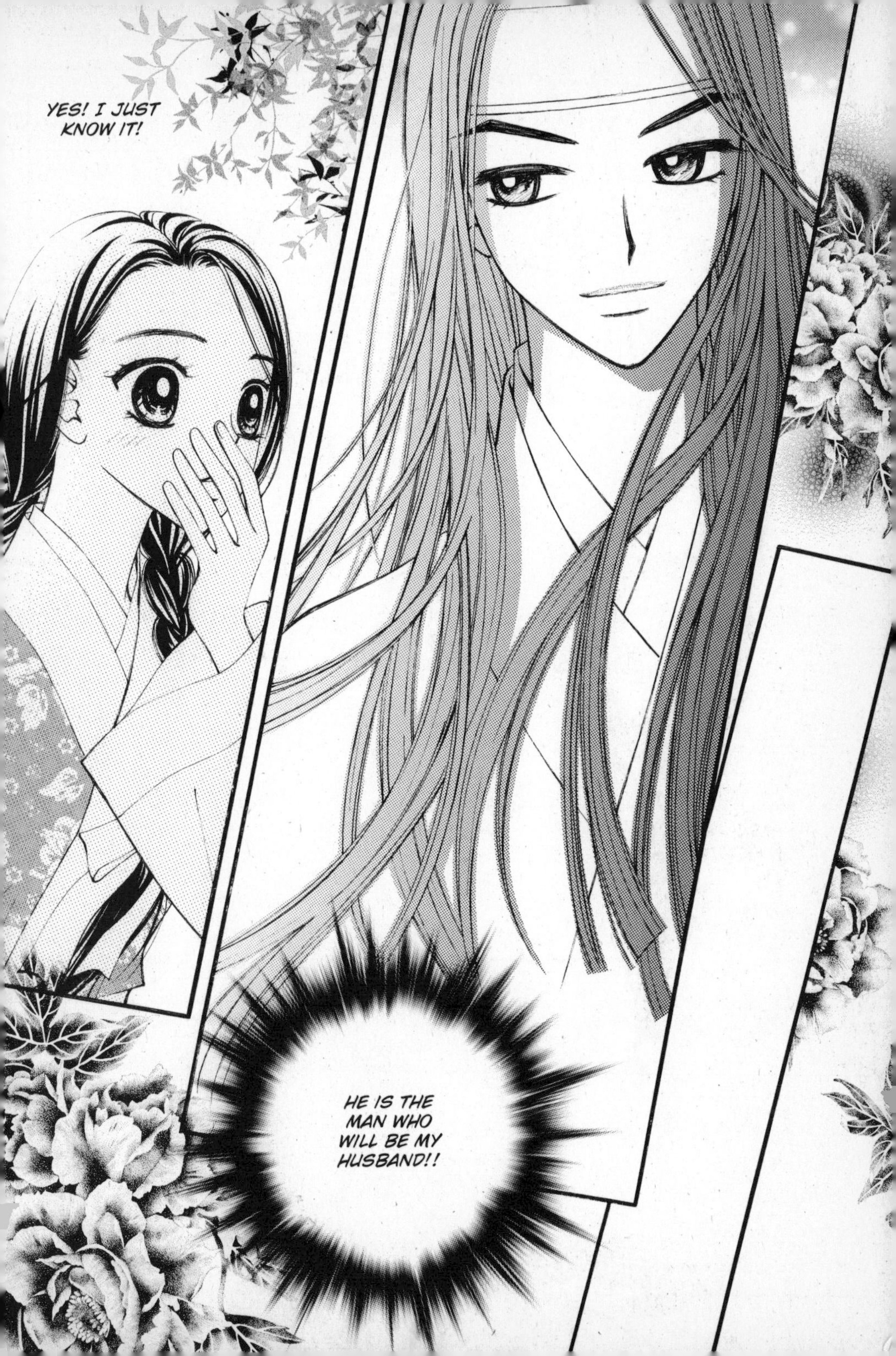
YES! I JUST KNOW IT!
HE IS THE MAN WHO WILL BE MY HUSBAND!!

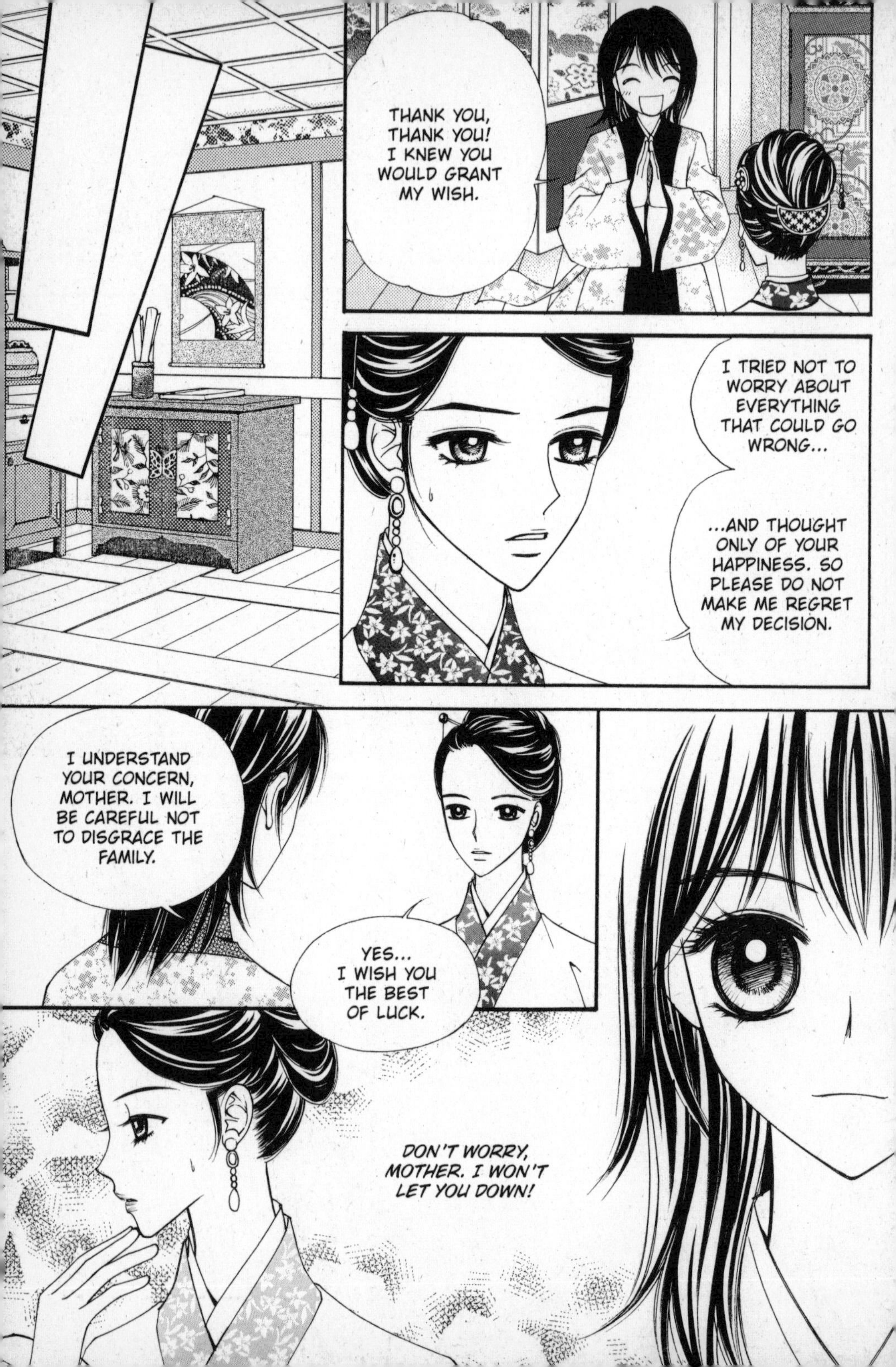
THANK YOU, THANK YOU! I KNEW YOU WOULD GRANT MY WISH.
I TRIED NOT TO WORRY ABOUT EVERYTHING THAT COULD GO WRONG...
...AND THOUGHT ONLY OF YOUR HAPPINESS. SO PLEASE DO NOT MAKE ME REGRET MY DECISION.
I UNDERSTAND YOUR CONCERN, MOTHER. I WILL BE CAREFUL NOT TO DISGRACE THE FAMILY.
YES... I WISH YOU THE BEST OF LUCK.
DON'T WORRY, MOTHER. I WON'T LET YOU DOWN!

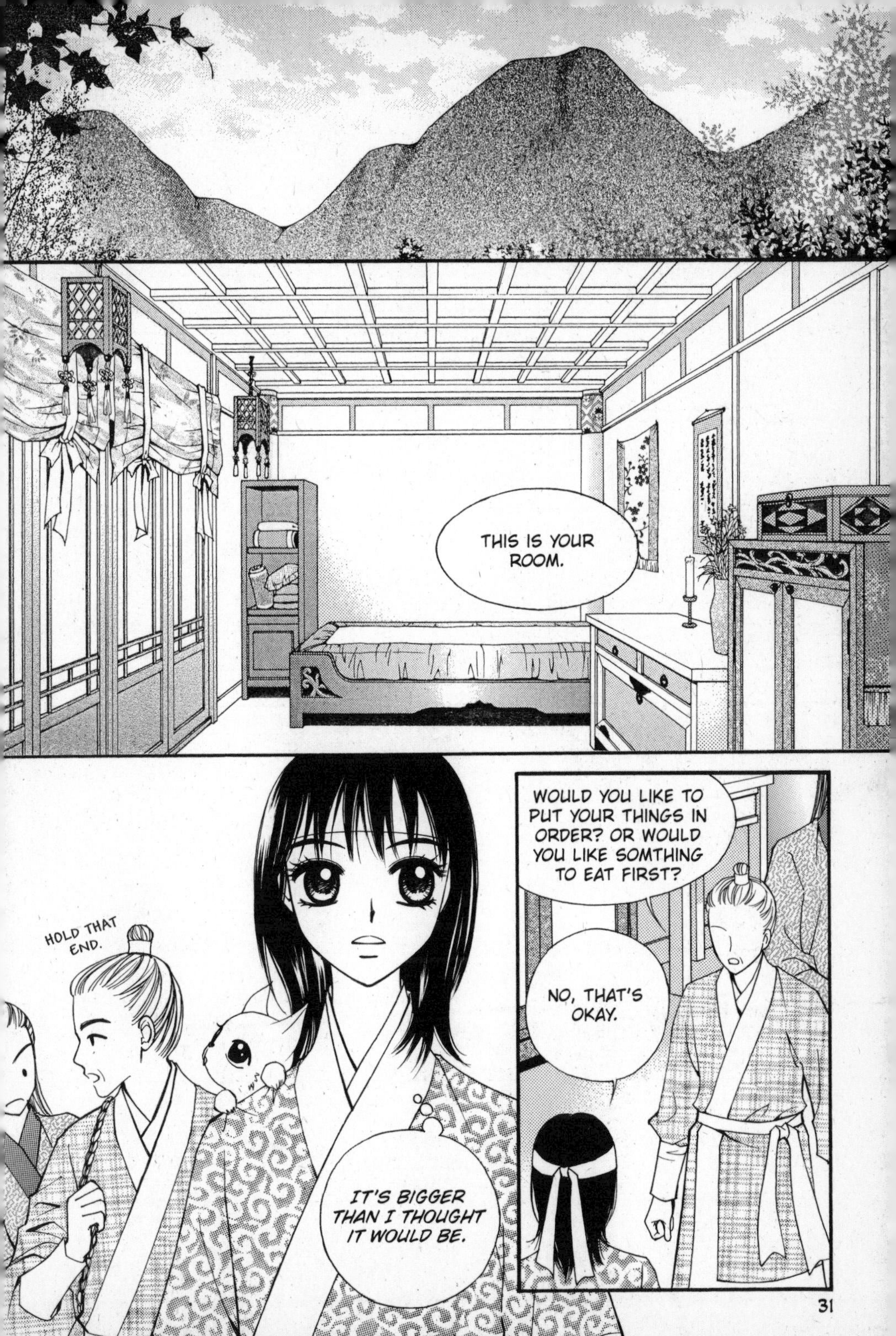
THIS IS YOUR ROOM.
HOLD THAT END.
IT'S BIGGER THAN I THOUGHT IT WOULD BE.
WOULD YOU LIKE TO PUT YOUR THINGS IN ORDER? OR WOULD YOU LIKE SOMTHING TO EAT FIRST?
NO, THAT'S OKAY.

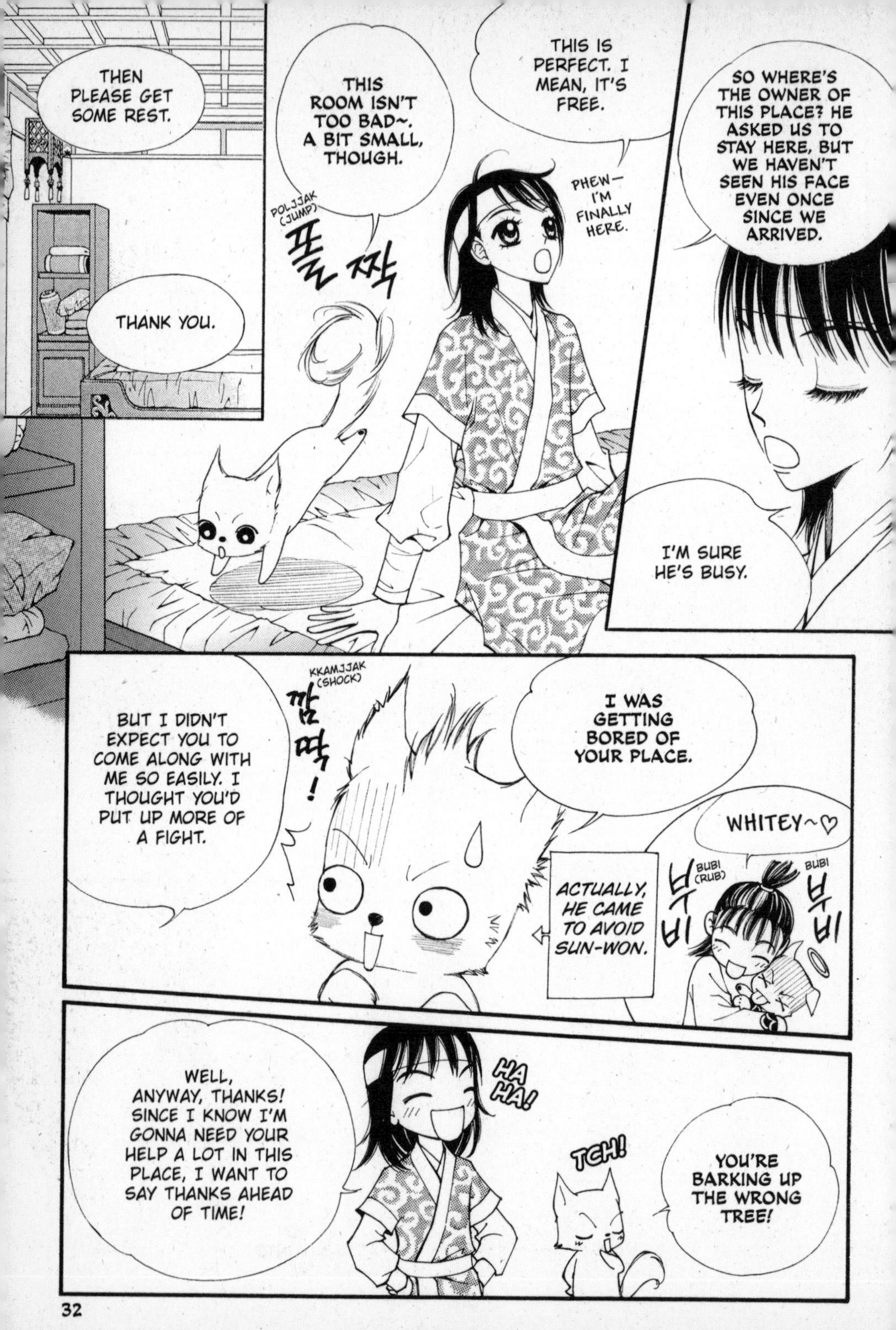
THEN PLEASE GET SOME REST.
THANK YOU.
THIS ROOM ISN'T TOO BAD~. A BIT SMALL, THOUGH.
POLJJAK (JUMP)
폴짝
THIS IS PERFECT. I MEAN, IT'S FREE.
PHEW— I'M FINALLY HERE.
SO WHERE'S THE OWNER OF THIS PLACE? HE ASKED US TO STAY HERE, BUT WE HAVEN'T SEEN HIS FACE EVEN ONCE SINCE WE ARRIVED.
I'M SURE HE'S BUSY.
BUT I DIDN'T EXPECT YOU TO COME ALONG WITH ME SO EASILY. I THOUGHT YOU'D PUT UP MORE OF A FIGHT.
KKAMJJAK (SHOCK)
깜짝!
I WAS GETTING BORED OF YOUR PLACE.
ACTUALLY, HE CAME TO AVOID SUN-WON.
WHITEY~♡
BUBI (RUB)
부비
BUBI
부비
WELL, ANYWAY, THANKS! SINCE I KNOW I'M GONNA NEED YOUR HELP A LOT IN THIS PLACE, I WANT TO SAY THANKS AHEAD OF TIME!
HA HA!
TCH!
YOU'RE BARKING UP THE WRONG TREE!

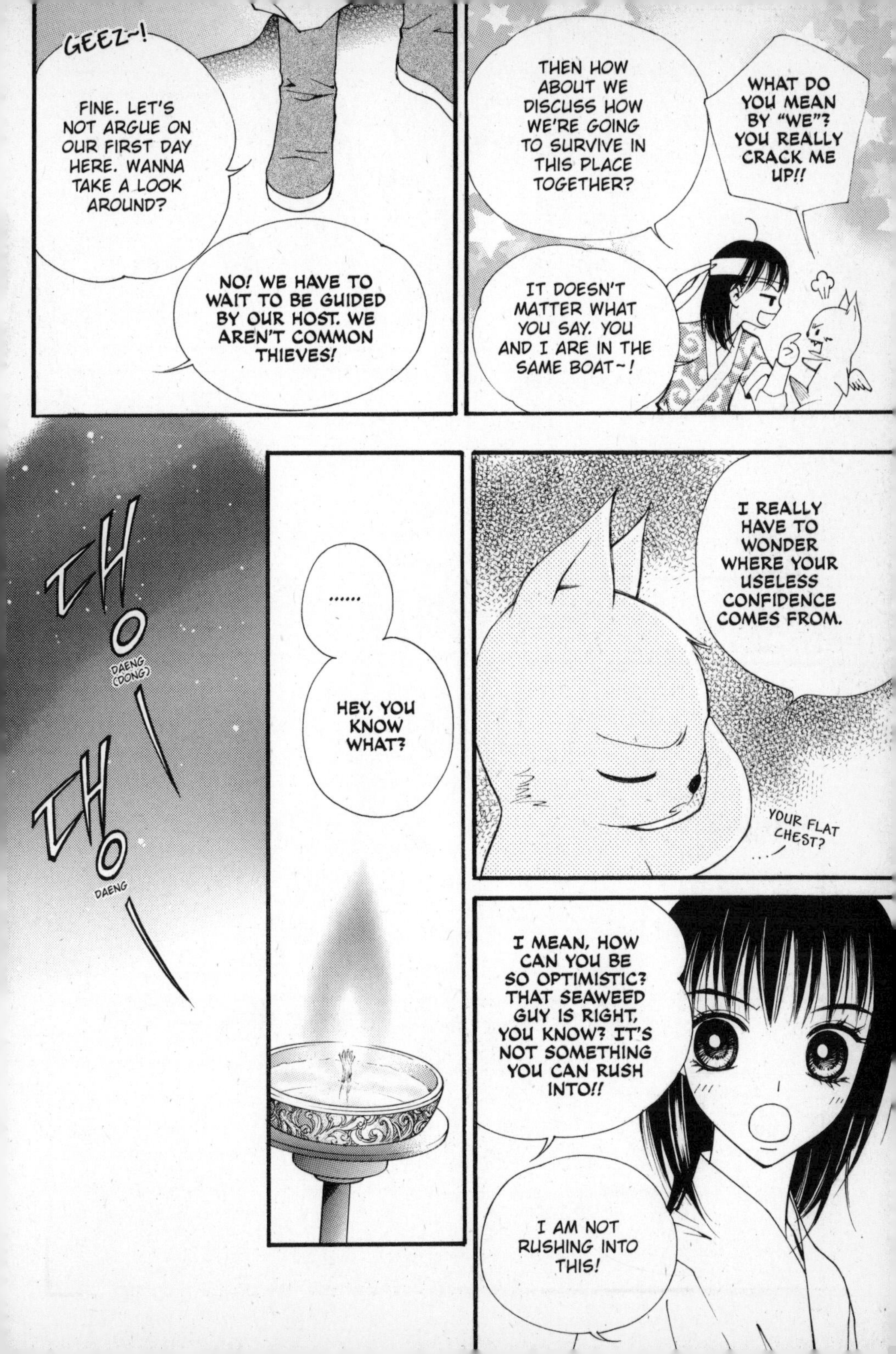
GEEZ~!
FINE. LET'S NOT ARGUE ON OUR FIRST DAY HERE. WANNA TAKE A LOOK AROUND?
NO! WE HAVE TO WAIT TO BE GUIDED BY OUR HOST. WE AREN'T COMMON THIEVES!
THEN HOW ABOUT WE DISCUSS HOW WE'RE GOING TO SURVIVE IN THIS PLACE TOGETHER?
WHAT DO YOU MEAN BY "WE"? YOU REALLY CRACK ME UP!!
IT DOESN'T MATTER WHAT YOU SAY. YOU AND I ARE IN THE SAME BOAT~!
DAENG (DONG)
DAENG
......
HEY, YOU KNOW WHAT?
I REALLY HAVE TO WONDER WHERE YOUR USELESS CONFIDENCE COMES FROM.
YOUR FLAT CHEST? ...
I MEAN, HOW CAN YOU BE SO OPTIMISTIC? THAT SEAWEED GUY IS RIGHT, YOU KNOW? IT'S NOT SOMETHING YOU CAN RUSH INTO!!
I AM NOT RUSHING INTO THIS!

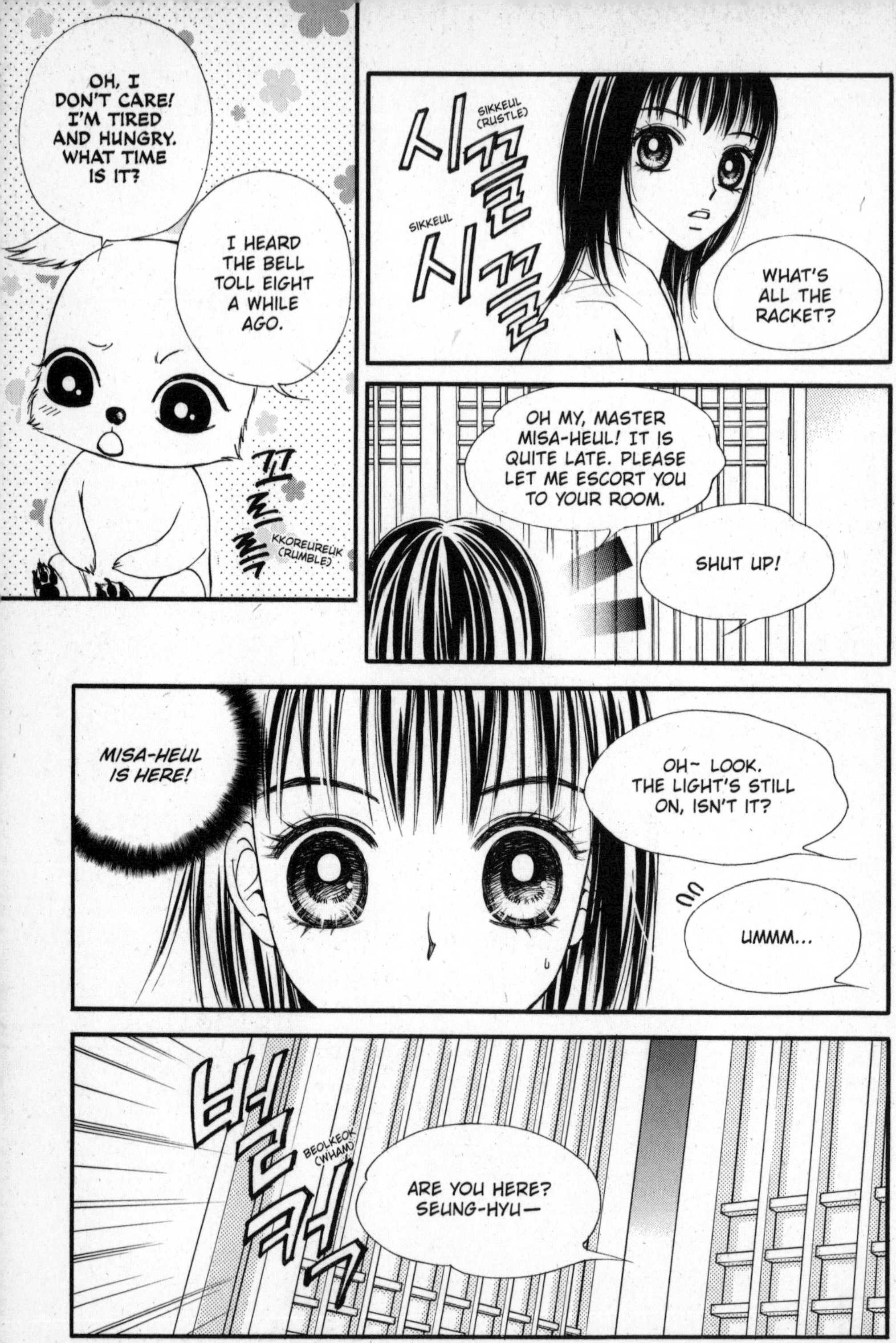
OH, I DON'T CARE! I'M TIRED AND HUNGRY. WHAT TIME IS IT?
I HEARD THE BELL TOLL EIGHT A WHILE AGO.
KKOREUREUK (RUMBLE)
시끌 시끌
SIKKEUL (RUSTLE)
SIKKEUL
WHAT'S ALL THE RACKET?
OH MY, MASTER MISA-HEUL! IT IS QUITE LATE. PLEASE LET ME ESCORT YOU TO YOUR ROOM.
SHUT UP!
MISA-HEUL IS HERE!
OH~ LOOK. THE LIGHT'S STILL ON, ISN'T IT?
UMMM...
벌컥
BEOLKEOK (WHAM)
ARE YOU HERE? SEUNG-HYU—

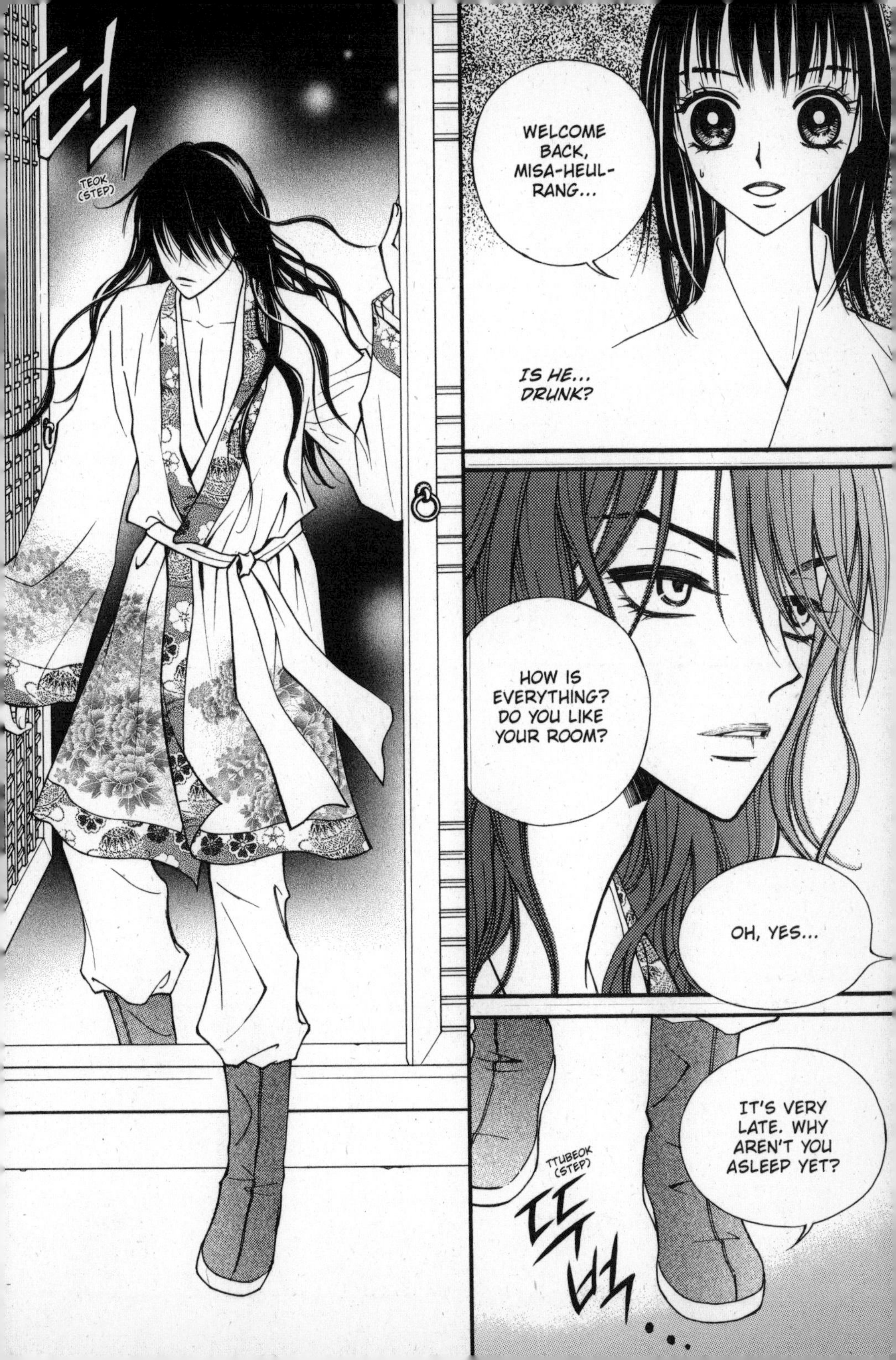
턱
TEOK (STEP)
WELCOME BACK, MISA-HEUL-RANG...
IS HE... DRUNK?
HOW IS EVERYTHING? DO YOU LIKE YOUR ROOM?
OH, YES...
TTUBEOK (STEP)
뚜벅
IT'S VERY LATE. WHY AREN'T YOU ASLEEP YET?

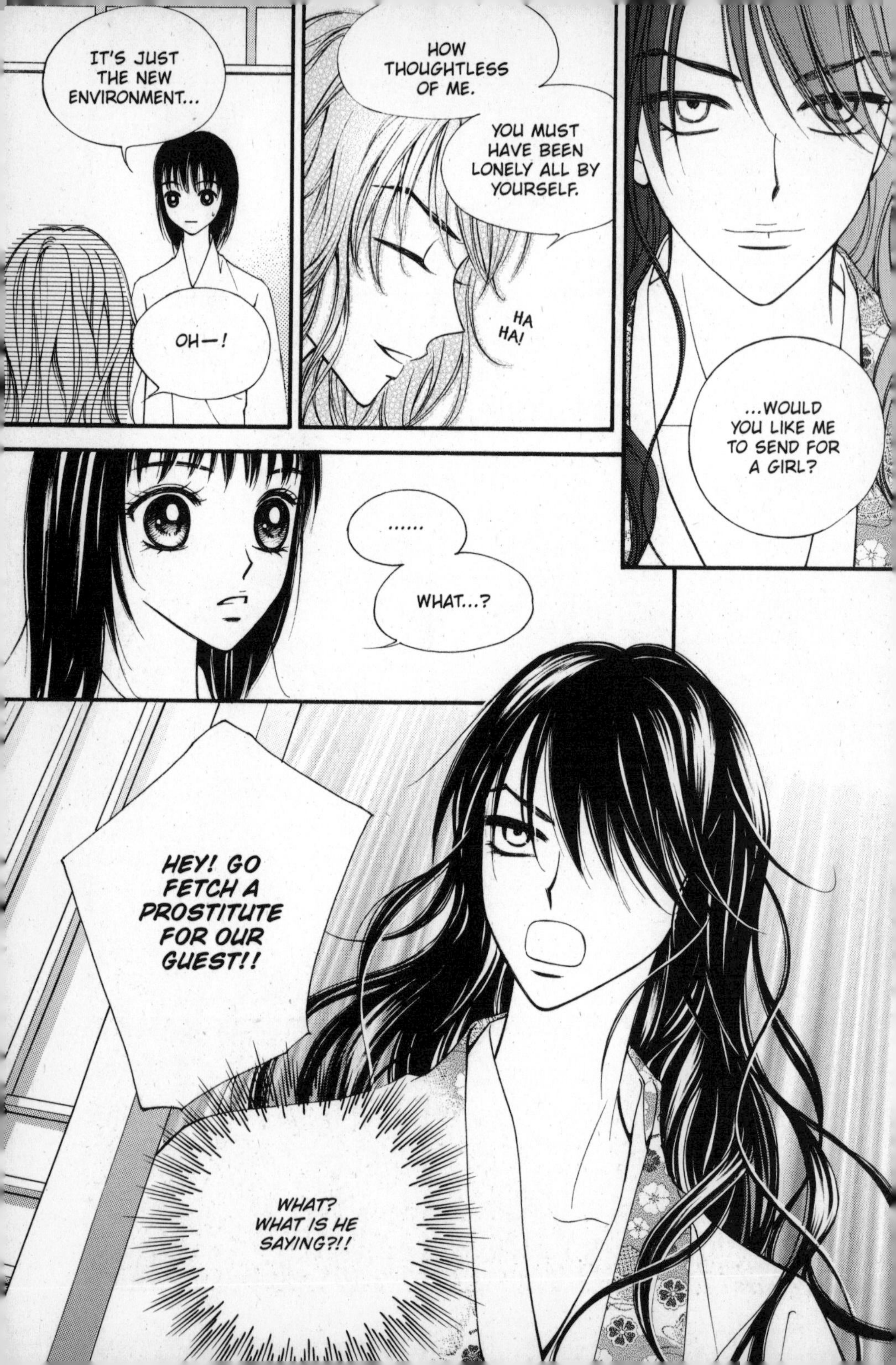
IT'S JUST THE NEW ENVIRONMENT...
OH—!
HOW THOUGHTLESS OF ME.
YOU MUST HAVE BEEN LONELY ALL BY YOURSELF.
HA HA!
...WOULD YOU LIKE ME TO SEND FOR A GIRL?
......
WHAT...?
HEY! GO FETCH A PROSTITUTE FOR OUR GUEST!!
WHAT? WHAT IS HE SAYING?!!

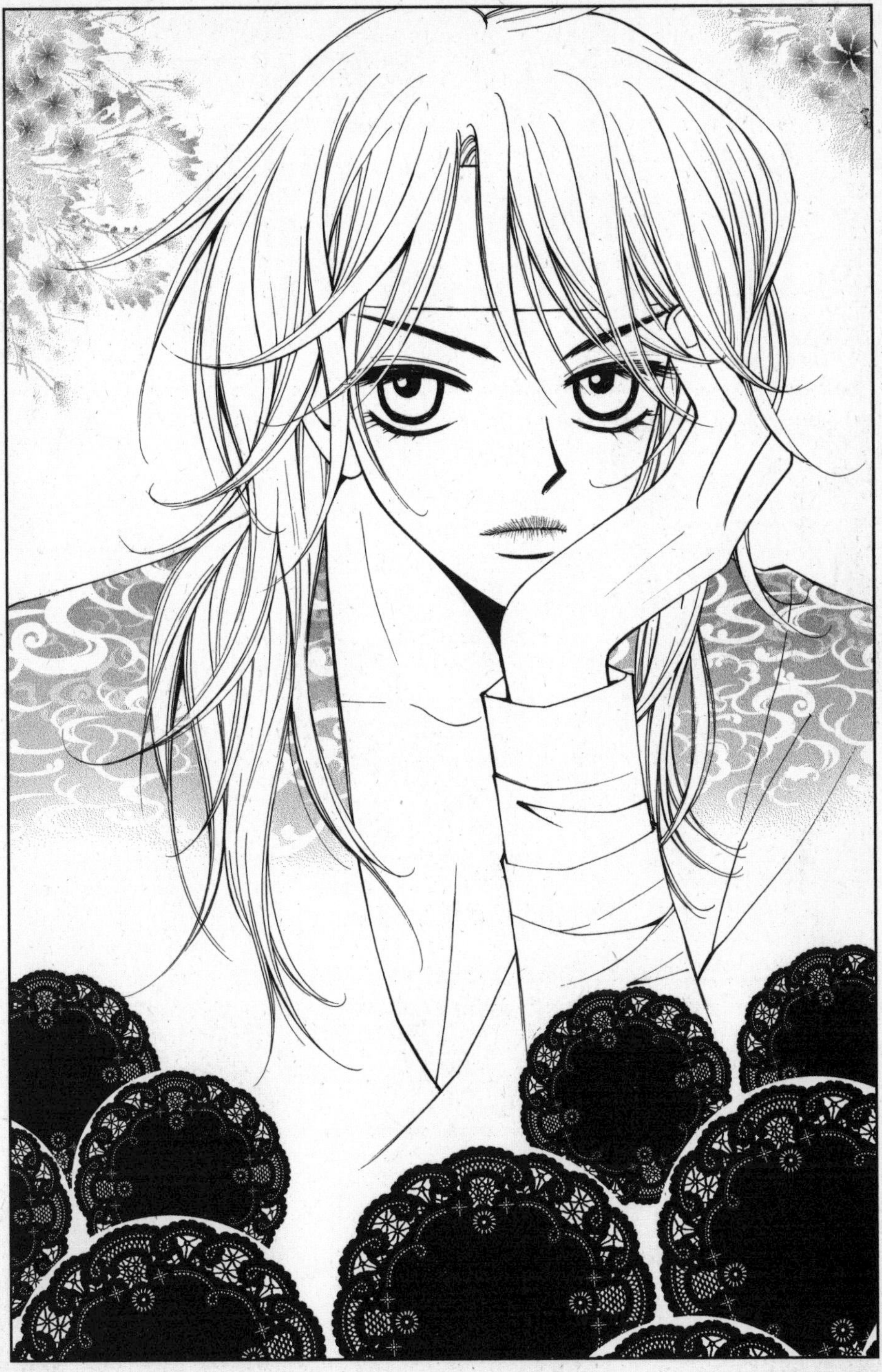

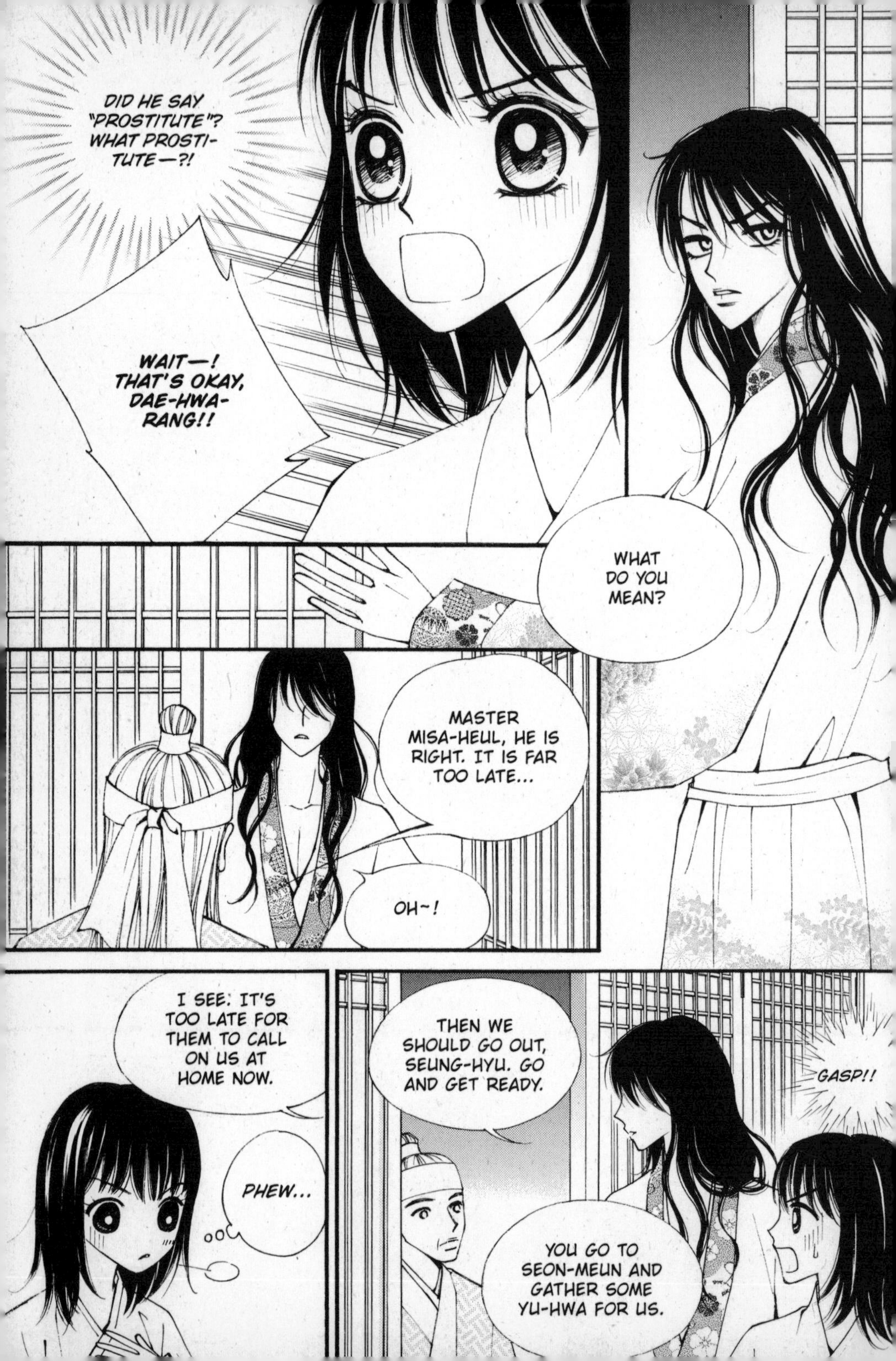
DID HE SAY "PROSTITUTE"? WHAT PROSTI-TUTE—?!
WAIT—! THAT'S OKAY, DAE-HWA-RANG!!
WHAT DO YOU MEAN?
MASTER MISA-HEUL, HE IS RIGHT. IT IS FAR TOO LATE...
OH~!
I SEE: IT'S TOO LATE FOR THEM TO CALL ON US AT HOME NOW.
PHEW...
THEN WE SHOULD GO OUT, SEUNG-HYU. GO AND GET READY.
GASP!!
YOU GO TO SEON-MEUN AND GATHER SOME YU-HWA FOR US.

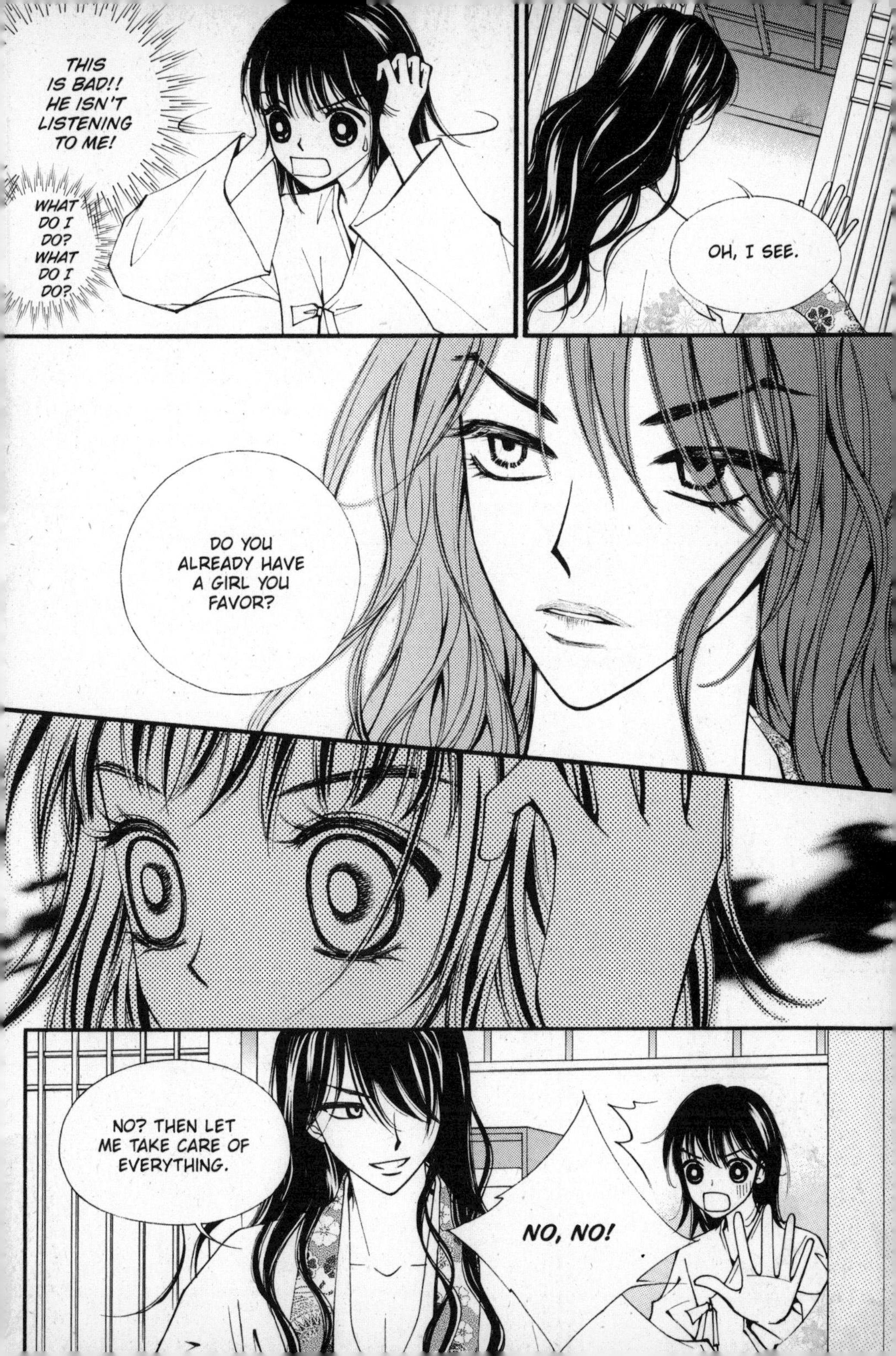
THIS IS BAD!! HE ISN'T LISTENING TO ME!
WHAT DO I DO? WHAT DO I DO?
OH, I SEE.
DO YOU ALREADY HAVE A GIRL YOU FAVOR?
NO? THEN LET ME TAKE CARE OF EVERYTHING.
NO, NO!

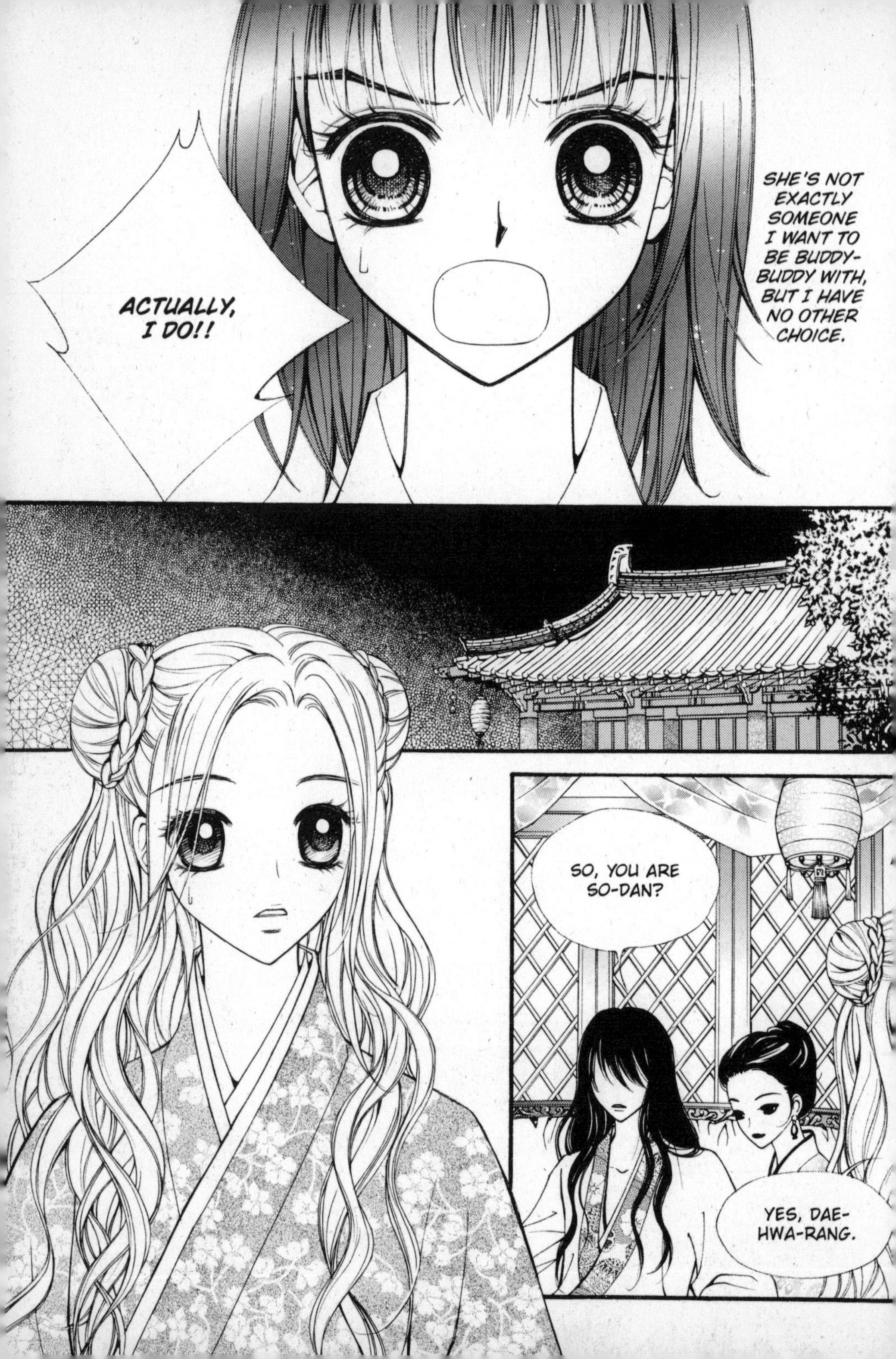
ACTUALLY, I DO!!
SHE'S NOT EXACTLY SOMEONE I WANT TO BE BUDDY-BUDDY WITH, BUT I HAVE NO OTHER CHOICE.
SO, YOU ARE SO-DAN?
YES, DAE-HWA-RANG.

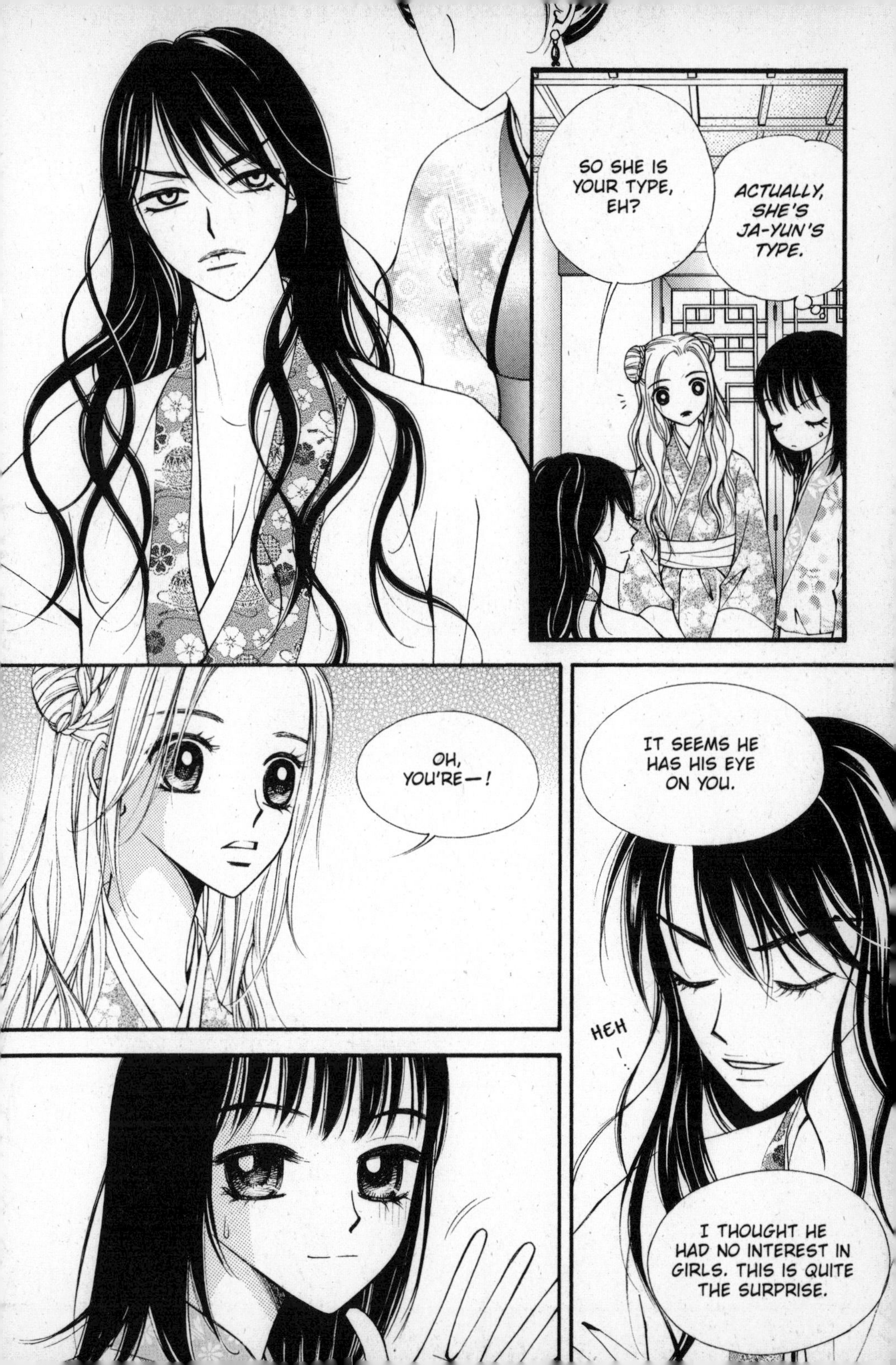
SO SHE IS YOUR TYPE, EH?
ACTUALLY, SHE'S JA-YUN'S TYPE.
OH, YOU'RE—!
IT SEEMS HE HAS HIS EYE ON YOU.
HEH
I THOUGHT HE HAD NO INTEREST IN GIRLS. THIS IS QUITE THE SURPRISE.

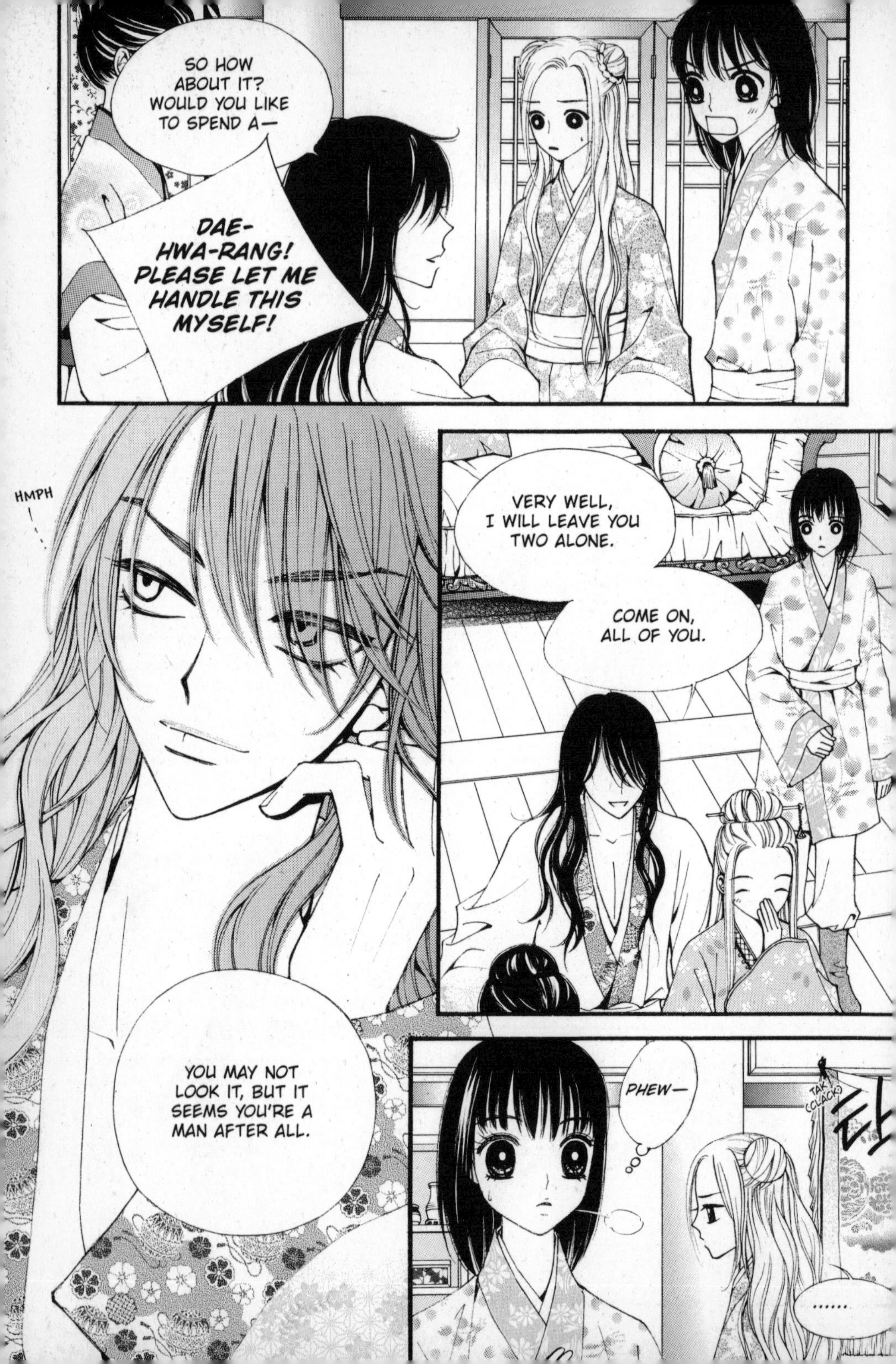
SO HOW ABOUT IT? WOULD YOU LIKE TO SPEND A—
DAE-HWA-RANG! PLEASE LET ME HANDLE THIS MYSELF!
HMPH
YOU MAY NOT LOOK IT, BUT IT SEEMS YOU'RE A MAN AFTER ALL.
VERY WELL, I WILL LEAVE YOU TWO ALONE.
COME ON, ALL OF YOU.
PHEW—
탁
TAK (CLACK)
......

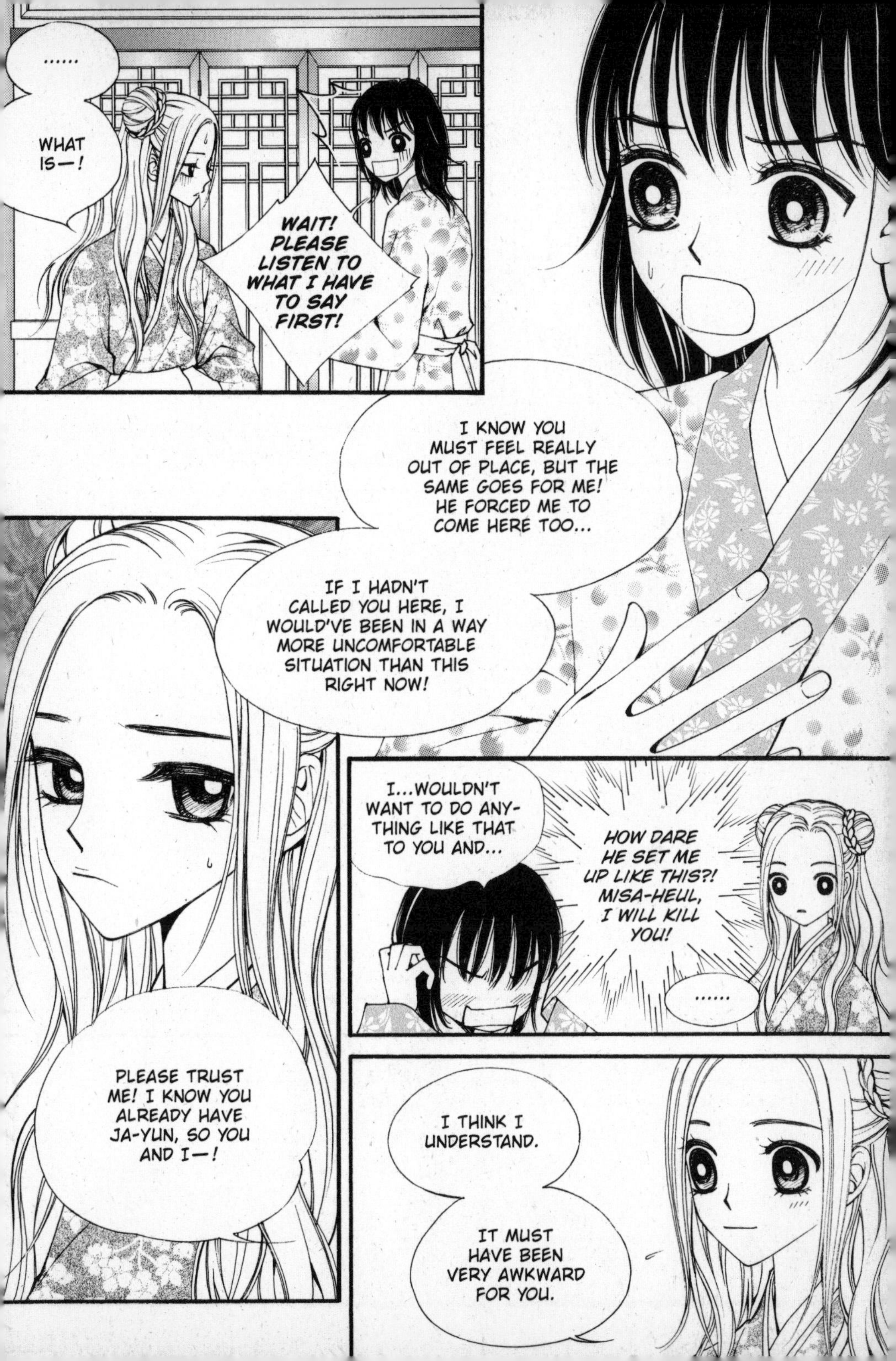
......
WHAT IS—!
WAIT! PLEASE LISTEN TO WHAT I HAVE TO SAY FIRST!
I KNOW YOU MUST FEEL REALLY OUT OF PLACE, BUT THE SAME GOES FOR ME! HE FORCED ME TO COME HERE TOO...
IF I HADN'T CALLED YOU HERE, I WOULD'VE BEEN IN A WAY MORE UNCOMFORTABLE SITUATION THAN THIS RIGHT NOW!
I...WOULDN'T WANT TO DO ANY-THING LIKE THAT TO YOU AND...
HOW DARE HE SET ME UP LIKE THIS?! MISA-HEUL, I WILL KILL YOU!
......
PLEASE TRUST ME! I KNOW YOU ALREADY HAVE JA-YUN, SO YOU AND I—!
I THINK I UNDERSTAND.
IT MUST HAVE BEEN VERY AWKWARD FOR YOU.

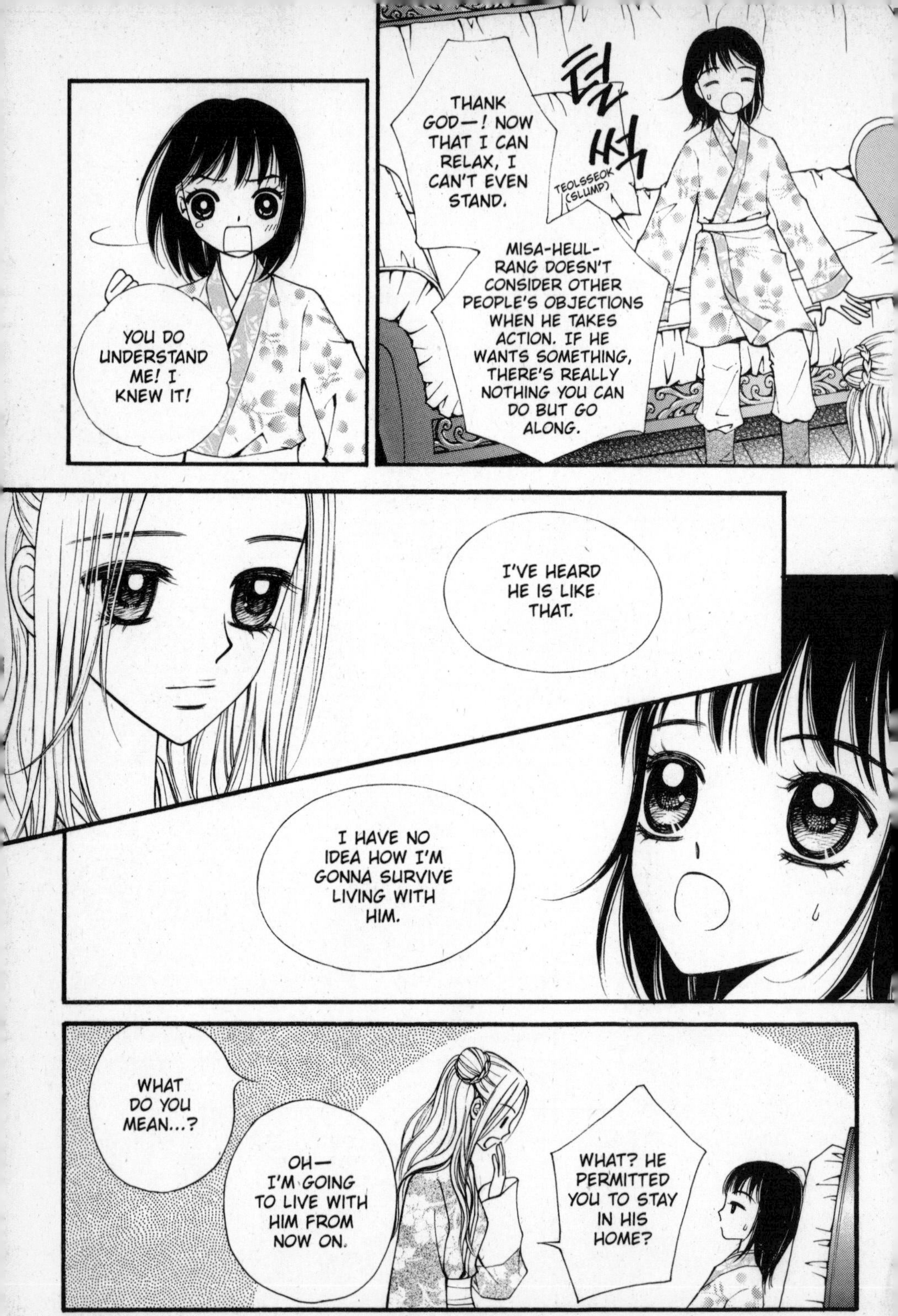
YOU DO UNDERSTAND ME! I KNEW IT!
THANK GOD—! NOW THAT I CAN RELAX, I CAN'T EVEN STAND.
털썩
TEOLSSEOK (SLUMP)
MISA-HEUL-RANG DOESN'T CONSIDER OTHER PEOPLE'S OBJECTIONS WHEN HE TAKES ACTION. IF HE WANTS SOMETHING, THERE'S REALLY NOTHING YOU CAN DO BUT GO ALONG.
I'VE HEARD HE IS LIKE THAT.
I HAVE NO IDEA HOW I'M GONNA SURVIVE LIVING WITH HIM.
WHAT DO YOU MEAN...?
OH— I'M GOING TO LIVE WITH HIM FROM NOW ON.
WHAT? HE PERMITTED YOU TO STAY IN HIS HOME?

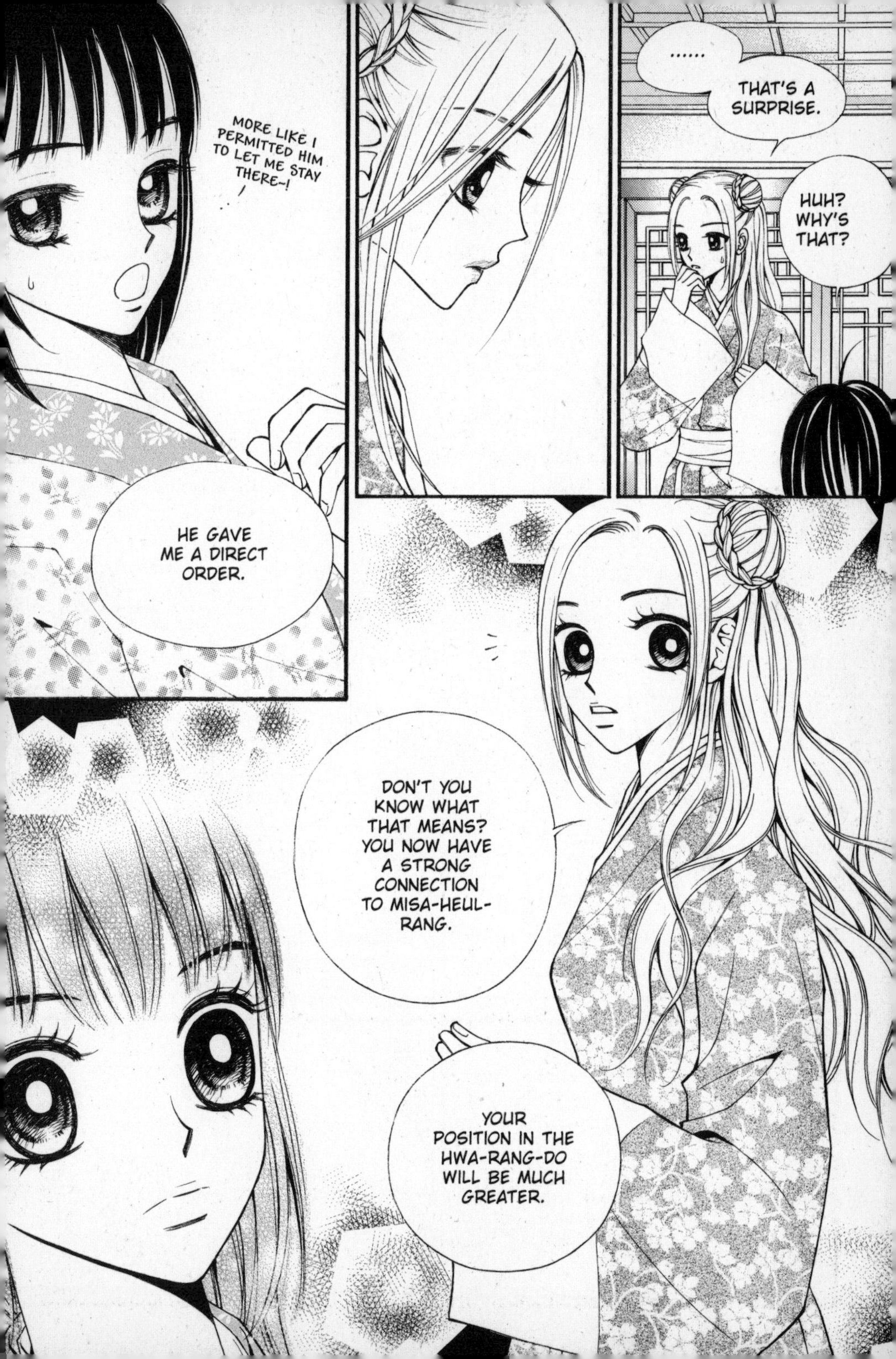
MORE LIKE I PERMITTED HIM TO LET ME STAY THERE~!
HE GAVE ME A DIRECT ORDER.
......
THAT'S A SURPRISE.
HUH? WHY'S THAT?
DON'T YOU KNOW WHAT THAT MEANS? YOU NOW HAVE A STRONG CONNECTION TO MISA-HEUL-RANG.
YOUR POSITION IN THE HWA-RANG-DO WILL BE MUCH GREATER.

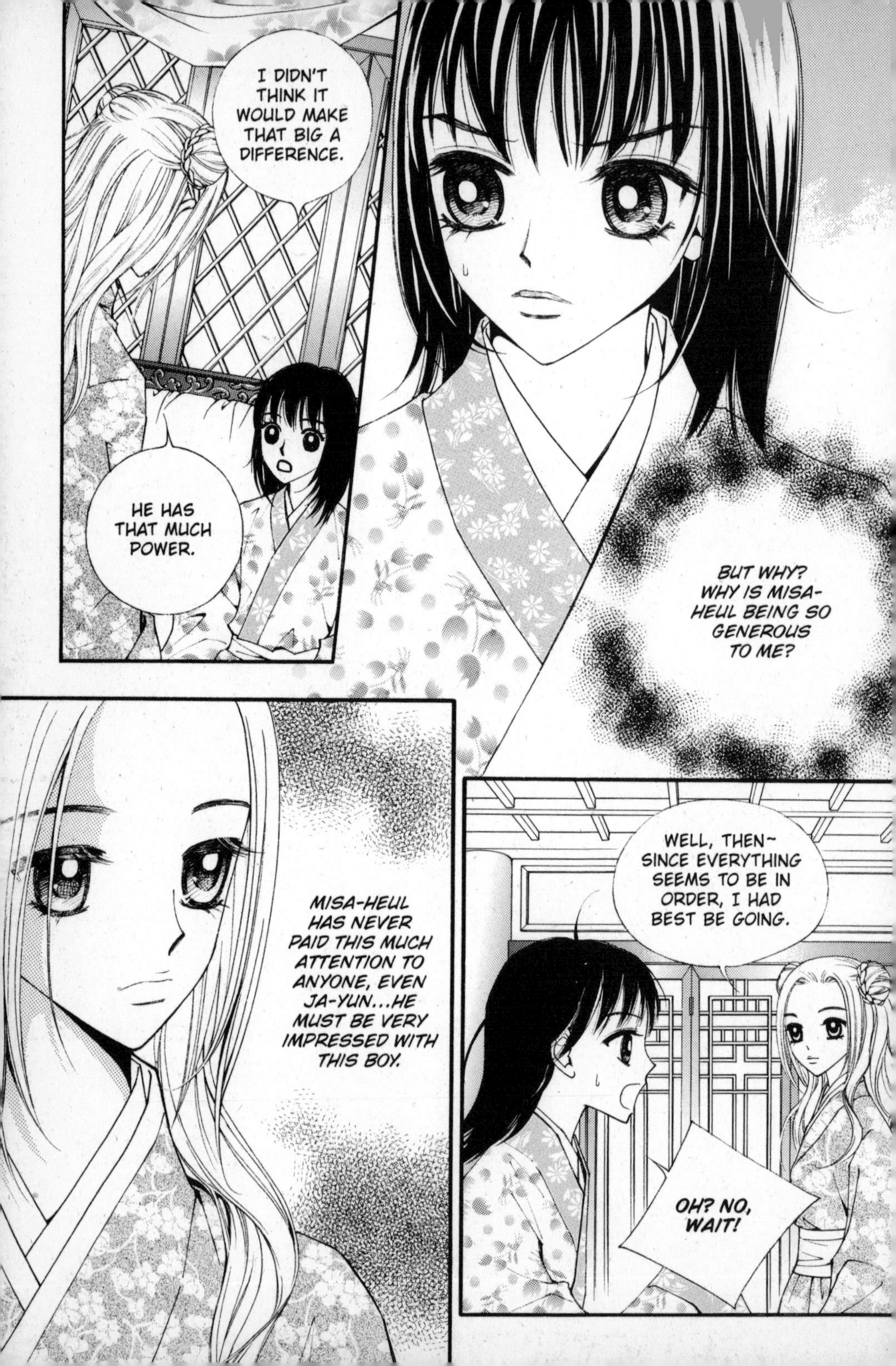
I DIDN'T THINK IT WOULD MAKE THAT BIG A DIFFERENCE.
HE HAS THAT MUCH POWER.
BUT WHY? WHY IS MISA-HEUL BEING SO GENEROUS TO ME?
MISA-HEUL HAS NEVER PAID THIS MUCH ATTENTION TO ANYONE, EVEN JA-YUN...HE MUST BE VERY IMPRESSED WITH THIS BOY.
WELL, THEN~ SINCE EVERYTHING SEEMS TO BE IN ORDER, I HAD BEST BE GOING.
OH? NO, WAIT!

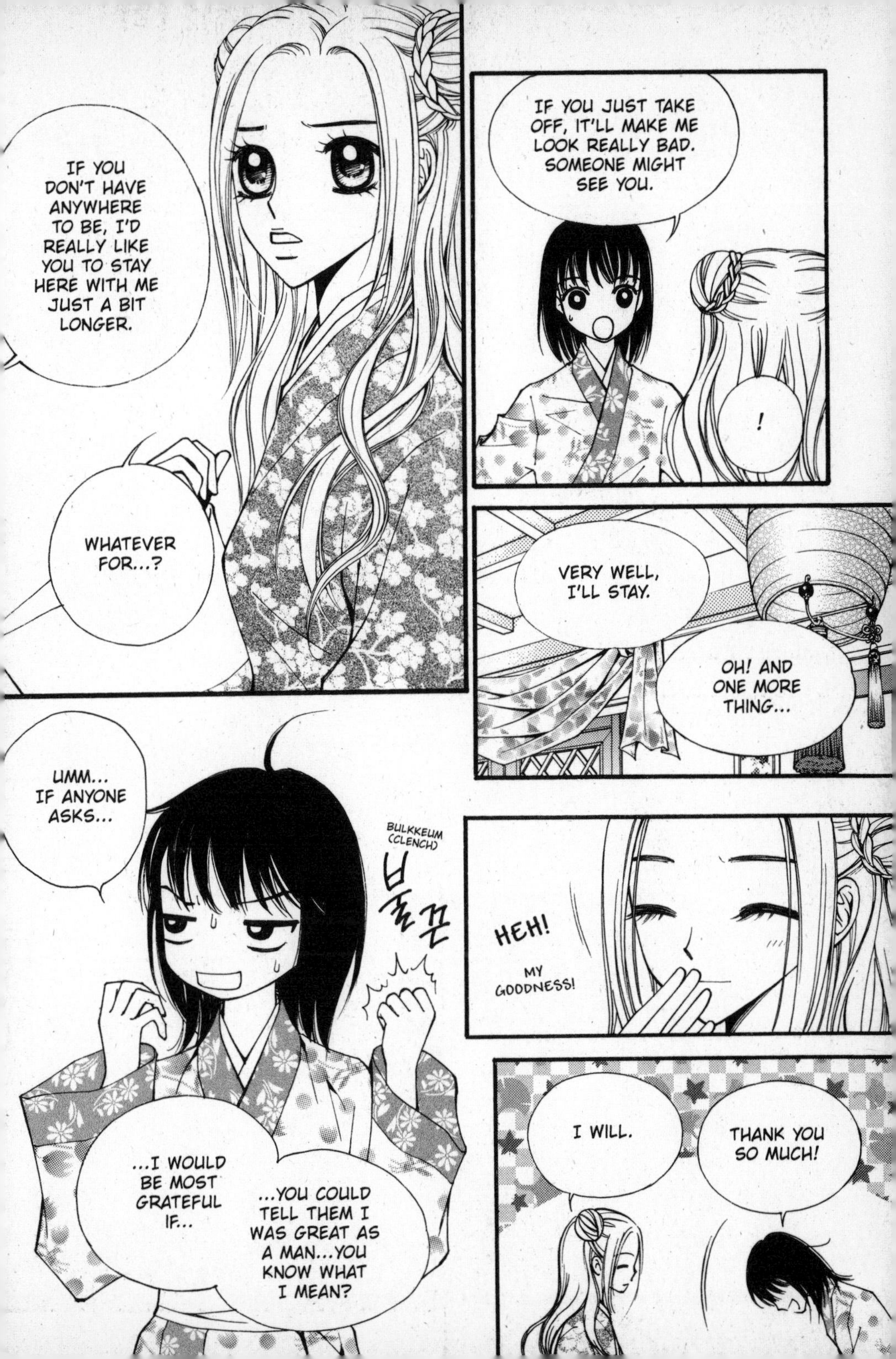
IF YOU DON'T HAVE ANYWHERE TO BE, I'D REALLY LIKE YOU TO STAY HERE WITH ME JUST A BIT LONGER.
WHATEVER FOR...?
IF YOU JUST TAKE OFF, IT'LL MAKE ME LOOK REALLY BAD. SOMEONE MIGHT SEE YOU.
!
VERY WELL, I'LL STAY.
OH! AND ONE MORE THING...
UMM... IF ANYONE ASKS...
BULKKEUM (CLENCH)
불끈
...I WOULD BE MOST GRATEFUL IF...
...YOU COULD TELL THEM I WAS GREAT AS A MAN...YOU KNOW WHAT I MEAN?
HEH!
MY GOODNESS!
I WILL.
THANK YOU SO MUCH!

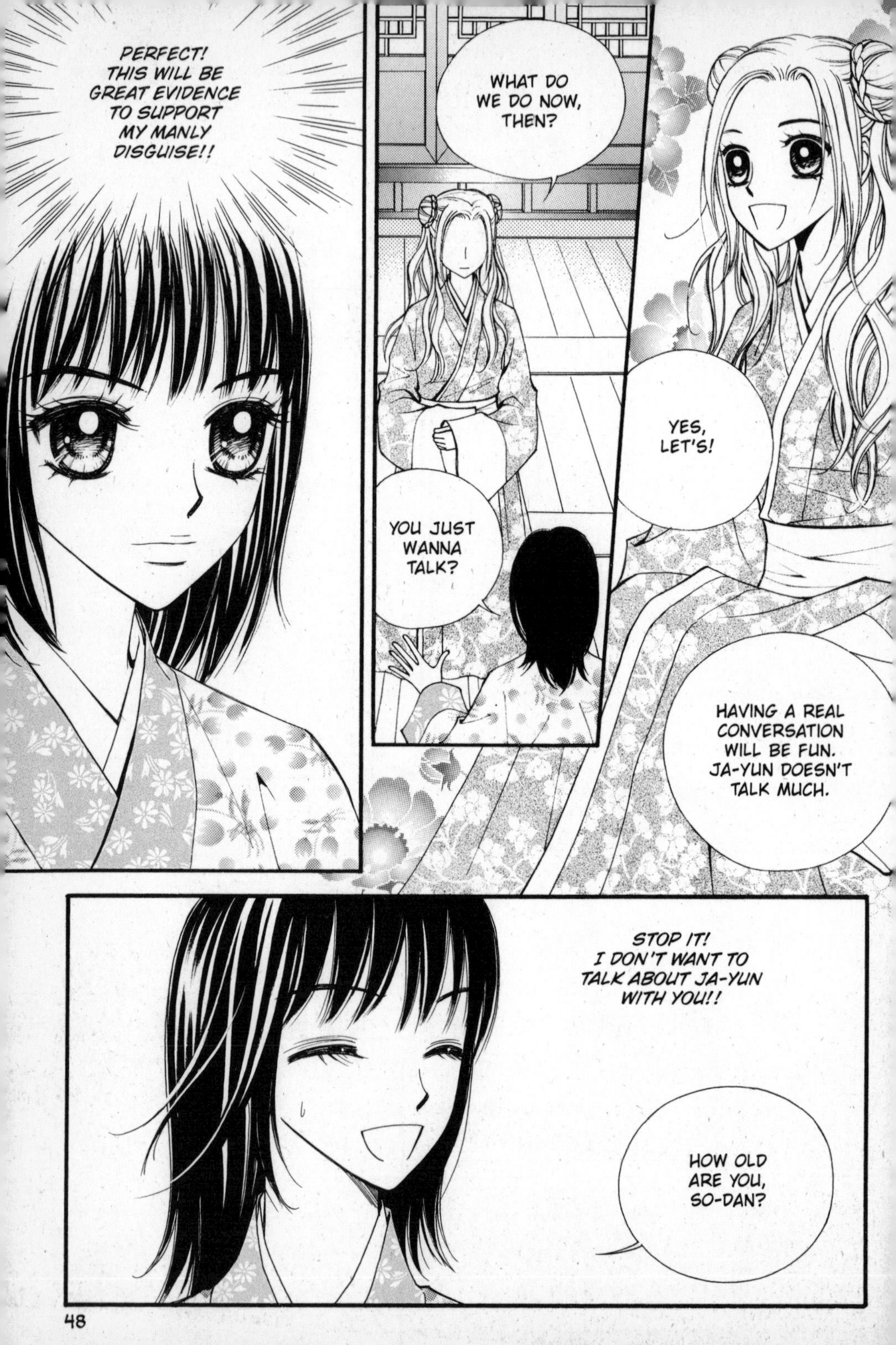
PERFECT! THIS WILL BE GREAT EVIDENCE TO SUPPORT MY MANLY DISGUISE!!
WHAT DO WE DO NOW, THEN?
YOU JUST WANNA TALK?
YES, LET'S!
HAVING A REAL CONVERSATION WILL BE FUN. JA-YUN DOESN'T TALK MUCH.
STOP IT! I DON'T WANT TO TALK ABOUT JA-YUN WITH YOU!!
HOW OLD ARE YOU, SO-DAN?

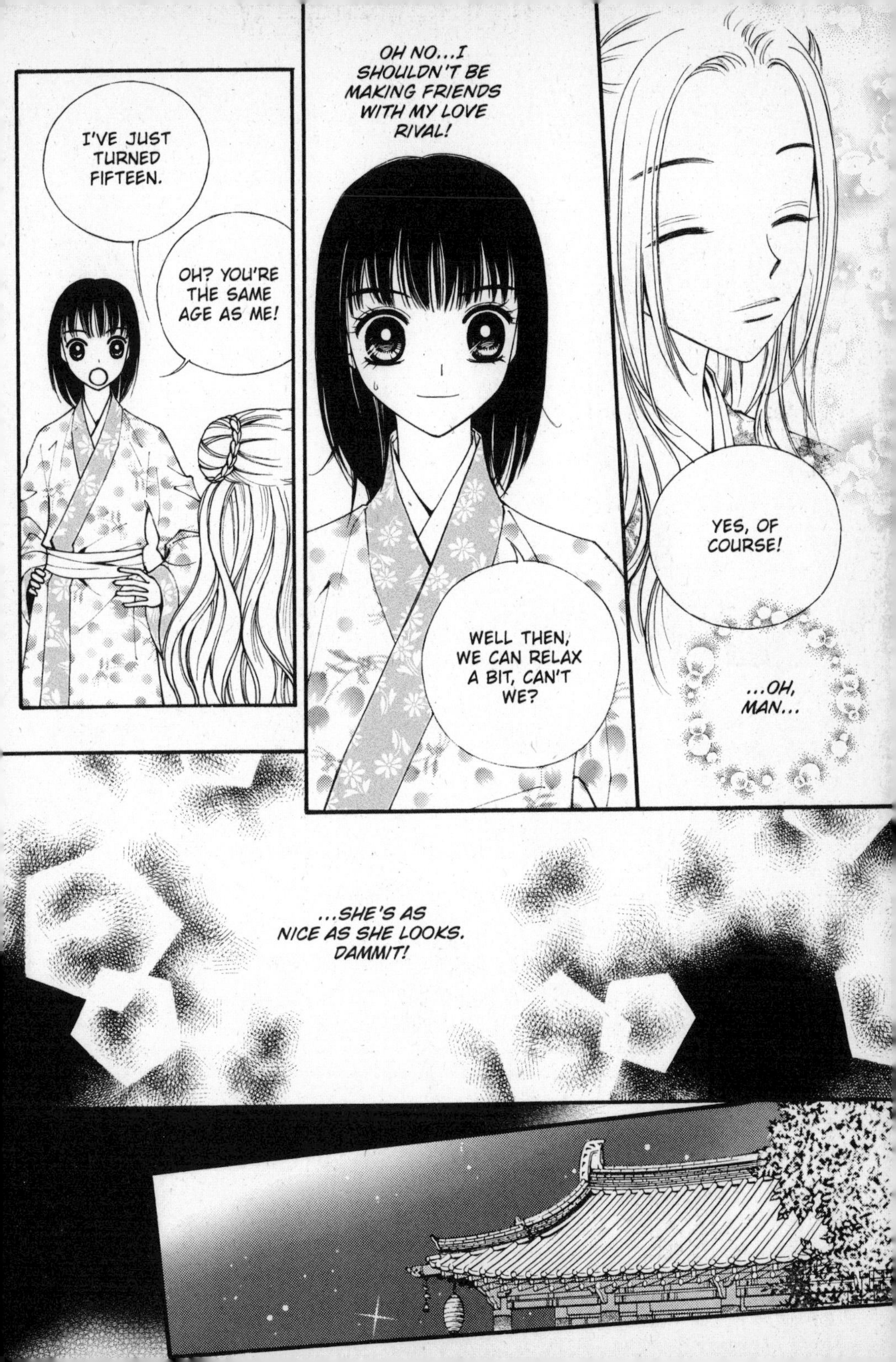
I'VE JUST TURNED FIFTEEN.
OH? YOU'RE THE SAME AGE AS ME!
OH NO...I SHOULDN'T BE MAKING FRIENDS WITH MY LOVE RIVAL!
WELL THEN, WE CAN RELAX A BIT, CAN'T WE?
YES, OF COURSE!
...OH, MAN...
...SHE'S AS NICE AS SHE LOOKS. DAMMIT!

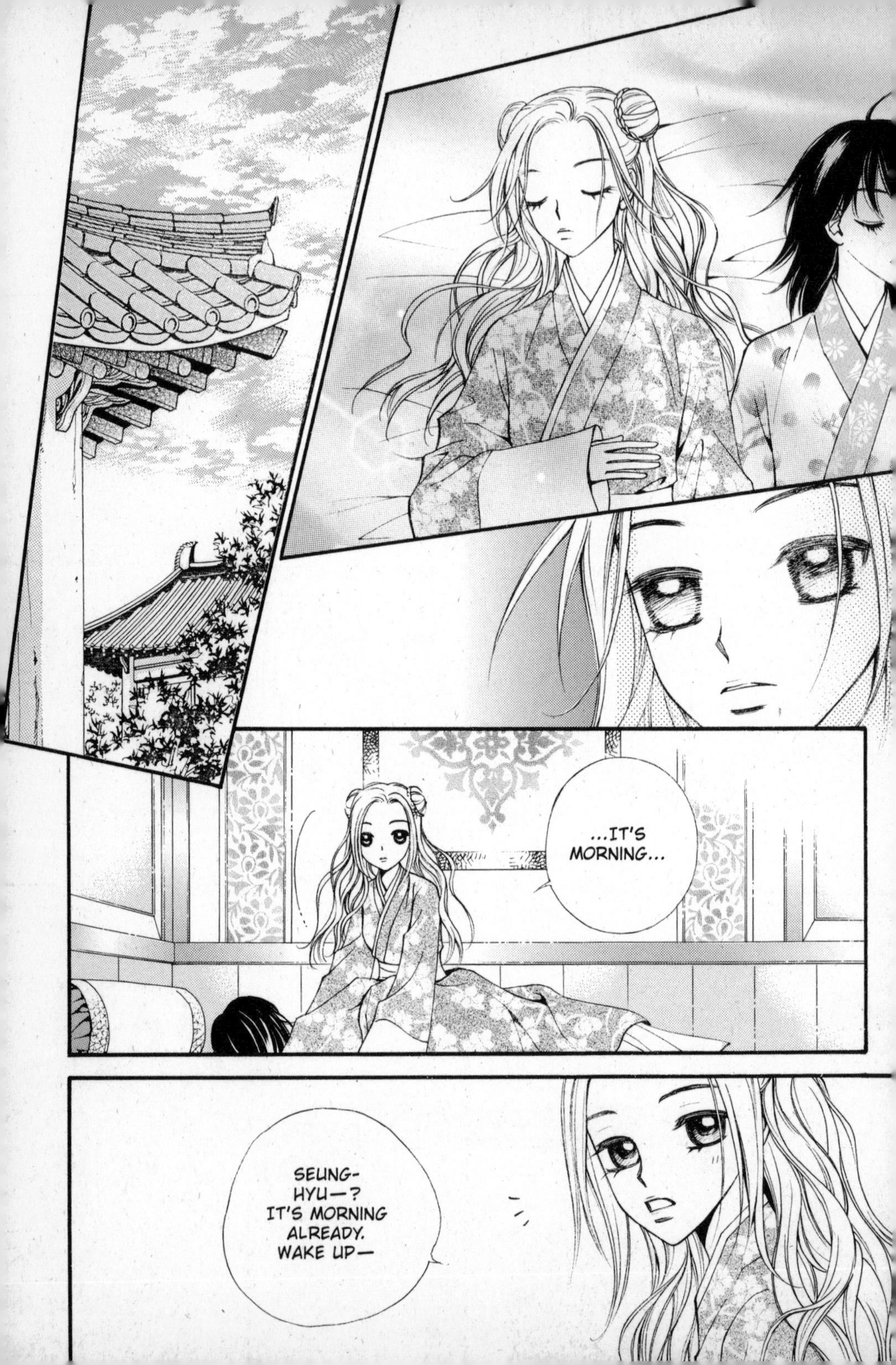

...IT'S MORNING...
SEUNG-HYU—? IT'S MORNING ALREADY. WAKE UP—

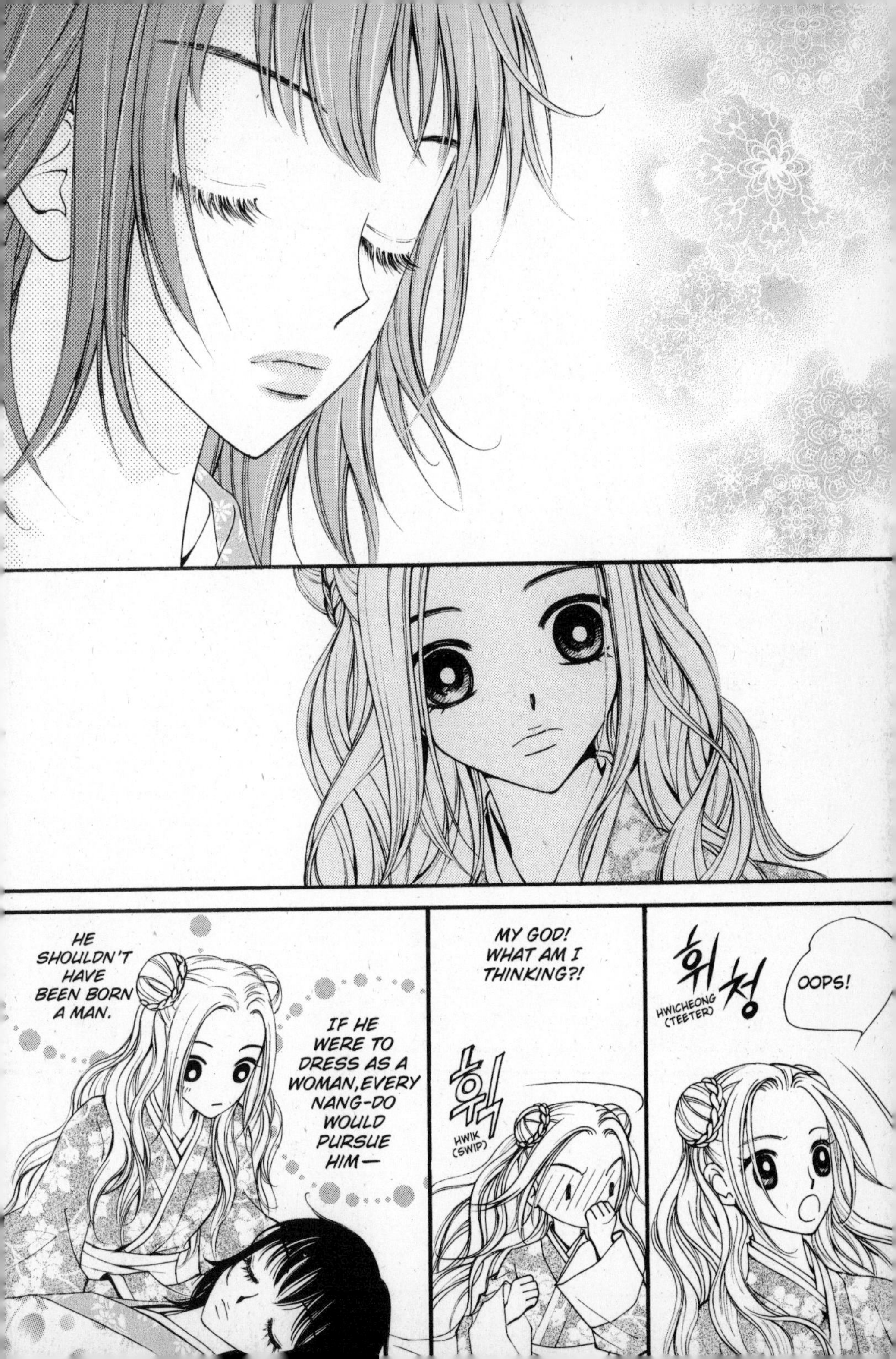

HE SHOULDN'T HAVE BEEN BORN A MAN.
IF HE WERE TO DRESS AS A WOMAN, EVERY NANG-DO WOULD PURSUE HIM—
MY GOD! WHAT AM I THINKING?!
휙
HWIK (SWIP)
휘청
HWICHEONG (TEETER)
OOPS!

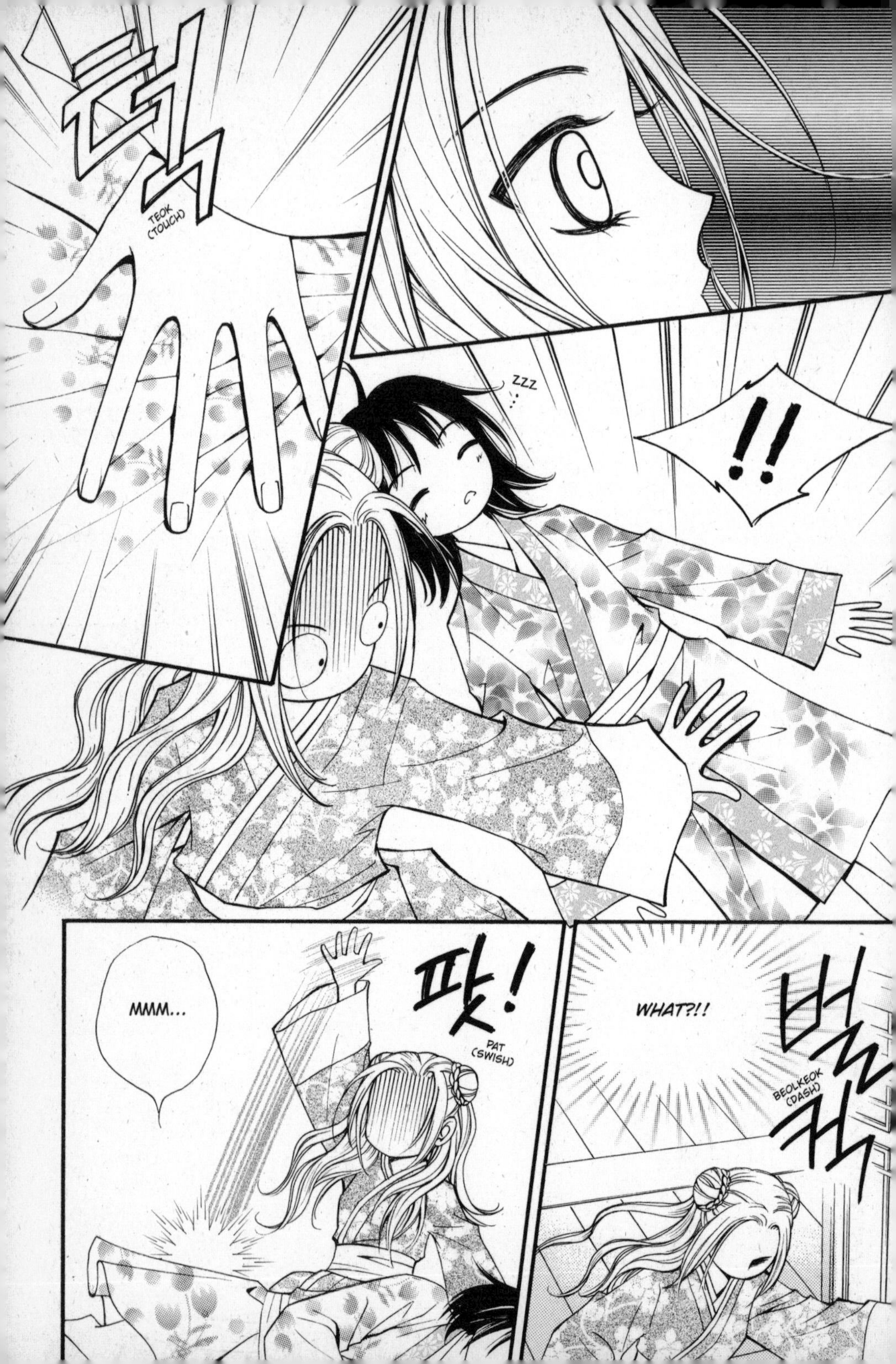

턱
TEOK (TOUCH)
ZZZ
!!
MMM...
팟!
PAT (SWISH)
WHAT?!!
벌컥
BEOLKEOK (DASH)

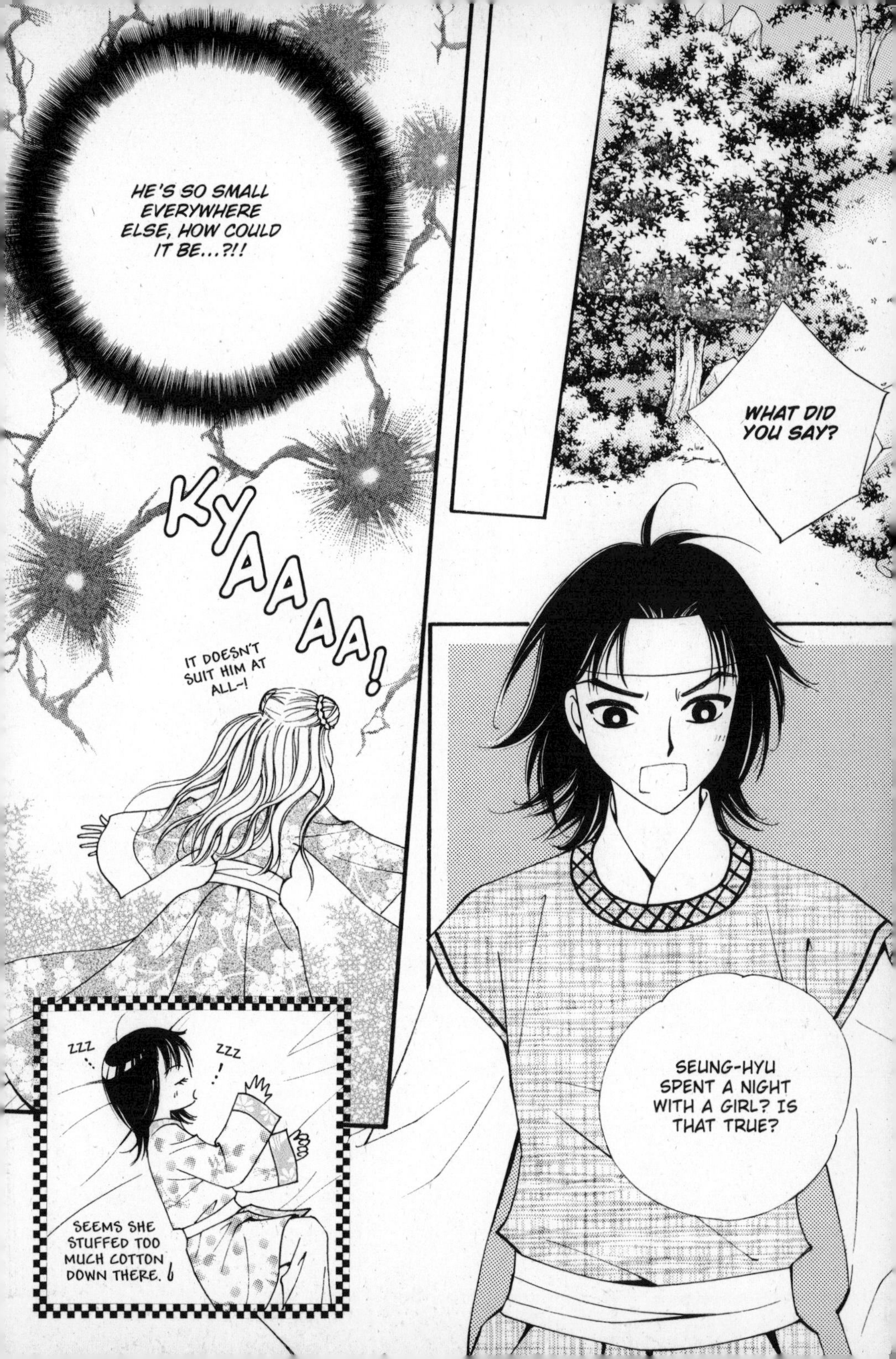
HE'S SO SMALL EVERYWHERE ELSE, HOW COULD IT BE...?!!
KYAAAAA!
IT DOESN'T SUIT HIM AT ALL~!
ZZZ...
ZZZ !
SEEMS SHE STUFFED TOO MUCH COTTON DOWN THERE.
WHAT DID YOU SAY?
SEUNG-HYU SPENT A NIGHT WITH A GIRL? IS THAT TRUE?

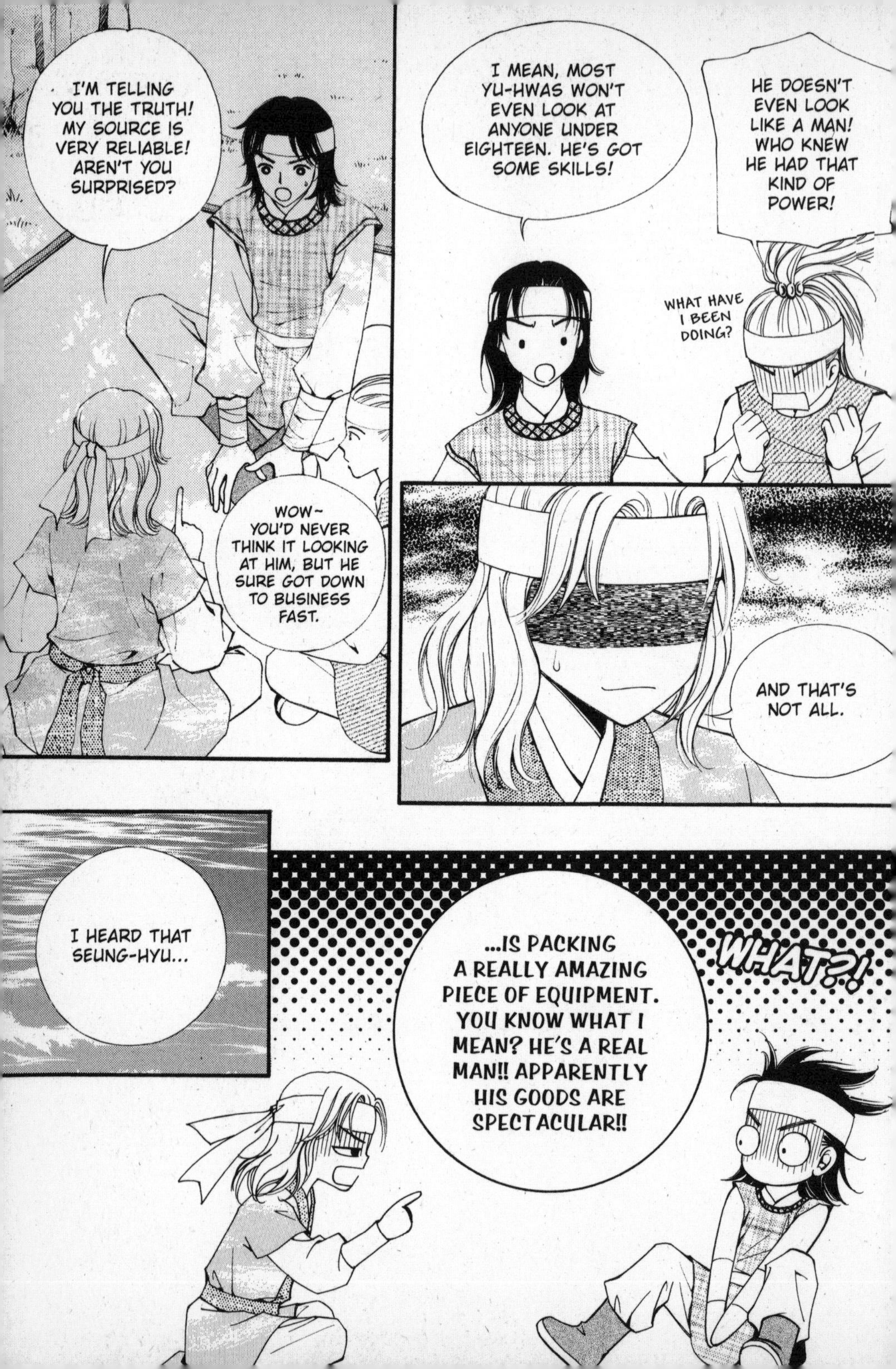
I'M TELLING YOU THE TRUTH! MY SOURCE IS VERY RELIABLE! AREN'T YOU SURPRISED?
WOW~ YOU'D NEVER THINK IT LOOKING AT HIM, BUT HE SURE GOT DOWN TO BUSINESS FAST.
I MEAN, MOST YU-HWAS WON'T EVEN LOOK AT ANYONE UNDER EIGHTEEN. HE'S GOT SOME SKILLS!
HE DOESN'T EVEN LOOK LIKE A MAN! WHO KNEW HE HAD THAT KIND OF POWER!
WHAT HAVE I BEEN DOING?
AND THAT'S NOT ALL.
I HEARD THAT SEUNG-HYU...
...IS PACKING A REALLY AMAZING PIECE OF EQUIPMENT. YOU KNOW WHAT I MEAN? HE'S A REAL MAN!! APPARENTLY HIS GOODS ARE SPECTACULAR!!
WHAT?!

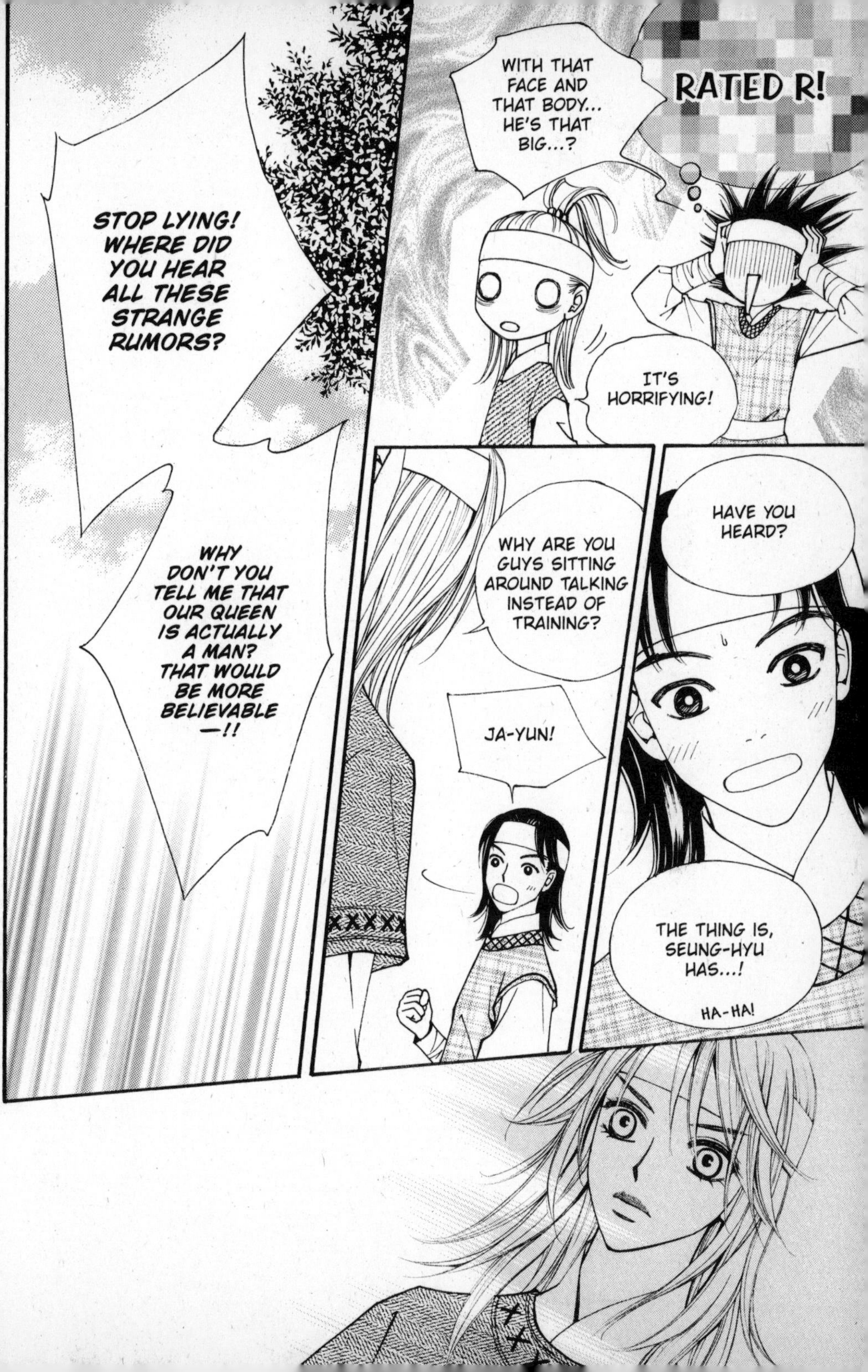
STOP LYING! WHERE DID YOU HEAR ALL THESE STRANGE RUMORS?
WHY DON'T YOU TELL ME THAT OUR QUEEN IS ACTUALLY A MAN? THAT WOULD BE MORE BELIEVABLE—!!
WITH THAT FACE AND THAT BODY... HE'S THAT BIG...?
RATED R!
IT'S HORRIFYING!
WHY ARE YOU GUYS SITTING AROUND TALKING INSTEAD OF TRAINING?
JA-YUN!
HAVE YOU HEARD?
THE THING IS, SEUNG-HYU HAS...!
HA-HA!

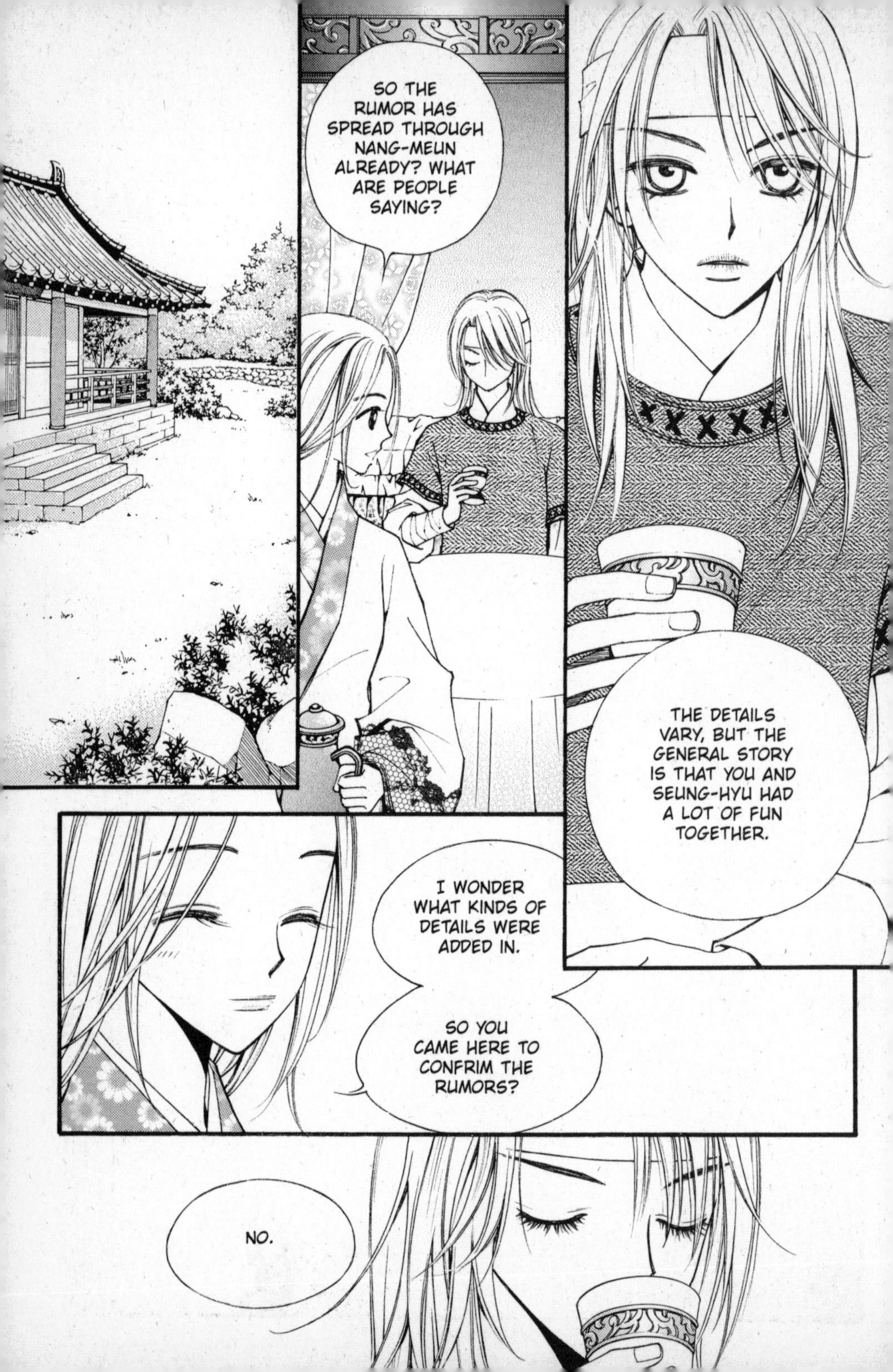
SO THE RUMOR HAS SPREAD THROUGH NANG-MEUN ALREADY? WHAT ARE PEOPLE SAYING?
THE DETAILS VARY, BUT THE GENERAL STORY IS THAT YOU AND SEUNG-HYU HAD A LOT OF FUN TOGETHER.
I WONDER WHAT KINDS OF DETAILS WERE ADDED IN.
SO YOU CAME HERE TO CONFIRM THE RUMORS?
NO.

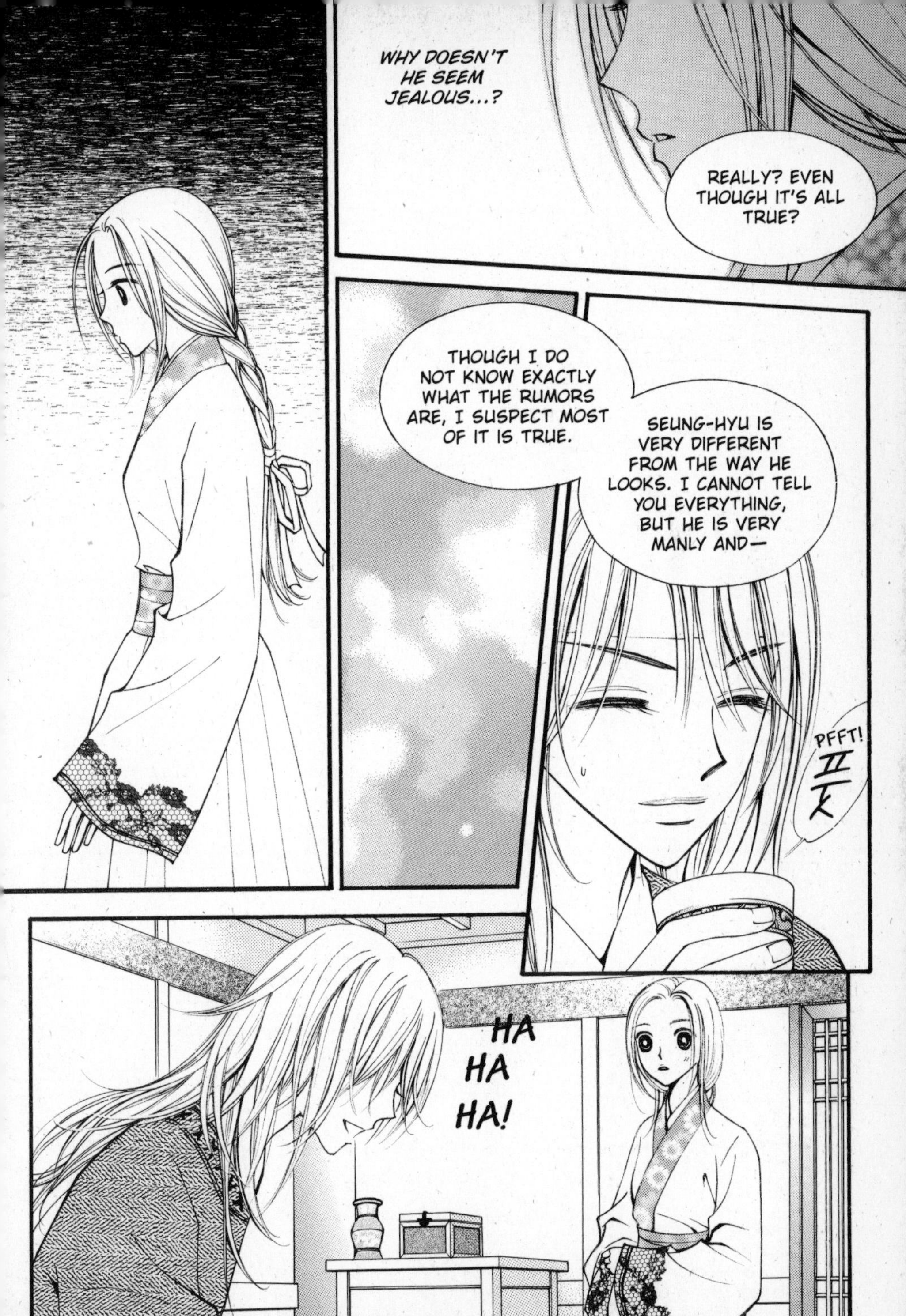
WHY DOESN'T HE SEEM JEALOUS...?
REALLY? EVEN THOUGH IT'S ALL TRUE?
THOUGH I DO NOT KNOW EXACTLY WHAT THE RUMORS ARE, I SUSPECT MOST OF IT IS TRUE.
SEUNG-HYU IS VERY DIFFERENT FROM THE WAY HE LOOKS. I CANNOT TELL YOU EVERYTHING, BUT HE IS VERY MANLY AND—
PFFT!
HA HA HA!

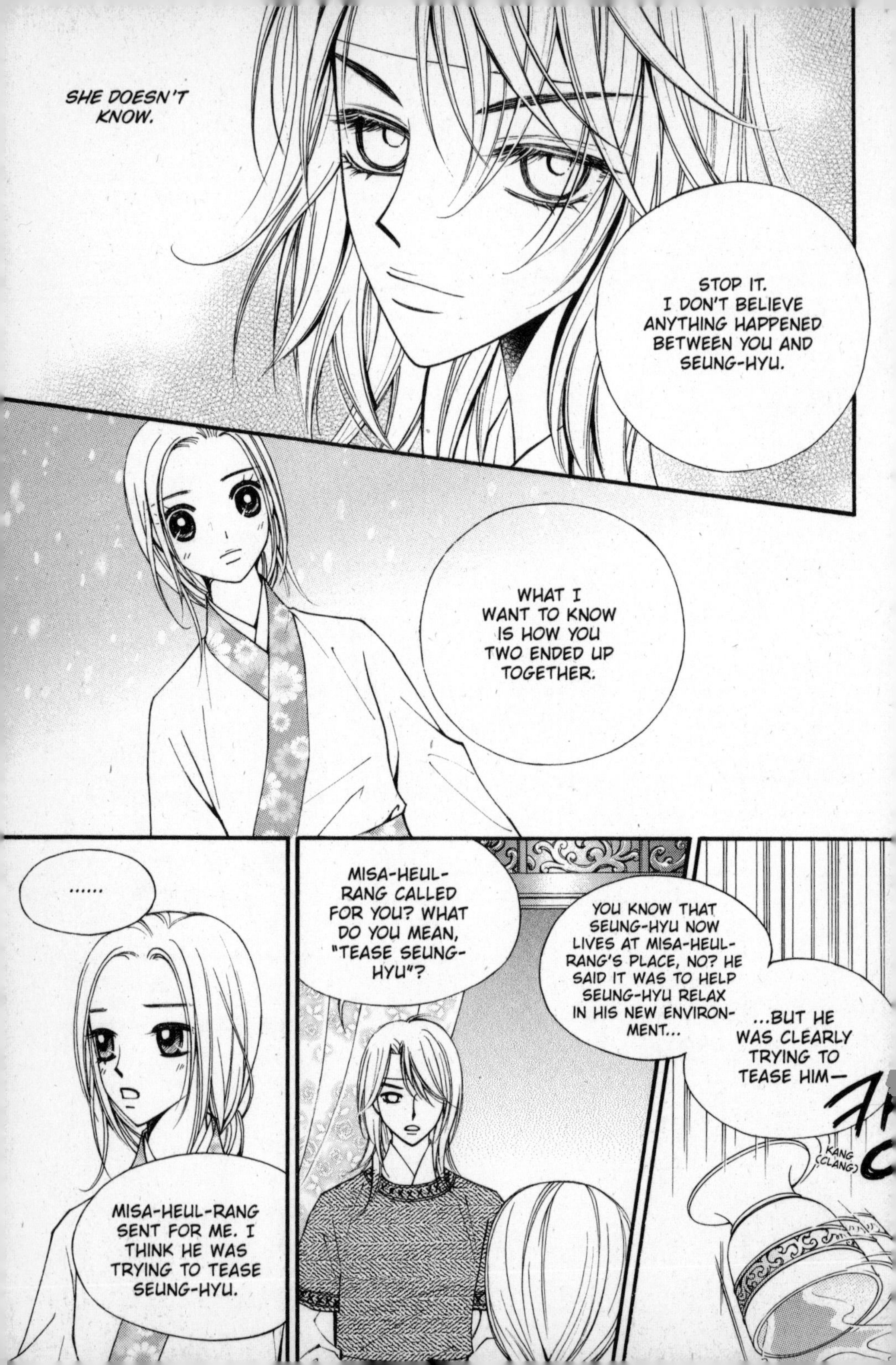
SHE DOESN'T KNOW.
STOP IT. I DON'T BELIEVE ANYTHING HAPPENED BETWEEN YOU AND SEUNG-HYU.
WHAT I WANT TO KNOW IS HOW YOU TWO ENDED UP TOGETHER.
......
MISA-HEUL-RANG SENT FOR ME. I THINK HE WAS TRYING TO TEASE SEUNG-HYU.
MISA-HEUL-RANG CALLED FOR YOU? WHAT DO YOU MEAN, "TEASE SEUNG-HYU"?
YOU KNOW THAT SEUNG-HYU NOW LIVES AT MISA-HEUL-RANG'S PLACE, NO? HE SAID IT WAS TO HELP SEUNG-HYU RELAX IN HIS NEW ENVIRONMENT...
...BUT HE WAS CLEARLY TRYING TO TEASE HIM—
KANG (CLANG)

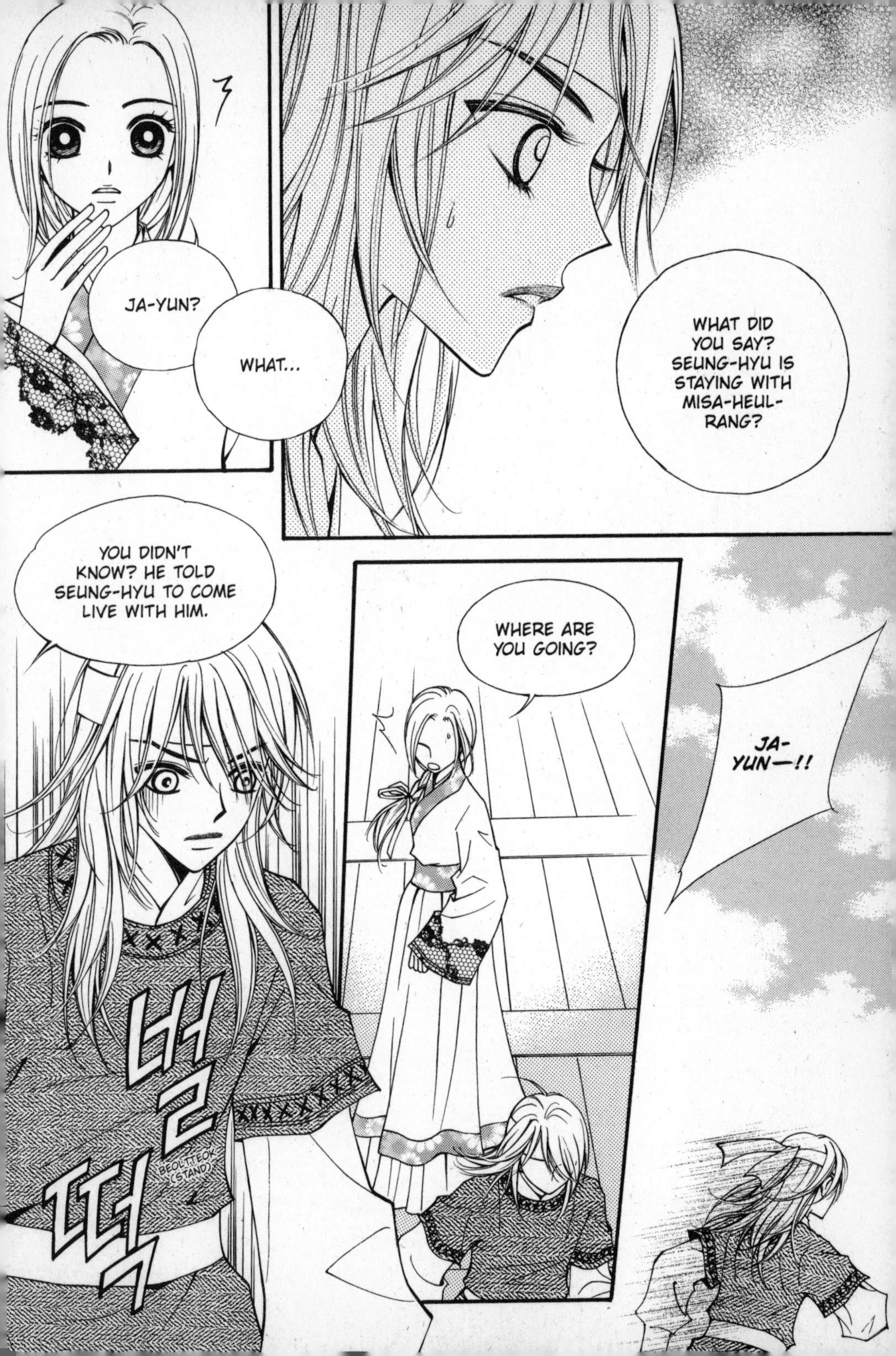
JA-YUN?
WHAT...
WHAT DID YOU SAY? SEUNG-HYU IS STAYING WITH MISA-HEUL-RANG?
YOU DIDN'T KNOW? HE TOLD SEUNG-HYU TO COME LIVE WITH HIM.
벌떡
BEOLTTEOK (STAND)
WHERE ARE YOU GOING?
JA-YUN—!!

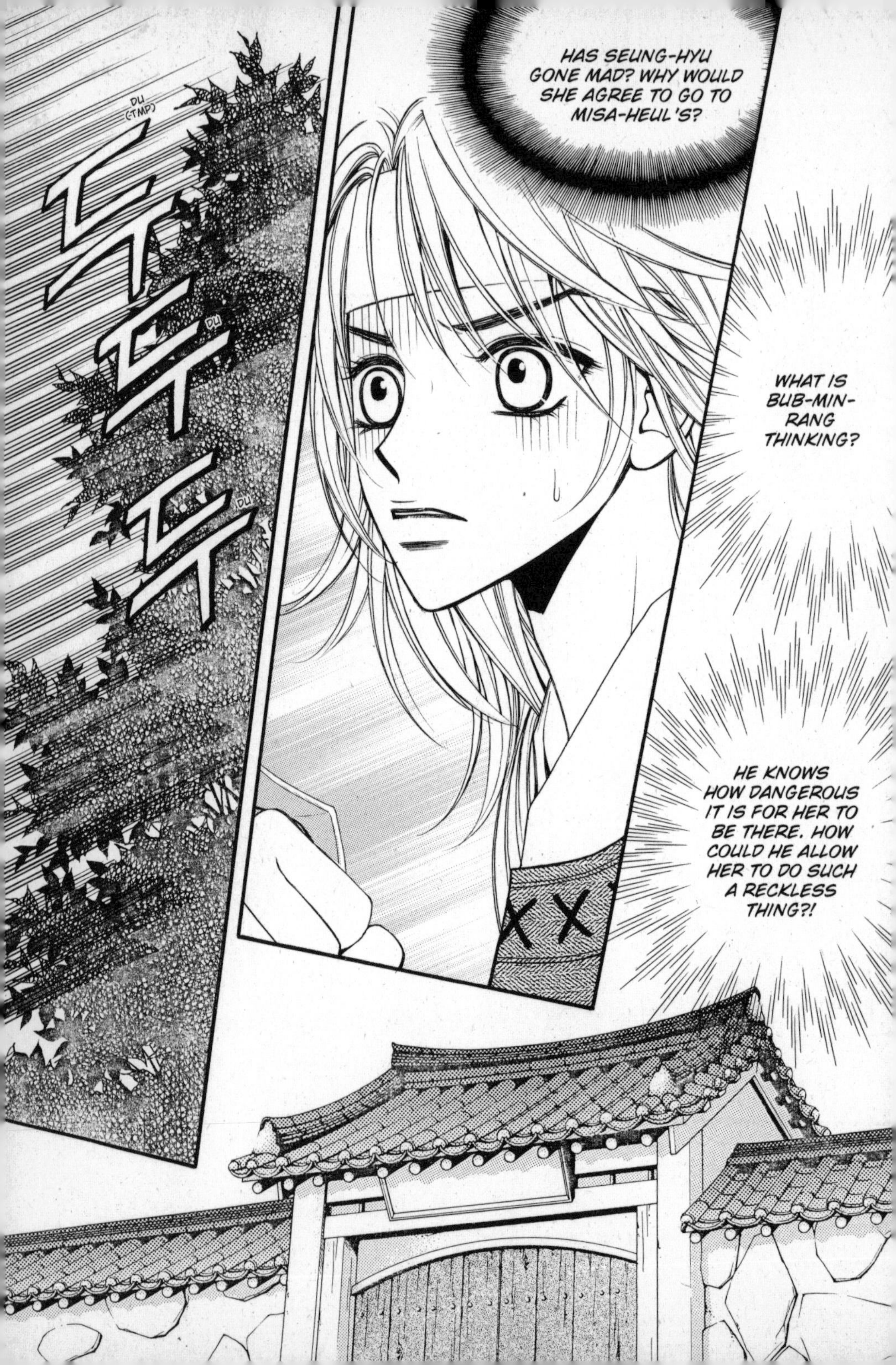
DU (TMP)
DU
DU
HAS SEUNG-HYU GONE MAD? WHY WOULD SHE AGREE TO GO TO MISA-HEUL'S?
WHAT IS BUB-MIN-RANG THINKING?
HE KNOWS HOW DANGEROUS IT IS FOR HER TO BE THERE. HOW COULD HE ALLOW HER TO DO SUCH A RECKLESS THING?!

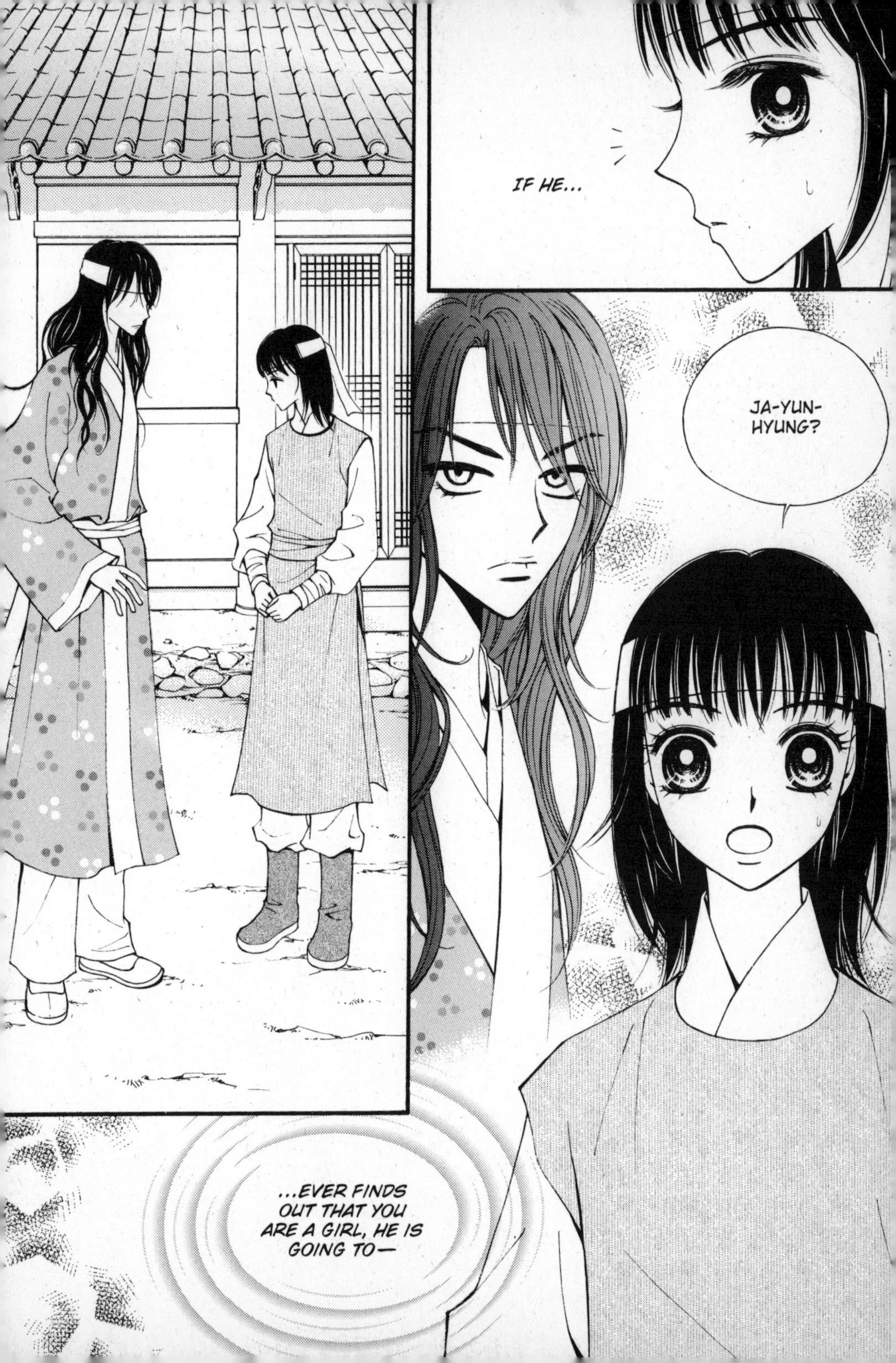
IF HE...
JA-YUN-HYUNG?
...EVER FINDS OUT THAT YOU ARE A GIRL, HE IS GOING TO—

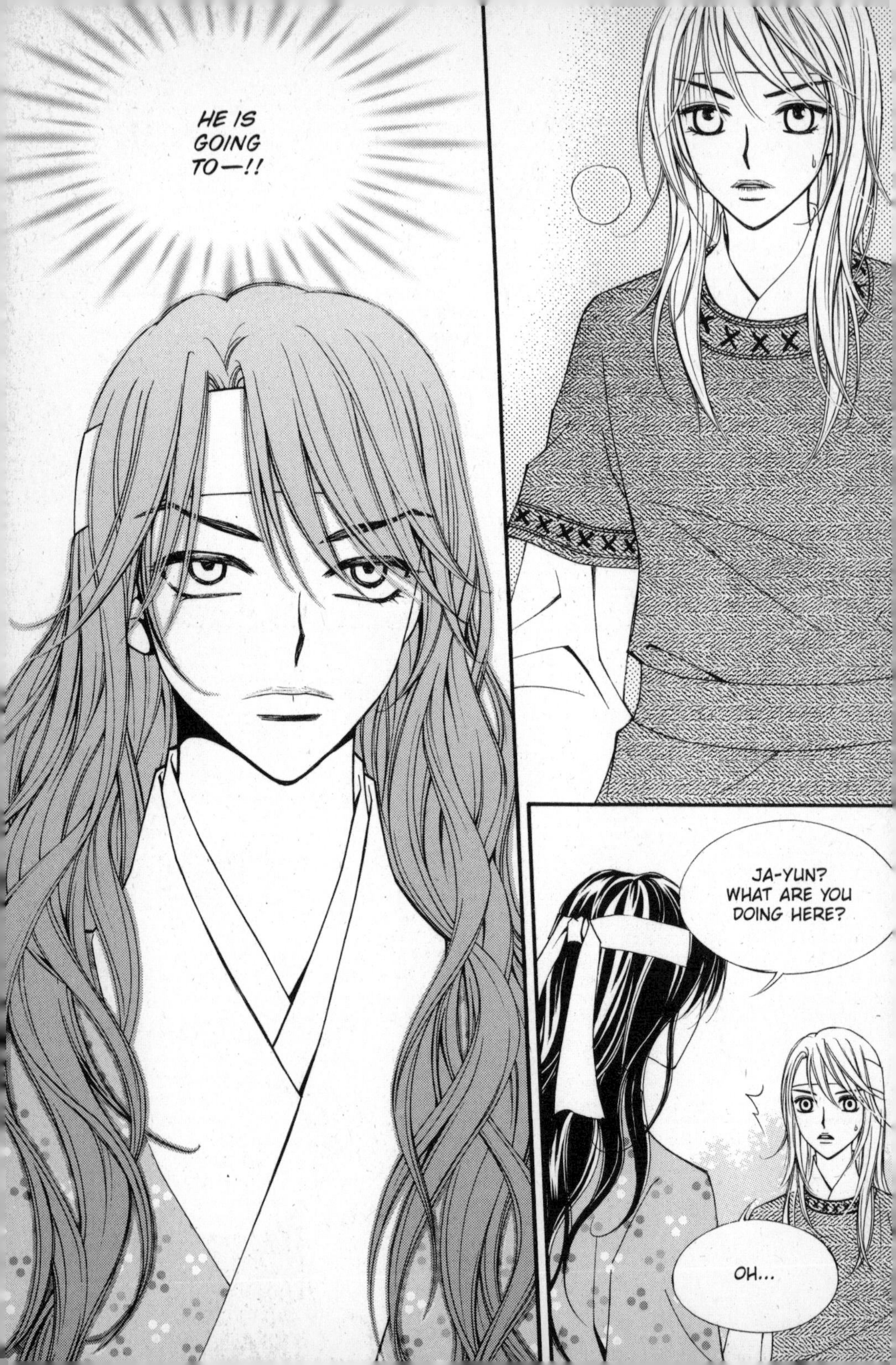
HE IS GOING TO—!!
JA-YUN? WHAT ARE YOU DOING HERE?
OH...

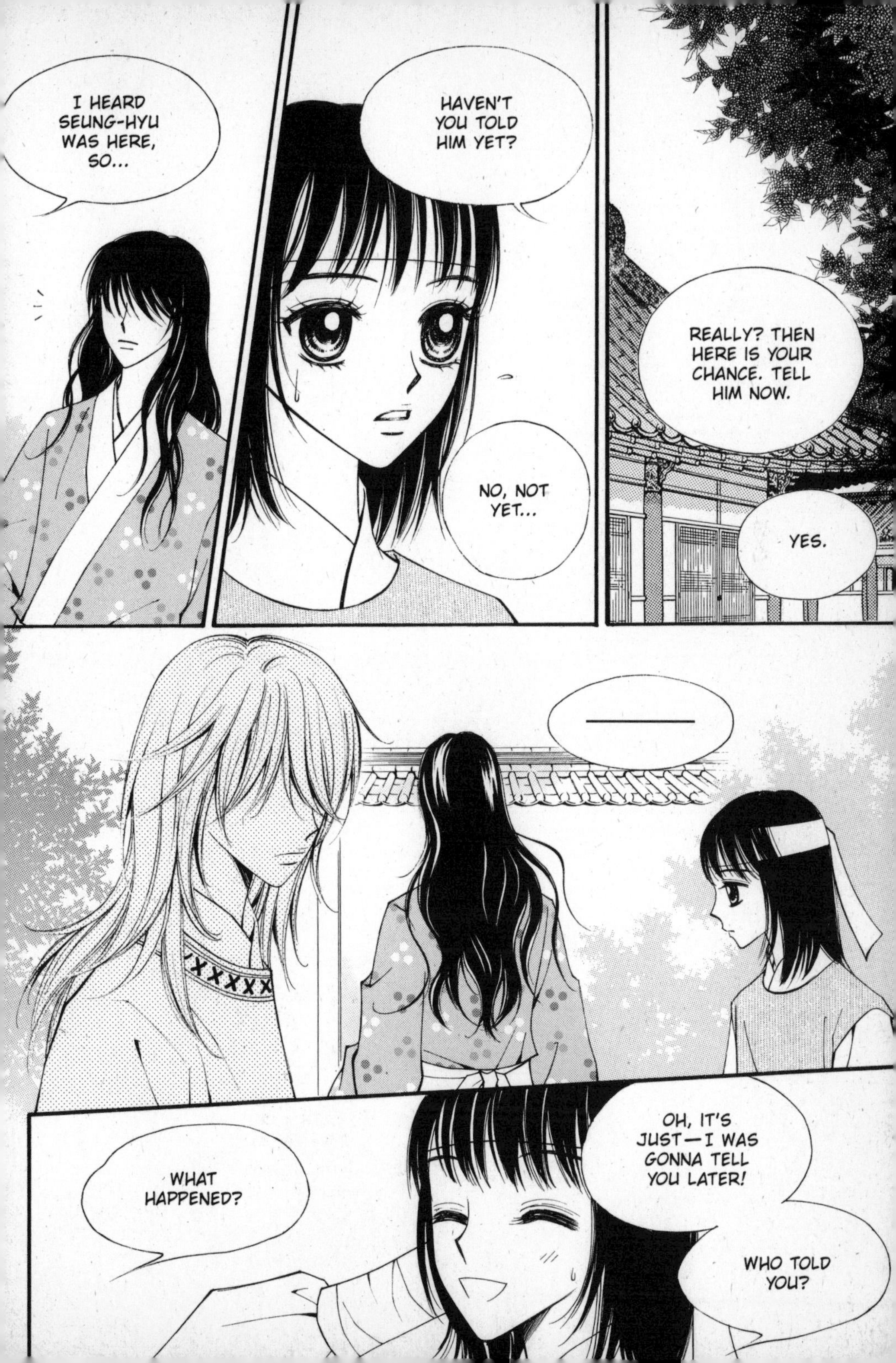
I HEARD SEUNG-HYU WAS HERE, SO...
HAVEN'T YOU TOLD HIM YET?
NO, NOT YET...
REALLY? THEN HERE IS YOUR CHANCE. TELL HIM NOW.
YES.
———
WHAT HAPPENED?
OH, IT'S JUST—I WAS GONNA TELL YOU LATER!
WHO TOLD YOU?

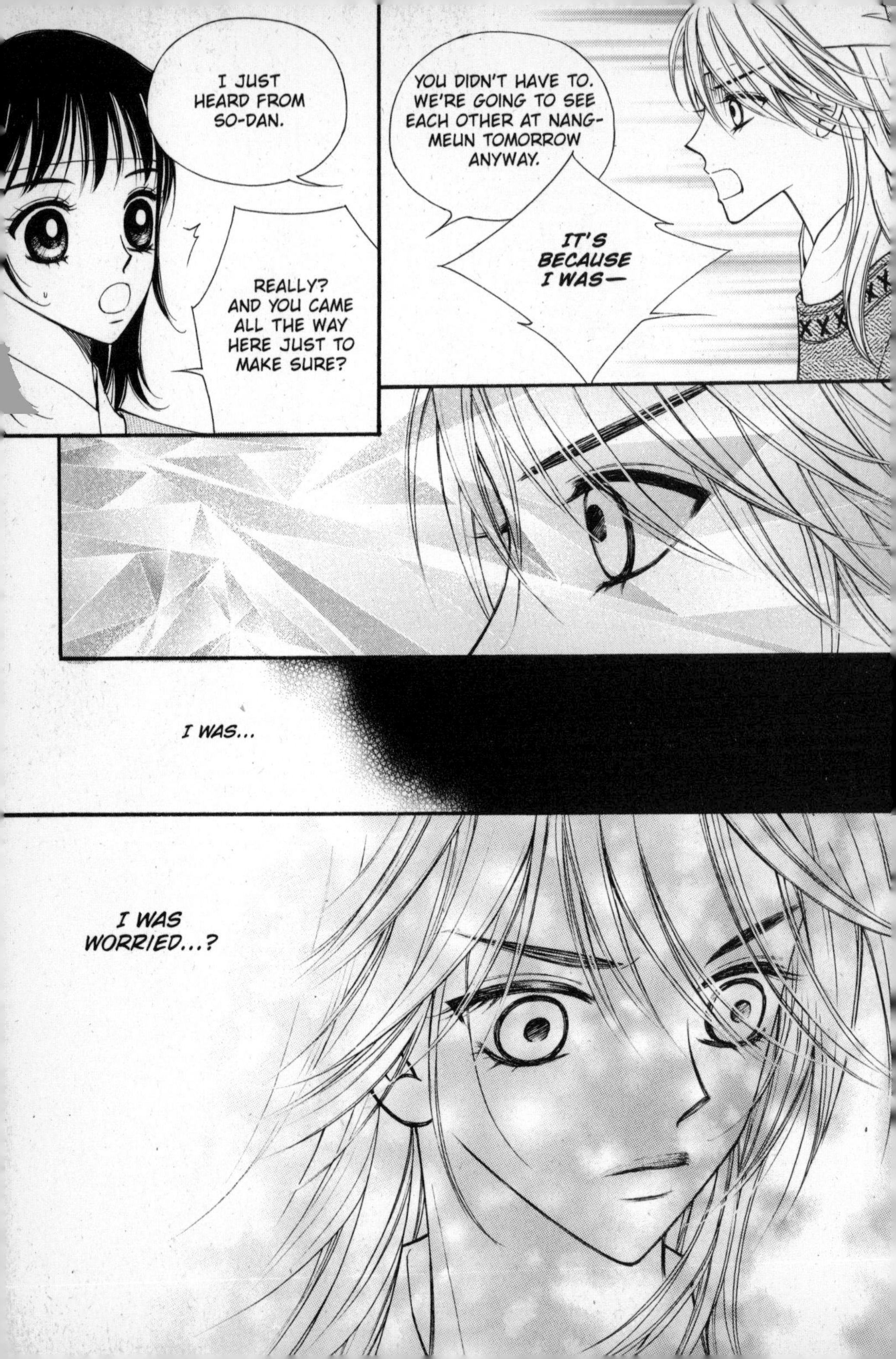
I JUST HEARD FROM SO-DAN.
REALLY? AND YOU CAME ALL THE WAY HERE JUST TO MAKE SURE?
YOU DIDN'T HAVE TO. WE'RE GOING TO SEE EACH OTHER AT NANG-MEUN TOMORROW ANYWAY.
IT'S BECAUSE I WAS—
I WAS...
I WAS WORRIED...?

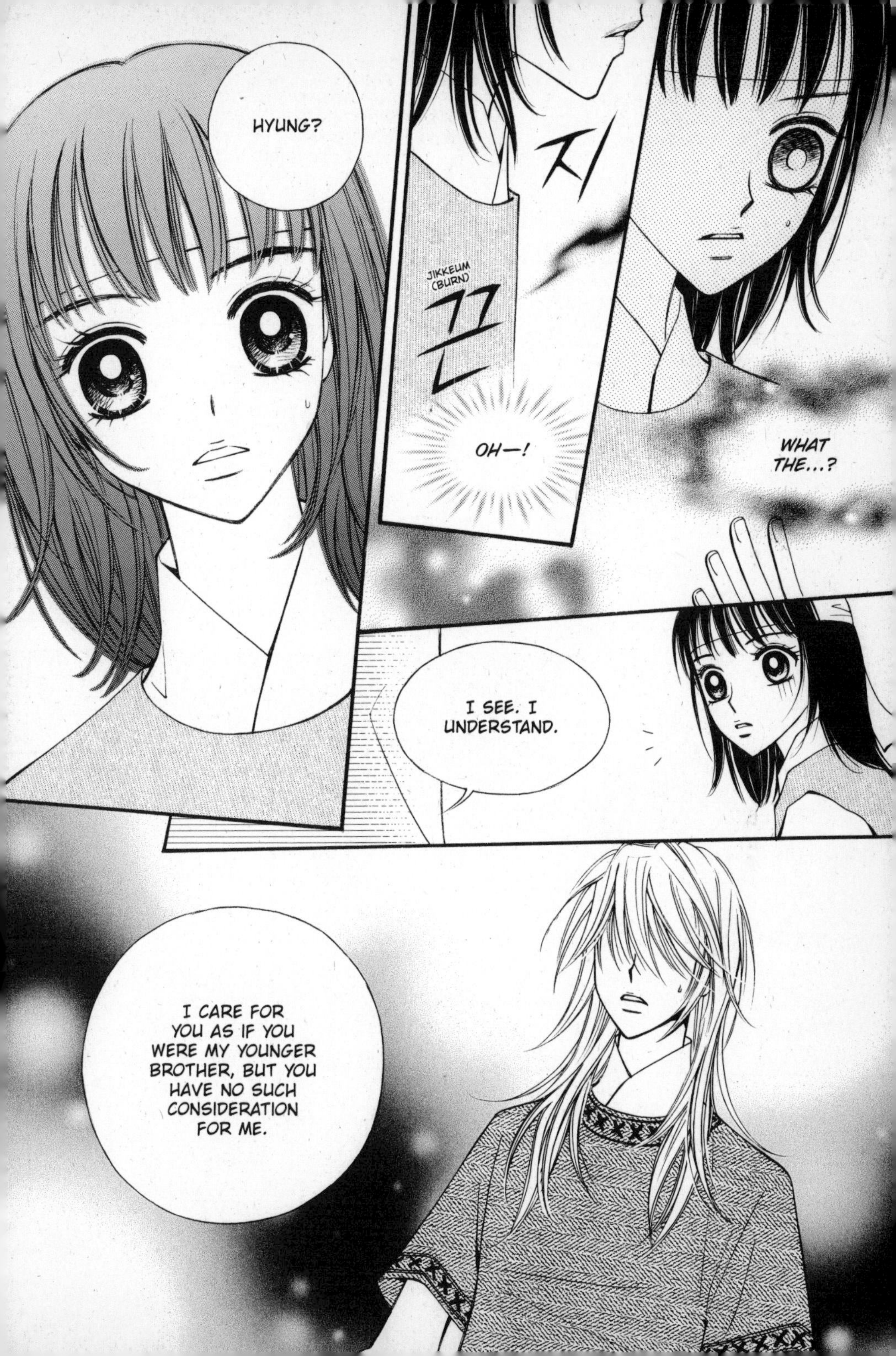
HYUNG?
JIKKEUM (BURN)
OH—!
WHAT THE...?
I SEE. I UNDERSTAND.
I CARE FOR YOU AS IF YOU WERE MY YOUNGER BROTHER, BUT YOU HAVE NO SUCH CONSIDERATION FOR ME.

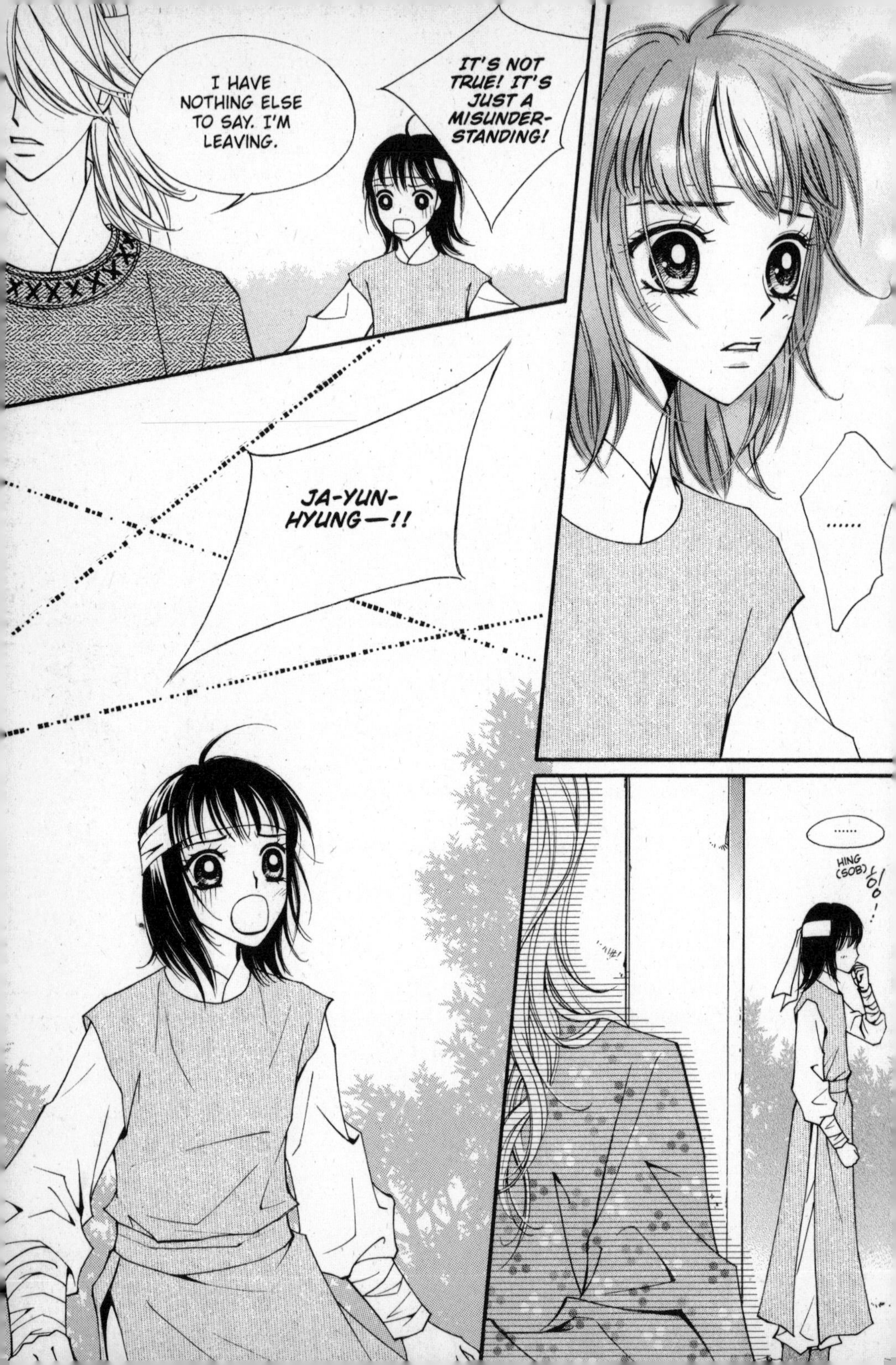
I HAVE NOTHING ELSE TO SAY. I'M LEAVING.
IT'S NOT TRUE! IT'S JUST A MISUNDERSTANDING!
JA-YUN-HYUNG—!!
......
......
HING (SOB)

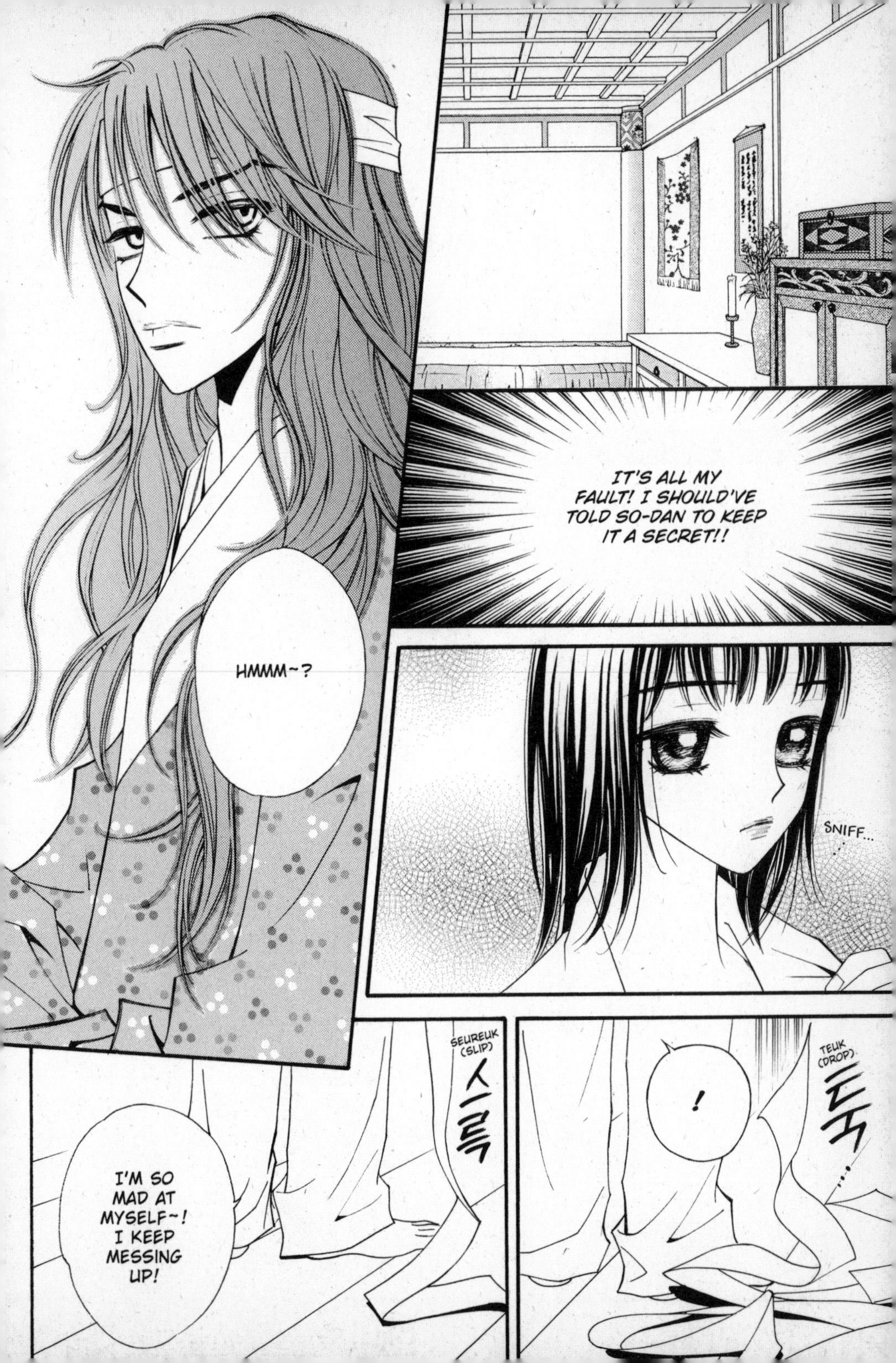
HMMM~?
IT'S ALL MY FAULT! I SHOULD'VE TOLD SO-DAN TO KEEP IT A SECRET!!
SNIFF...
I'M SO MAD AT MYSELF~! I KEEP MESSING UP!
SEUREUK (SLIP)
스르륵
!
TEUK (DROP)

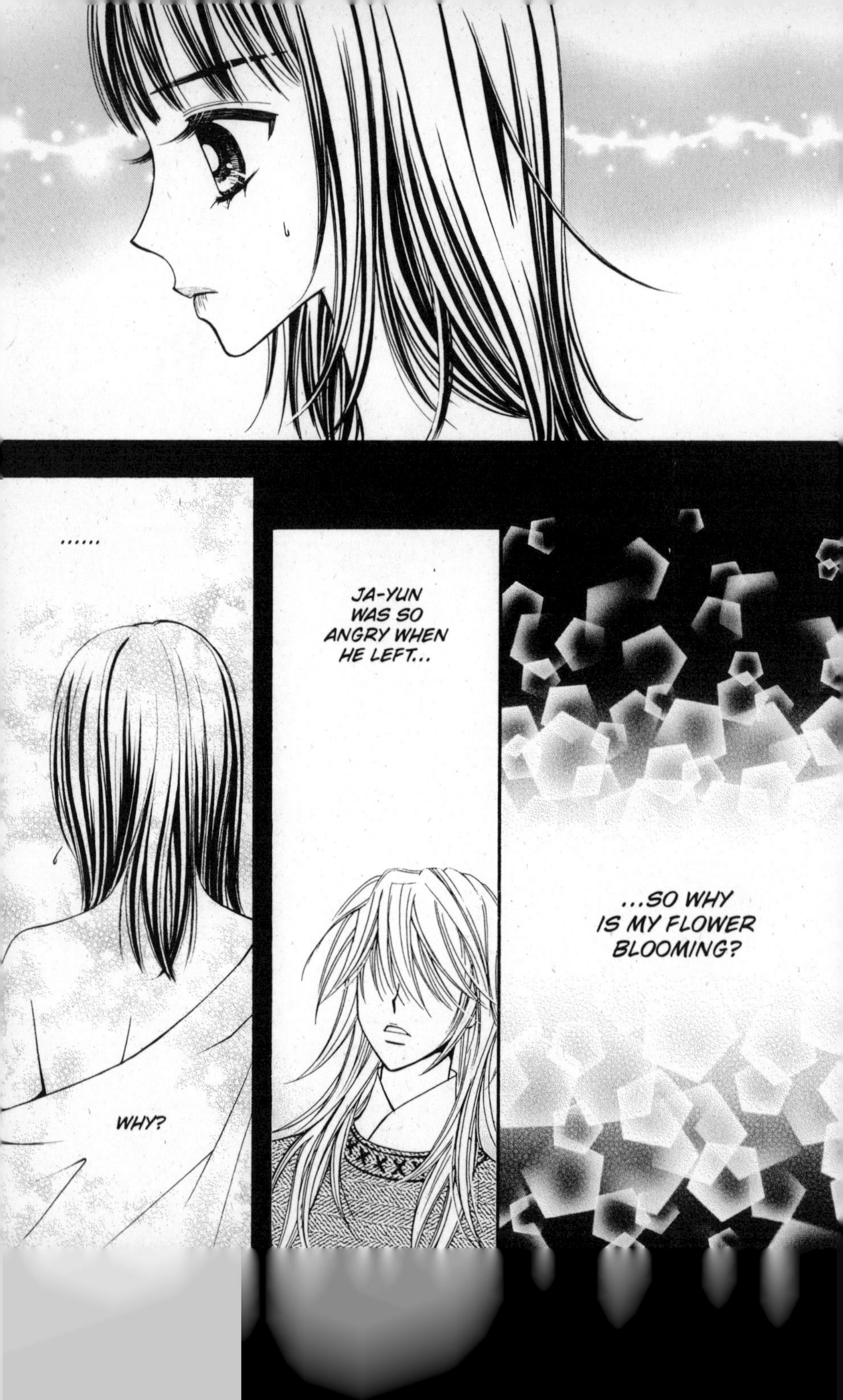
......
WHY?
JA-YUN WAS SO ANGRY WHEN HE LEFT...
...SO WHY IS MY FLOWER BLOOMING?

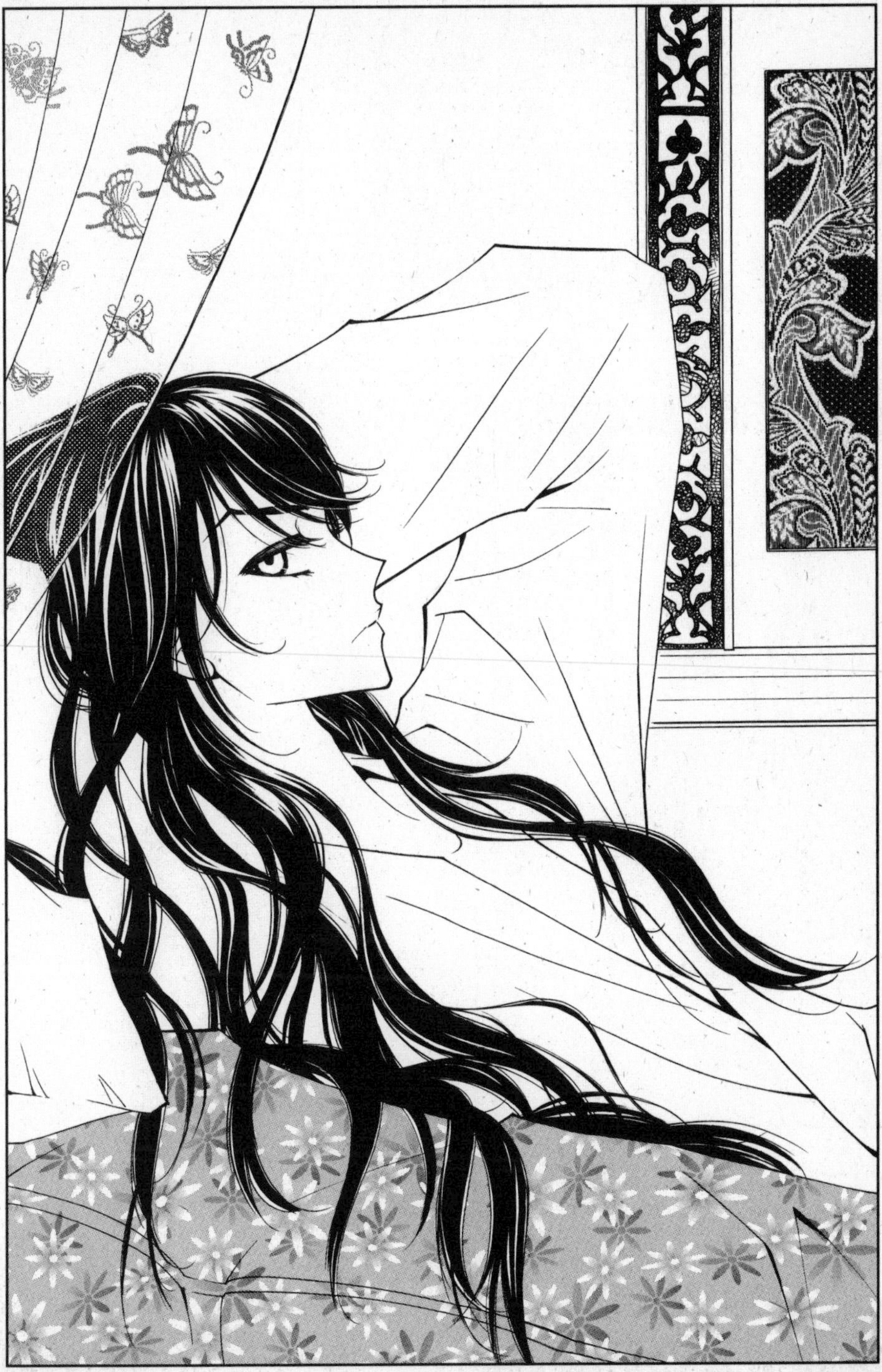

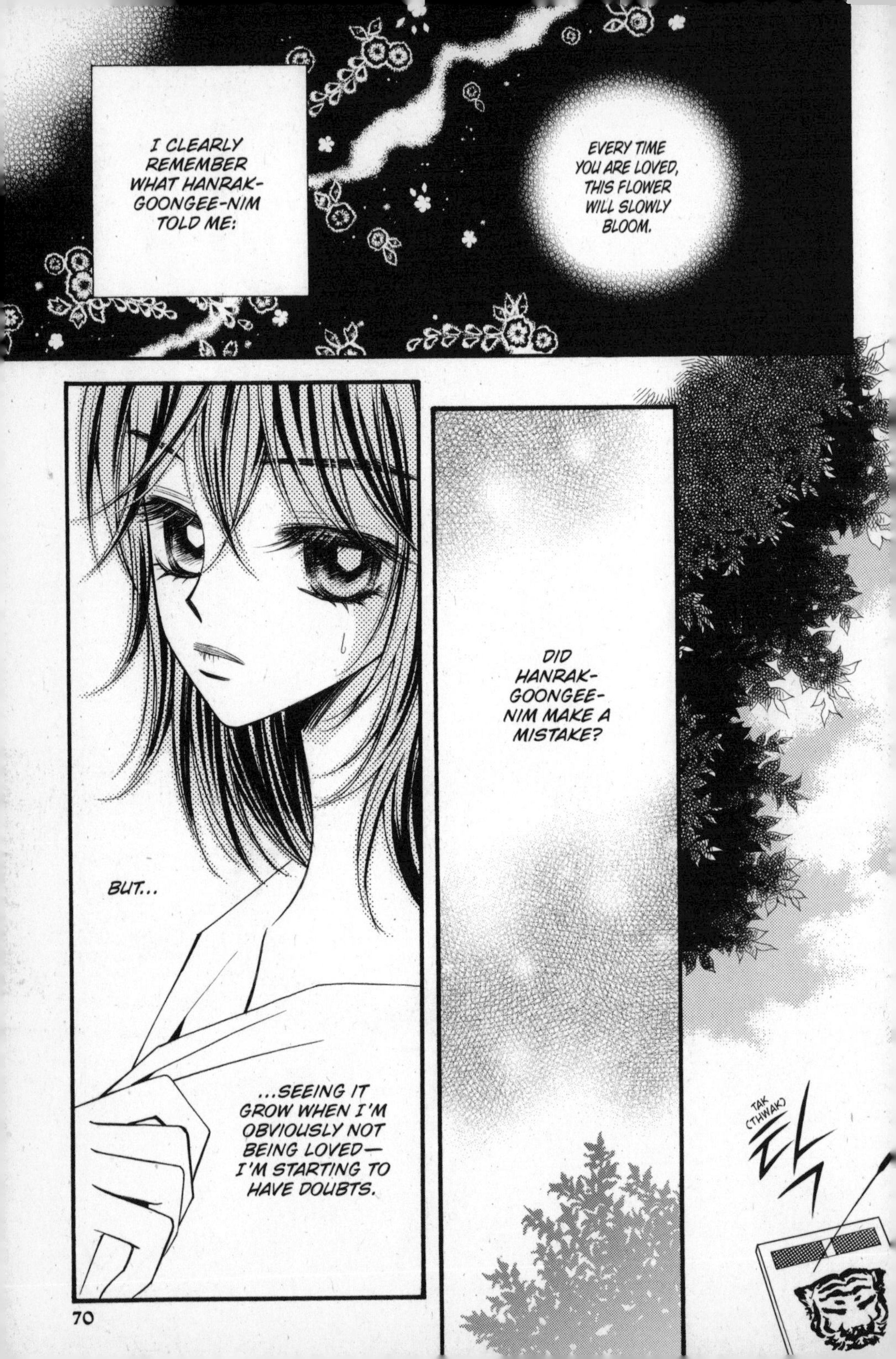
I CLEARLY REMEMBER WHAT HANRAK-GOONGEE-NIM TOLD ME:
EVERY TIME YOU ARE LOVED, THIS FLOWER WILL SLOWLY BLOOM.
BUT...
...SEEING IT GROW WHEN I'M OBVIOUSLY NOT BEING LOVED— I'M STARTING TO HAVE DOUBTS.
DID HANRAK-GOONGEE-NIM MAKE A MISTAKE?
TAK (THWAK)

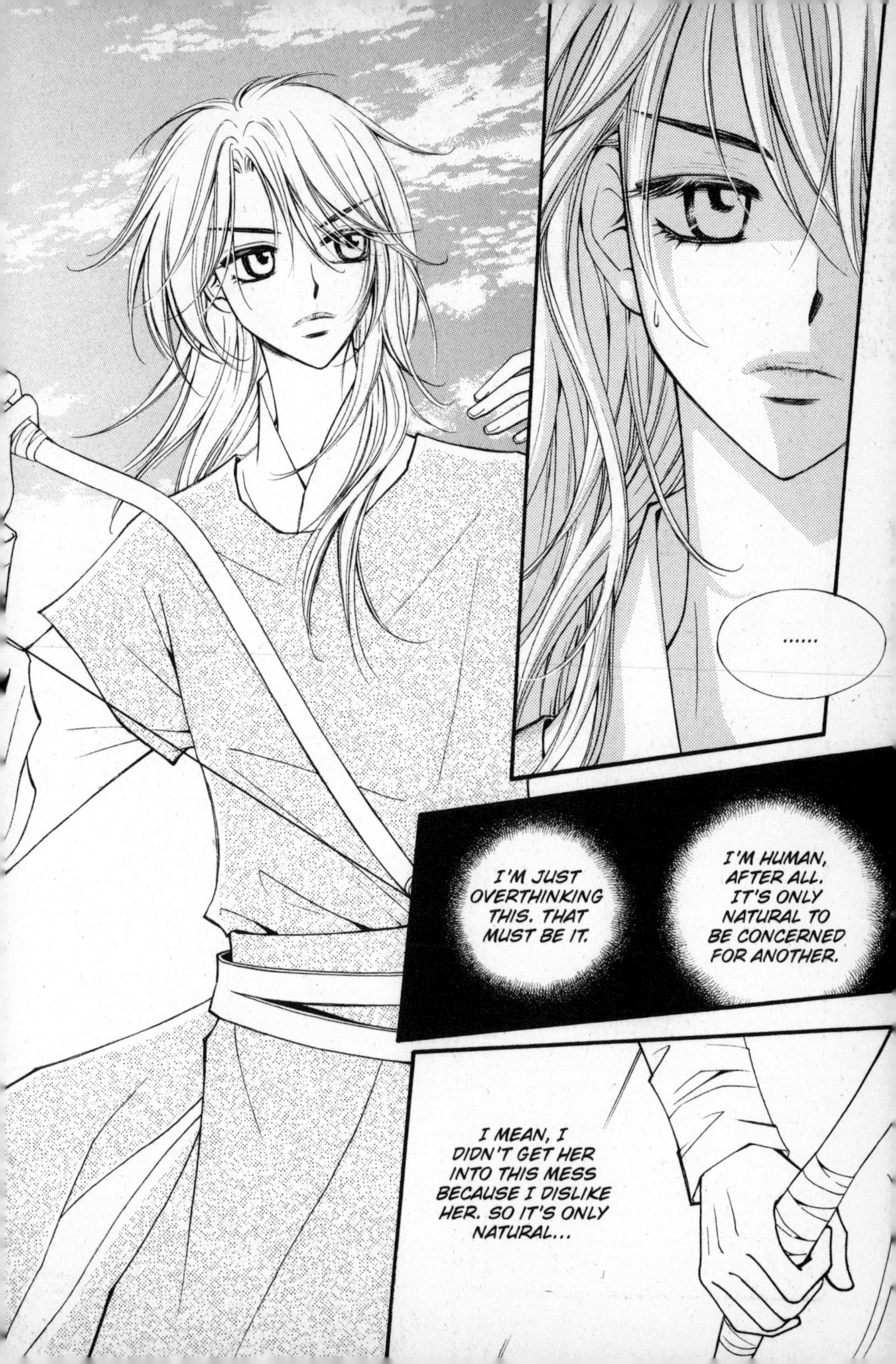
......
I'M JUST OVERTHINKING THIS. THAT MUST BE IT.
I'M HUMAN, AFTER ALL. IT'S ONLY NATURAL TO BE CONCERNED FOR ANOTHER.
I MEAN, I DIDN'T GET HER INTO THIS MESS BECAUSE I DISLIKE HER. SO IT'S ONLY NATURAL...

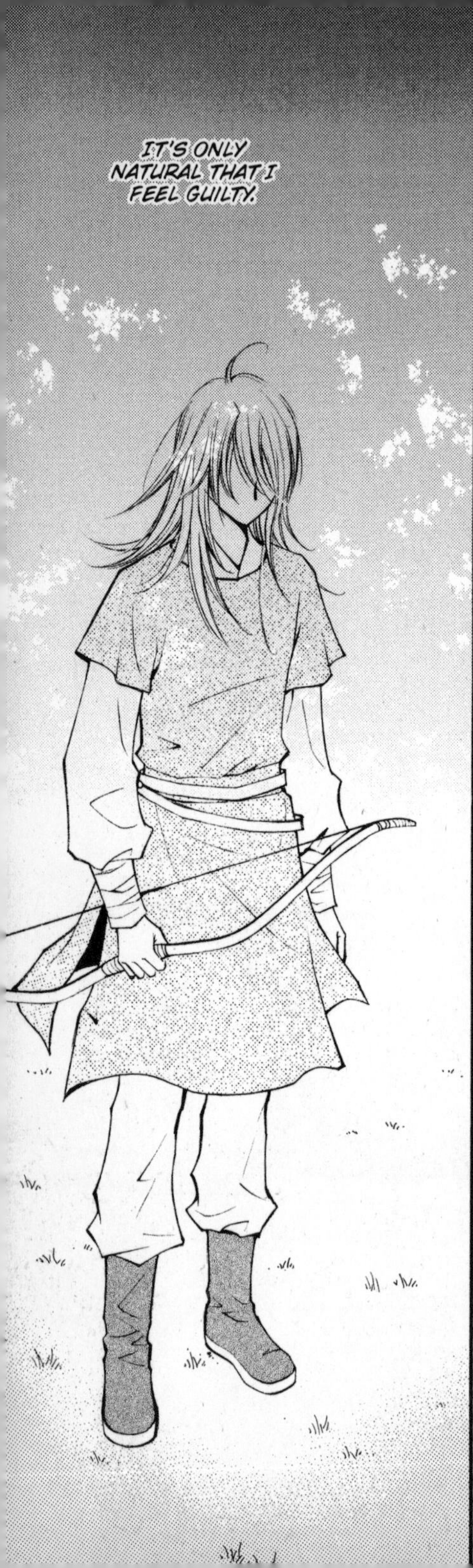
IT'S ONLY NATURAL THAT I FEEL GUILTY.

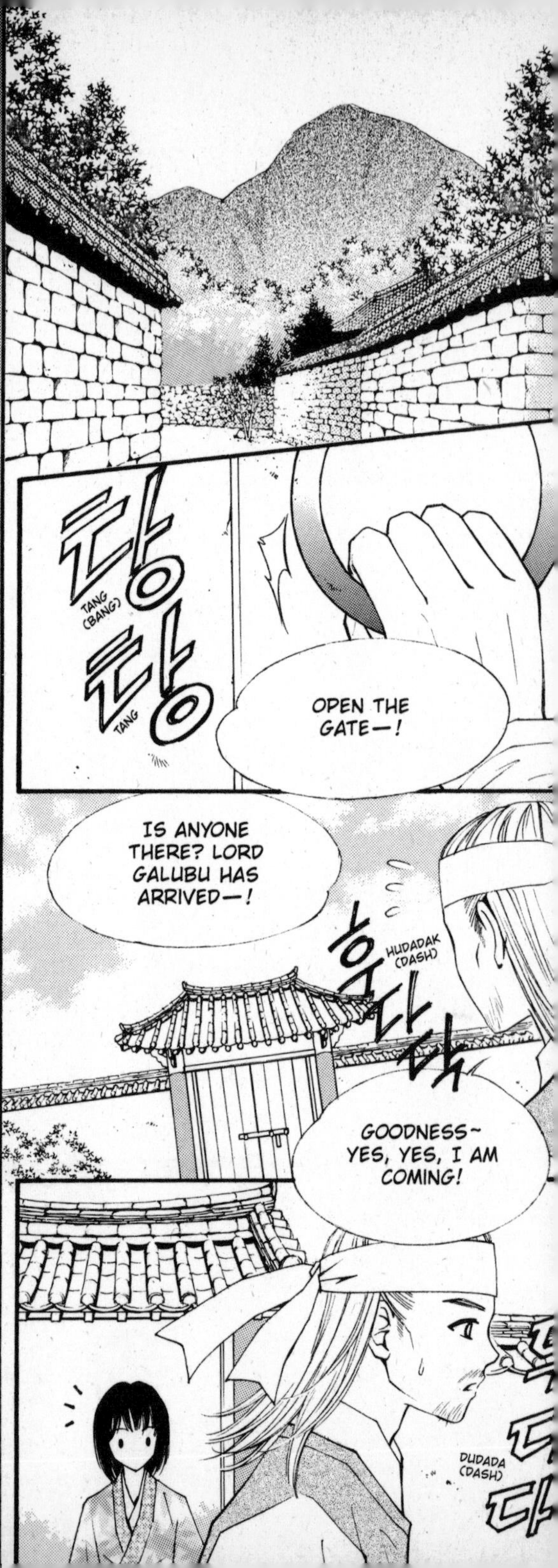
탕
TANG (BANG)
탕
TANG
OPEN THE GATE—!
IS ANYONE THERE? LORD GALUBU HAS ARRIVED—!
HUDADAK (DASH)
GOODNESS~ YES, YES, I AM COMING!
DUDADA (DASH)

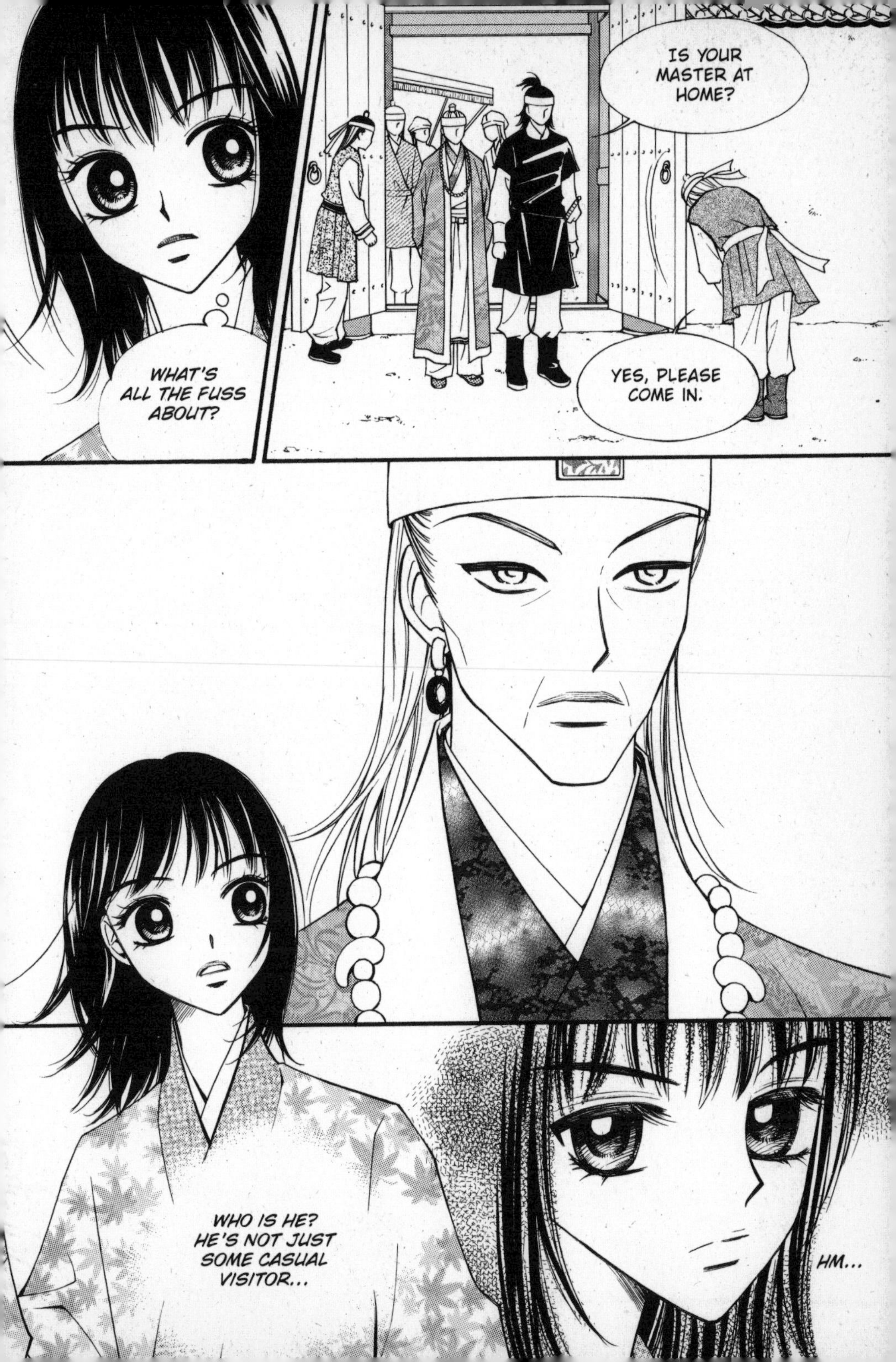
WHAT'S ALL THE FUSS ABOUT?
IS YOUR MASTER AT HOME?
YES, PLEASE COME IN.
WHO IS HE? HE'S NOT JUST SOME CASUAL VISITOR...
HM...

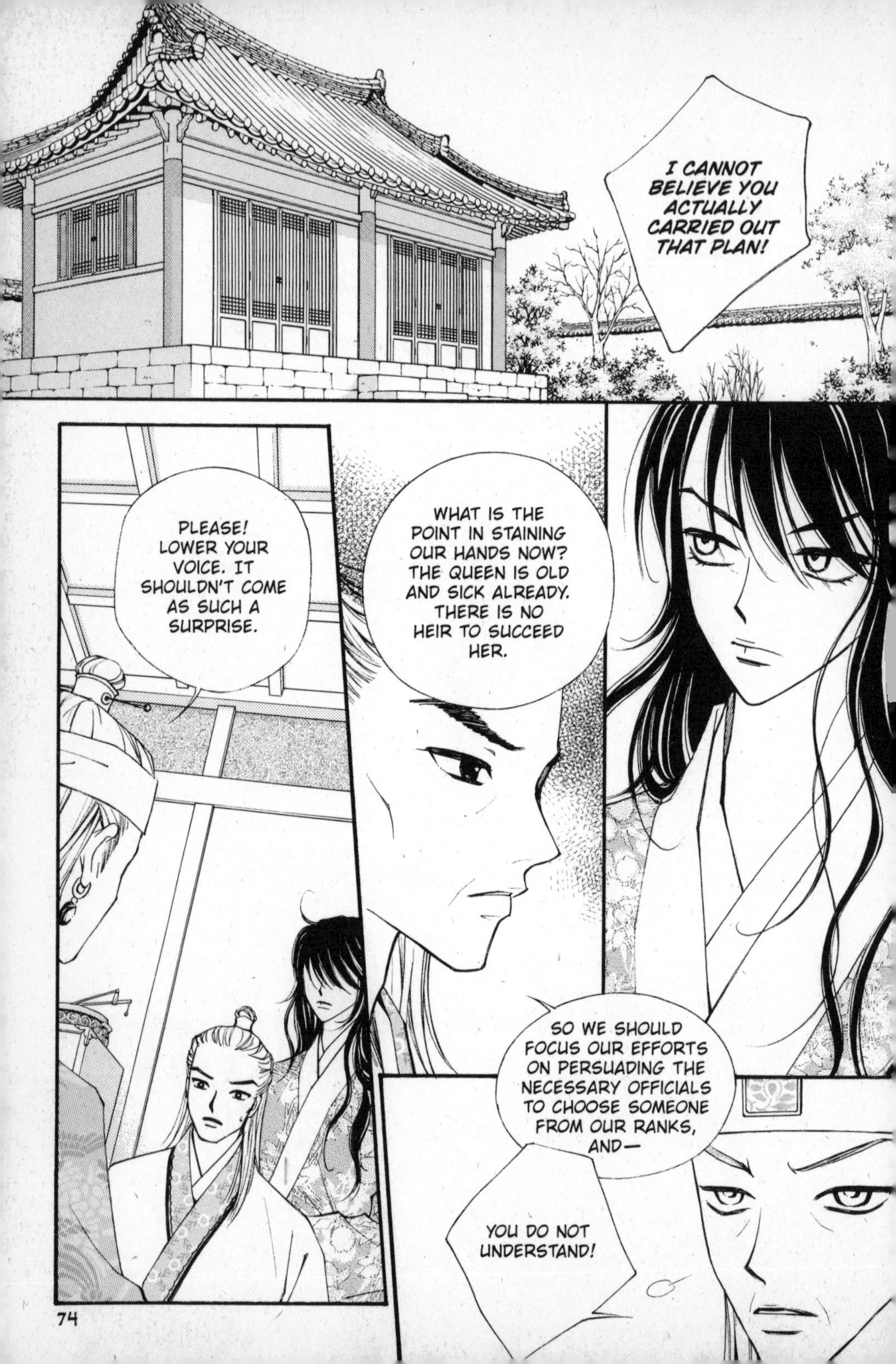
I CANNOT BELIEVE YOU ACTUALLY CARRIED OUT THAT PLAN!
PLEASE! LOWER YOUR VOICE. IT SHOULDN'T COME AS SUCH A SURPRISE.
WHAT IS THE POINT IN STAINING OUR HANDS NOW? THE QUEEN IS OLD AND SICK ALREADY. THERE IS NO HEIR TO SUCCEED HER.
SO WE SHOULD FOCUS OUR EFFORTS ON PERSUADING THE NECESSARY OFFICIALS TO CHOOSE SOMEONE FROM OUR RANKS, AND—
YOU DO NOT UNDERSTAND!

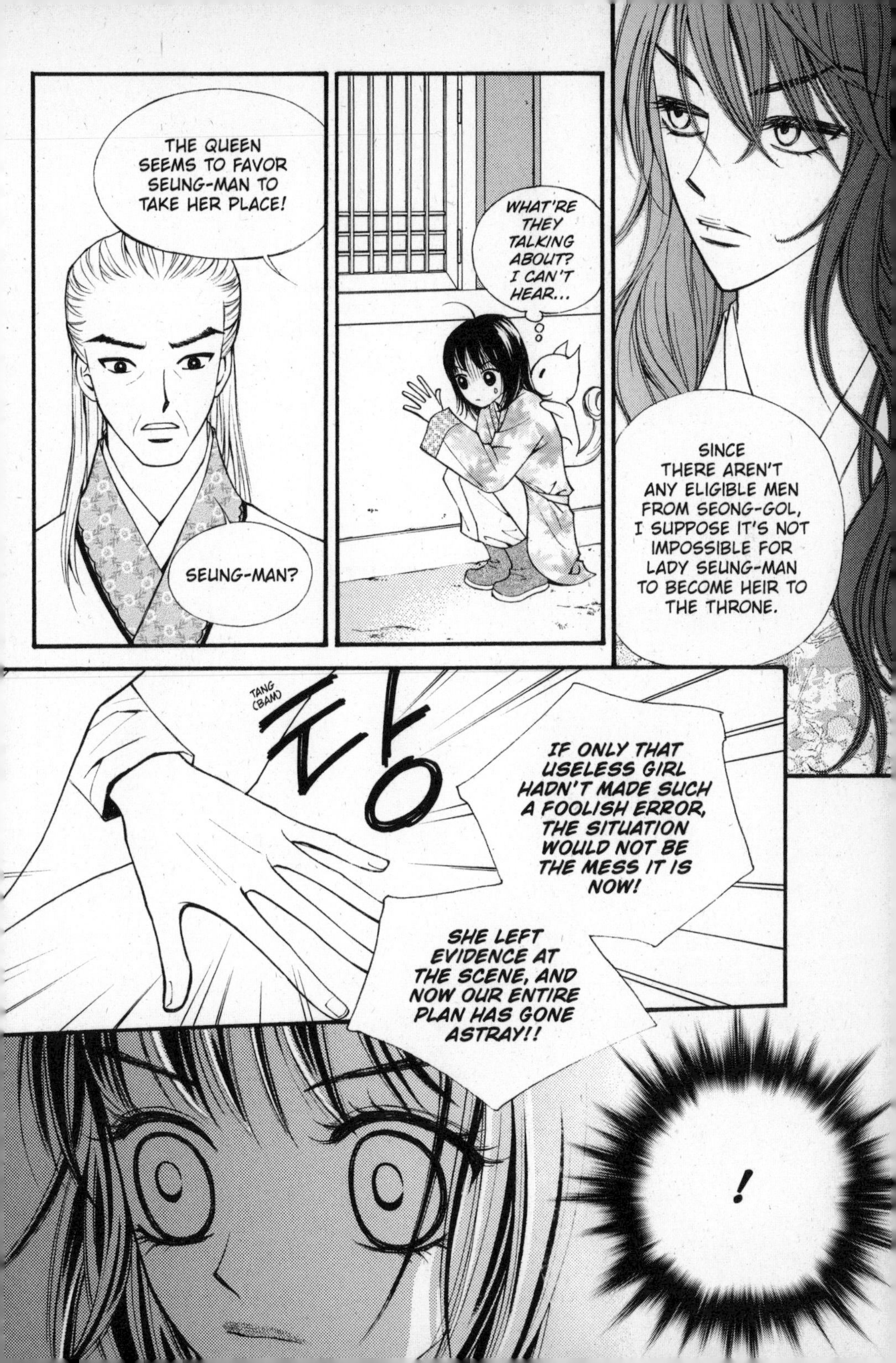
THE QUEEN SEEMS TO FAVOR SEUNG-MAN TO TAKE HER PLACE!
SEUNG-MAN?
WHAT'RE THEY TALKING ABOUT? I CAN'T HEAR...
SINCE THERE AREN'T ANY ELIGIBLE MEN FROM SEONG-GOL, I SUPPOSE IT'S NOT IMPOSSIBLE FOR LADY SEUNG-MAN TO BECOME HEIR TO THE THRONE.
탕
TANG (BAM)
IF ONLY THAT USELESS GIRL HADN'T MADE SUCH A FOOLISH ERROR, THE SITUATION WOULD NOT BE THE MESS IT IS NOW!
SHE LEFT EVIDENCE AT THE SCENE, AND NOW OUR ENTIRE PLAN HAS GONE ASTRAY!!
!

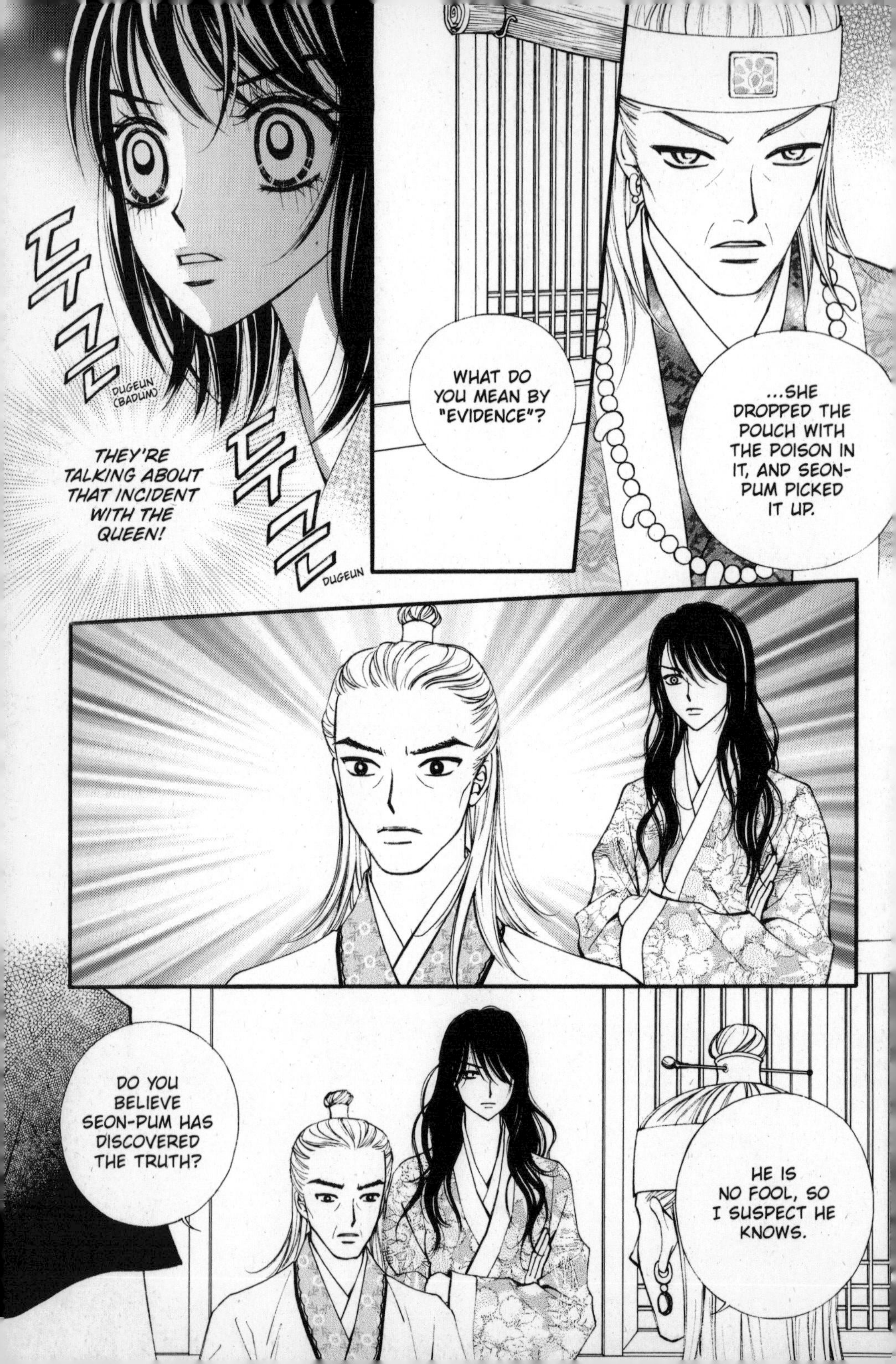
DUGEUN (BADUM)
THEY'RE TALKING ABOUT THAT INCIDENT WITH THE QUEEN!
DUGEUN
WHAT DO YOU MEAN BY "EVIDENCE"?
...SHE DROPPED THE POUCH WITH THE POISON IN IT, AND SEON-PUM PICKED IT UP.
DO YOU BELIEVE SEON-PUM HAS DISCOVERED THE TRUTH?
HE IS NO FOOL, SO I SUSPECT HE KNOWS.

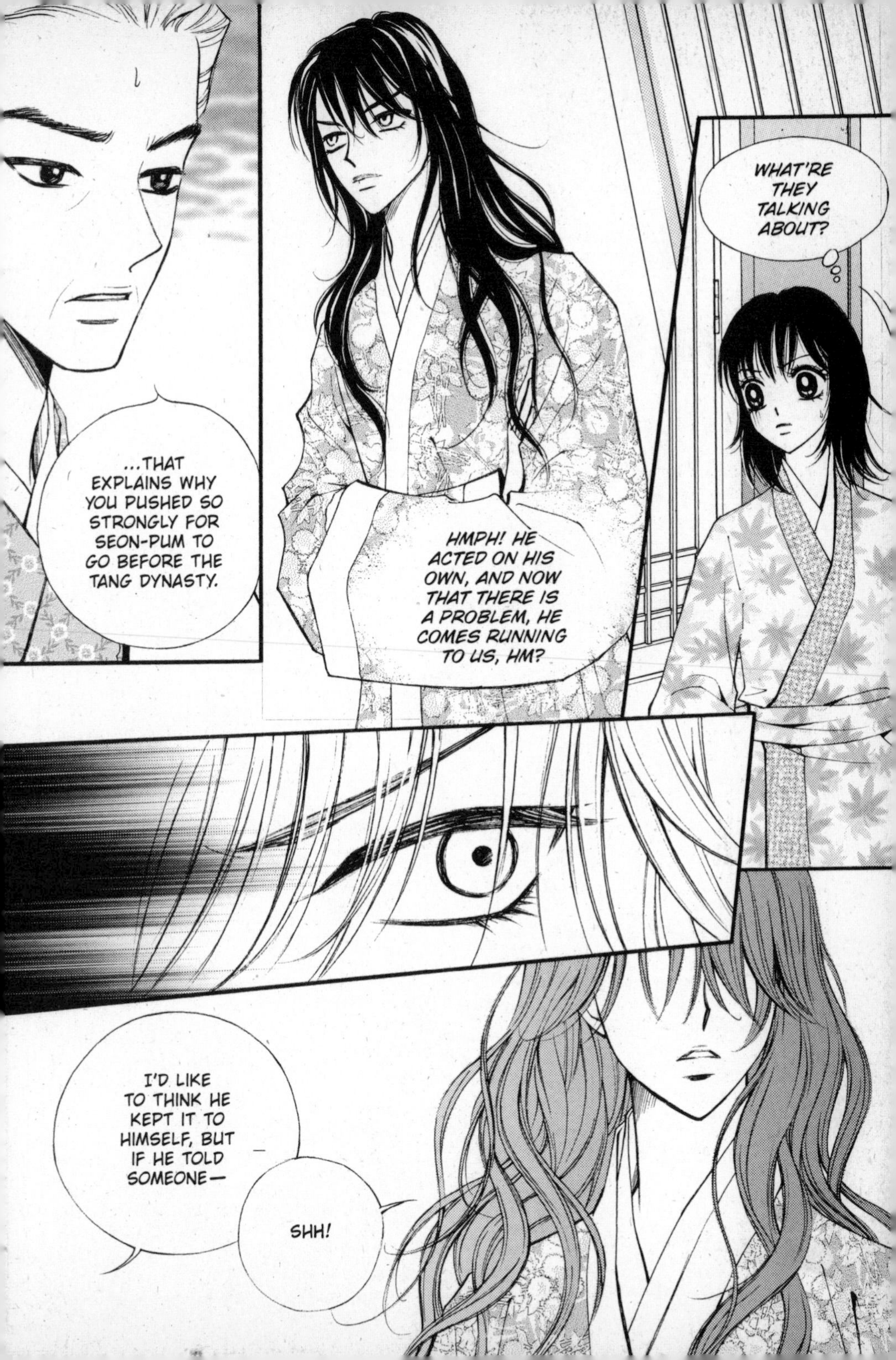
...THAT EXPLAINS WHY YOU PUSHED SO STRONGLY FOR SEON-PUM TO GO BEFORE THE TANG DYNASTY.
HMPH! HE ACTED ON HIS OWN, AND NOW THAT THERE IS A PROBLEM, HE COMES RUNNING TO US, HM?
WHAT'RE THEY TALKING ABOUT?
I'D LIKE TO THINK HE KEPT IT TO HIMSELF, BUT IF HE TOLD SOMEONE—
SHH!

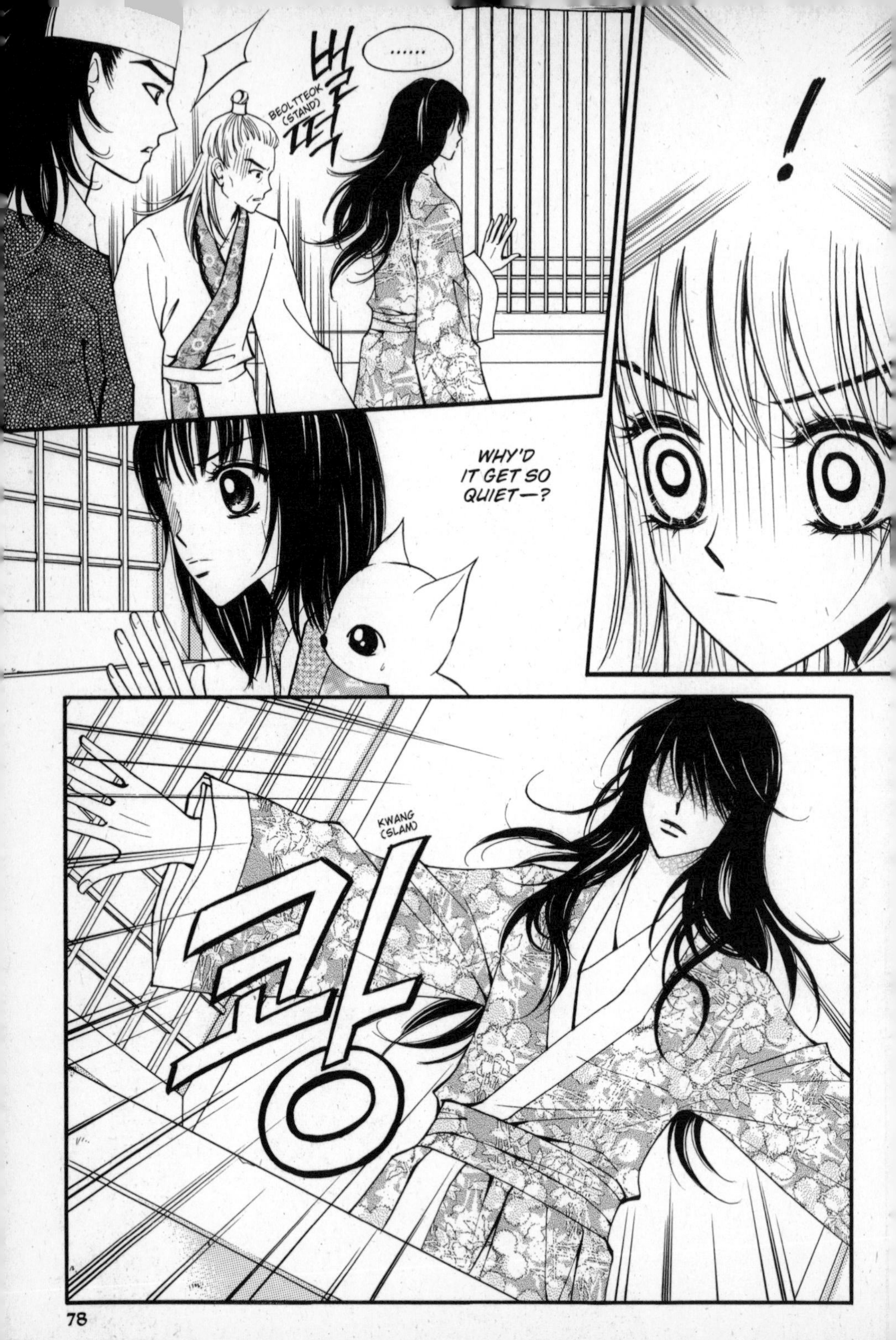
......
벌떡
BEOLTTEOK (STAND)
WHY'D IT GET SO QUIET—?
!
광
KWANG (SLAM)

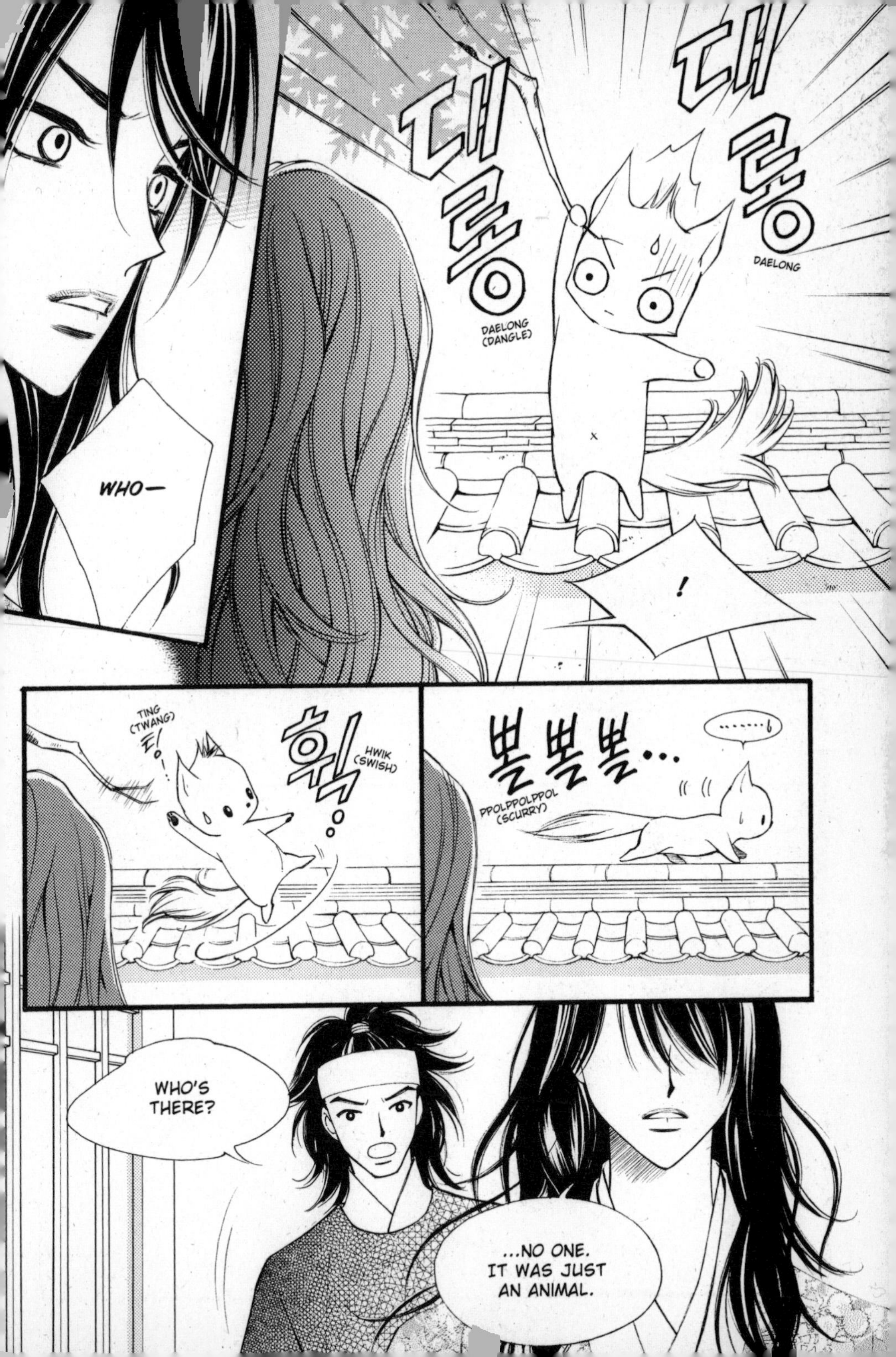
WHO—
대롱
DAELONG (DANGLE)
대롱
DAELONG
!
TING (TWANG)
휙
HWIK (SWISH)
뽈뽈뽈...
PPOLPPOLPPOL (SCURRY)
......
WHO'S THERE?
...NO ONE. IT WAS JUST AN ANIMAL.

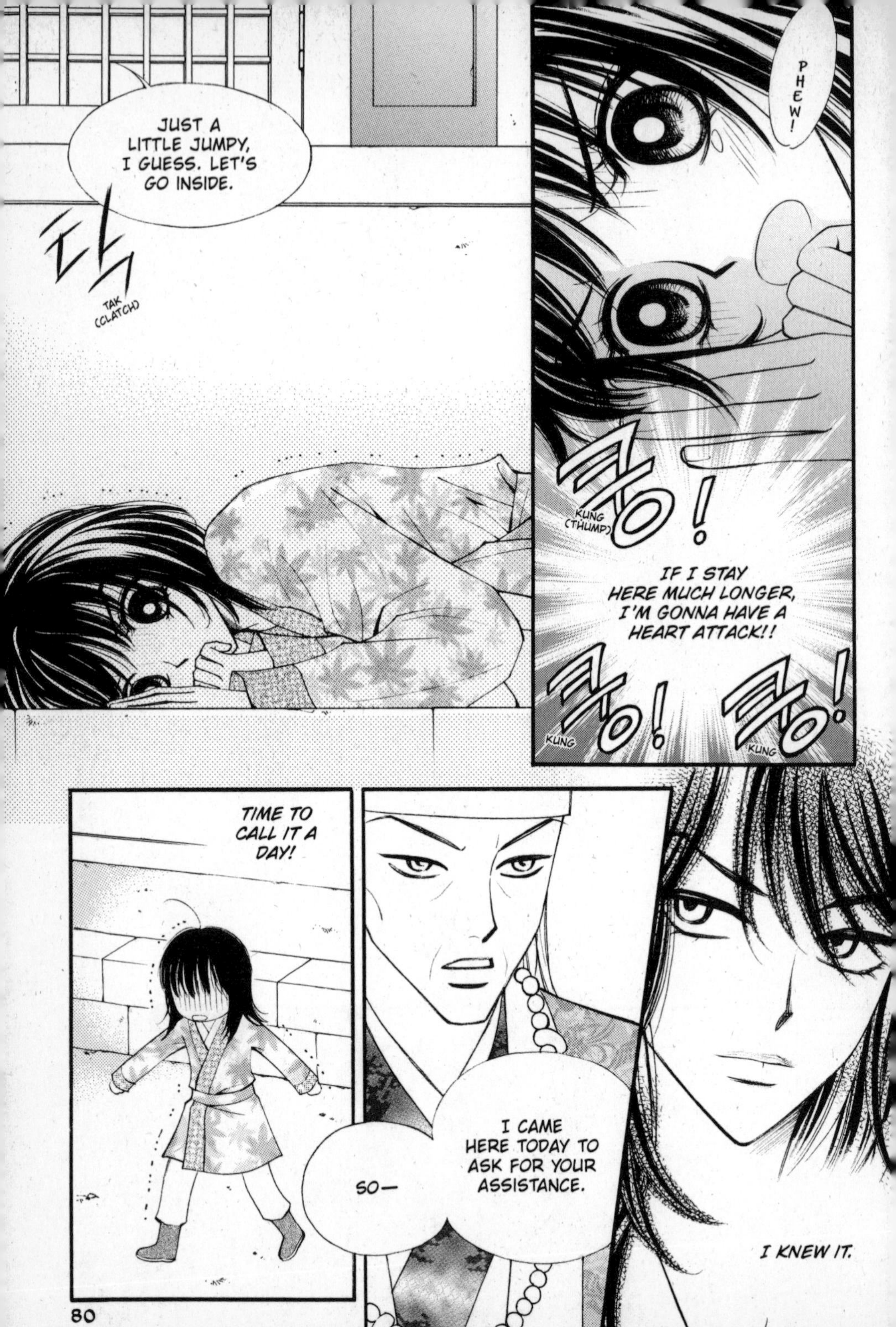
JUST A LITTLE JUMPY, I GUESS. LET'S GO INSIDE.
TAK (CLATCH)
PHEW!
KUNG (THUMP)
IF I STAY HERE MUCH LONGER, I'M GONNA HAVE A HEART ATTACK!!
KUNG
KUNG
TIME TO CALL IT A DAY!
SO—
I CAME HERE TODAY TO ASK FOR YOUR ASSISTANCE.
I KNEW IT.

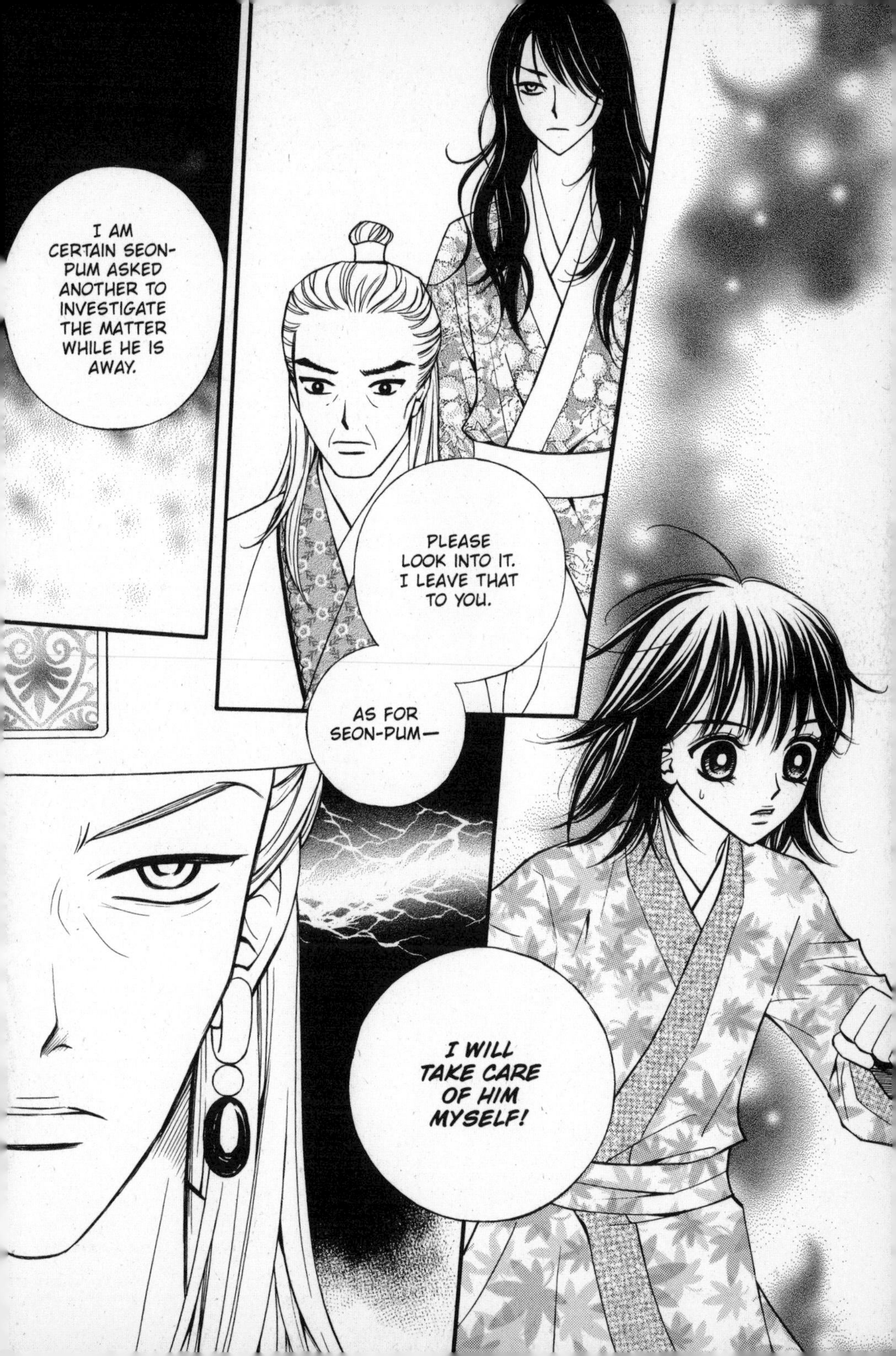
I AM CERTAIN SEON-PUM ASKED ANOTHER TO INVESTIGATE THE MATTER WHILE HE IS AWAY.
PLEASE LOOK INTO IT. I LEAVE THAT TO YOU.
AS FOR SEON-PUM—
I WILL TAKE CARE OF HIM MYSELF!

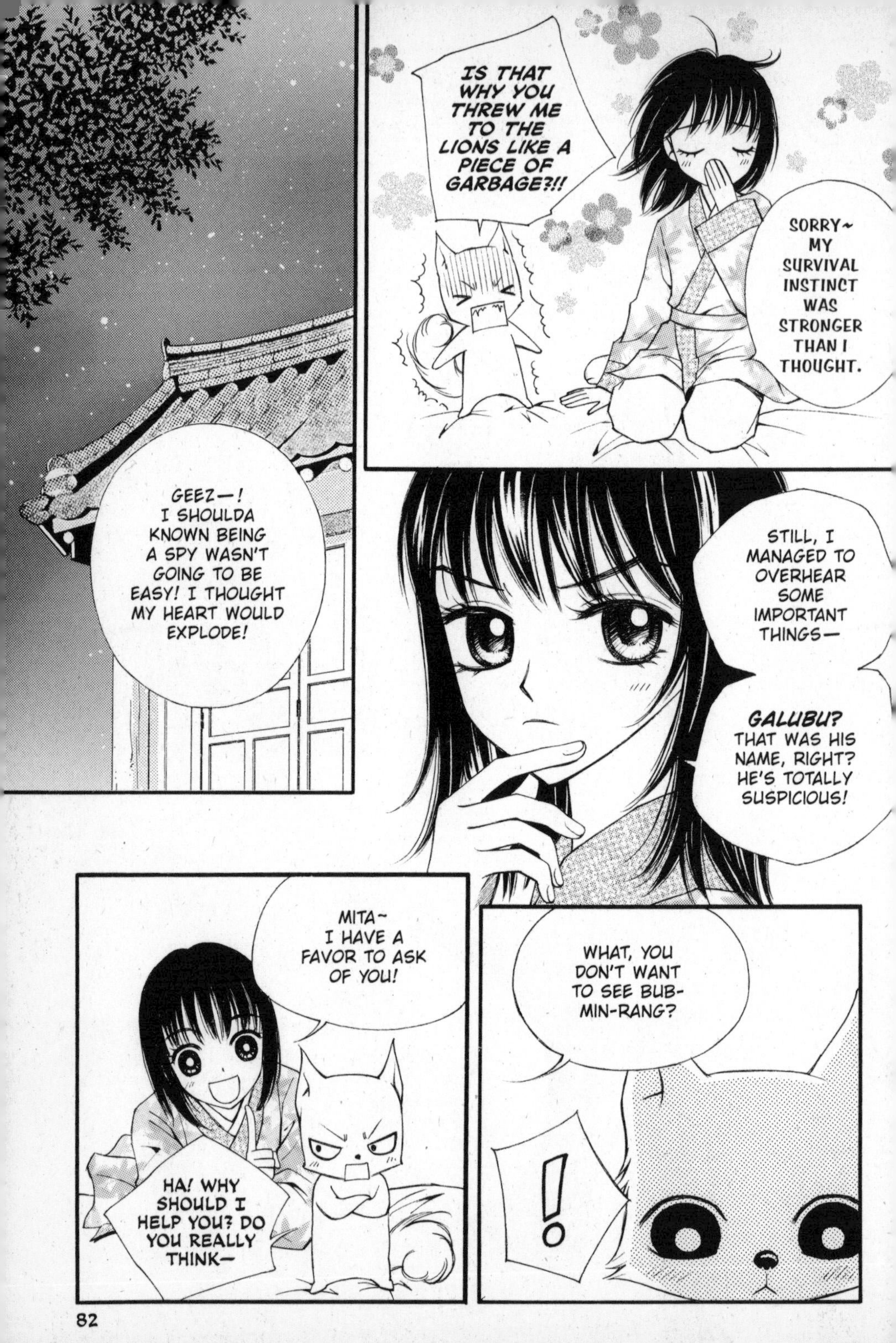
GEEZ—! I SHOULDA KNOWN BEING A SPY WASN'T GOING TO BE EASY! I THOUGHT MY HEART WOULD EXPLODE!
IS THAT WHY YOU THREW ME TO THE LIONS LIKE A PIECE OF GARBAGE?!!
SORRY~ MY SURVIVAL INSTINCT WAS STRONGER THAN I THOUGHT.
STILL, I MANAGED TO OVERHEAR SOME IMPORTANT THINGS—
GALUBU? THAT WAS HIS NAME, RIGHT? HE'S TOTALLY SUSPICIOUS!
MITA~ I HAVE A FAVOR TO ASK OF YOU!
HA! WHY SHOULD I HELP YOU? DO YOU REALLY THINK—
WHAT, YOU DON'T WANT TO SEE BUB-MIN-RANG?
!

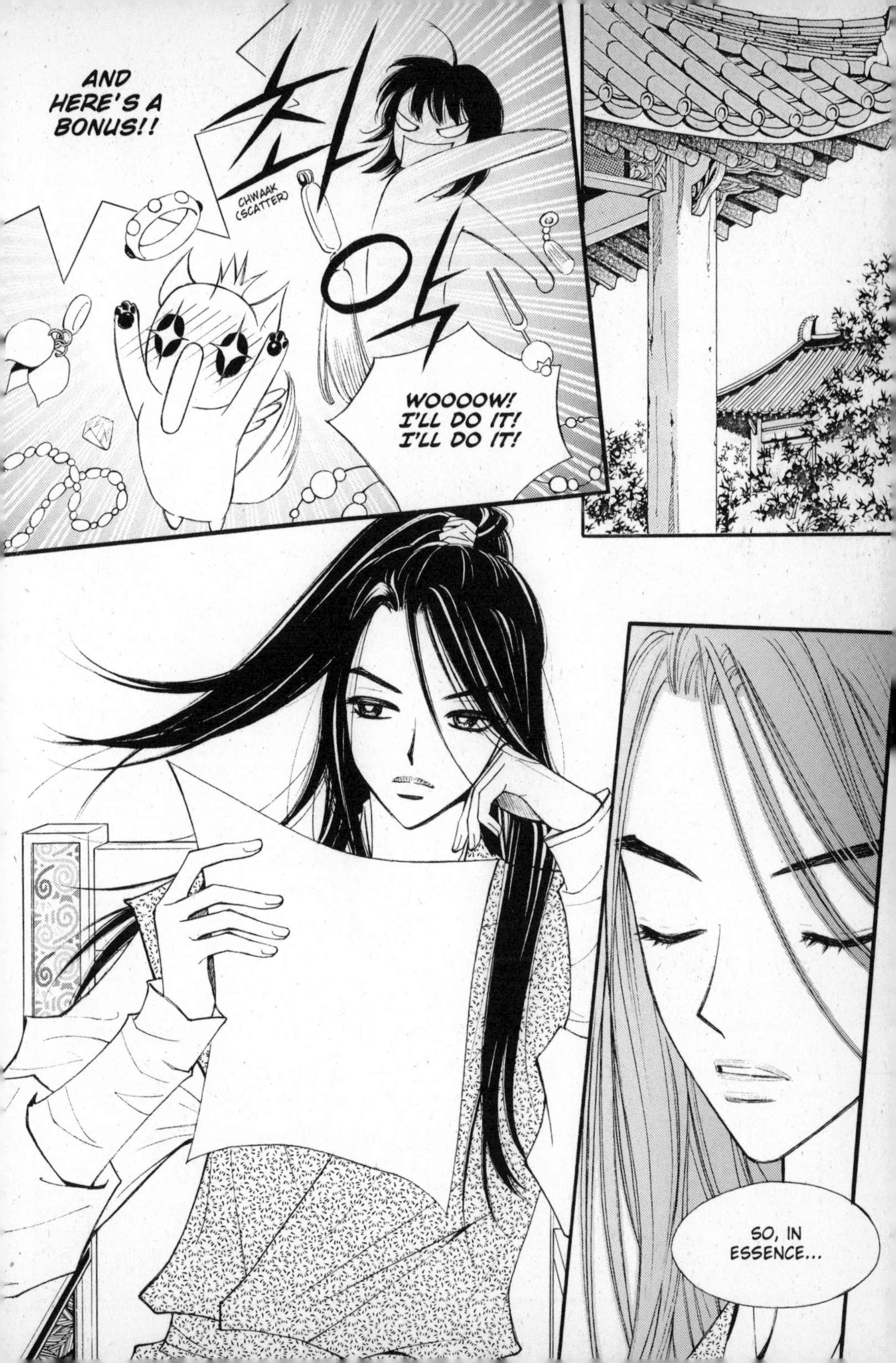
AND HERE'S A BONUS!!
CHWAAK (SCATTER)
WOOOOW! I'LL DO IT! I'LL DO IT!
SO, IN ESSENCE...

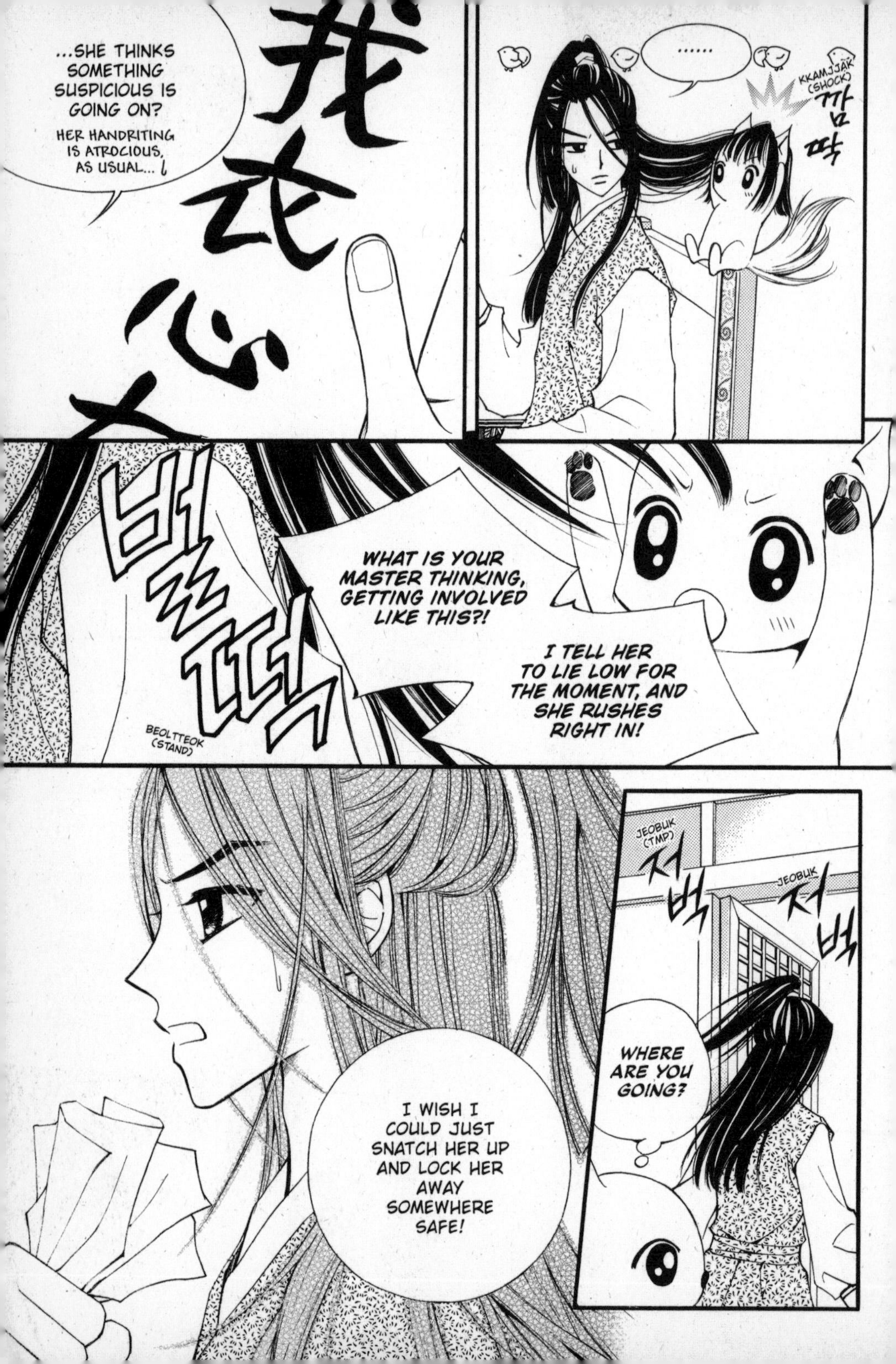
...SHE THINKS SOMETHING SUSPICIOUS IS GOING ON?
HER HANDRITING IS ATROCIOUS, AS USUAL...
......
KKAMJJAK (SHOCK)
BEOLTTEOK (STAND)
WHAT IS YOUR MASTER THINKING, GETTING INVOLVED LIKE THIS?!
I TELL HER TO LIE LOW FOR THE MOMENT, AND SHE RUSHES RIGHT IN!
I WISH I COULD JUST SNATCH HER UP AND LOCK HER AWAY SOMEWHERE SAFE!
JEOBUK (TMP)
저벅
JEOBUK
저벅
WHERE ARE YOU GOING?

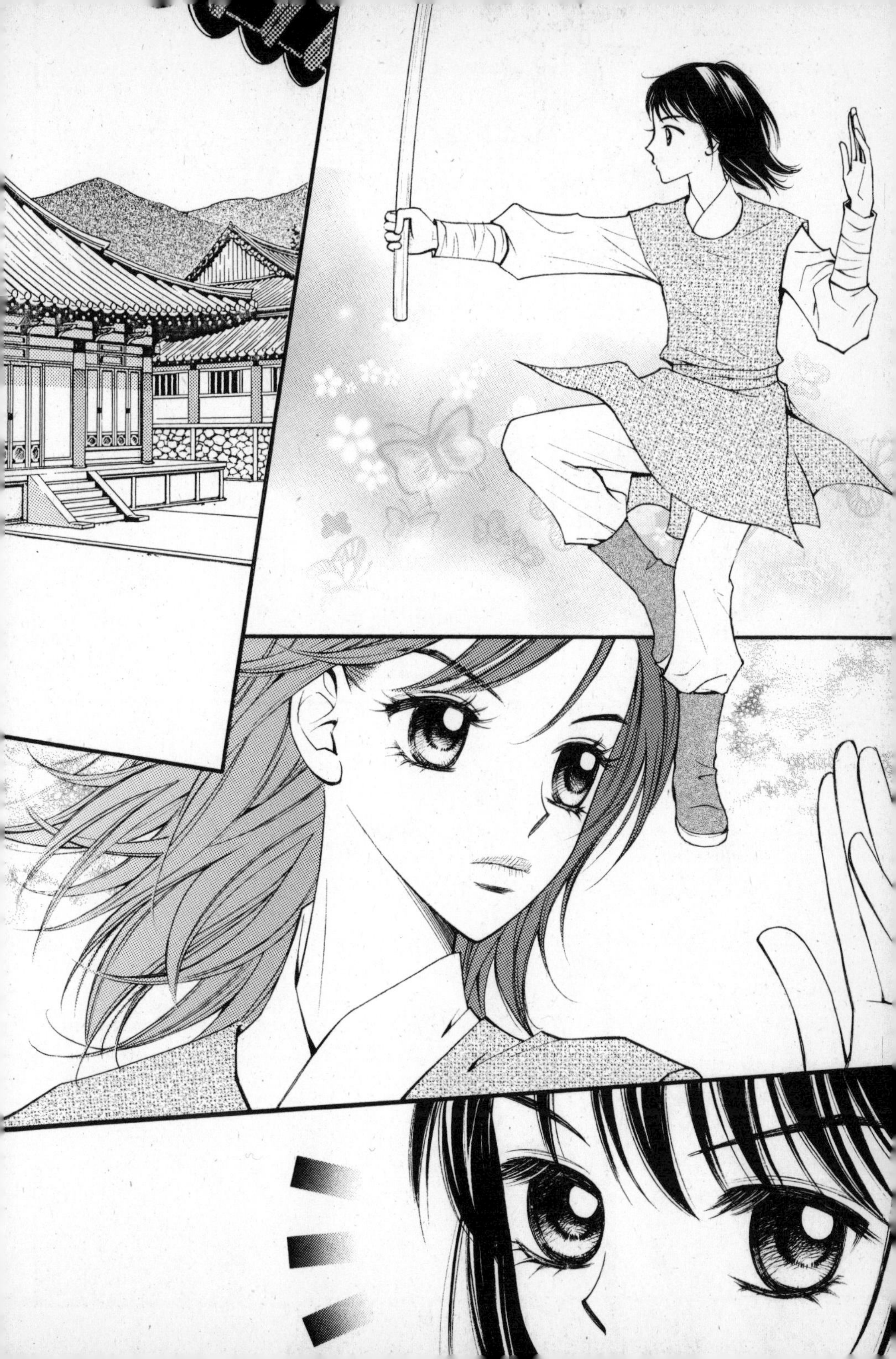

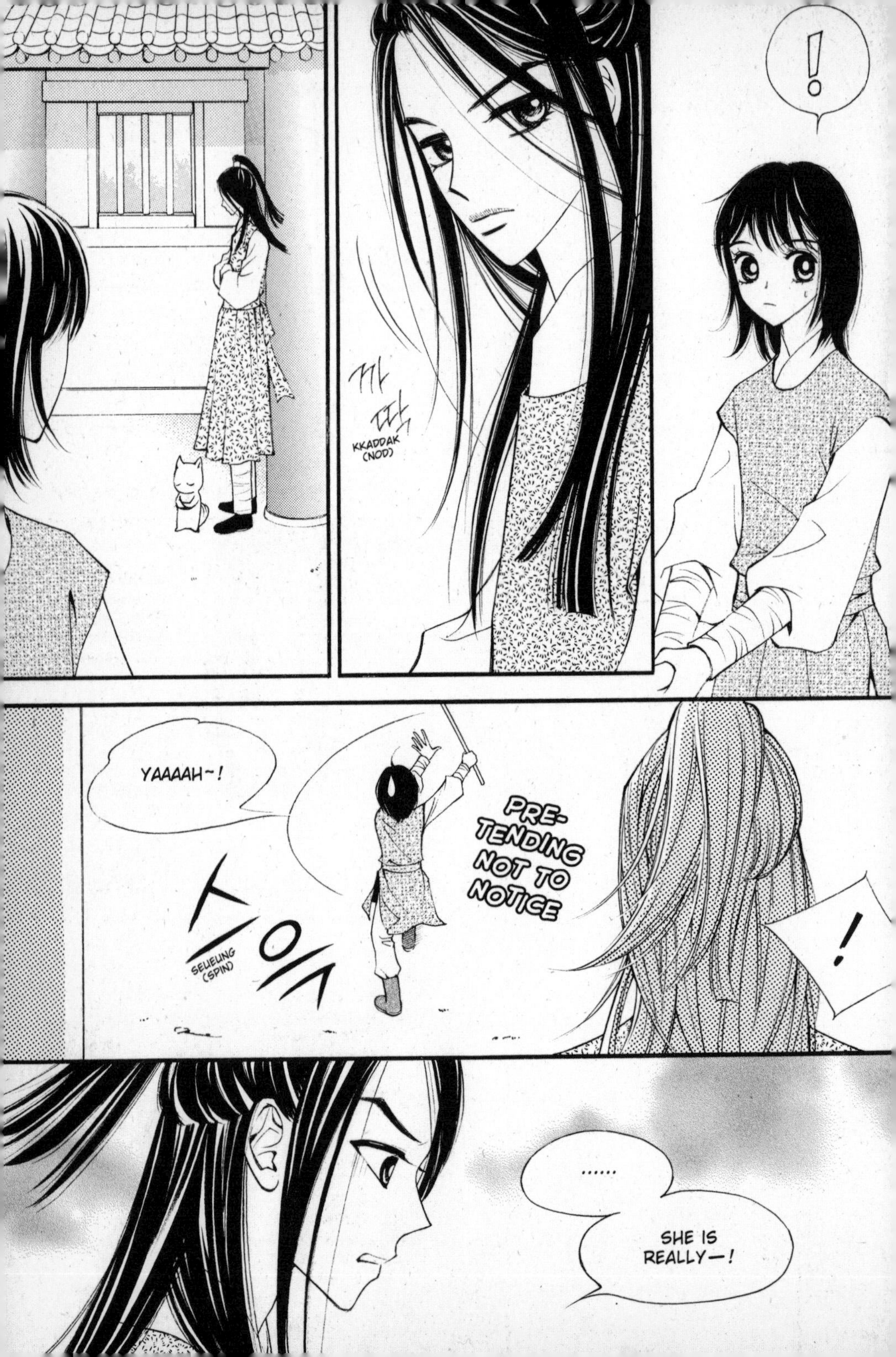

까딱
KKADDAK (NOD)
!
YAAAAH~!
PRE-TENDING NOT TO NOTICE
SEUEUNG (SPIN)
!
......
SHE IS REALLY—!

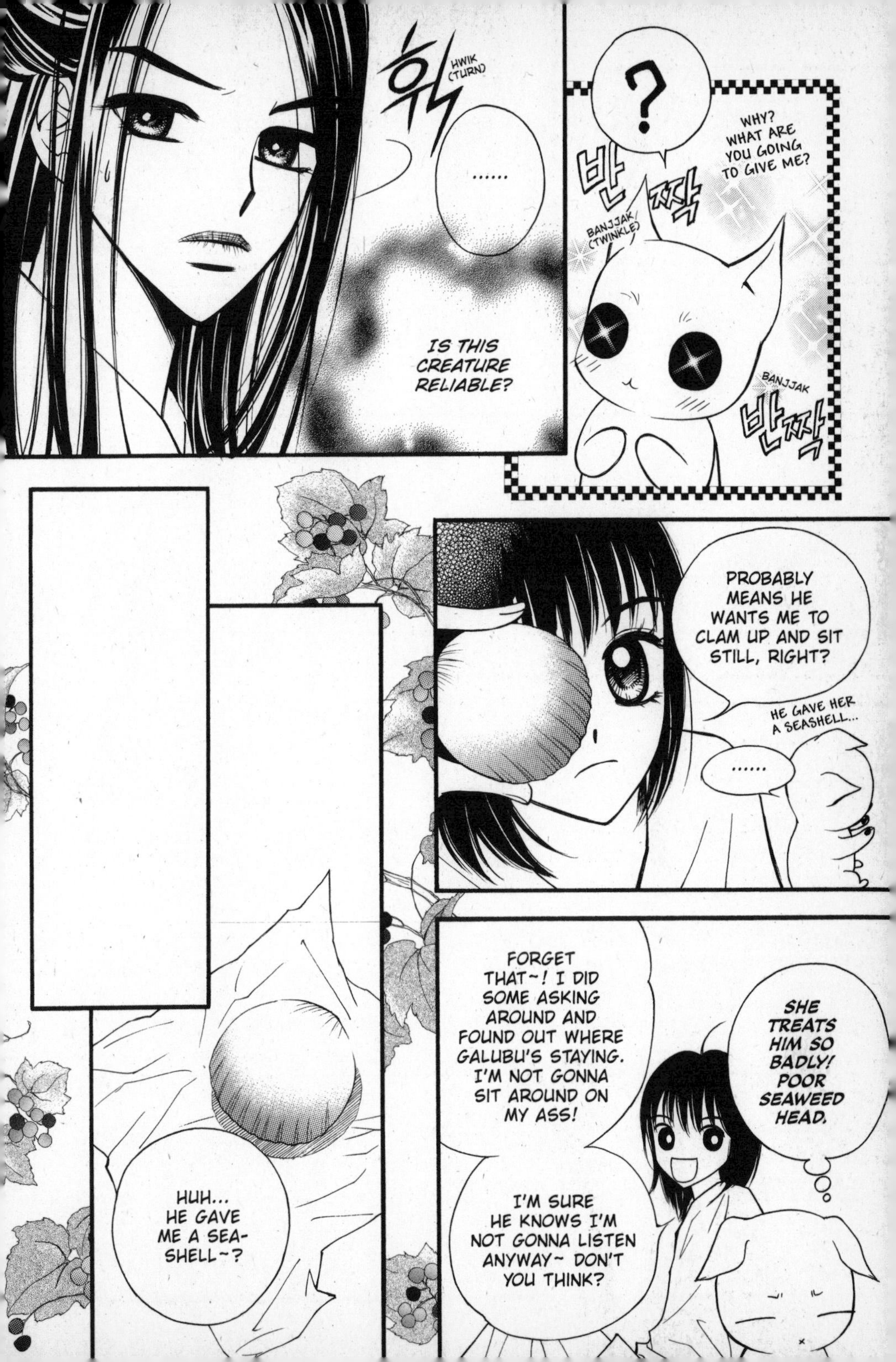

휙
HWIK (TURN)
......
IS THIS CREATURE RELIABLE?
?
반짝
BANJJAK (TWINKLE)
WHY? WHAT ARE YOU GOING TO GIVE ME?
반짝
BANJJAK
HUH... HE GAVE ME A SEA-SHELL~?
PROBABLY MEANS HE WANTS ME TO CLAM UP AND SIT STILL, RIGHT?
HE GAVE HER A SEASHELL...
......
FORGET THAT~! I DID SOME ASKING AROUND AND FOUND OUT WHERE GALUBU'S STAYING. I'M NOT GONNA SIT AROUND ON MY ASS!
SHE TREATS HIM SO BADLY! POOR SEAWEED HEAD.
I'M SURE HE KNOWS I'M NOT GONNA LISTEN ANYWAY~ DON'T YOU THINK?

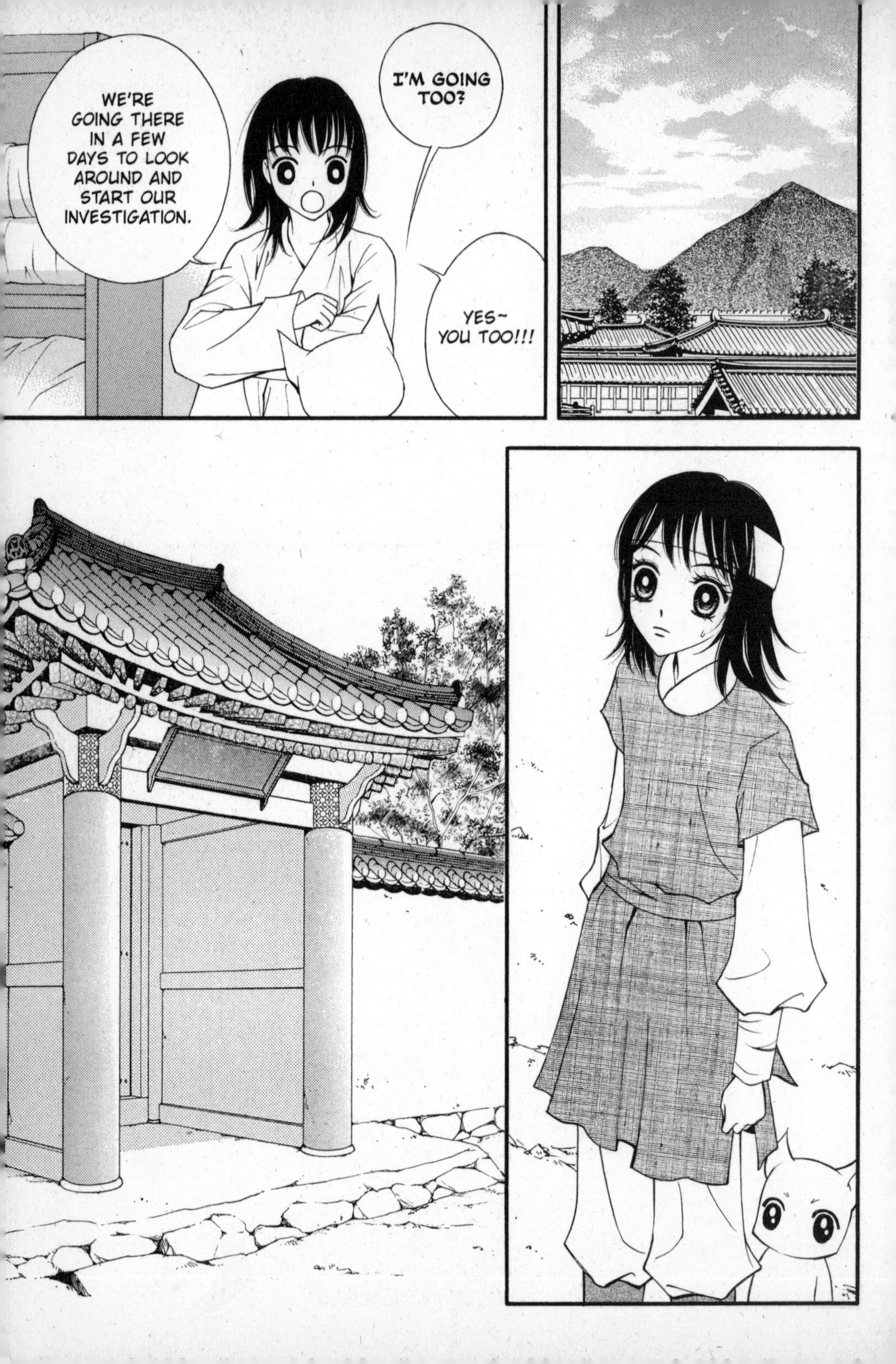
WE'RE GOING THERE IN A FEW DAYS TO LOOK AROUND AND START OUR INVESTIGATION.
I'M GOING TOO?
YES~ YOU TOO!!!

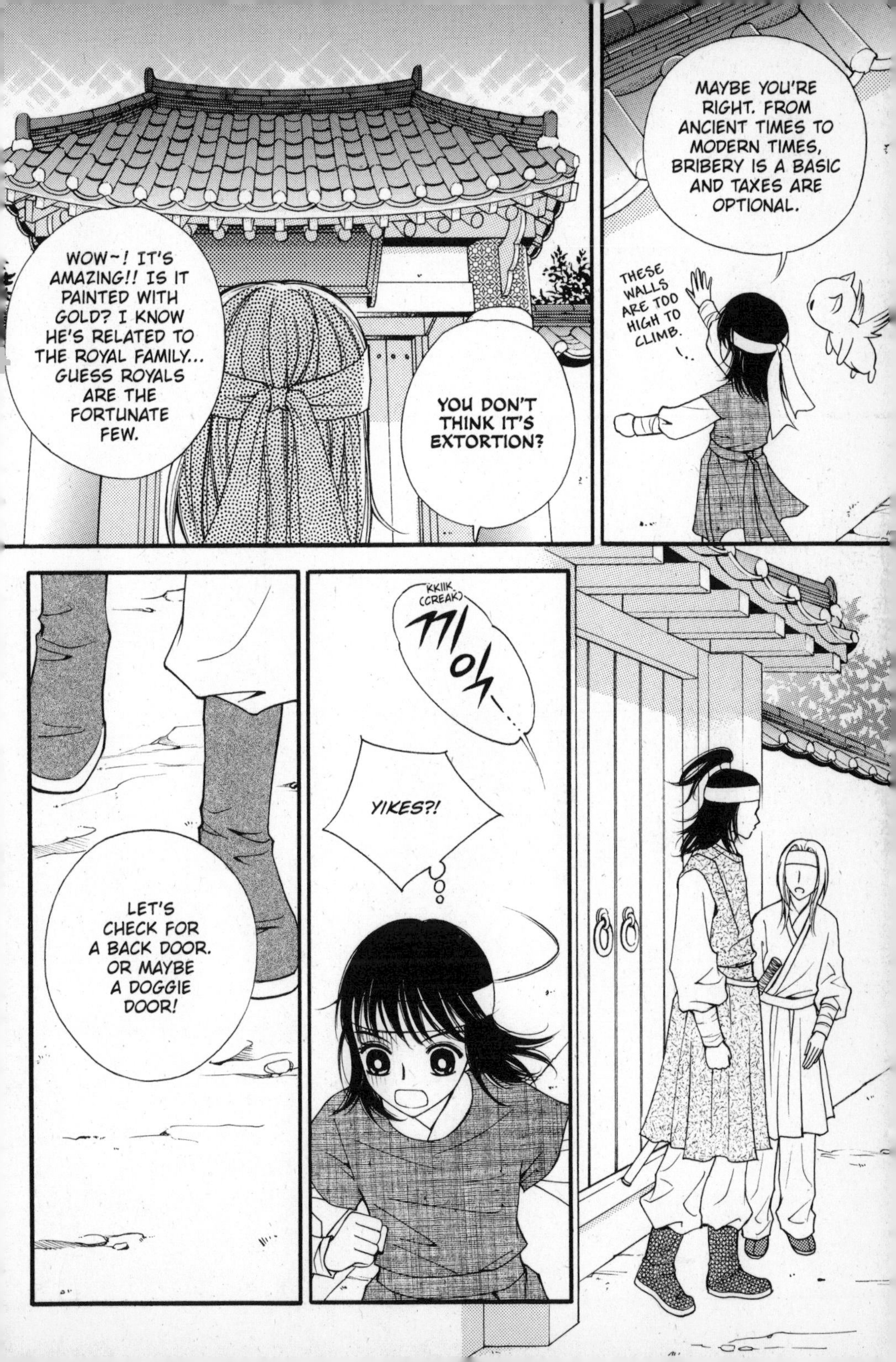
WOW~! IT'S AMAZING!! IS IT PAINTED WITH GOLD? I KNOW HE'S RELATED TO THE ROYAL FAMILY... GUESS ROYALS ARE THE FORTUNATE FEW.
YOU DON'T THINK IT'S EXTORTION?
MAYBE YOU'RE RIGHT. FROM ANCIENT TIMES TO MODERN TIMES, BRIBERY IS A BASIC AND TAXES ARE OPTIONAL.
THESE WALLS ARE TOO HIGH TO CLIMB.
LET'S CHECK FOR A BACK DOOR. OR MAYBE A DOGGIE DOOR!
KKIIK (CREAK)
YIKES?!

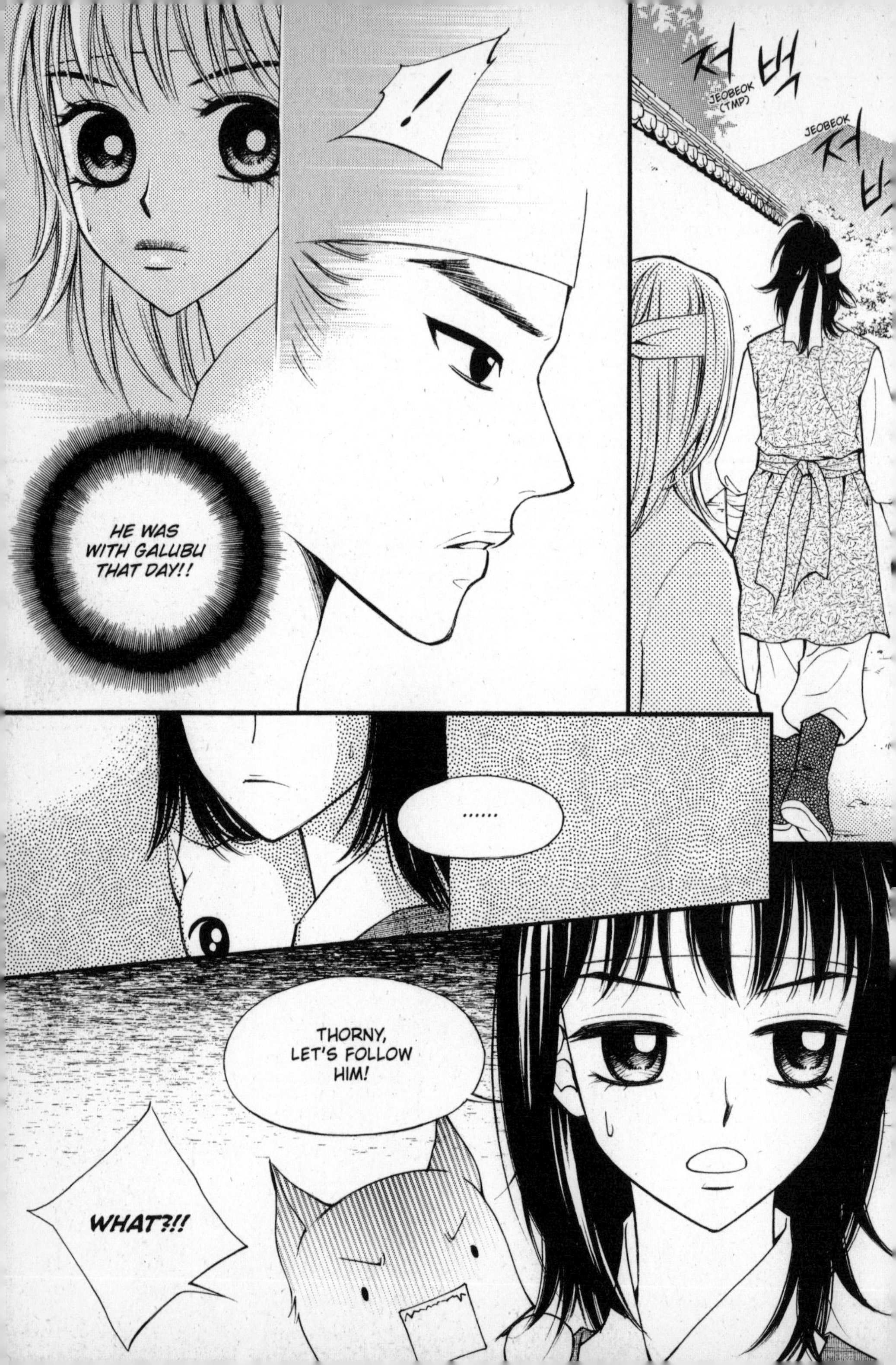
!
HE WAS WITH GALUBU THAT DAY!!
저벅
JEOBEOK (TMP)
JEOBEOK
......
THORNY, LET'S FOLLOW HIM!
WHAT?!!

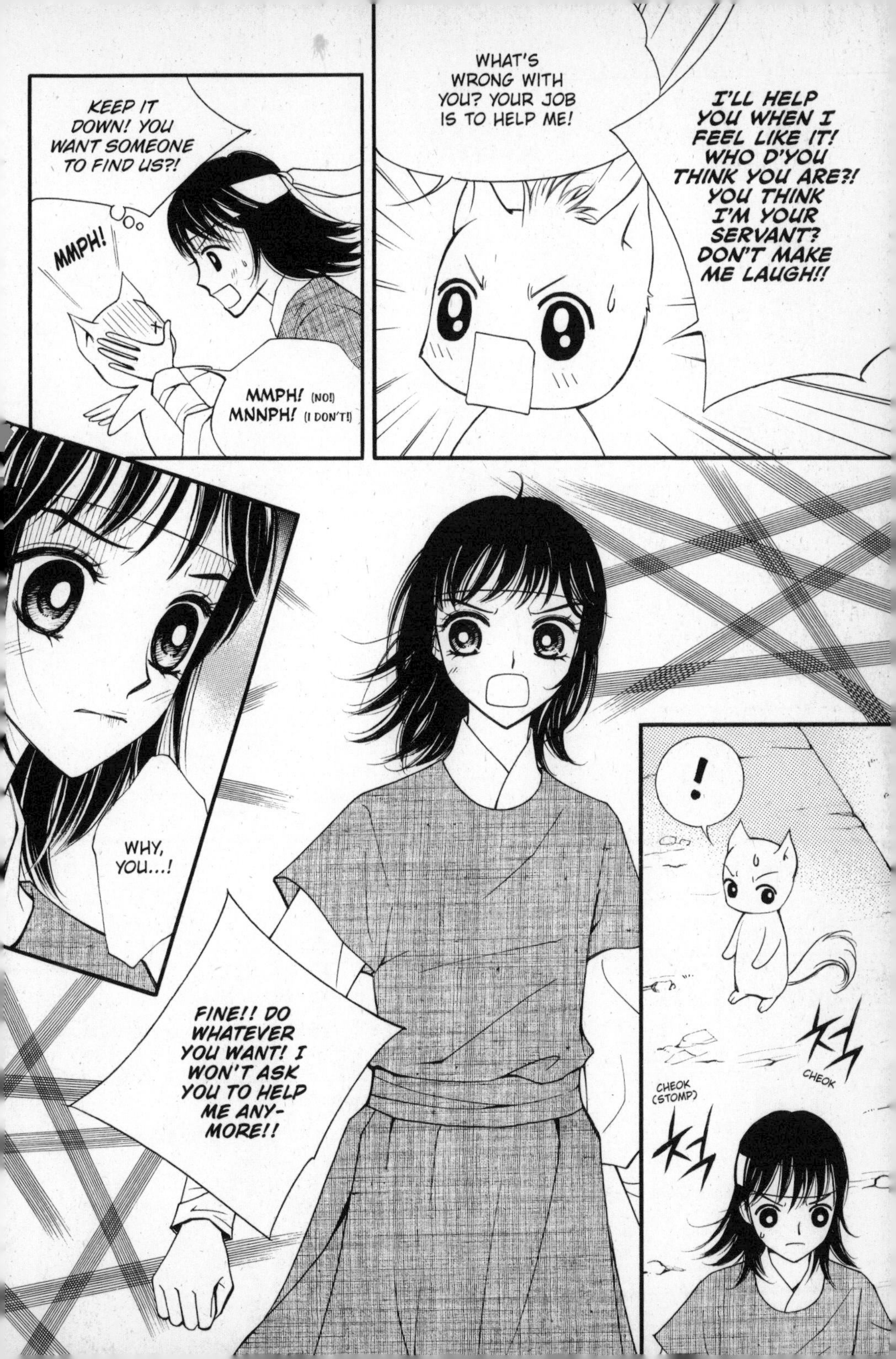
KEEP IT DOWN! YOU WANT SOMEONE TO FIND US?!
MMPH!
MMPH! (NO!) MNNPH! (I DON'T!)
WHAT'S WRONG WITH YOU? YOUR JOB IS TO HELP ME!
I'LL HELP YOU WHEN I FEEL LIKE IT! WHO D'YOU THINK YOU ARE?! YOU THINK I'M YOUR SERVANT? DON'T MAKE ME LAUGH!!
WHY, YOU...!
FINE!! DO WHATEVER YOU WANT! I WON'T ASK YOU TO HELP ME ANY-MORE!!
!
CHEOK
CHEOK (STOMP)

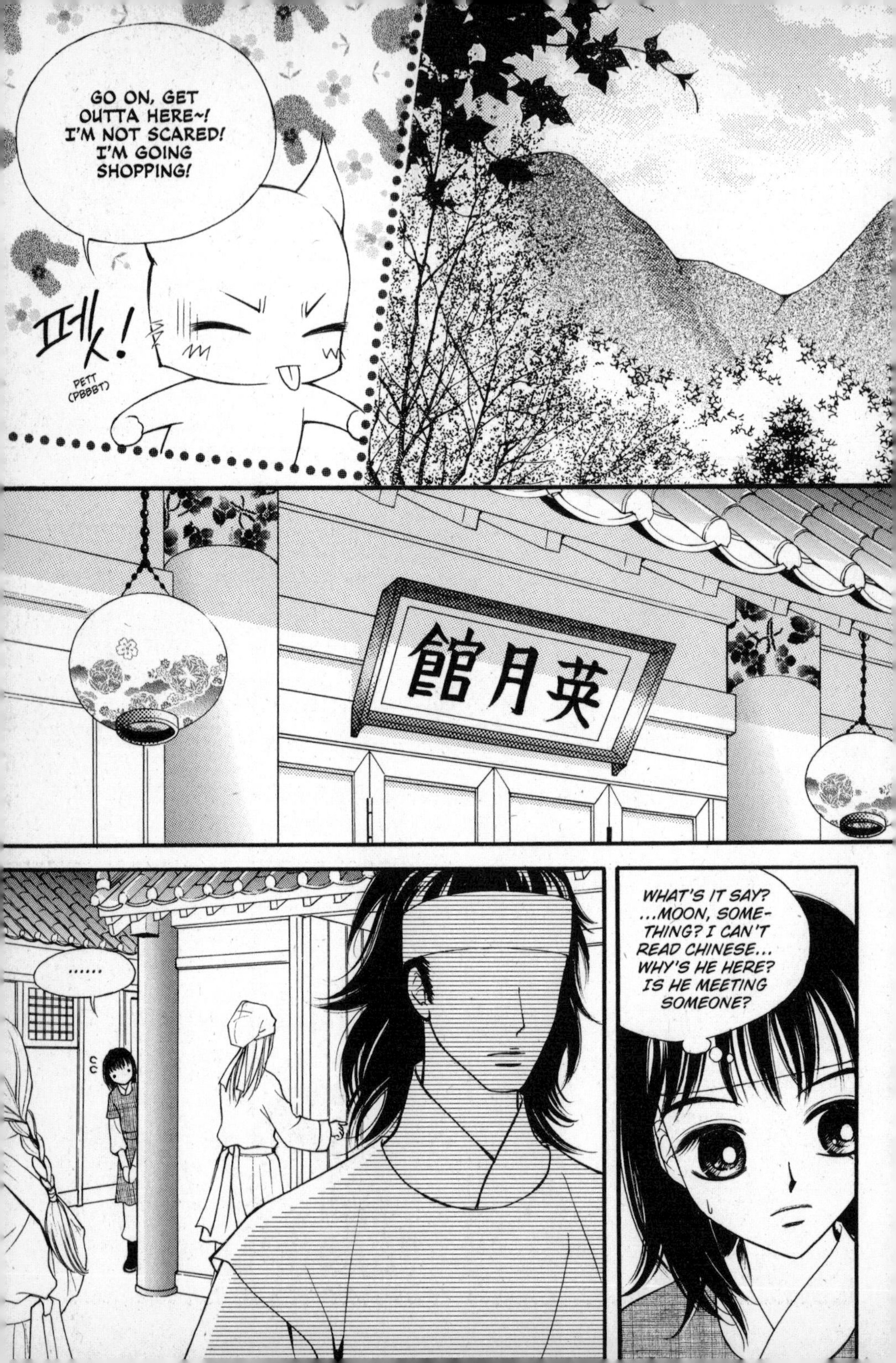
GO ON, GET OUTTA HERE~! I'M NOT SCARED! I'M GOING SHOPPING!
페ㅅ!
PETT (PBBBT)
館月英
......
WHAT'S IT SAY? ...MOON, SOMETHING? I CAN'T READ CHINESE... WHY'S HE HERE? IS HE MEETING SOMEONE?

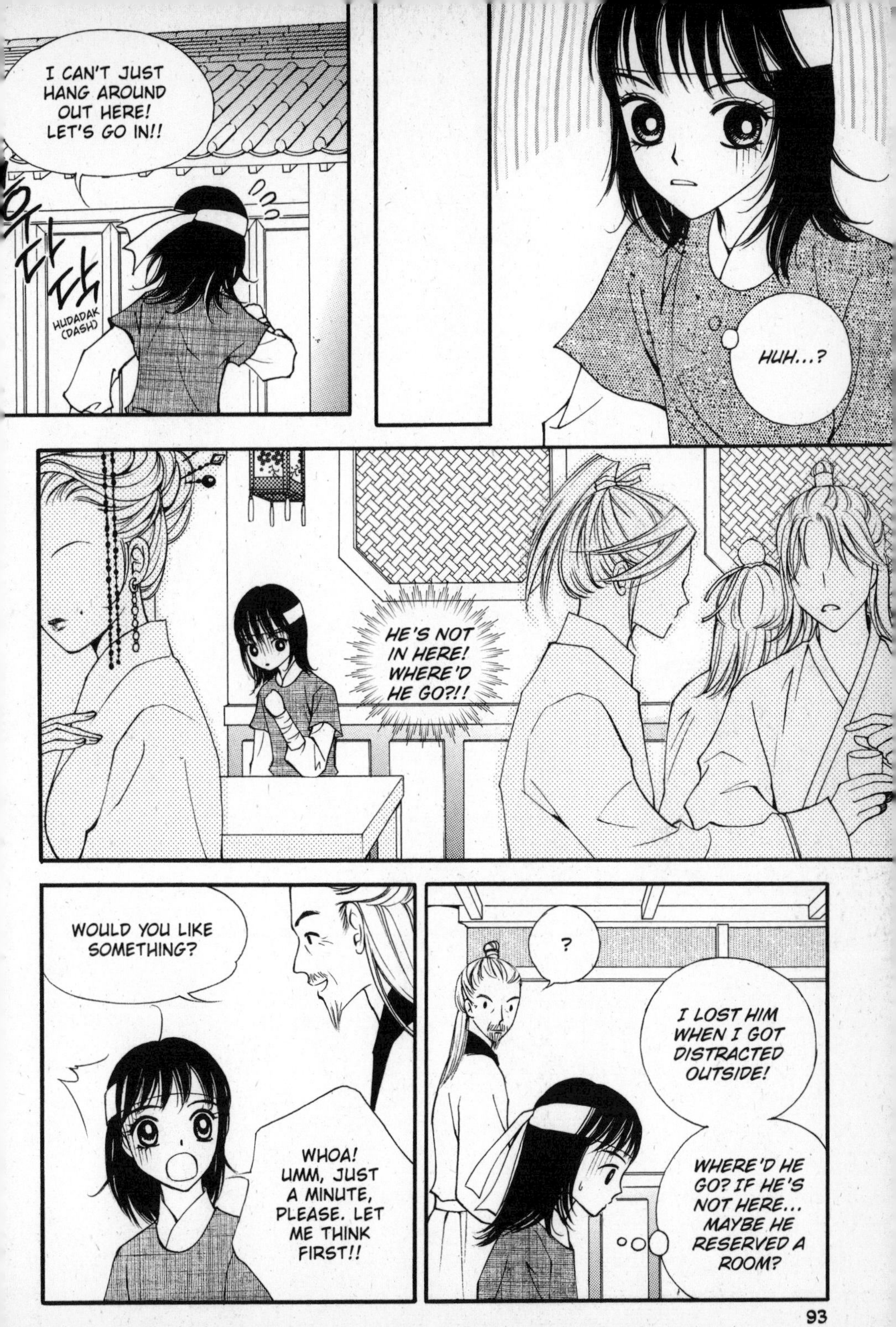
I CAN'T JUST HANG AROUND OUT HERE! LET'S GO IN!!
HUDADAK (DASH)
HUH...?
HE'S NOT IN HERE! WHERE'D HE GO?!!
WOULD YOU LIKE SOMETHING?
WHOA! UMM, JUST A MINUTE, PLEASE. LET ME THINK FIRST!!
?
I LOST HIM WHEN I GOT DISTRACTED OUTSIDE!
WHERE'D HE GO? IF HE'S NOT HERE... MAYBE HE RESERVED A ROOM?

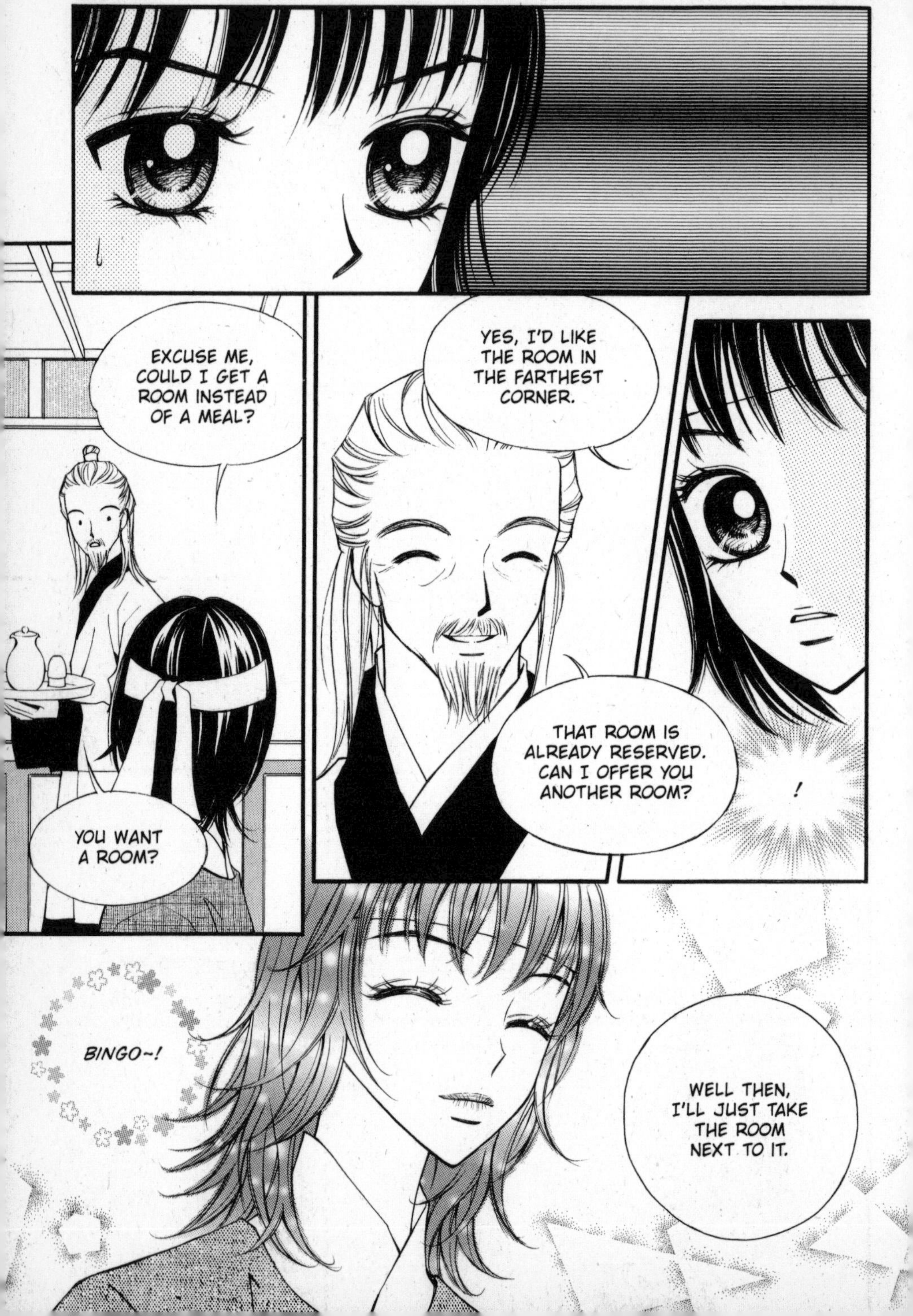
EXCUSE ME, COULD I GET A ROOM INSTEAD OF A MEAL?
YOU WANT A ROOM?
YES, I'D LIKE THE ROOM IN THE FARTHEST CORNER.
THAT ROOM IS ALREADY RESERVED. CAN I OFFER YOU ANOTHER ROOM?
!
BINGO~!
WELL THEN, I'LL JUST TAKE THE ROOM NEXT TO IT.

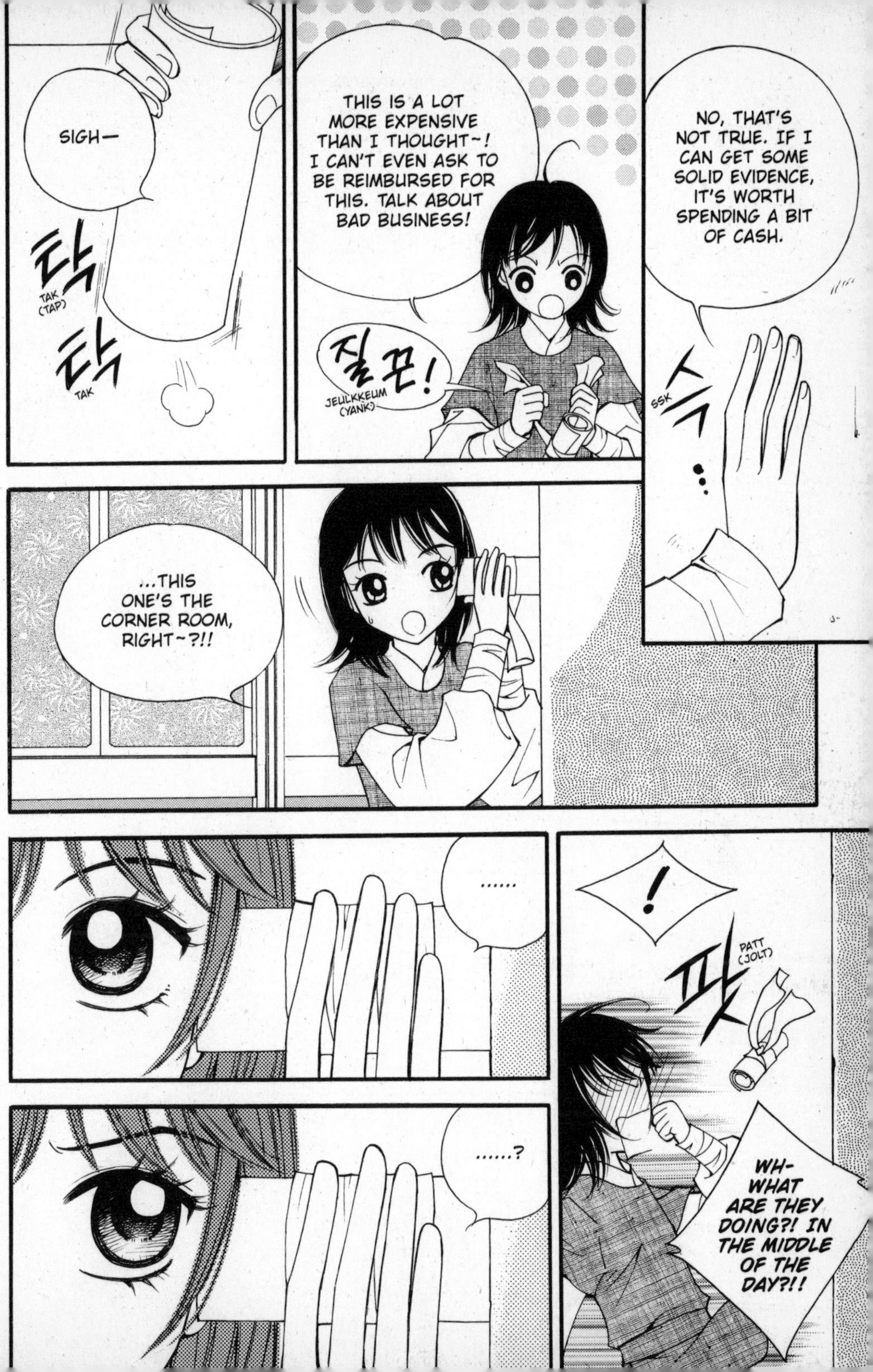
SIGH—
탁
TAK (TAP)
탁
TAK
THIS IS A LOT MORE EXPENSIVE THAN I THOUGHT~! I CAN'T EVEN ASK TO BE REIMBURSED FOR THIS. TALK ABOUT BAD BUSINESS!
질끈!
JEULKKEUM (YANK)
NO, THAT'S NOT TRUE. IF I CAN GET SOME SOLID EVIDENCE, IT'S WORTH SPENDING A BIT OF CASH.
스
SSK
...THIS ONE'S THE CORNER ROOM, RIGHT~?!!
......
......?
!
팟
PATT (JOLT)
WH-WHAT ARE THEY DOING?! IN THE MIDDLE OF THE DAY?!!

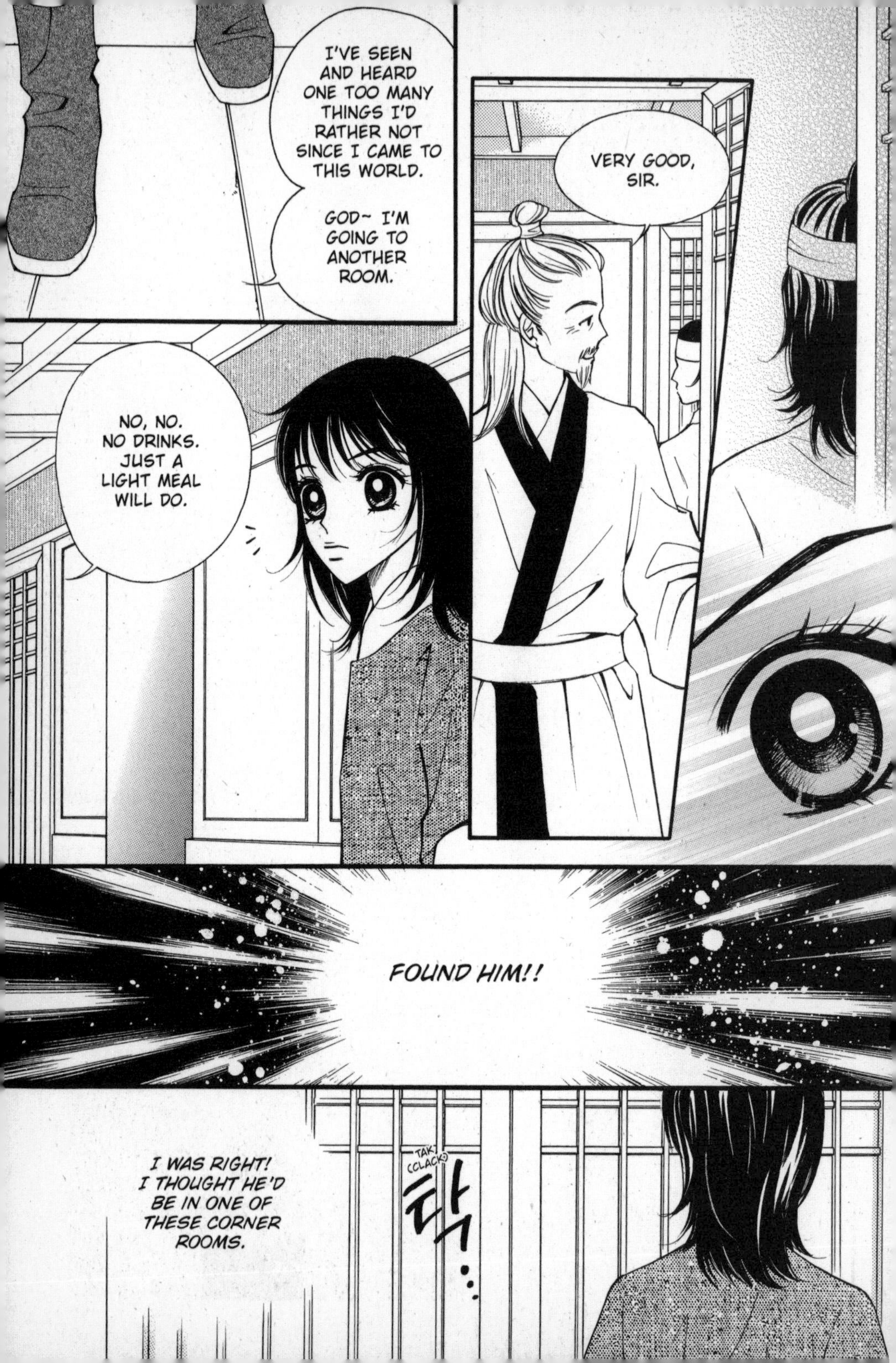
I'VE SEEN AND HEARD ONE TOO MANY THINGS I'D RATHER NOT SINCE I CAME TO THIS WORLD.
GOD~ I'M GOING TO ANOTHER ROOM.
NO, NO. NO DRINKS. JUST A LIGHT MEAL WILL DO.
VERY GOOD, SIR.
FOUND HIM!!
I WAS RIGHT! I THOUGHT HE'D BE IN ONE OF THESE CORNER ROOMS.
TAK (CLACK)
탁...

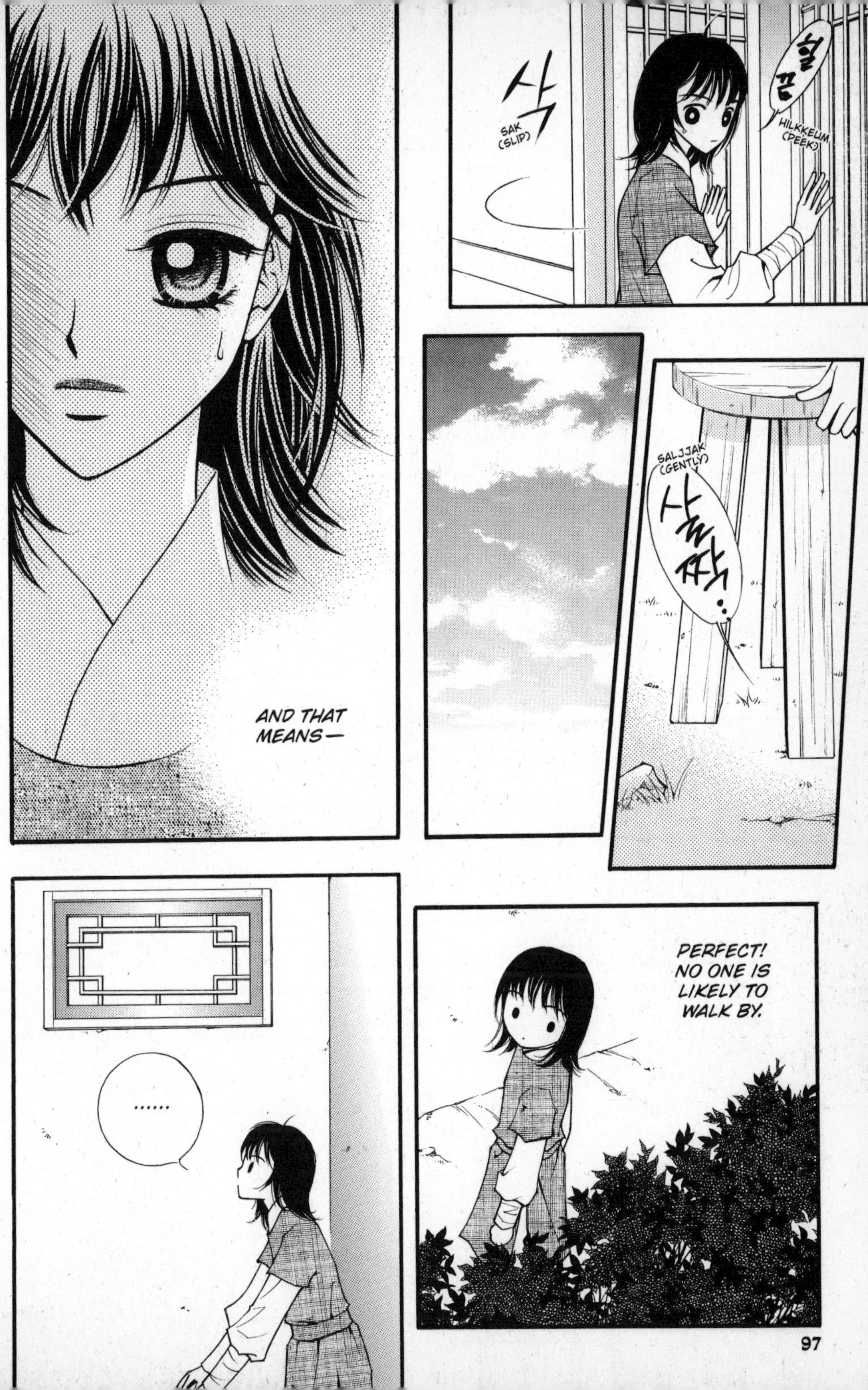
AND THAT MEANS—
삭
SAK (SLIP)
힐끔
HILKKEUM (PEEK)
SALJJAK (GENTLY)
살짝..
......
PERFECT! NO ONE IS LIKELY TO WALK BY.

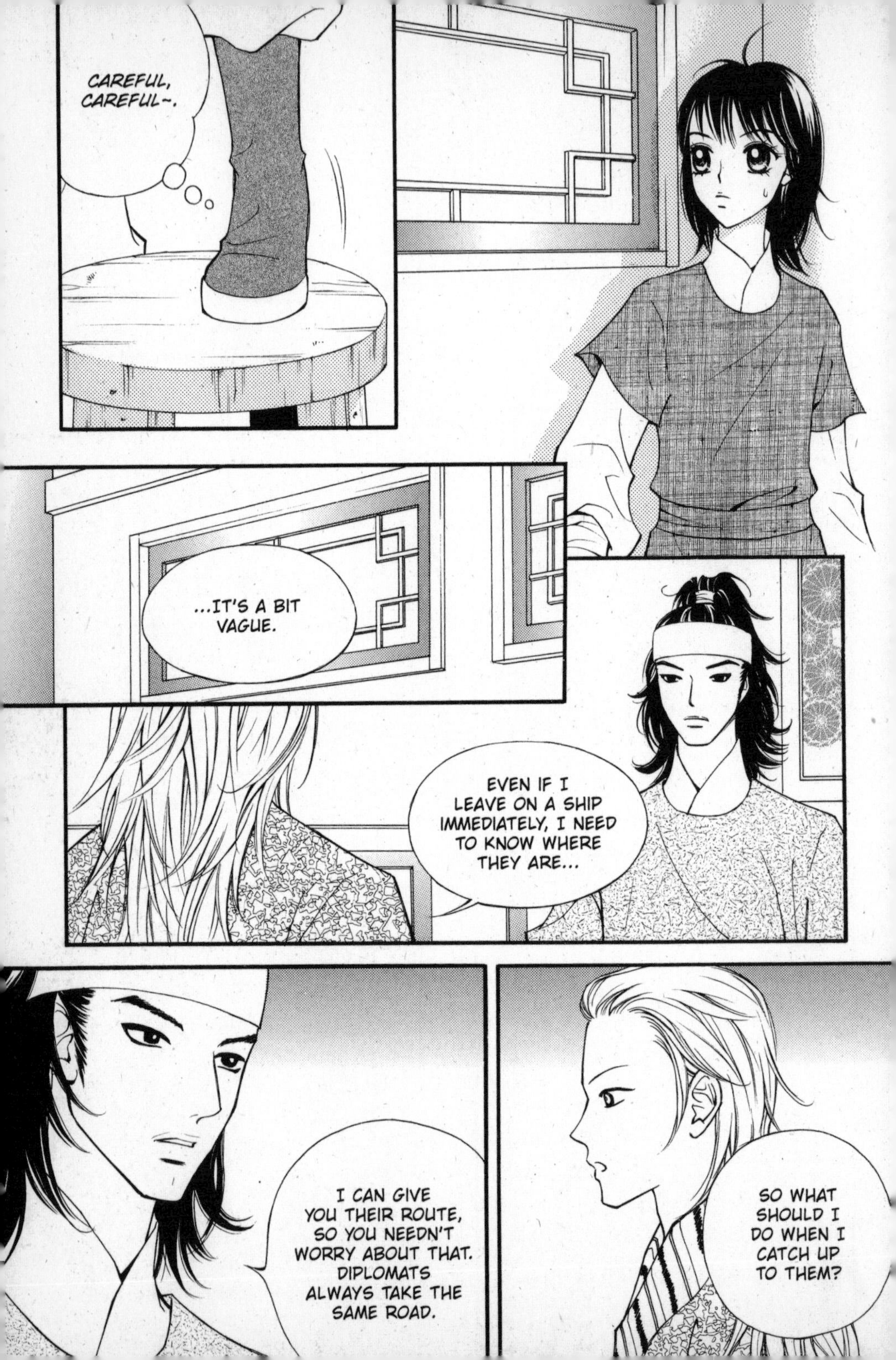
CAREFUL, CAREFUL~.
...IT'S A BIT VAGUE.
EVEN IF I LEAVE ON A SHIP IMMEDIATELY, I NEED TO KNOW WHERE THEY ARE...
I CAN GIVE YOU THEIR ROUTE, SO YOU NEEDN'T WORRY ABOUT THAT. DIPLOMATS ALWAYS TAKE THE SAME ROAD.
SO WHAT SHOULD I DO WHEN I CATCH UP TO THEM?

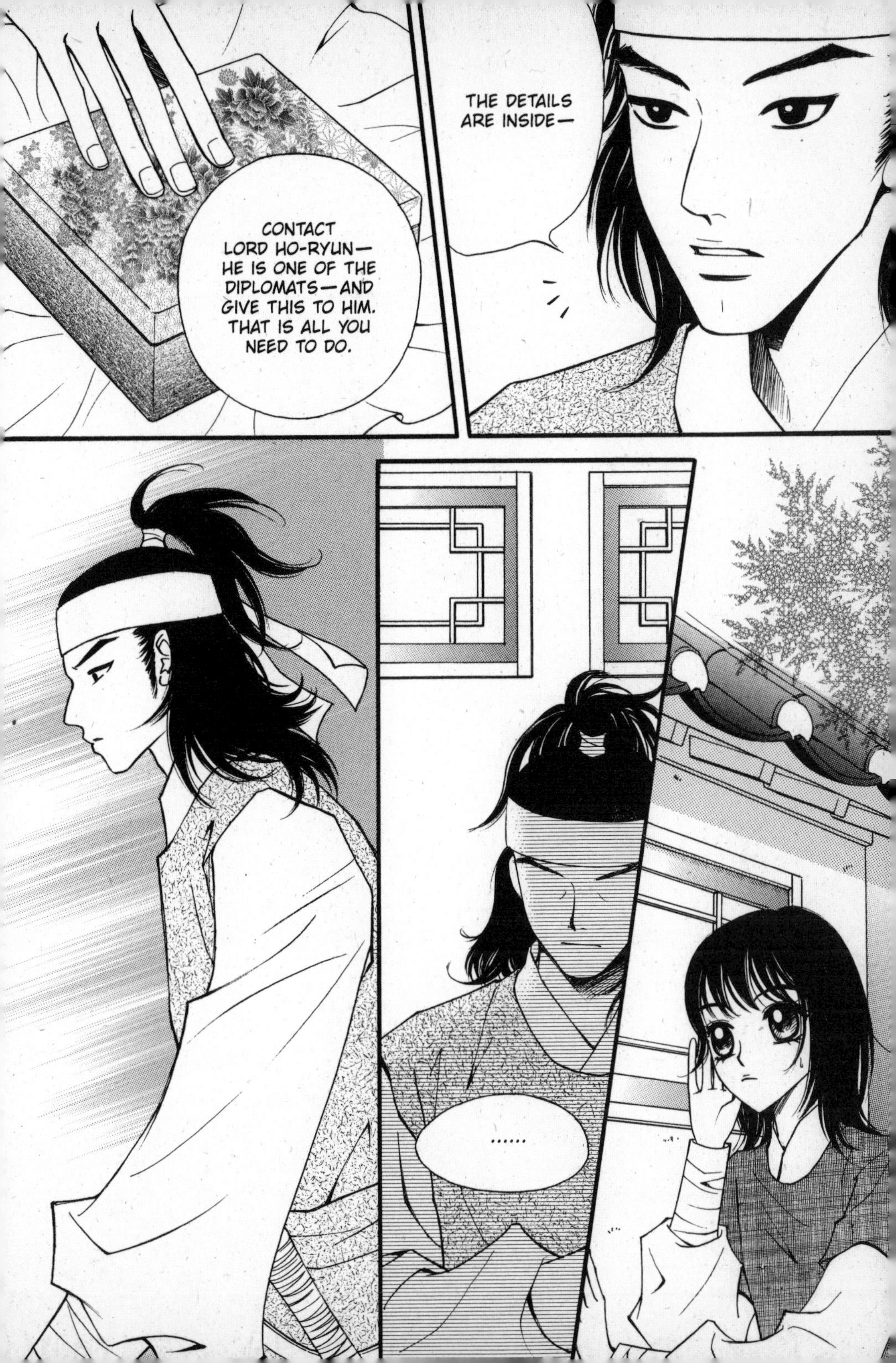
CONTACT LORD HO-RYUN—HE IS ONE OF THE DIPLOMATS—AND GIVE THIS TO HIM. THAT IS ALL YOU NEED TO DO.
THE DETAILS ARE INSIDE—
......

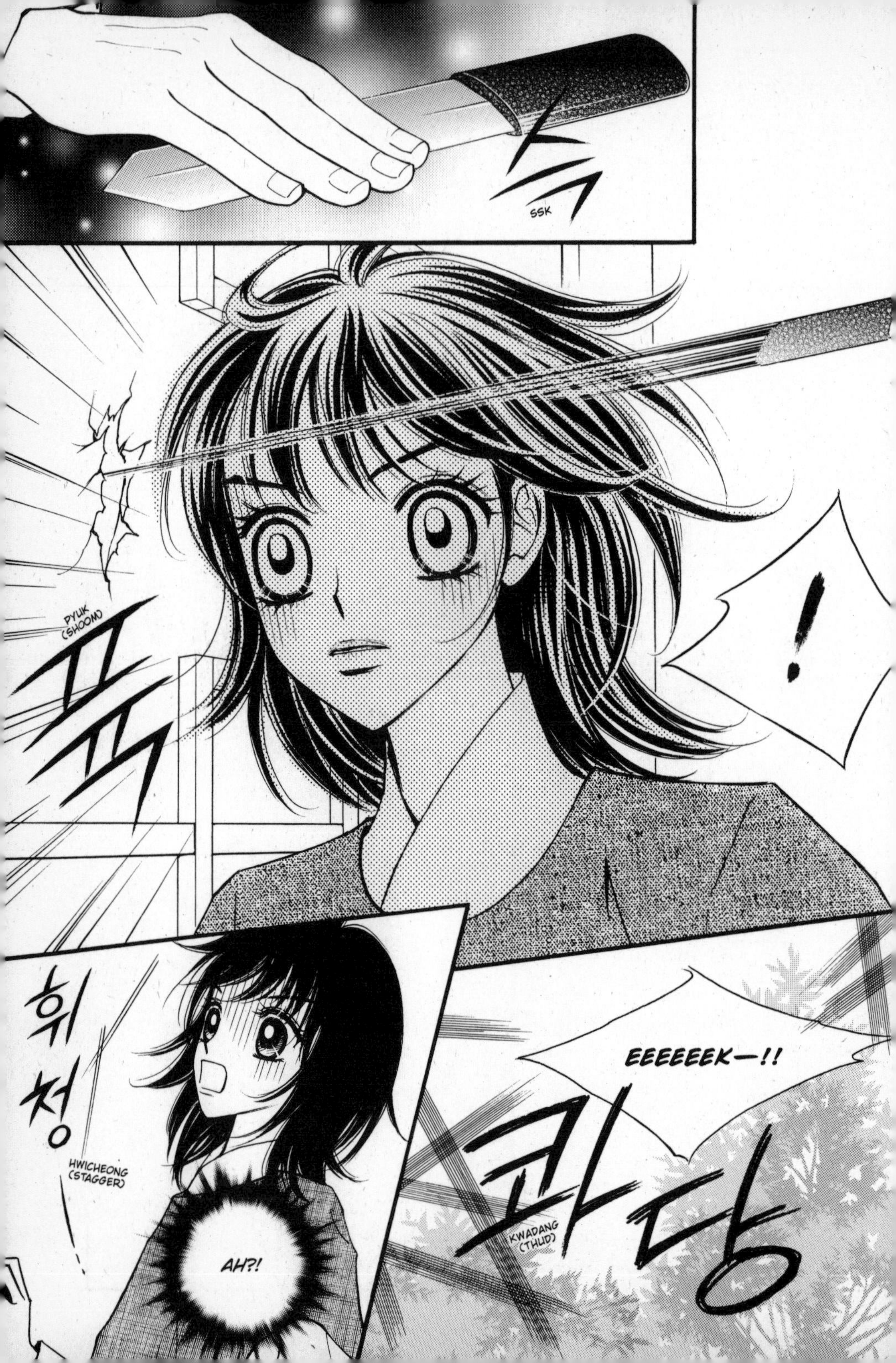
SSK
PYUIK (SHOOM)
!
휘청
HWICHEONG (STAGGER)
AH?!
EEEEEEK—!!
콰당
KWADANG (THUD)

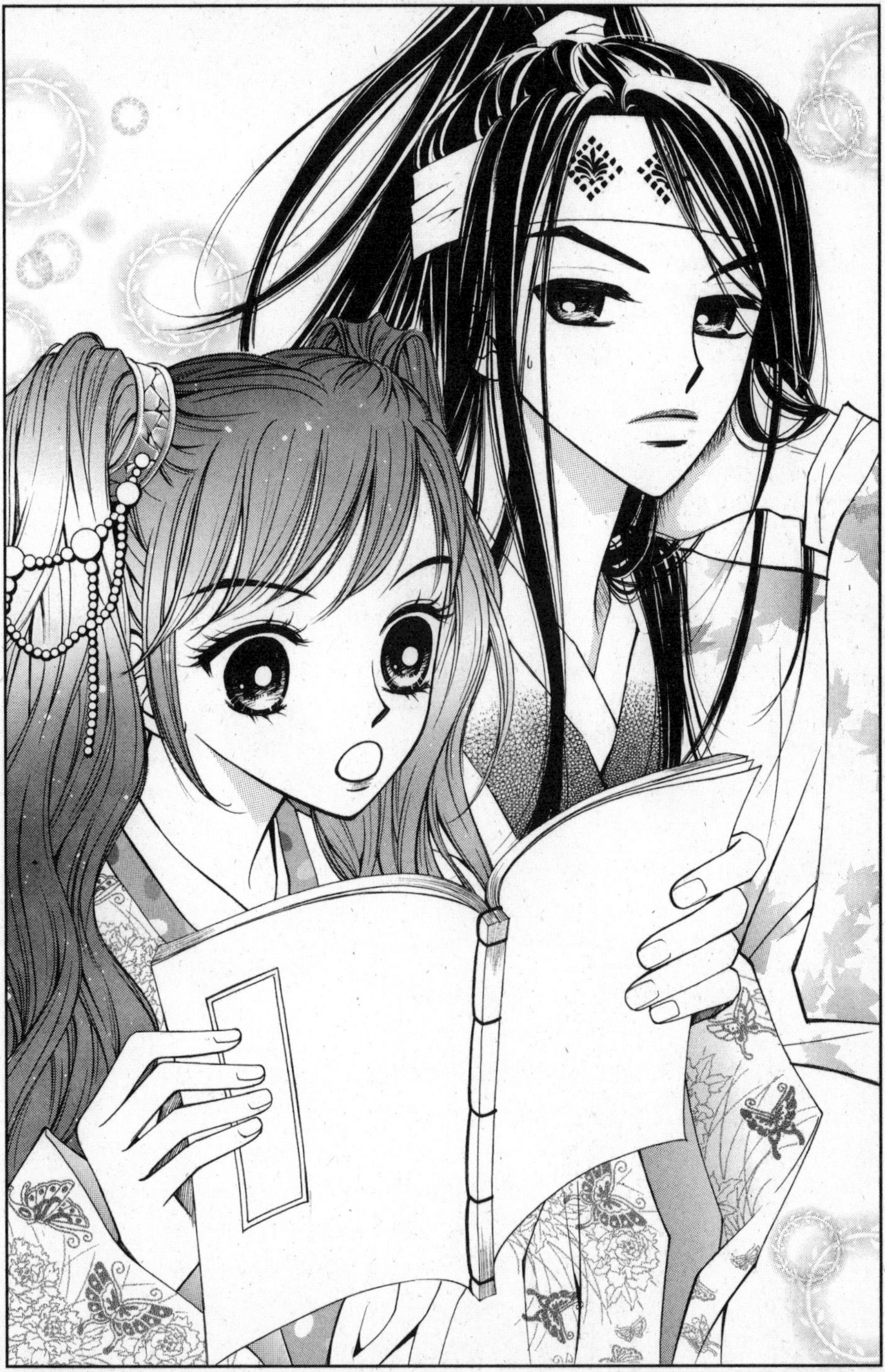

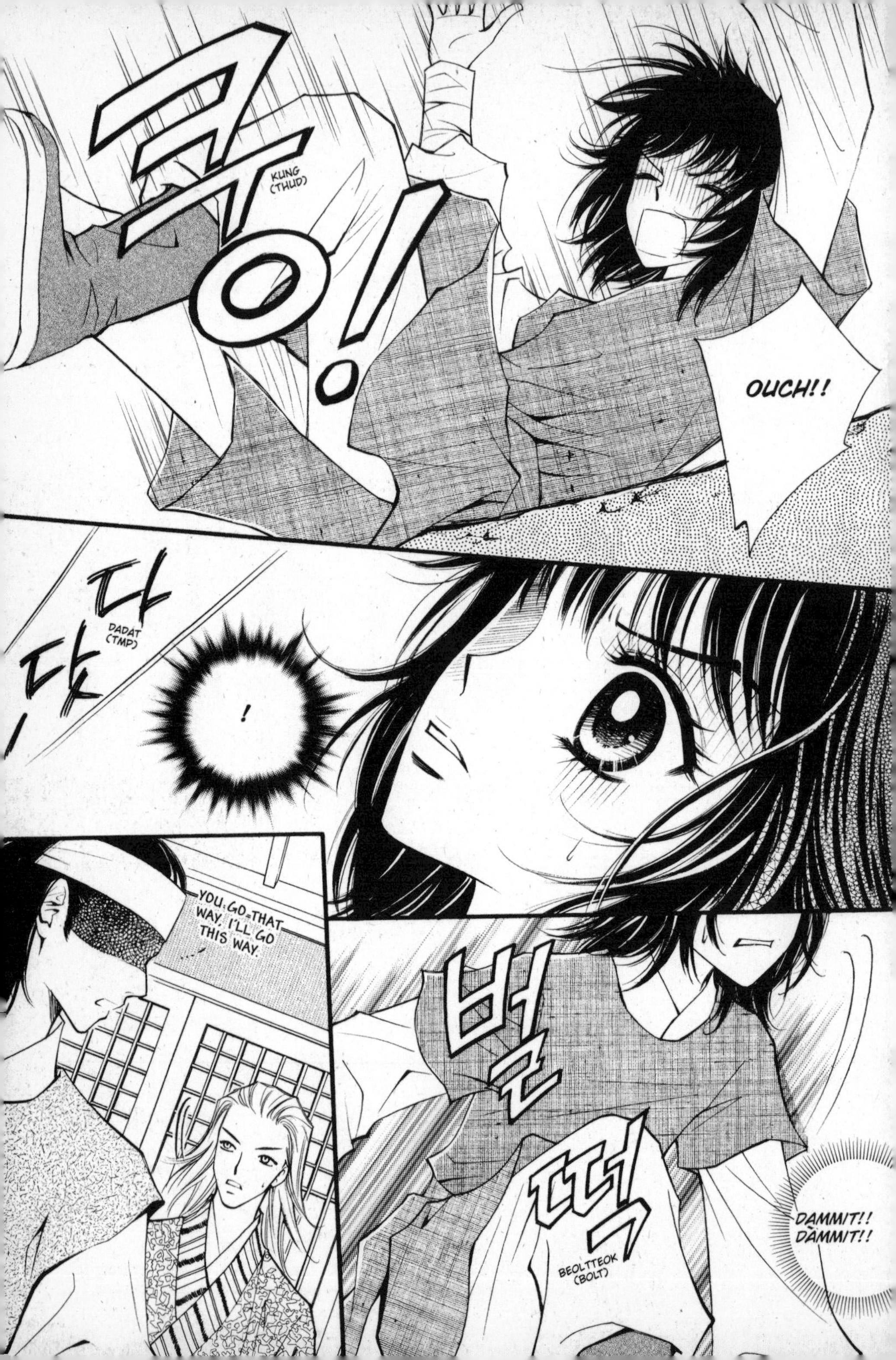
쿵!
KUNG (THUD)
OUCH!!
다닥
DADAT (TMP)
!
YOU GO THAT WAY, I'LL GO THIS WAY.
벌떡
BEOLTTEOK (BOLT)
DAMMIT!! DAMMIT!!

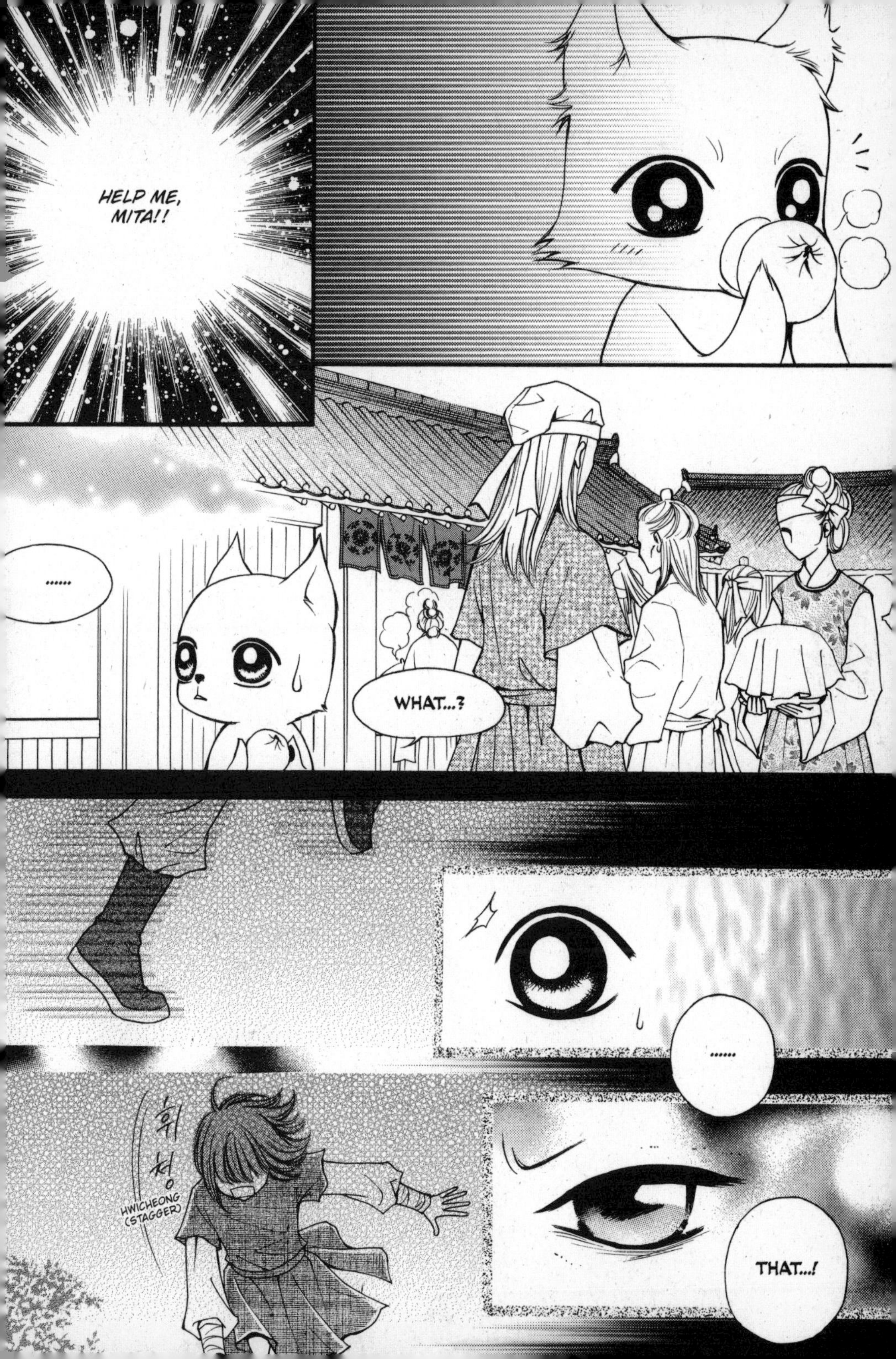
HELP ME, MITA!!
......
WHAT...?
......
휘청
HWICHEONG (STAGGER)
THAT...!

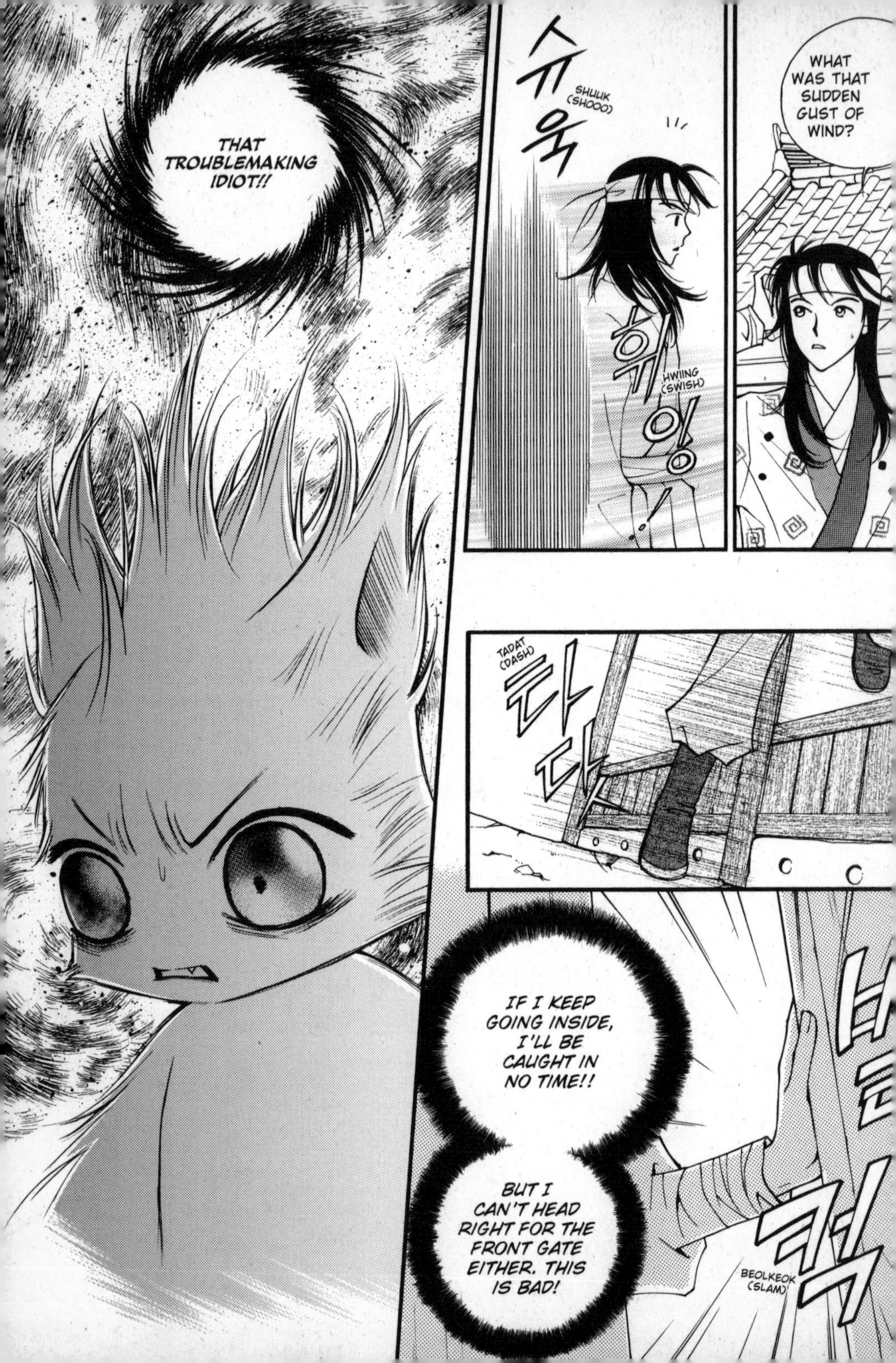
THAT TROUBLEMAKING IDIOT!!
SHUUK (SHOOO)
HWIING (SWISH)
WHAT WAS THAT SUDDEN GUST OF WIND?
TADAT (DASH)
IF I KEEP GOING INSIDE, I'LL BE CAUGHT IN NO TIME!!
BUT I CAN'T HEAD RIGHT FOR THE FRONT GATE EITHER. THIS IS BAD!
BEOLKEOK (SLAM)

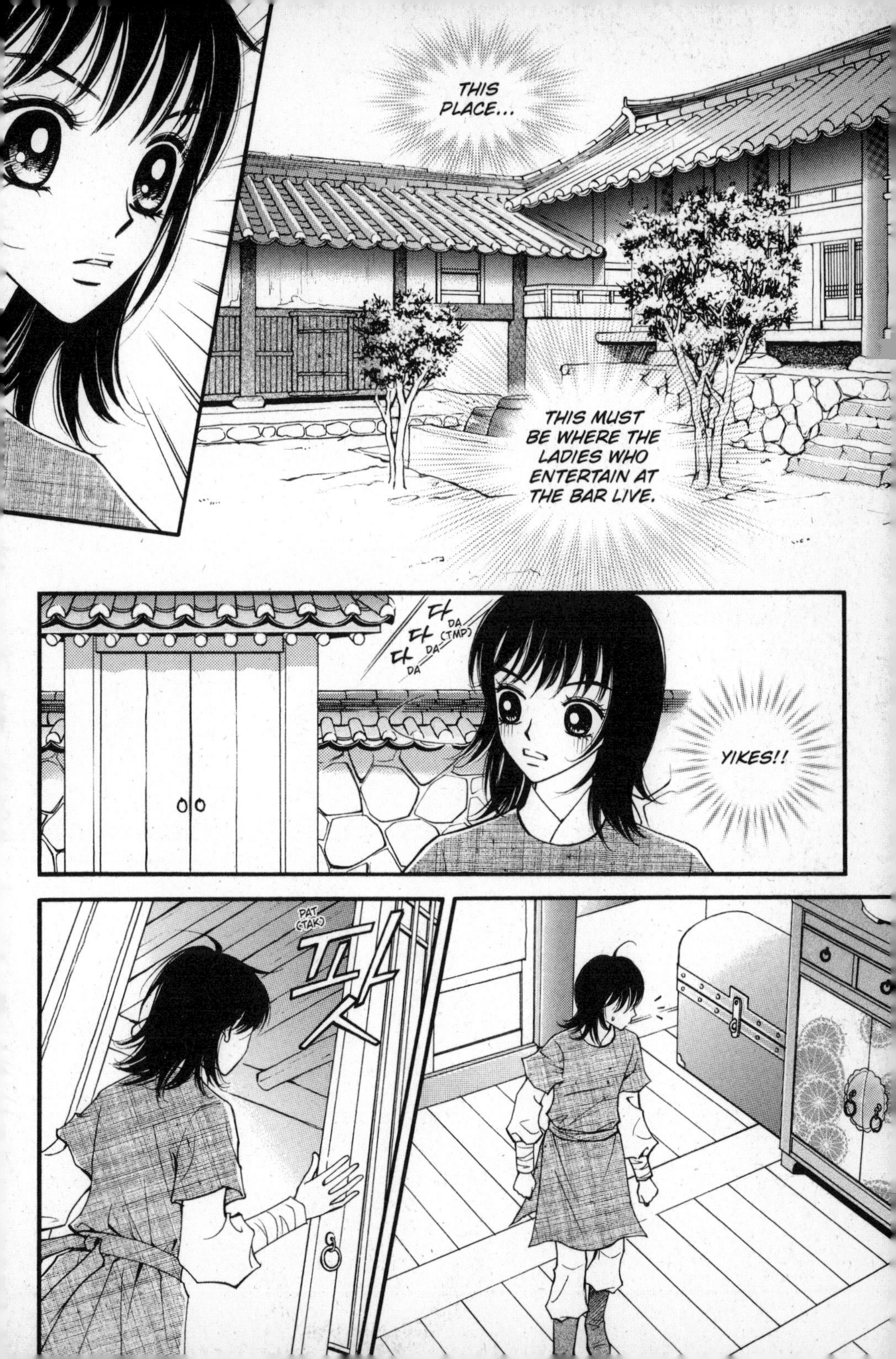
THIS PLACE...
THIS MUST BE WHERE THE LADIES WHO ENTERTAIN AT THE BAR LIVE.
다 DA 다 DA 다 DA (TMP)
YIKES!!
PAT (TAK)
파
삭

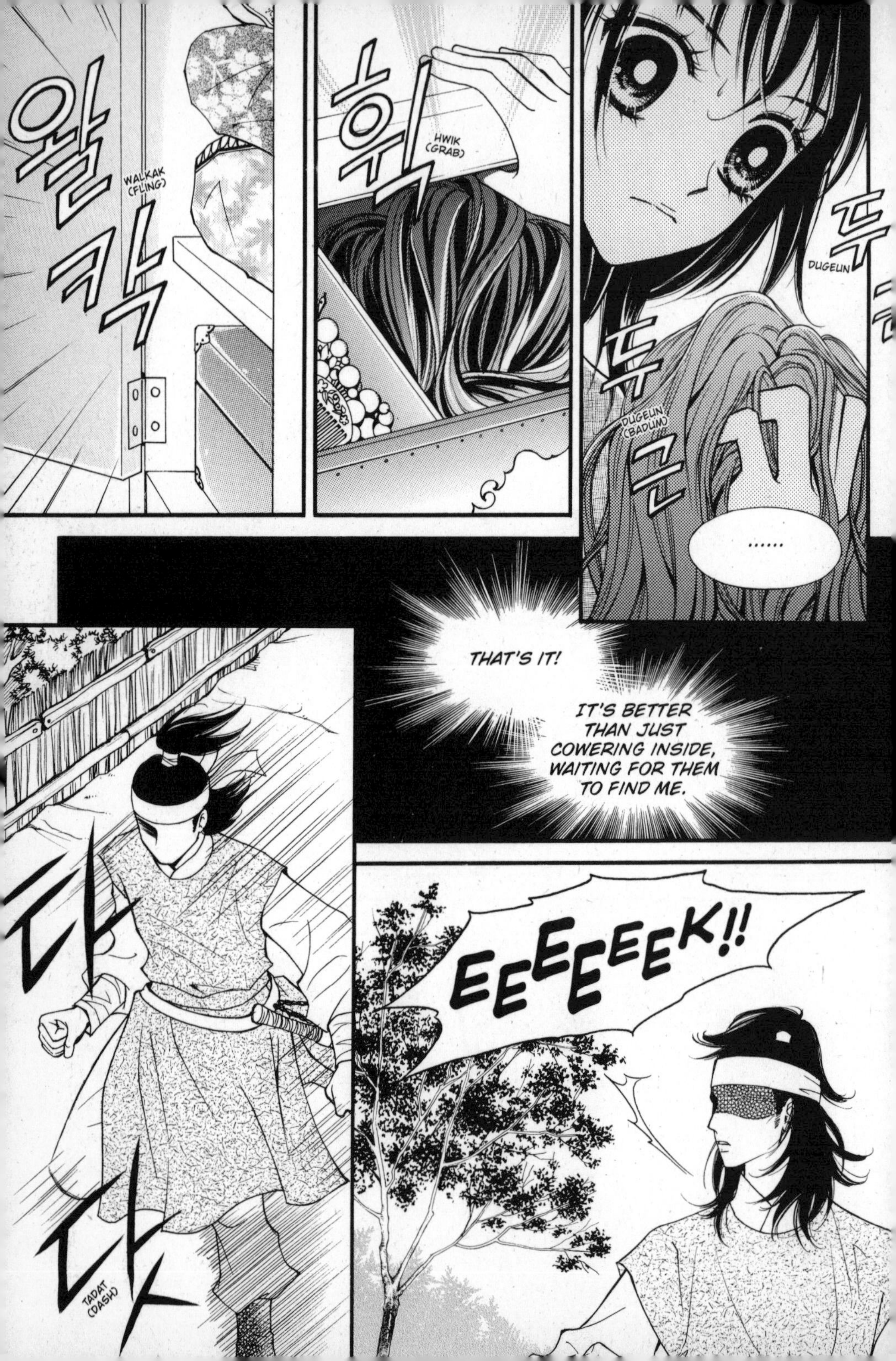

왈칵
WALKAK (FLING)
휙
HWIK (GRAB)
두근
DUGEUN
두근
DUGEUN (BADUM)
......
타닷
TADAT (DASH)
THAT'S IT!
IT'S BETTER THAN JUST COWERING INSIDE, WAITING FOR THEM TO FIND ME.
EEEEEEEEK!!

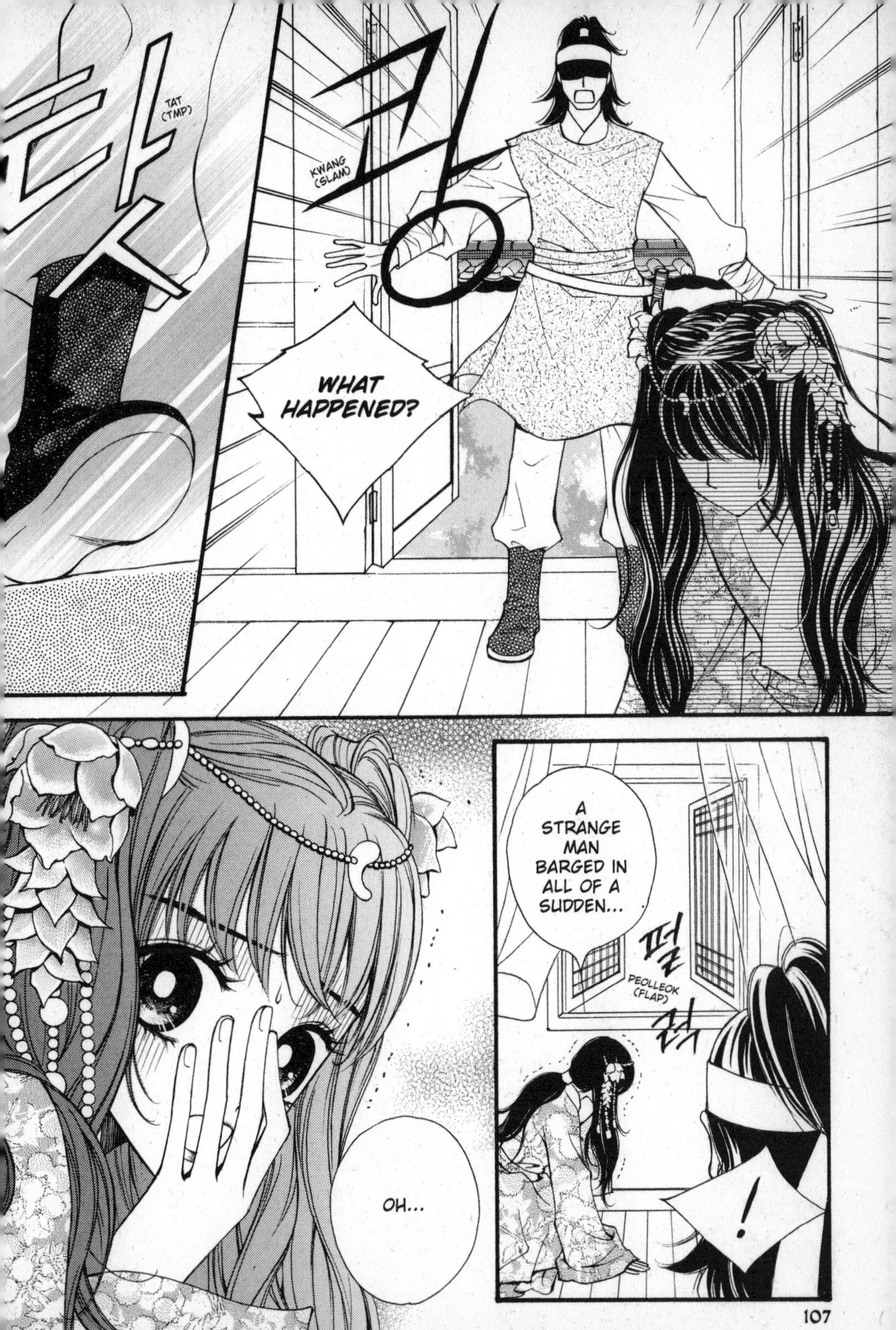

탁
TAT (TMP)
쾅
KWANG (SLAM)
WHAT HAPPENED?
OH...
A STRANGE MAN BARGED IN ALL OF A SUDDEN...
펄럭
PEOLLEOK (FLAP)
!

PAT
(JUMP)

크ㅎ

KUNG
(THUMP)

TAK
(TMP)

TAK
TAK
TAK
TAK

!

AH...WHEW. NOW I GOTTA GET OUT OF HERE FAST...

IT SHOULD BE CLEAR TO MAKE A BREAK FOR THE FRONT DOOR NOW, RIGHT?

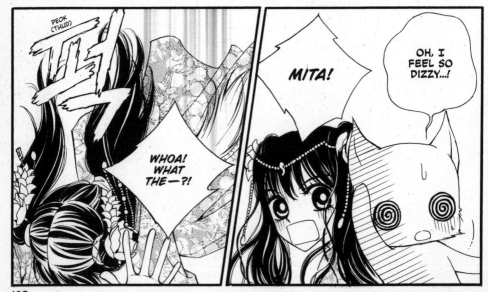

PEOK
(THUD)

WHOA! WHAT THE—?!

MITA!

OH, I FEEL SO DIZZY...!

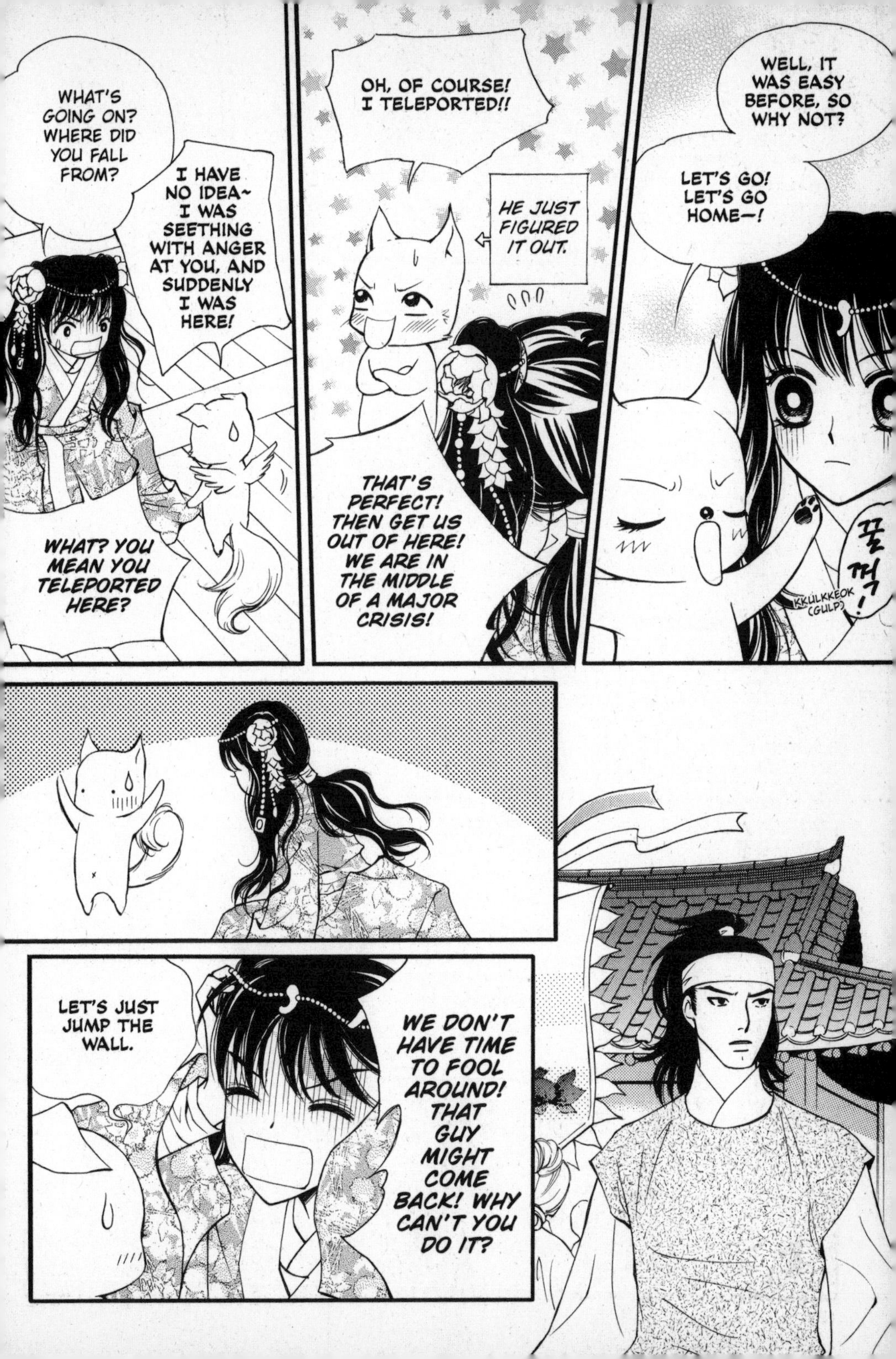
WHAT'S GOING ON? WHERE DID YOU FALL FROM?
I HAVE NO IDEA~ I WAS SEETHING WITH ANGER AT YOU, AND SUDDENLY I WAS HERE!
WHAT? YOU MEAN YOU TELEPORTED HERE?
OH, OF COURSE! I TELEPORTED!!
HE JUST FIGURED IT OUT.
THAT'S PERFECT! THEN GET US OUT OF HERE! WE ARE IN THE MIDDLE OF A MAJOR CRISIS!
WELL, IT WAS EASY BEFORE, SO WHY NOT?
LET'S GO! LET'S GO HOME—!
꿀꺽!
KKULKKEOK (GULP)
LET'S JUST JUMP THE WALL.
WE DON'T HAVE TIME TO FOOL AROUND! THAT GUY MIGHT COME BACK! WHY CAN'T YOU DO IT?

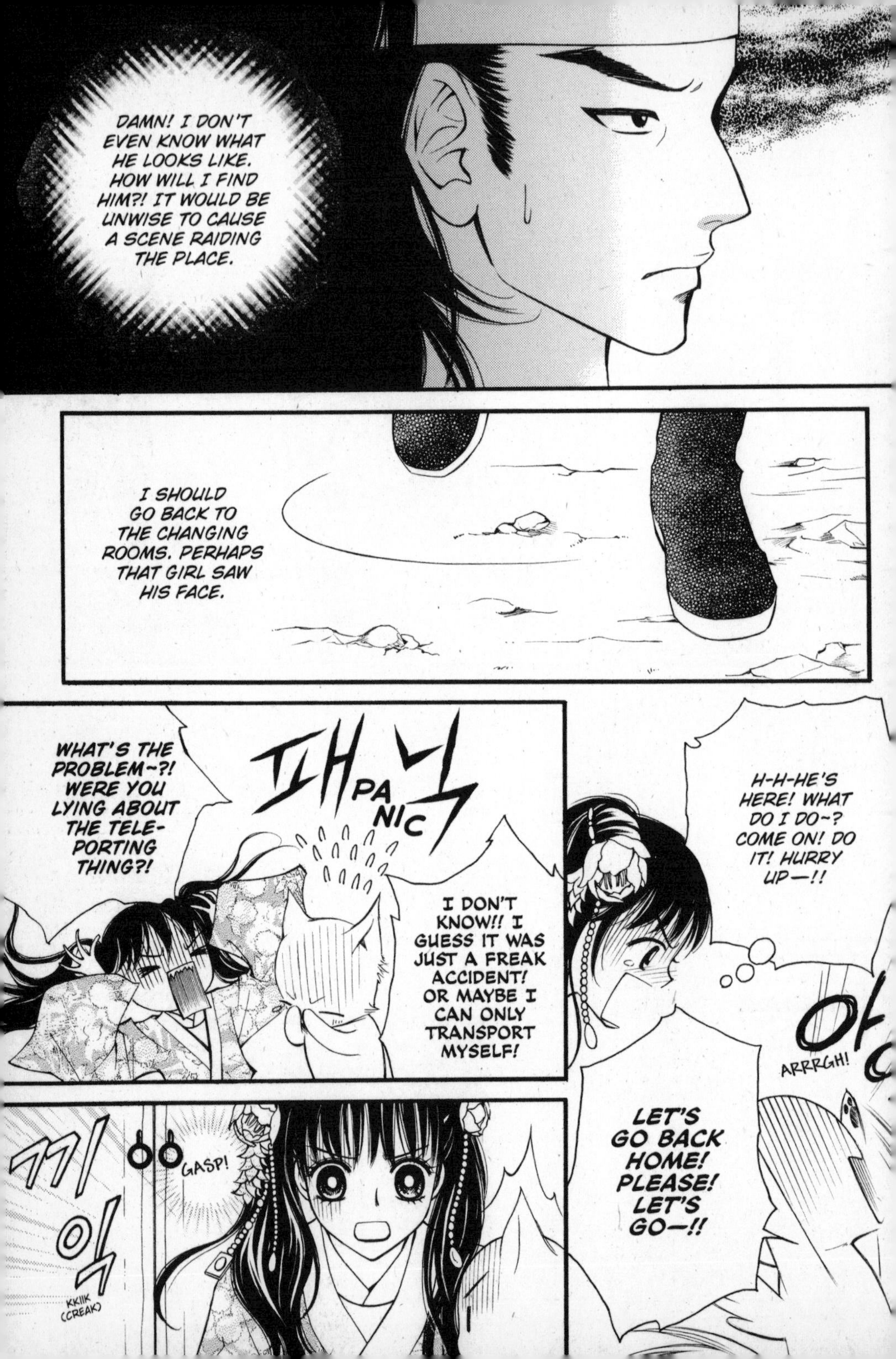
DAMN! I DON'T EVEN KNOW WHAT HE LOOKS LIKE. HOW WILL I FIND HIM?! IT WOULD BE UNWISE TO CAUSE A SCENE RAIDING THE PLACE.
I SHOULD GO BACK TO THE CHANGING ROOMS. PERHAPS THAT GIRL SAW HIS FACE.
WHAT'S THE PROBLEM~?! WERE YOU LYING ABOUT THE TELE-PORTING THING?!
PANIC
I DON'T KNOW!! I GUESS IT WAS JUST A FREAK ACCIDENT! OR MAYBE I CAN ONLY TRANSPORT MYSELF!
GASP!
KKIIK (CREAK)
H-H-HE'S HERE! WHAT DO I DO~? COME ON! DO IT! HURRY UP—!!
ARRRGH!
LET'S GO BACK HOME! PLEASE! LET'S GO—!!

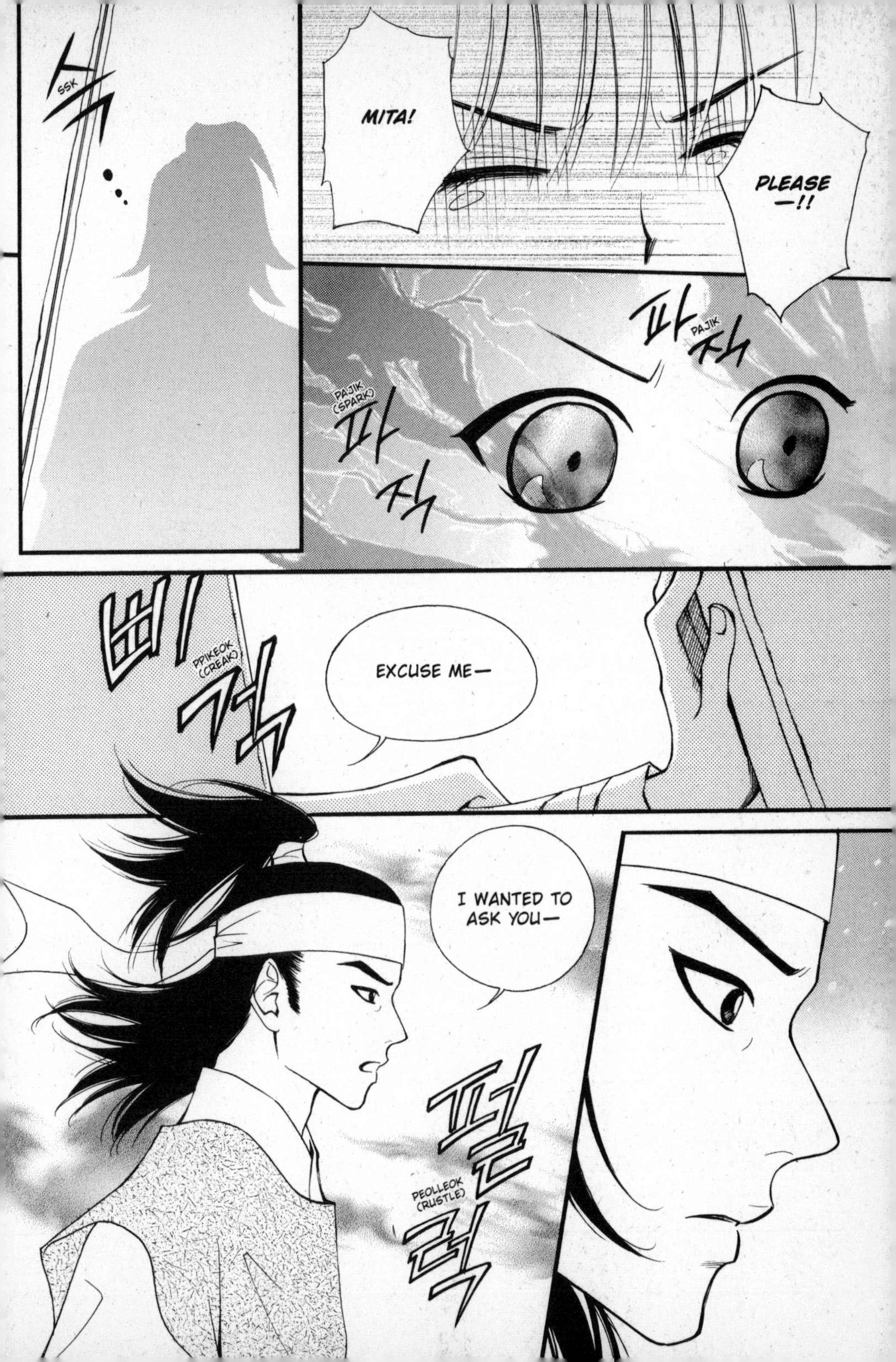
스윽
SSK
• • •
MITA!
PLEASE —!!
파직
PAJIK
파직
PAJIK (SPARK)
삐걱
PPIKEOK (CREAK)
EXCUSE ME—
I WANTED TO ASK YOU—
펄럭
PEOLLEOK (RUSTLE)

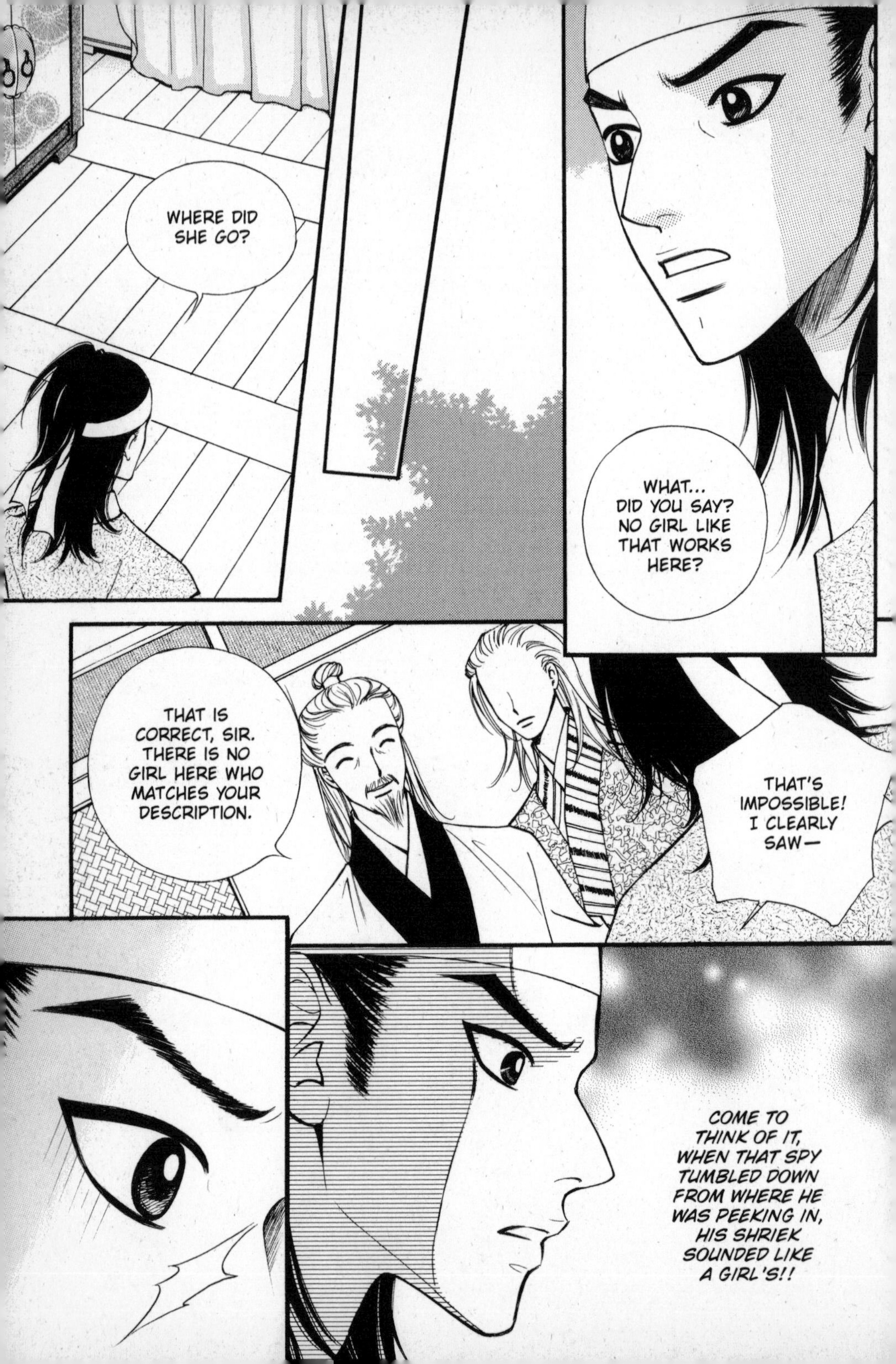
WHERE DID SHE GO?
WHAT... DID YOU SAY? NO GIRL LIKE THAT WORKS HERE?
THAT IS CORRECT, SIR. THERE IS NO GIRL HERE WHO MATCHES YOUR DESCRIPTION.
THAT'S IMPOSSIBLE! I CLEARLY SAW—
COME TO THINK OF IT, WHEN THAT SPY TUMBLED DOWN FROM WHERE HE WAS PEEKING IN, HIS SHRIEK SOUNDED LIKE A GIRL'S!!

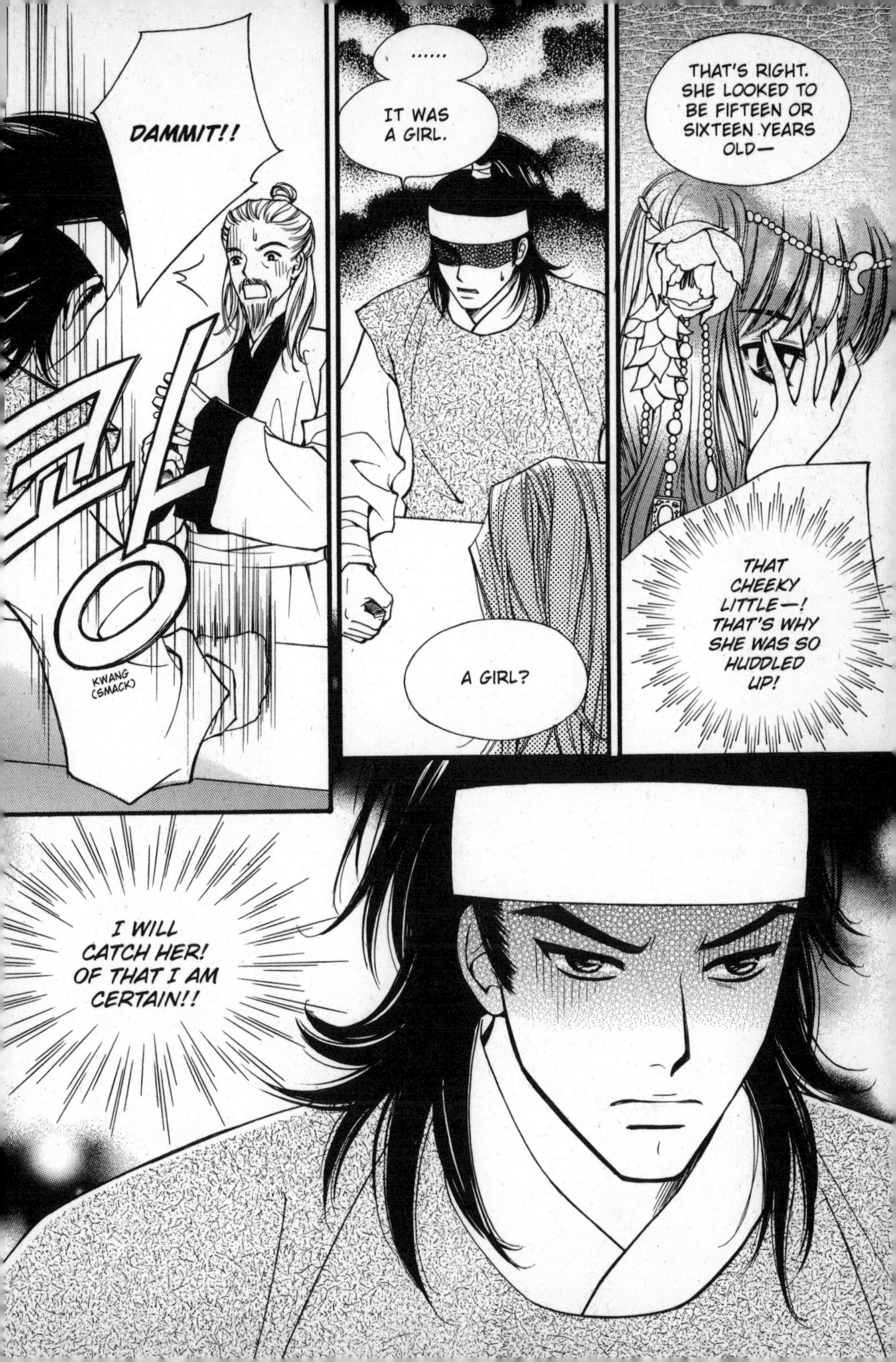
DAMMIT!!
KWANG (SMACK)
......
IT WAS A GIRL.
A GIRL?
THAT'S RIGHT. SHE LOOKED TO BE FIFTEEN OR SIXTEEN YEARS OLD—
THAT CHEEKY LITTLE—! THAT'S WHY SHE WAS SO HUDDLED UP!
I WILL CATCH HER! OF THAT I AM CERTAIN!!

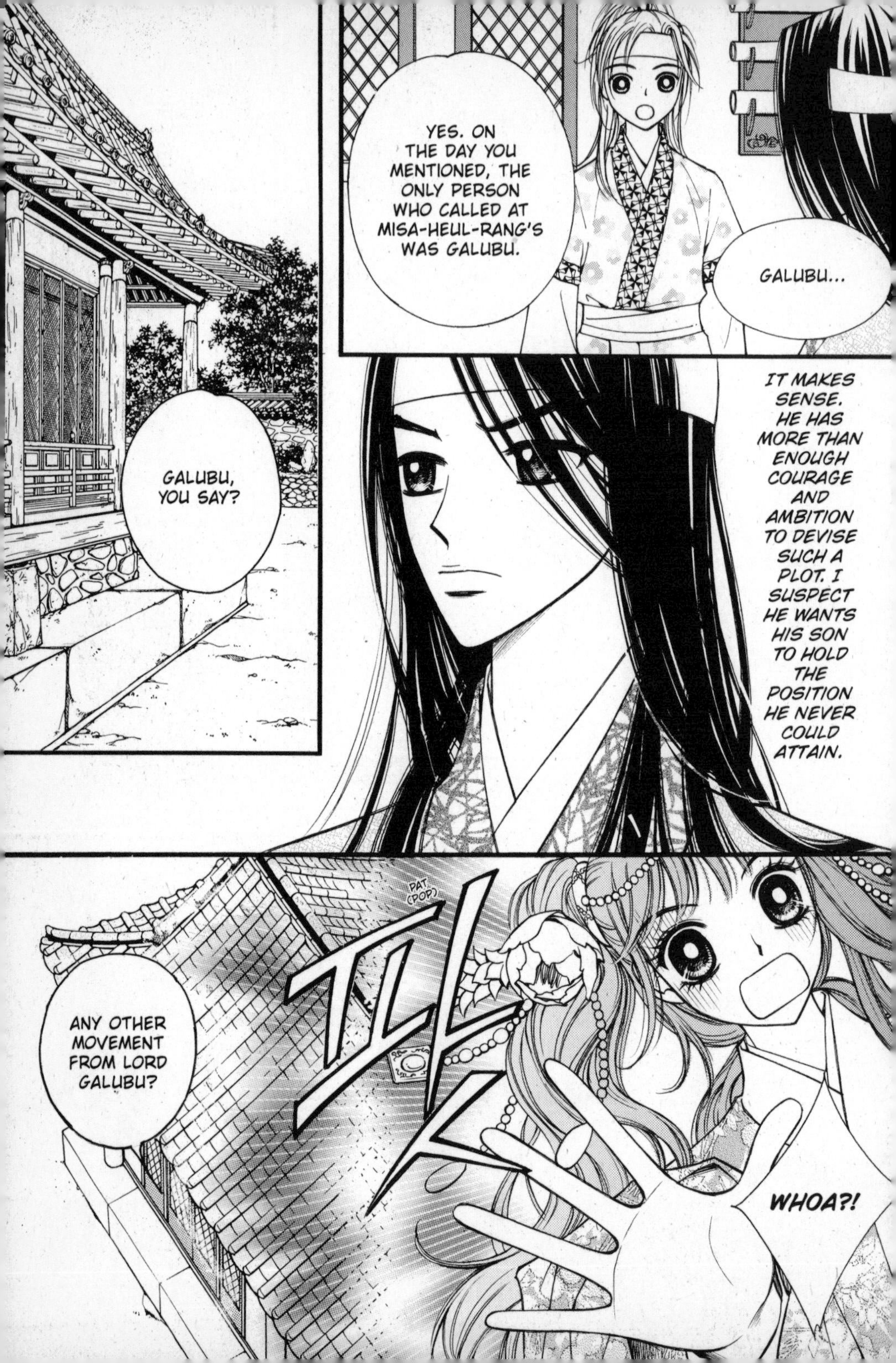
GALUBU, YOU SAY?
YES. ON THE DAY YOU MENTIONED, THE ONLY PERSON WHO CALLED AT MISA-HEUL-RANG'S WAS GALUBU.
GALUBU...
IT MAKES SENSE. HE HAS MORE THAN ENOUGH COURAGE AND AMBITION TO DEVISE SUCH A PLOT. I SUSPECT HE WANTS HIS SON TO HOLD THE POSITION HE NEVER COULD ATTAIN.
ANY OTHER MOVEMENT FROM LORD GALUBU?
PAT (POP)
WHOA?!

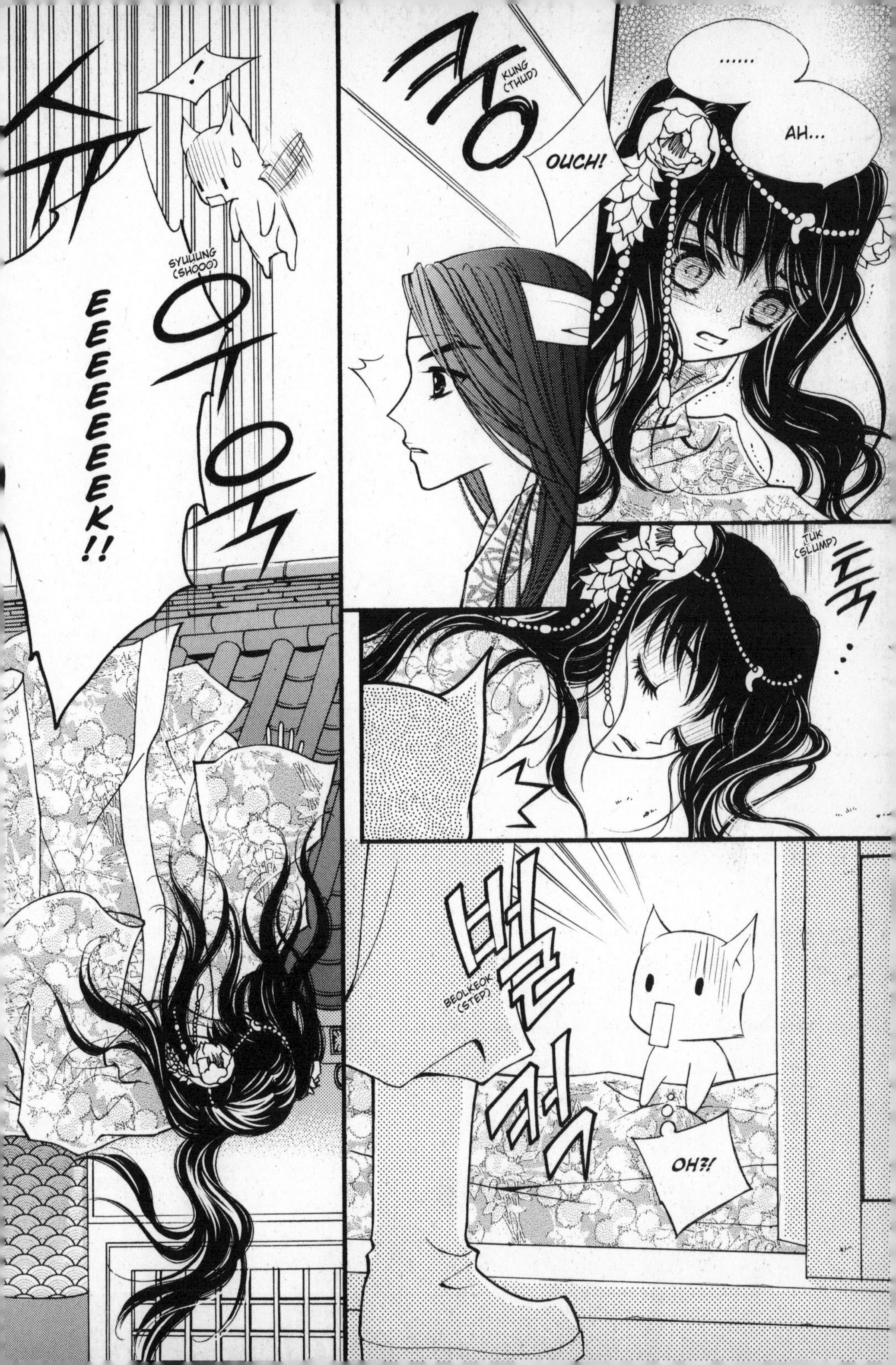
!
SYUUUNG (SHOOO)
EEEEEEEEEK!!
KUNG (THUD)
OUCH!
......
AH...
TUK (SLUMP)
...
BEOLKEOK (STEP)
OH?!

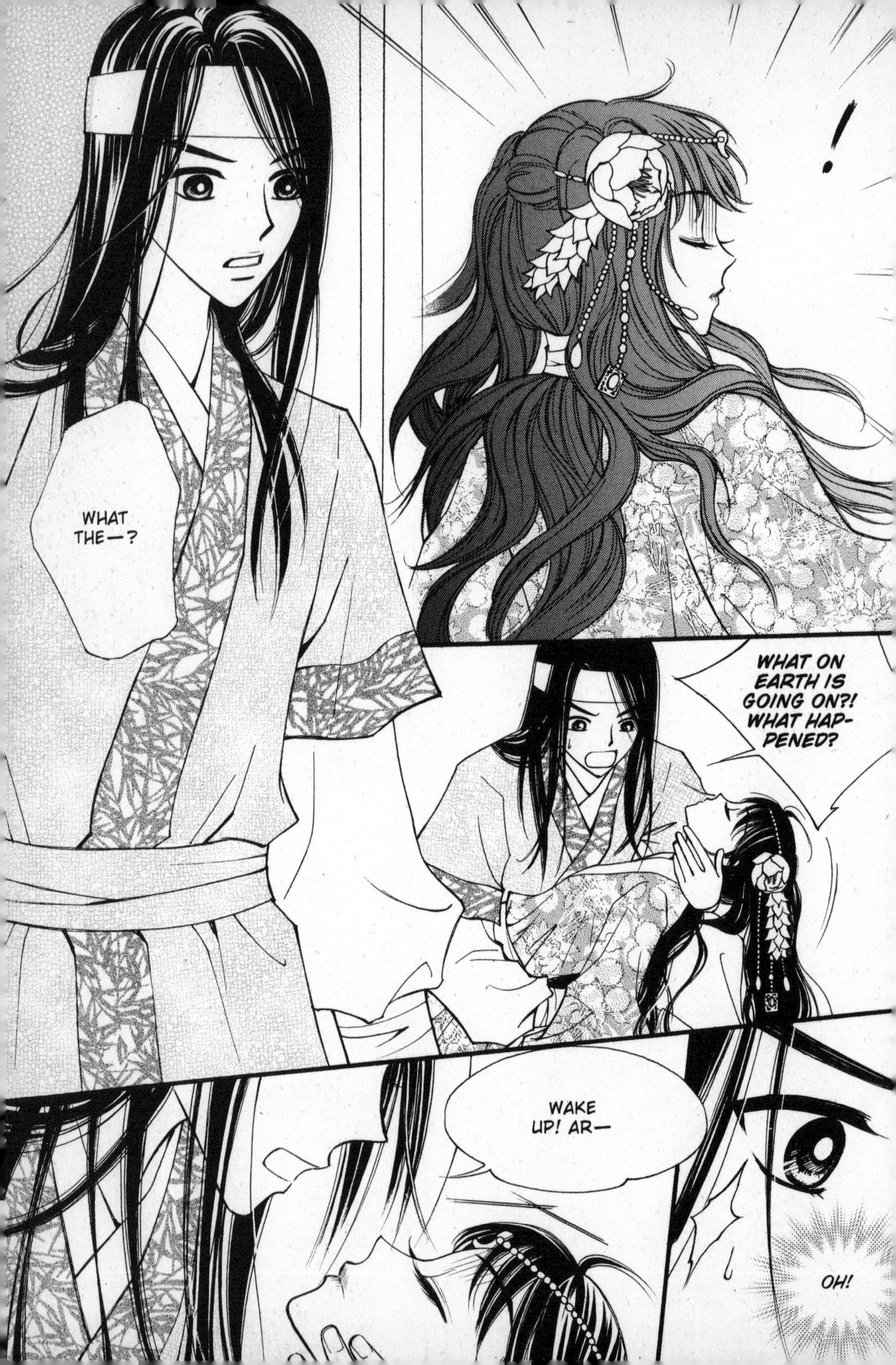
WHAT THE—?
!
WHAT ON EARTH IS GOING ON?! WHAT HAP-PENED?
WAKE UP! AR—
OH!

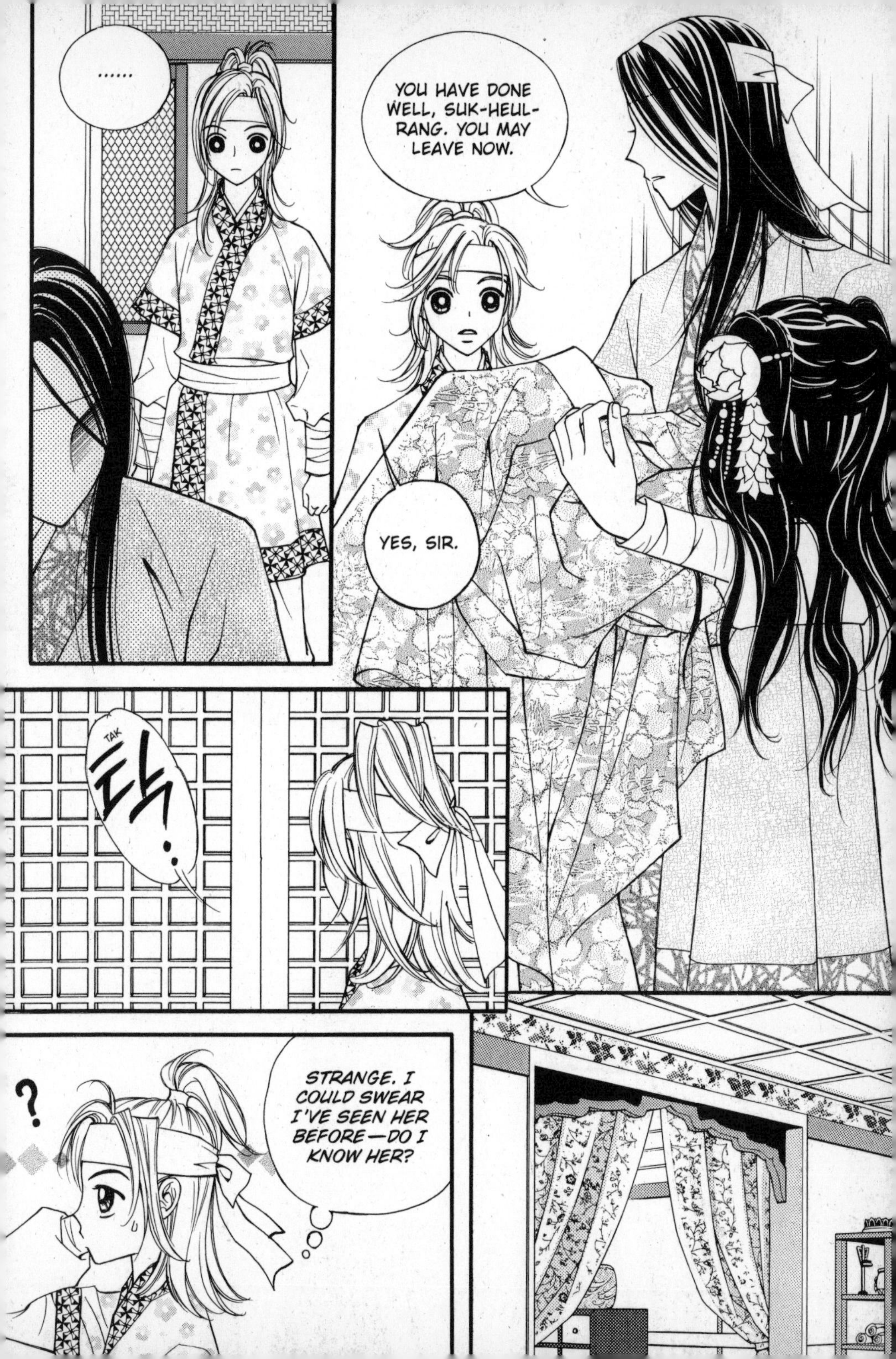
......
YOU HAVE DONE WELL, SUK-HEUL-RANG. YOU MAY LEAVE NOW.
YES, SIR.
TAK
탁!..
?
STRANGE. I COULD SWEAR I'VE SEEN HER BEFORE—DO I KNOW HER?

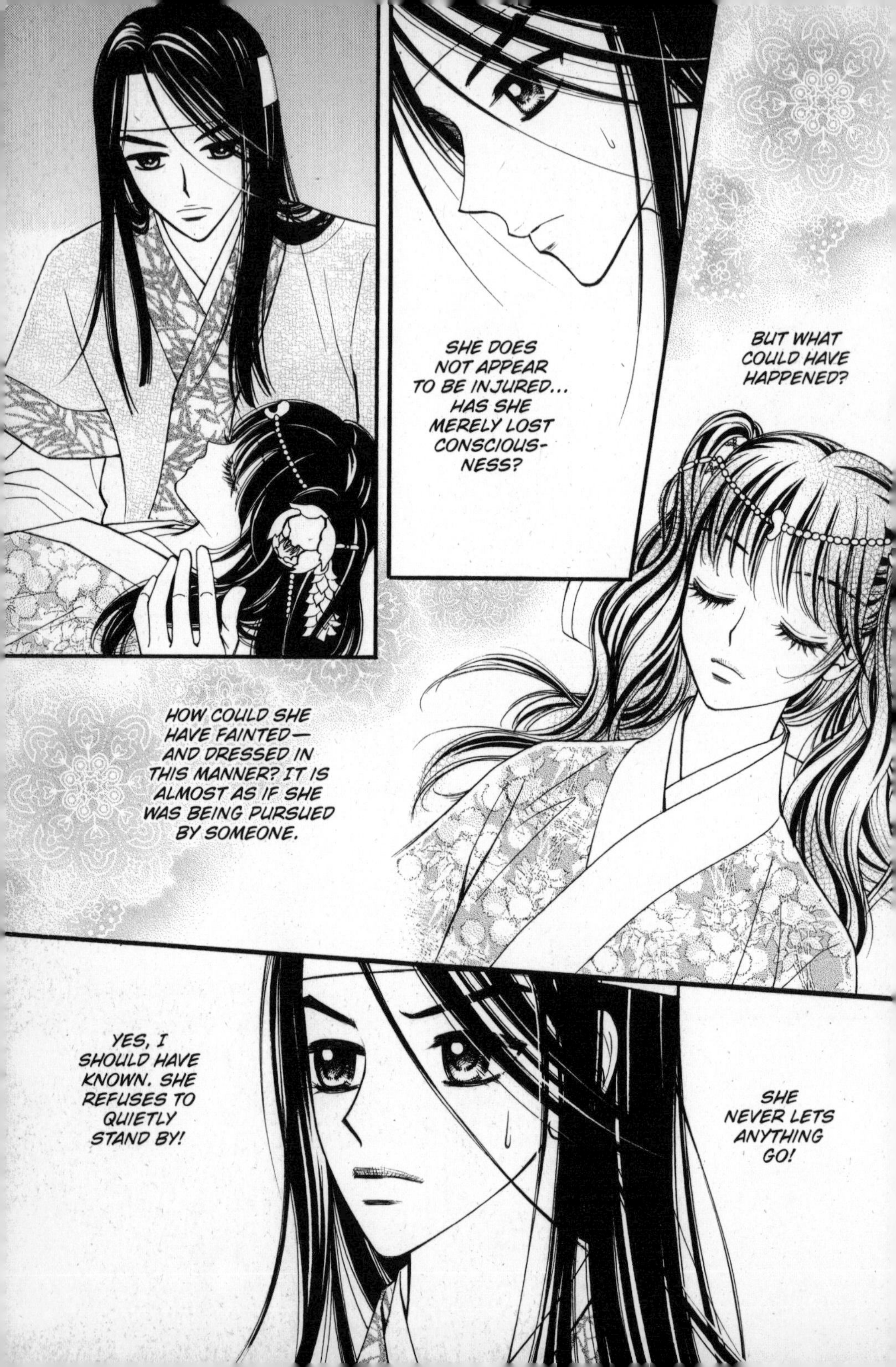

SHE DOES NOT APPEAR TO BE INJURED... HAS SHE MERELY LOST CONSCIOUS-NESS?
BUT WHAT COULD HAVE HAPPENED?
HOW COULD SHE HAVE FAINTED—AND DRESSED IN THIS MANNER? IT IS ALMOST AS IF SHE WAS BEING PURSUED BY SOMEONE.
YES, I SHOULD HAVE KNOWN. SHE REFUSES TO QUIETLY STAND BY!
SHE NEVER LETS ANYTHING GO!

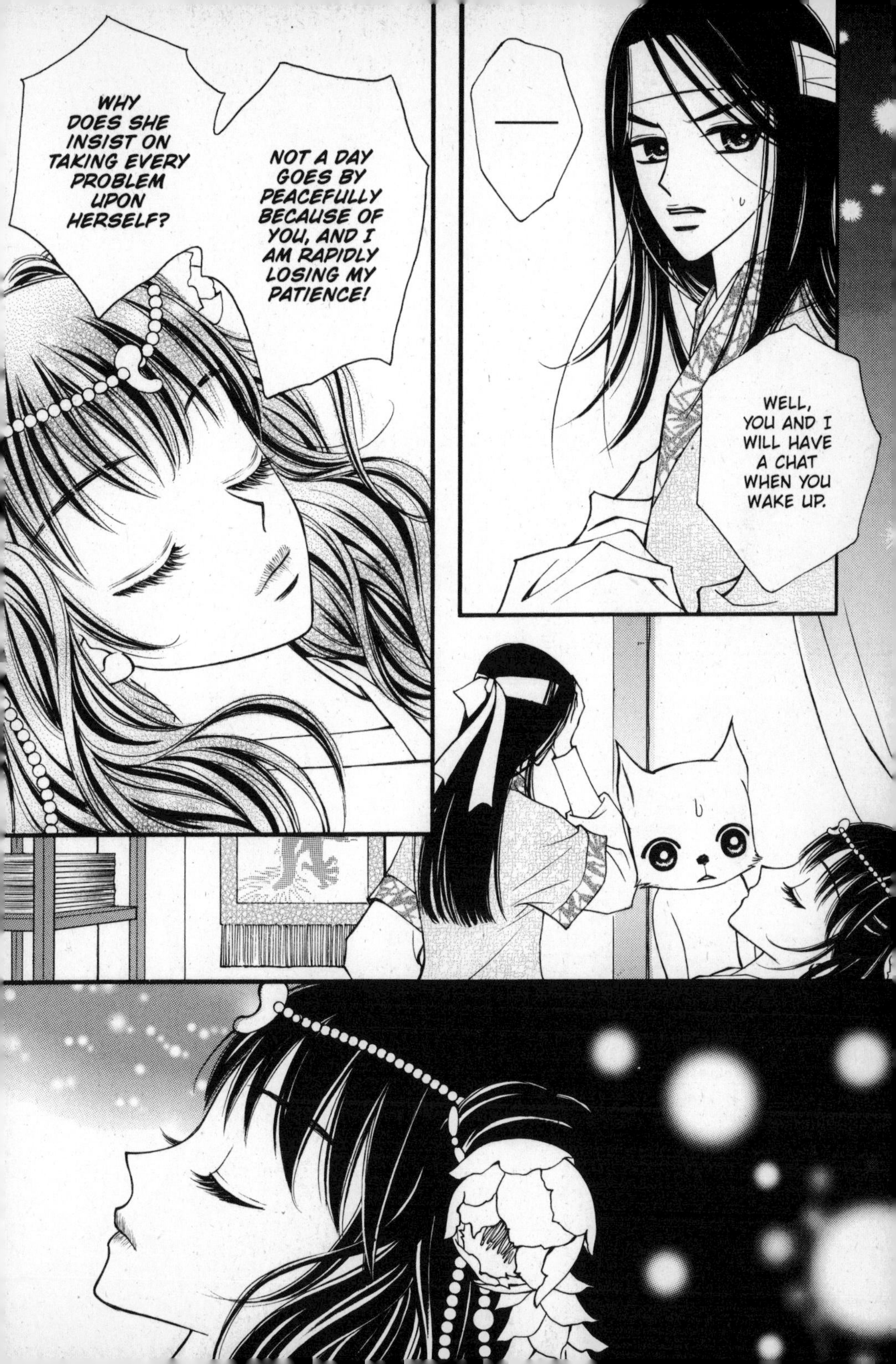
WHY DOES SHE INSIST ON TAKING EVERY PROBLEM UPON HERSELF?
NOT A DAY GOES BY PEACEFULLY BECAUSE OF YOU, AND I AM RAPIDLY LOSING MY PATIENCE!
—
WELL, YOU AND I WILL HAVE A CHAT WHEN YOU WAKE UP.

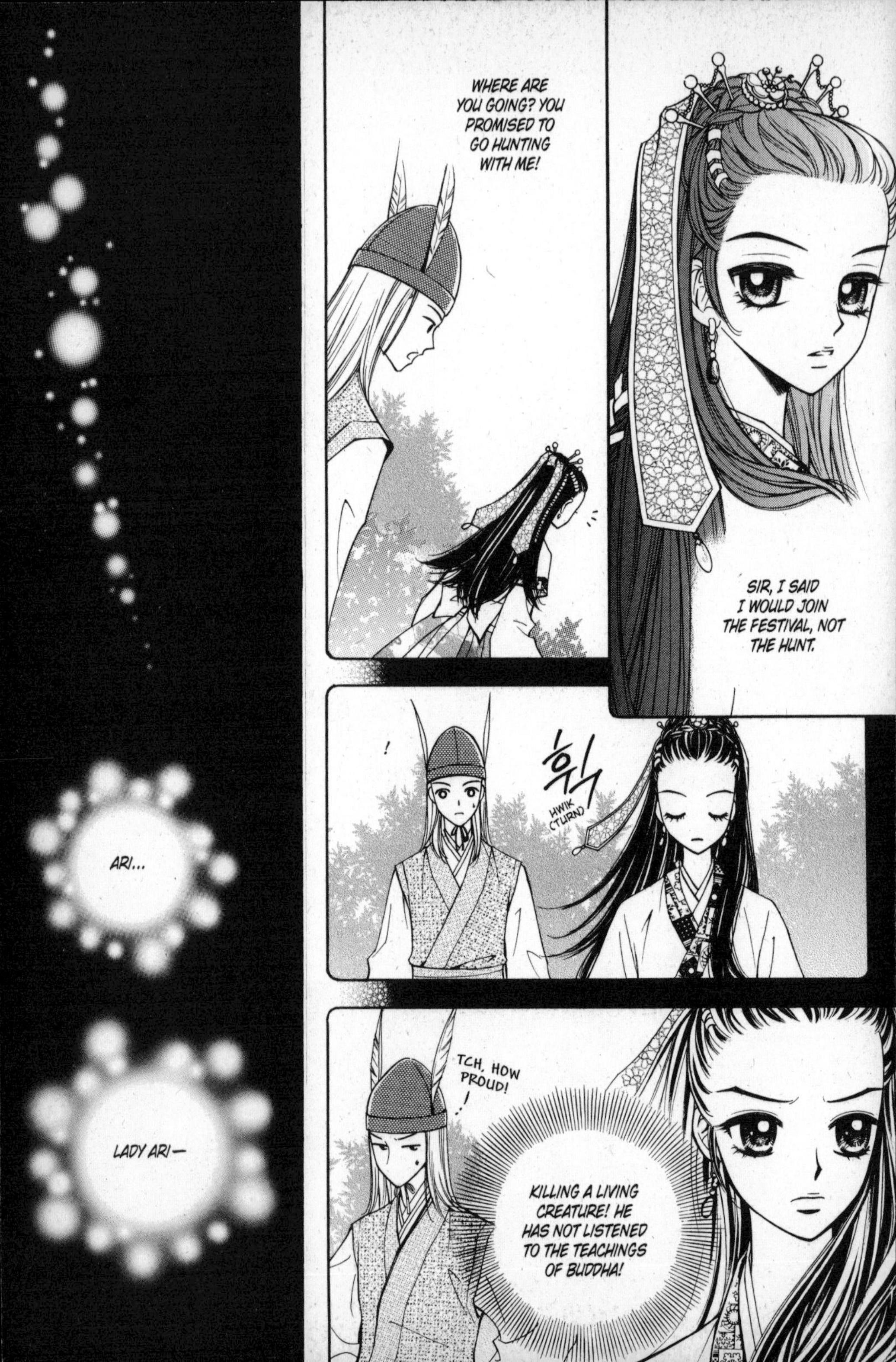
ARI...
LADY ARI—
WHERE ARE YOU GOING? YOU PROMISED TO GO HUNTING WITH ME!
SIR, I SAID I WOULD JOIN THE FESTIVAL, NOT THE HUNT.
!
휙
HWIK (TURN)
TCH, HOW PROUD!
KILLING A LIVING CREATURE! HE HAS NOT LISTENED TO THE TEACHINGS OF BUDDHA!

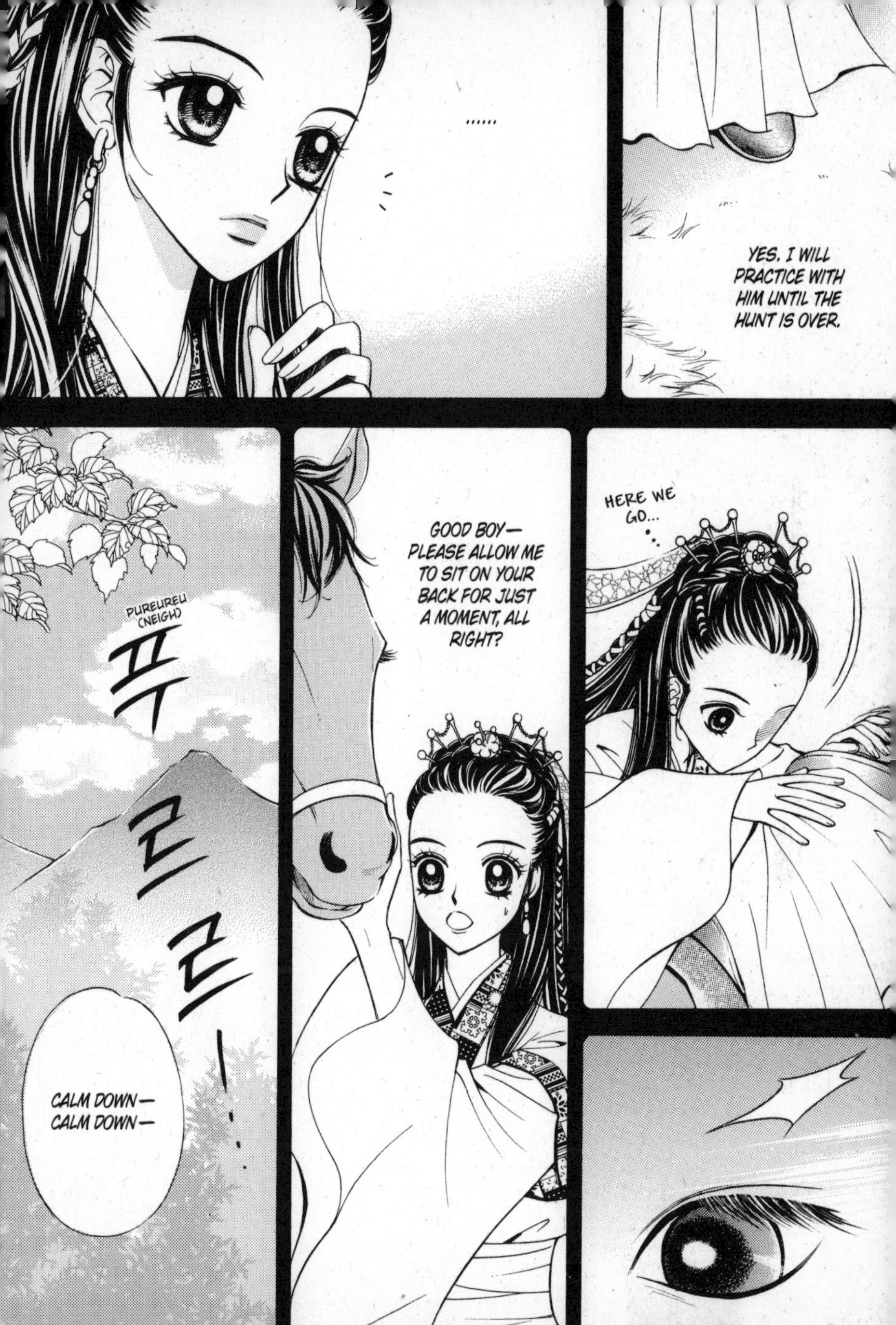
......
YES. I WILL PRACTICE WITH HIM UNTIL THE HUNT IS OVER.
PUREUREU (NEIGH)
CALM DOWN— CALM DOWN—
GOOD BOY— PLEASE ALLOW ME TO SIT ON YOUR BACK FOR JUST A MOMENT, ALL RIGHT?
HERE WE GO...

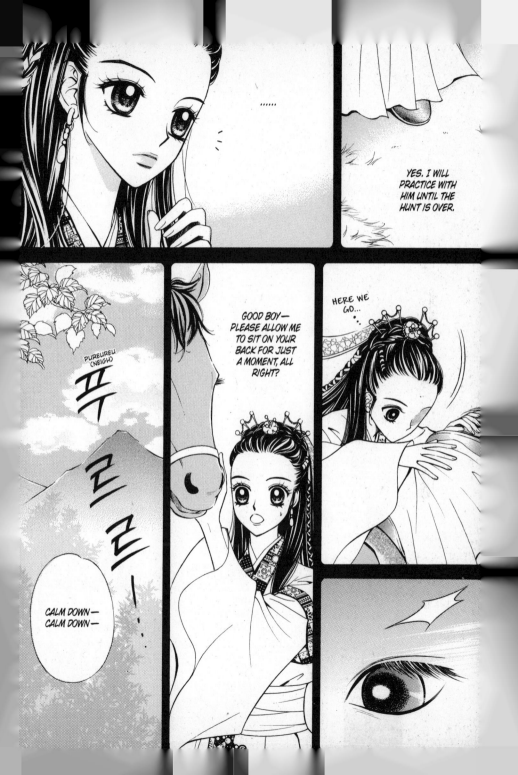

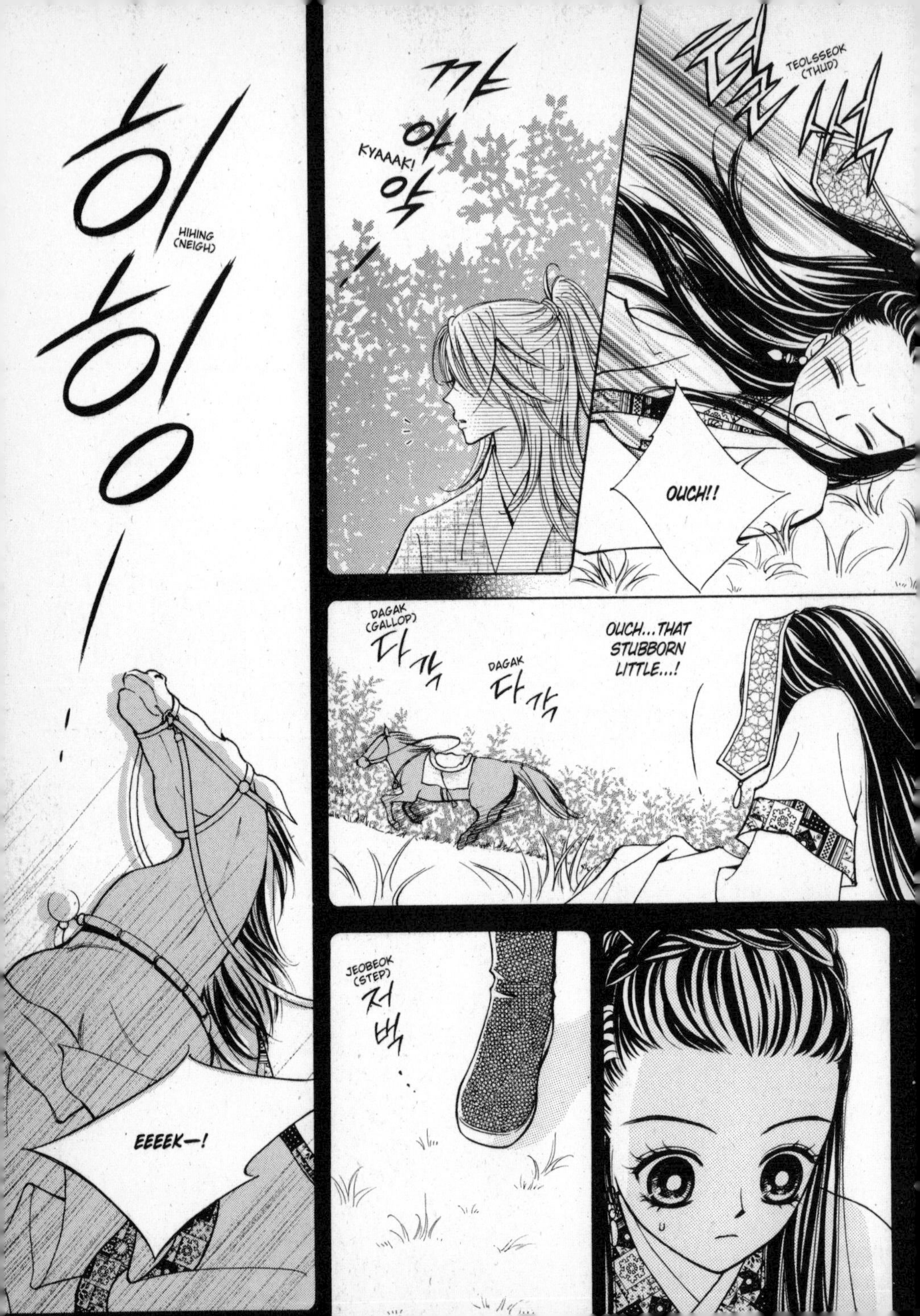
HIHING (NEIGH)
EEEEK—!
꺄아악
KYAAAK!
TEOLSSEOK (THUD)
OUCH!!
DAGAK (GALLOP)
다각
DAGAK
다각
OUCH...THAT STUBBORN LITTLE...!
JEOBEOK (STEP)
저벅...

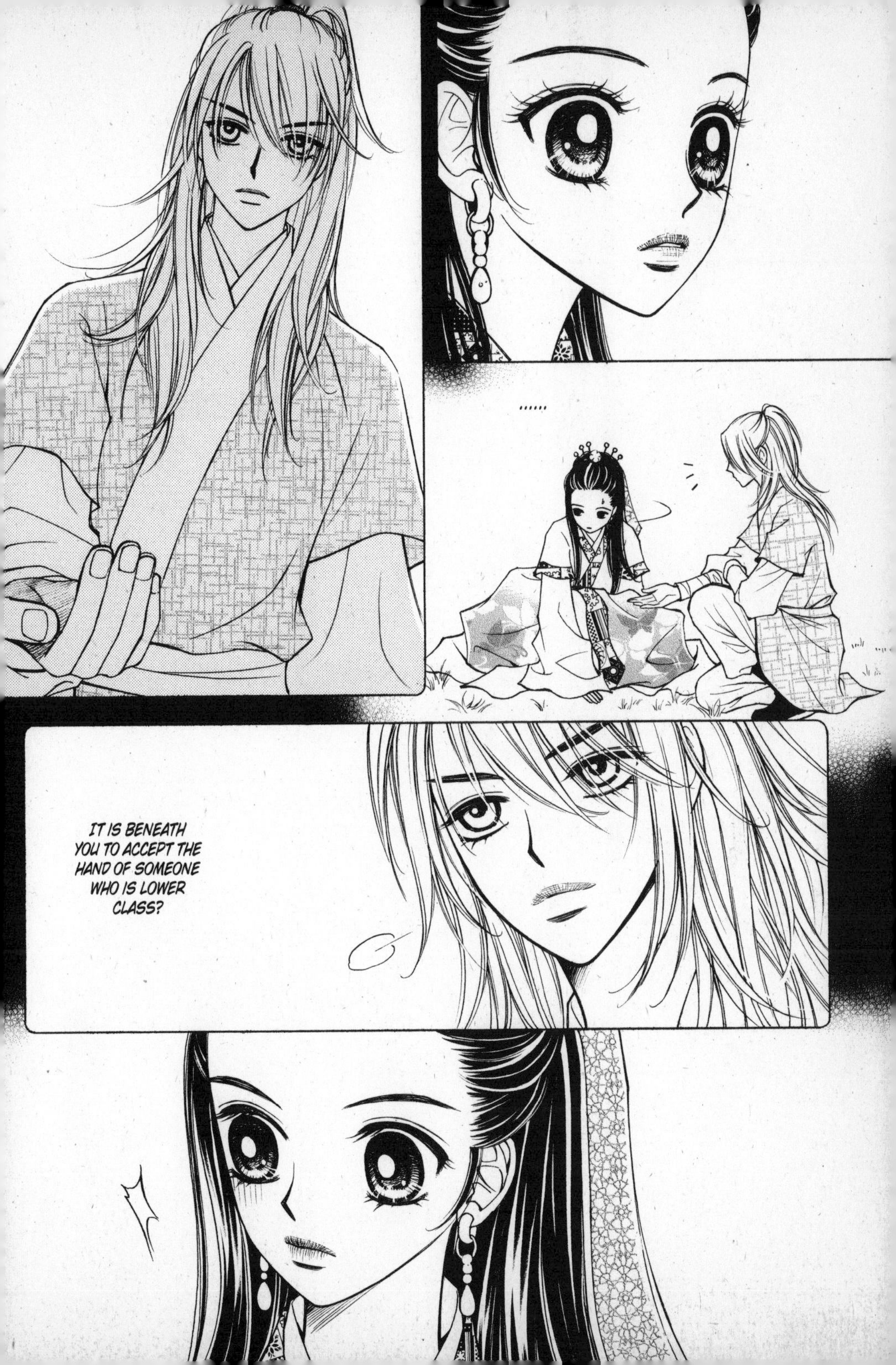
......
IT IS BENEATH YOU TO ACCEPT THE HAND OF SOMEONE WHO IS LOWER CLASS?

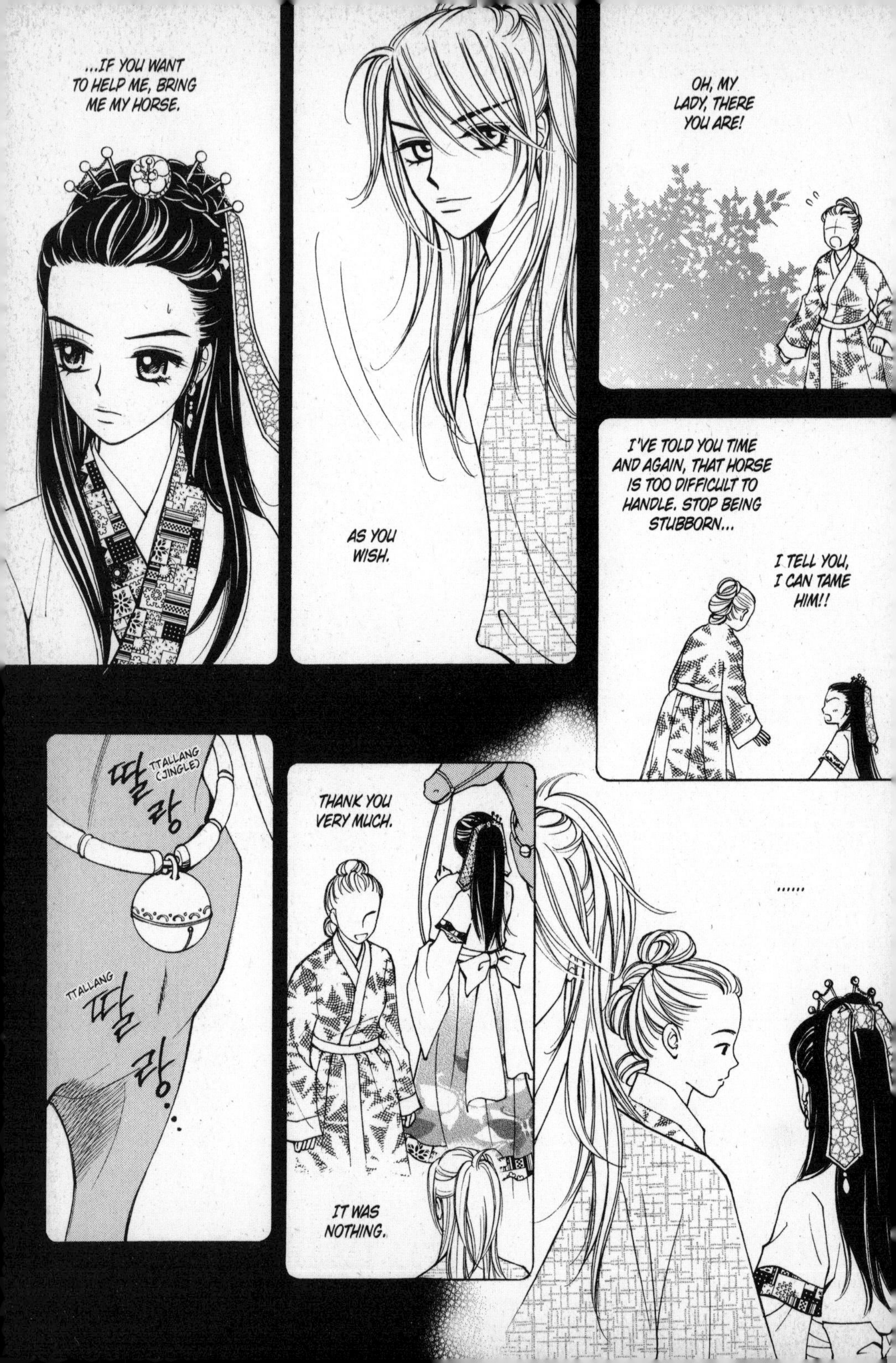

...IF YOU WANT TO HELP ME, BRING ME MY HORSE.
AS YOU WISH.
OH, MY LADY, THERE YOU ARE!
I'VE TOLD YOU TIME AND AGAIN, THAT HORSE IS TOO DIFFICULT TO HANDLE. STOP BEING STUBBORN...
I TELL YOU, I CAN TAME HIM!!
딸랑
TTALLANG (JINGLE)
TTALLANG
딸랑
THANK YOU VERY MUCH.
IT WAS NOTHING.
......

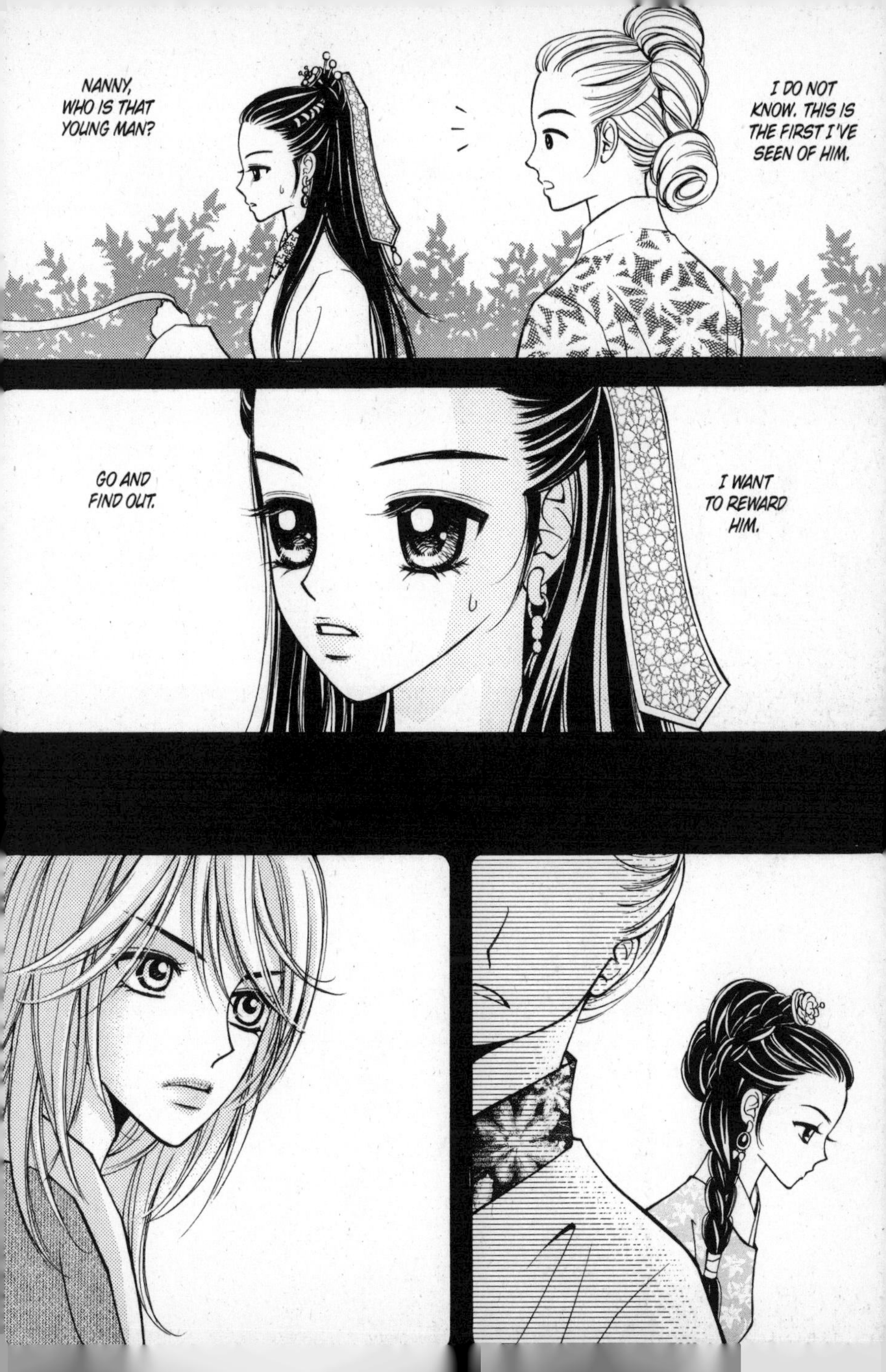
NANNY, WHO IS THAT YOUNG MAN?
I DO NOT KNOW. THIS IS THE FIRST I'VE SEEN OF HIM.
GO AND FIND OUT.
I WANT TO REWARD HIM.

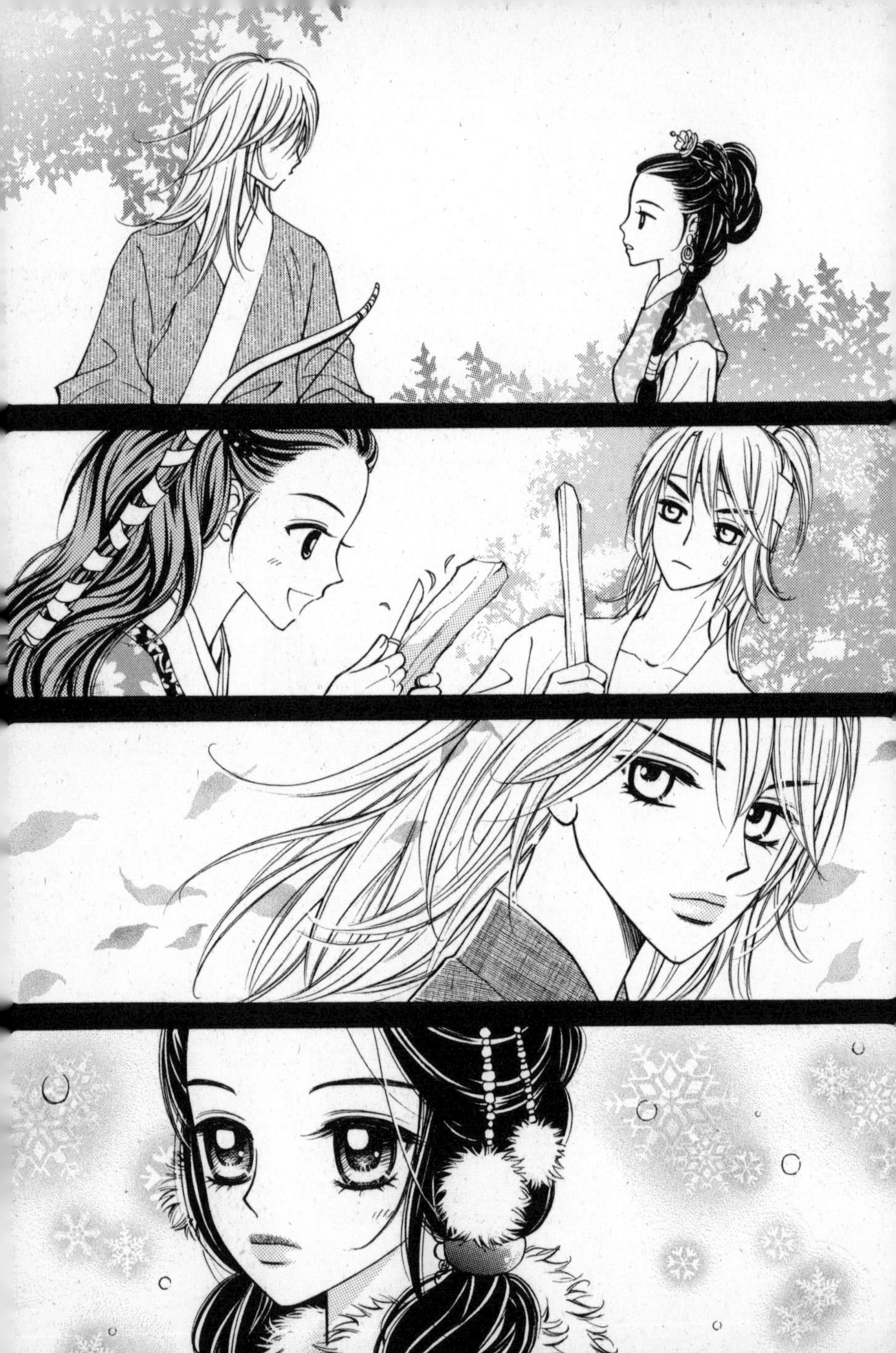

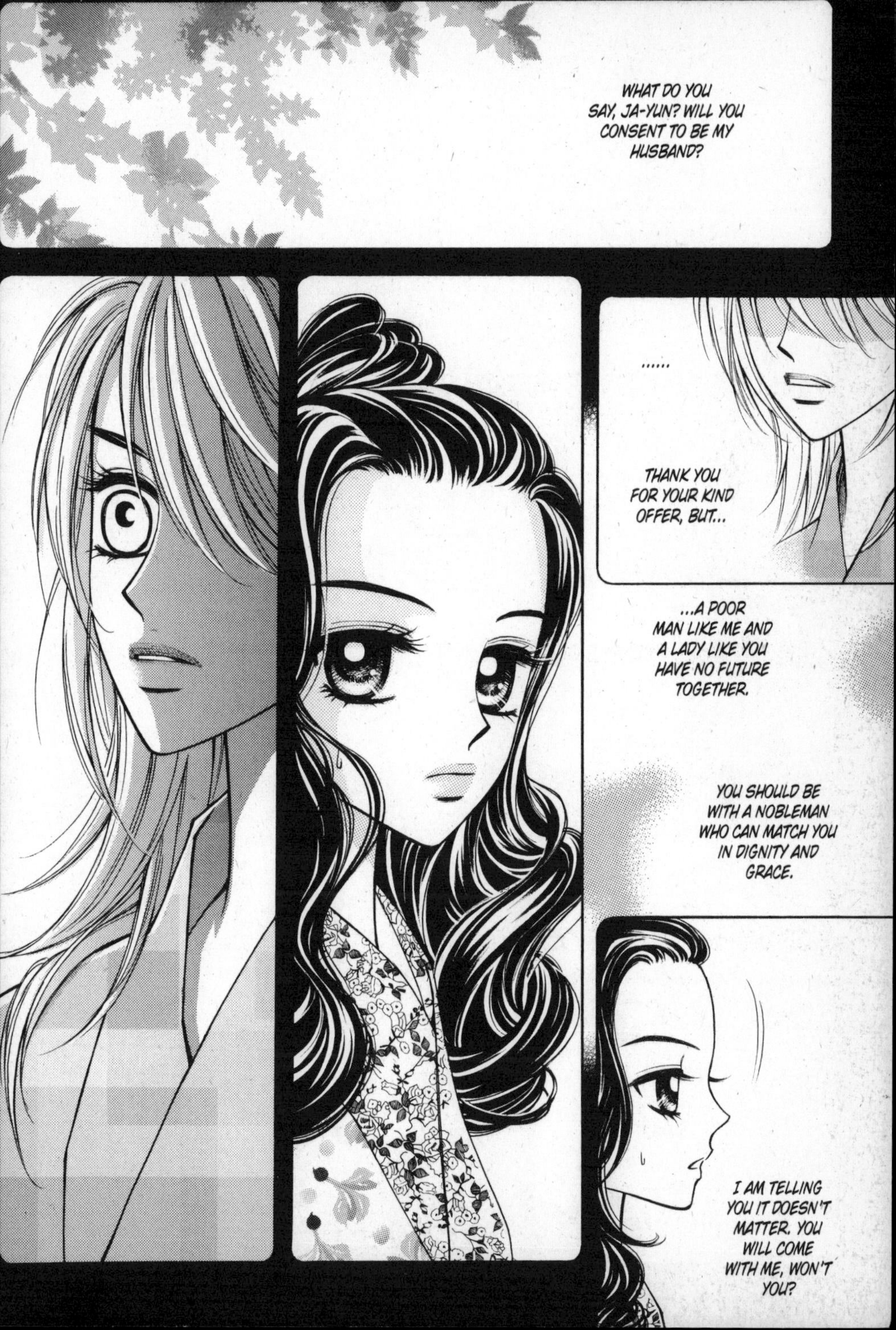
WHAT DO YOU SAY, JA-YUN? WILL YOU CONSENT TO BE MY HUSBAND?
......
THANK YOU FOR YOUR KIND OFFER, BUT...
...A POOR MAN LIKE ME AND A LADY LIKE YOU HAVE NO FUTURE TOGETHER.
YOU SHOULD BE WITH A NOBLEMAN WHO CAN MATCH YOU IN DIGNITY AND GRACE.
I AM TELLING YOU IT DOESN'T MATTER. YOU WILL COME WITH ME, WON'T YOU?

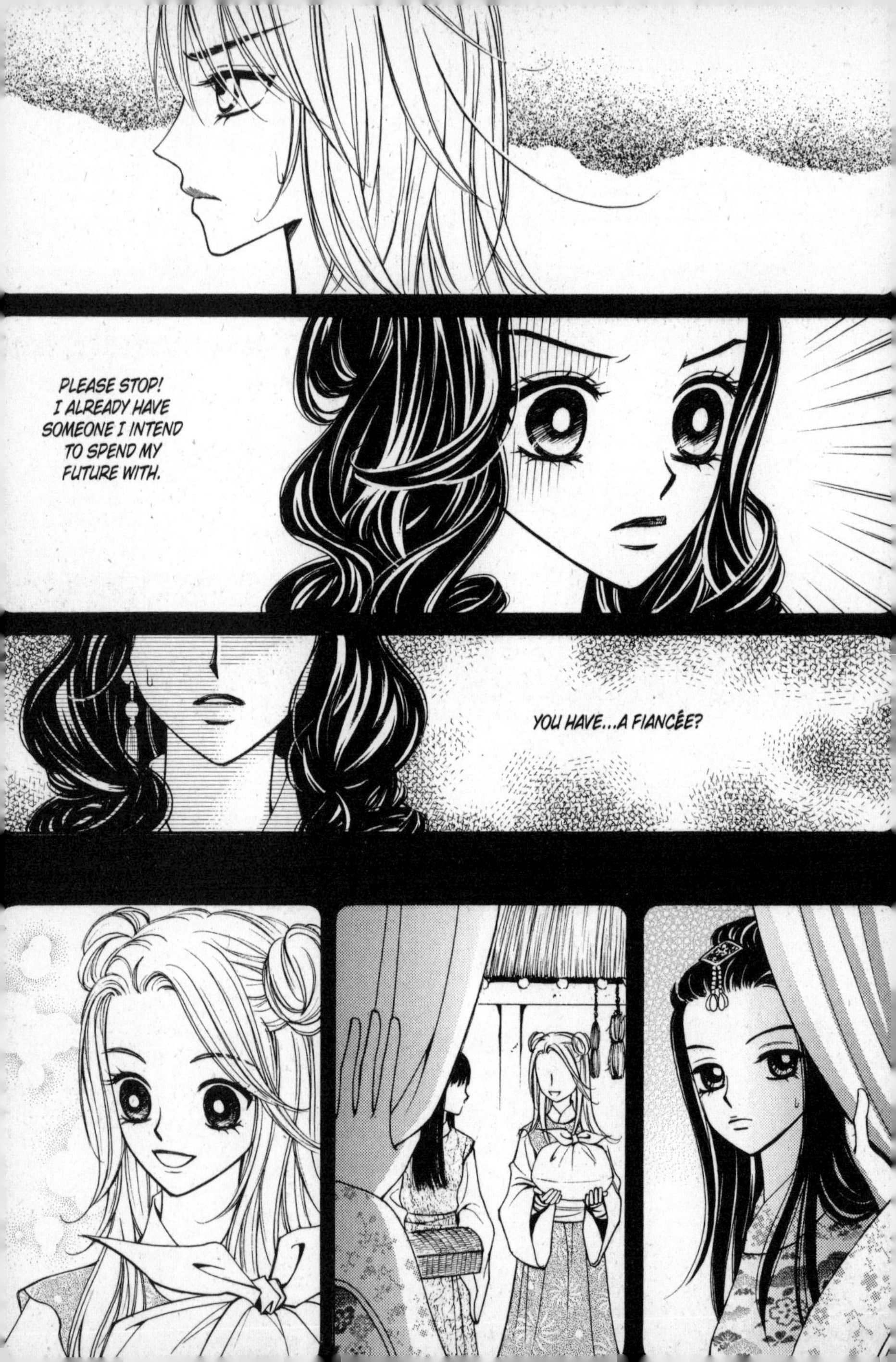
PLEASE STOP! I ALREADY HAVE SOMEONE I INTEND TO SPEND MY FUTURE WITH.
YOU HAVE...A FIANCÉE?

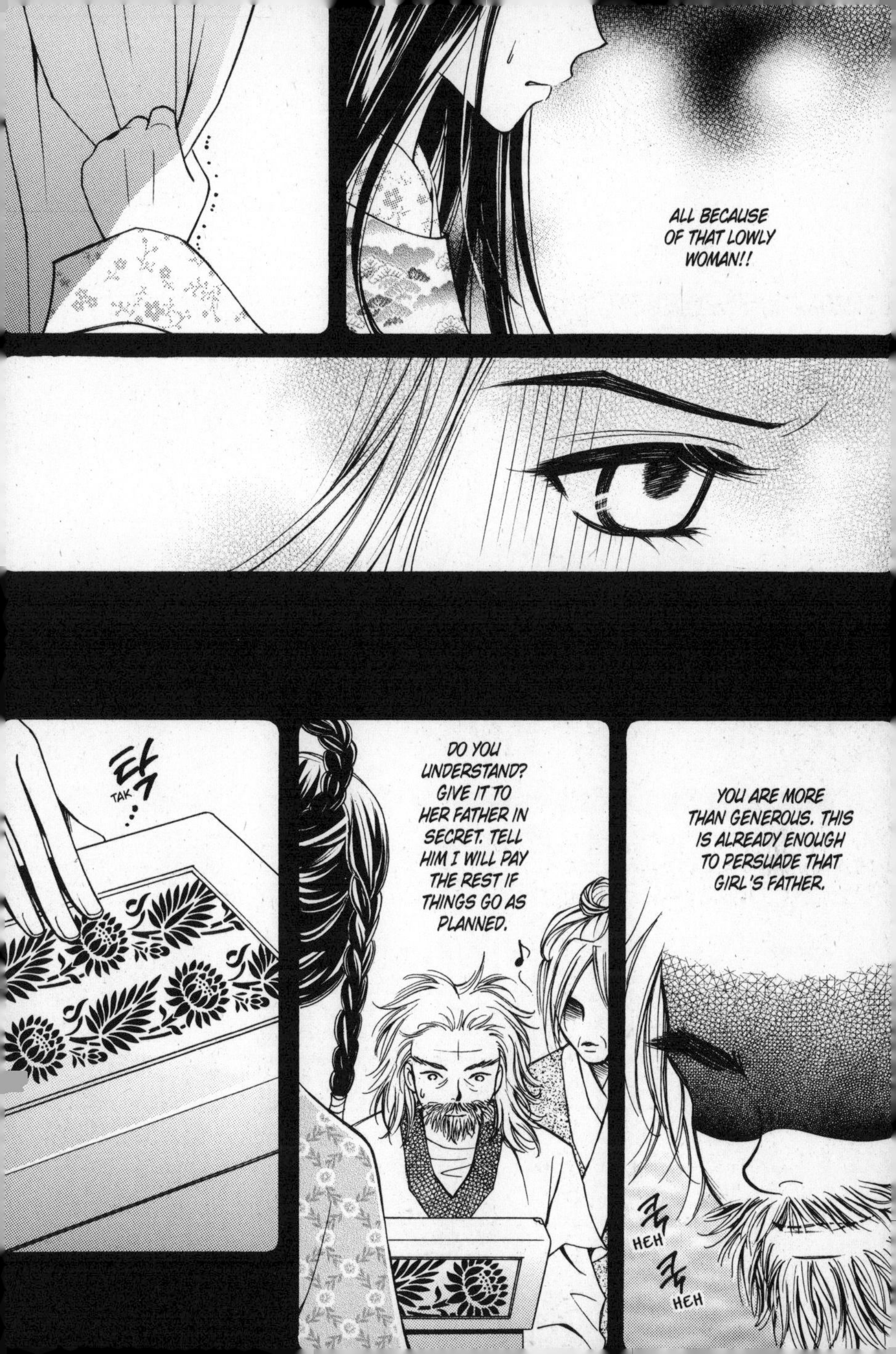
ALL BECAUSE OF THAT LOWLY WOMAN!!
탁
TAK
DO YOU UNDERSTAND? GIVE IT TO HER FATHER IN SECRET. TELL HIM I WILL PAY THE REST IF THINGS GO AS PLANNED.
YOU ARE MORE THAN GENEROUS. THIS IS ALREADY ENOUGH TO PERSUADE THAT GIRL'S FATHER.
크
HEH
크
HEH

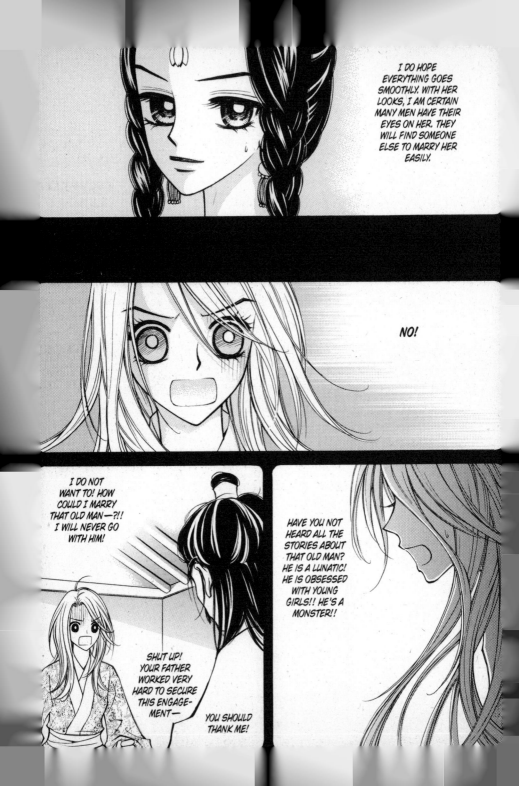

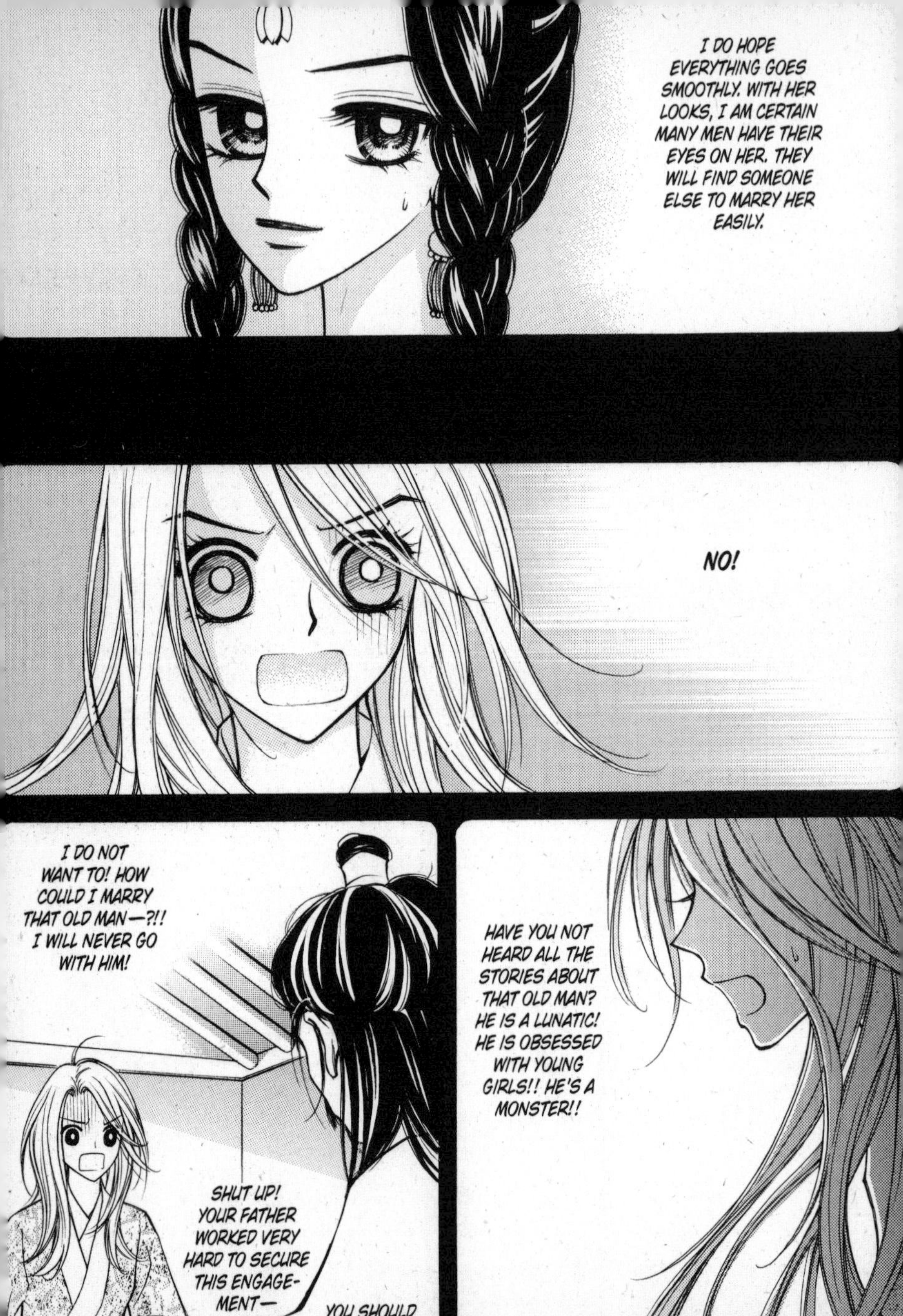
I DO HOPE EVERYTHING GOES SMOOTHLY. WITH HER LOOKS, I AM CERTAIN MANY MEN HAVE THEIR EYES ON HER. THEY WILL FIND SOMEONE ELSE TO MARRY HER EASILY.
NO!
I DO NOT WANT TO! HOW COULD I MARRY THAT OLD MAN—?!! I WILL NEVER GO WITH HIM!
SHUT UP! YOUR FATHER WORKED VERY HARD TO SECURE THIS ENGAGE-MENT—
YOU SHOULD THANK ME!
HAVE YOU NOT HEARD ALL THE STORIES ABOUT THAT OLD MAN? HE IS A LUNATIC! HE IS OBSESSED WITH YOUNG GIRLS!! HE'S A MONSTER!!

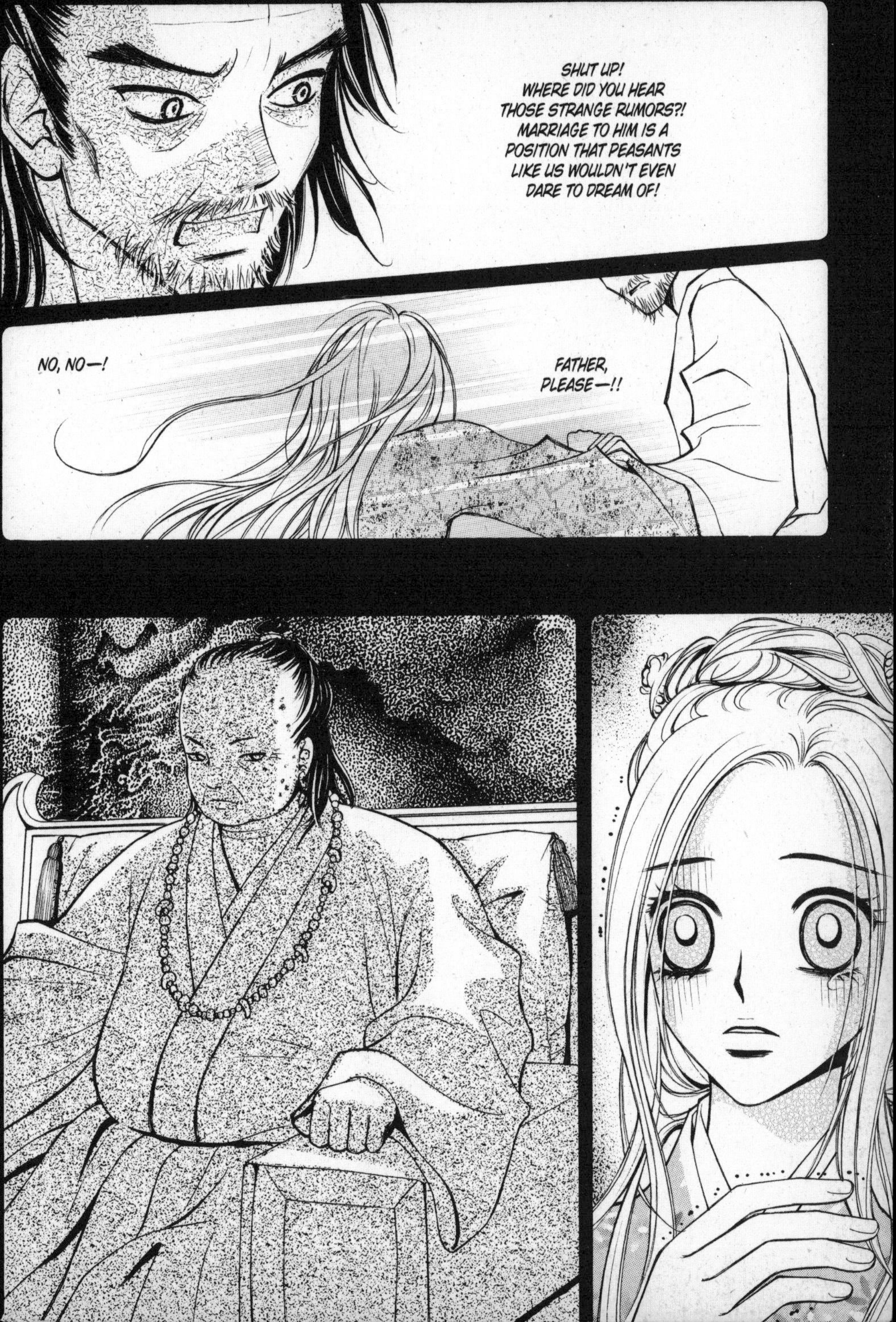
SHUT UP! WHERE DID YOU HEAR THOSE STRANGE RUMORS?! MARRIAGE TO HIM IS A POSITION THAT PEASANTS LIKE US WOULDN'T EVEN DARE TO DREAM OF!
NO, NO—!
FATHER, PLEASE—!!

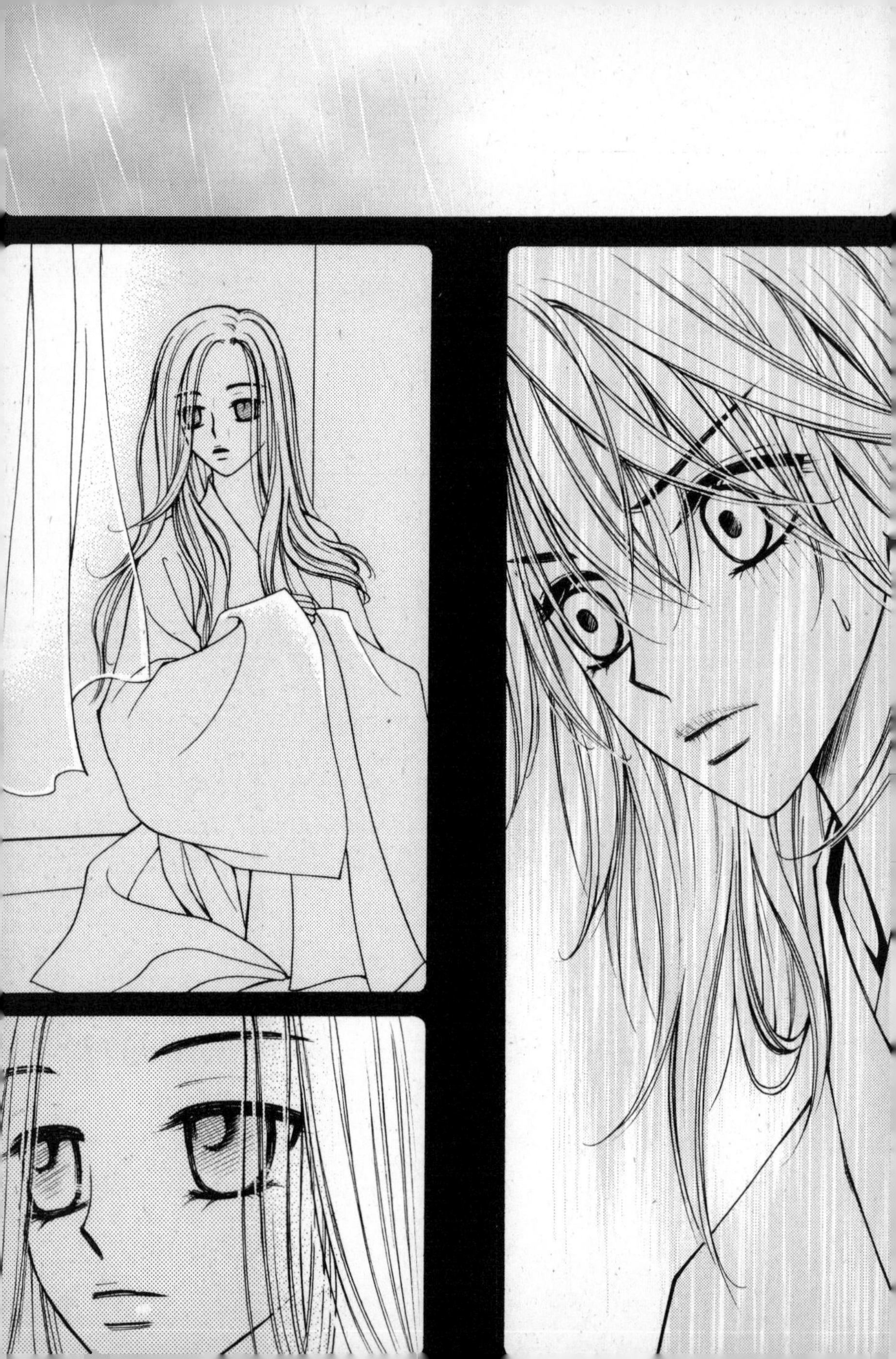

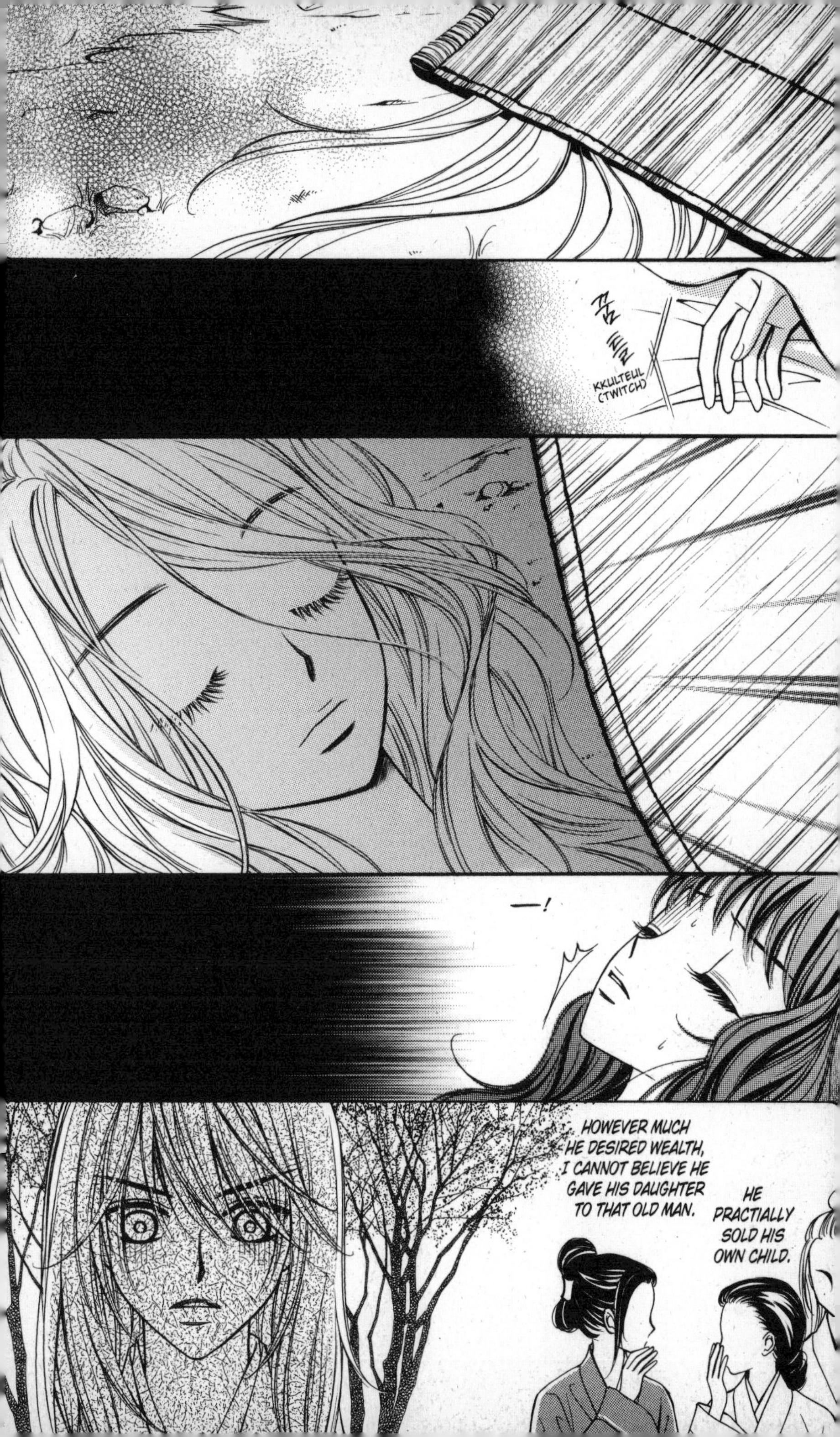
끌틀
KKULTEUL (TWITCH)
—!
HOWEVER MUCH HE DESIRED WEALTH, I CANNOT BELIEVE HE GAVE HIS DAUGHTER TO THAT OLD MAN.
HE PRACTIALLY SOLD HIS OWN CHILD.

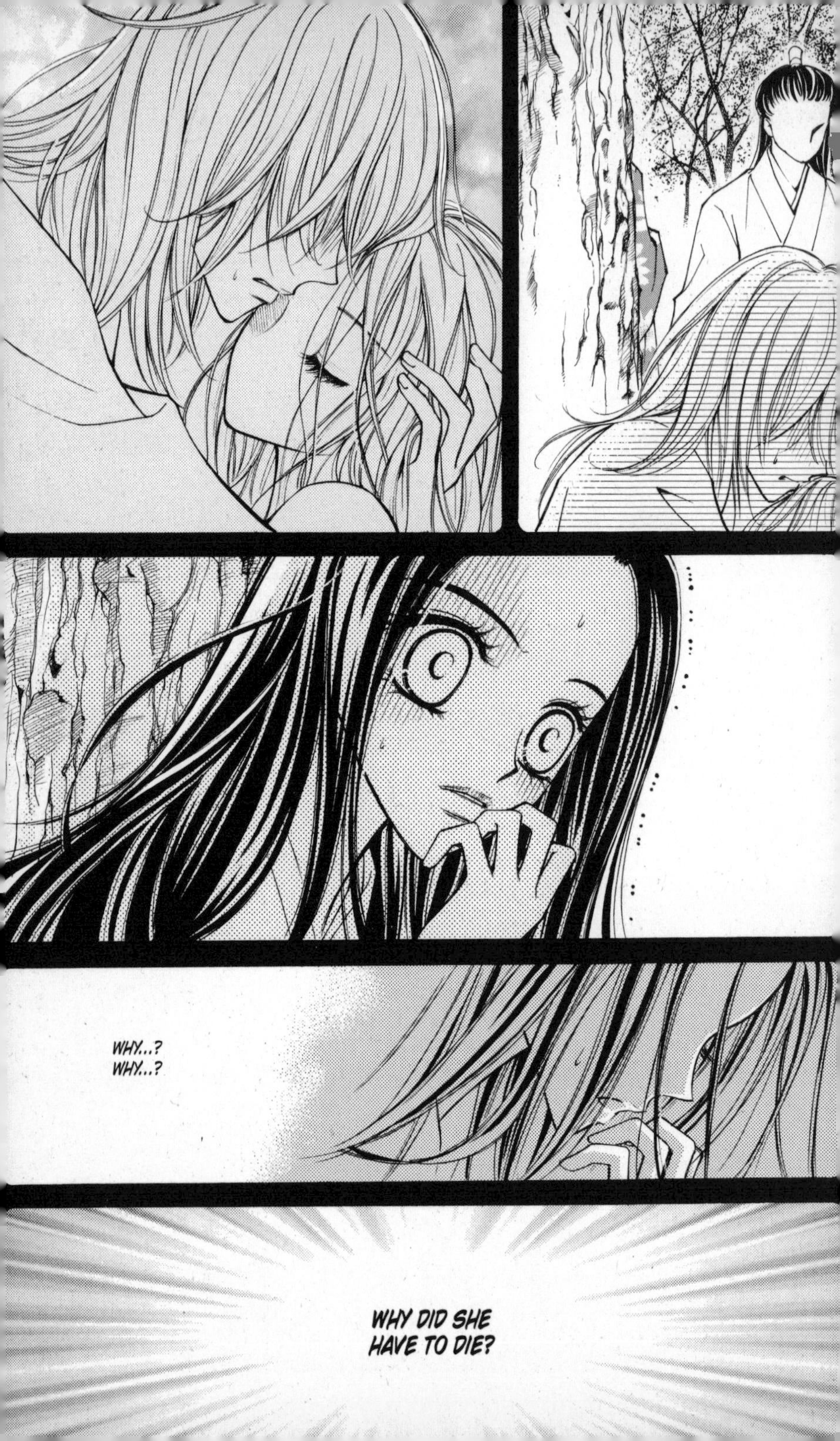
WHY...?
WHY...?
WHY DID SHE
HAVE TO DIE?

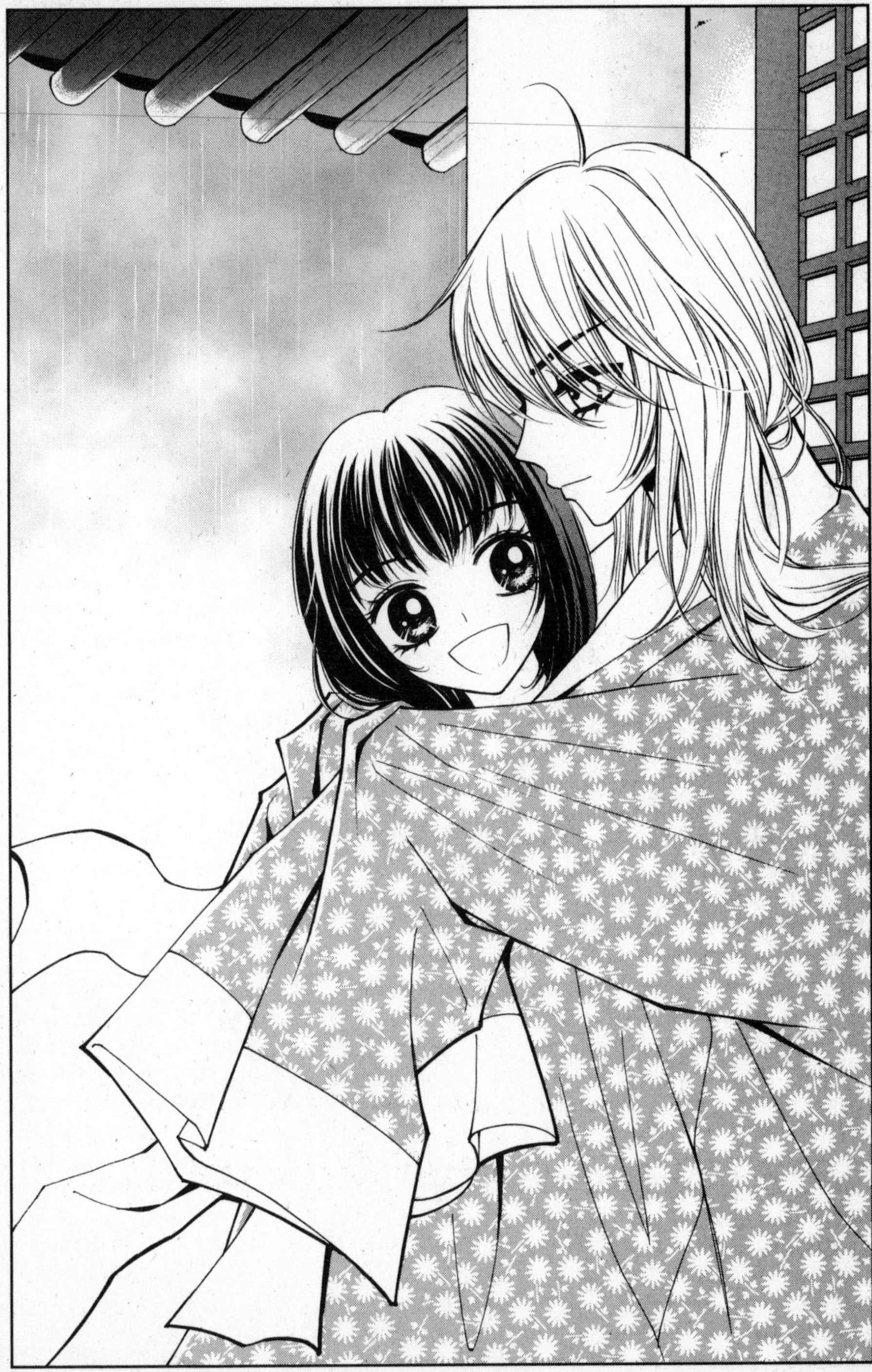

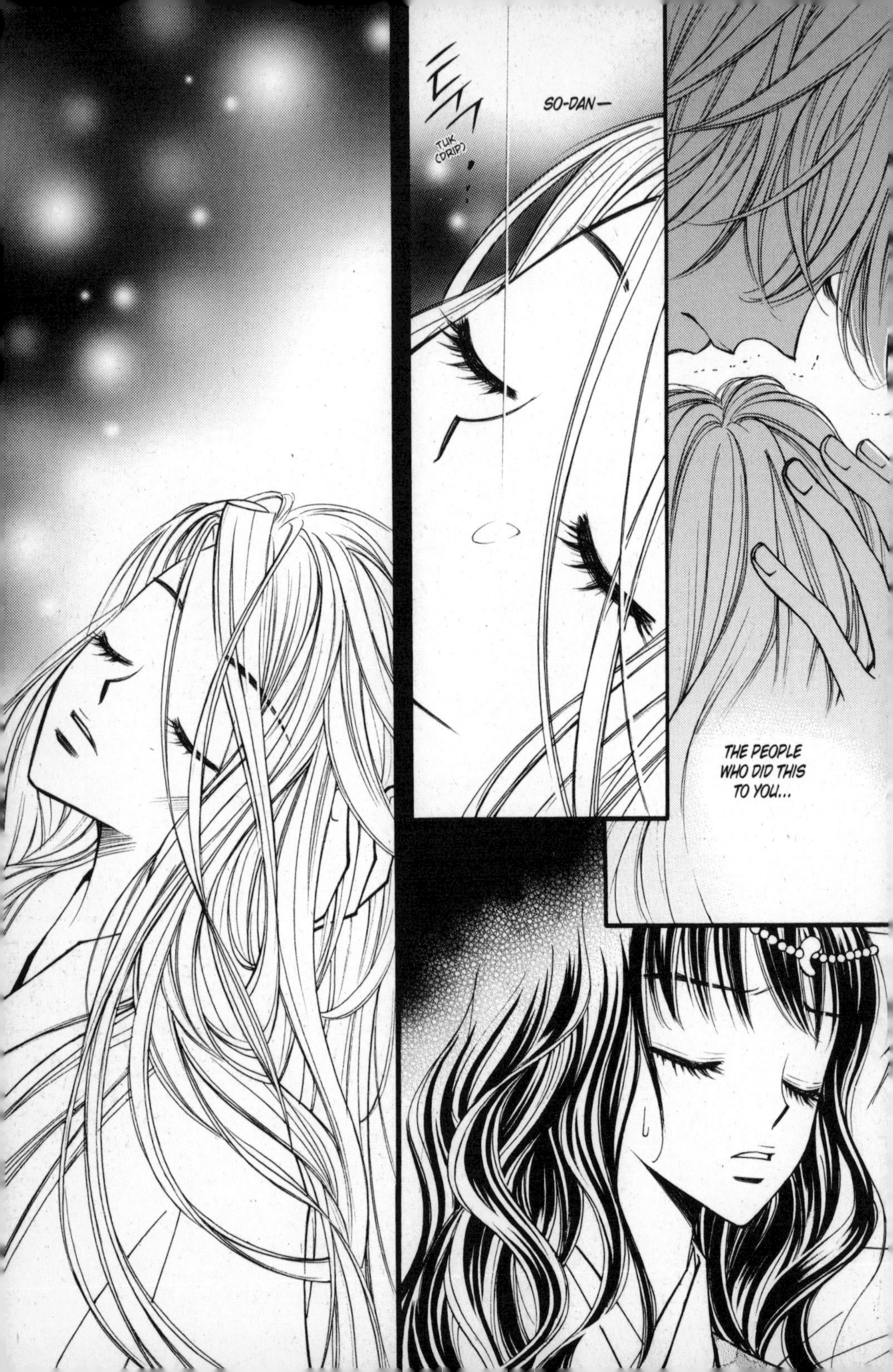
TUK (DRIP)
SO-DAN—
THE PEOPLE WHO DID THIS TO YOU...

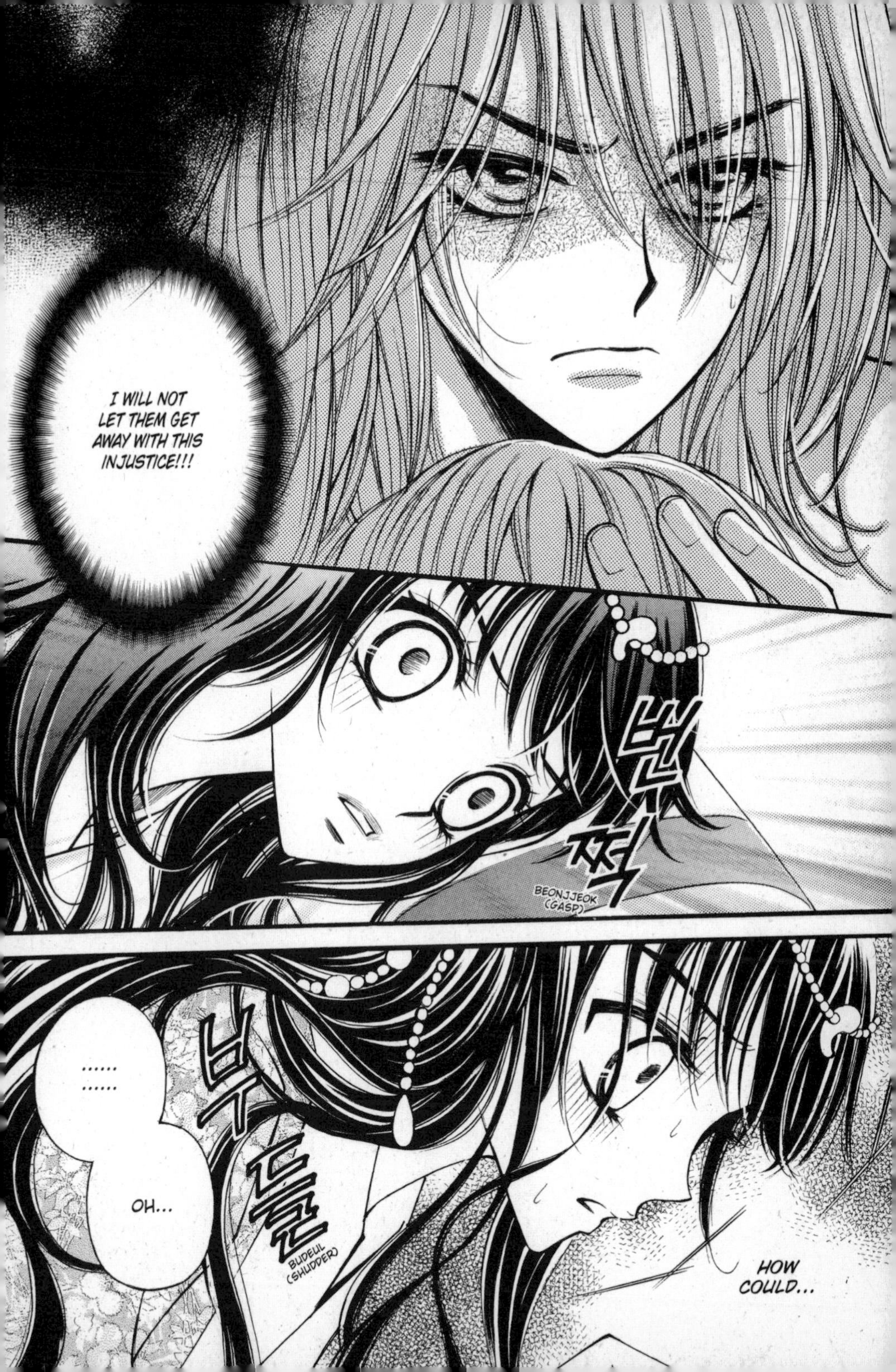
I WILL NOT LET THEM GET AWAY WITH THIS INJUSTICE!!!
번쩍
BEONJJEOK (GASP)
......
......
OH...
부들
BUDEUL (SHUDDER)
HOW COULD...

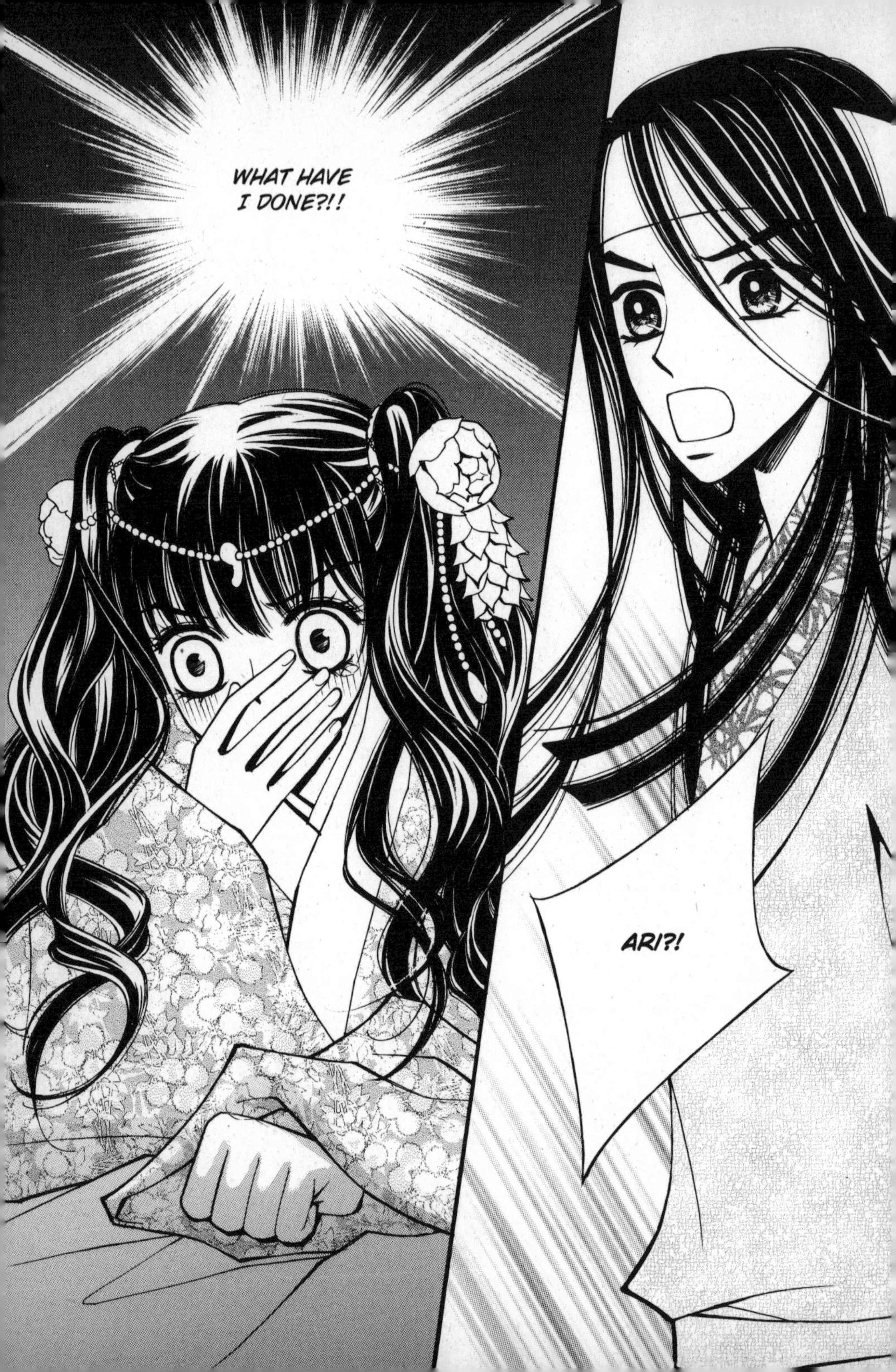
WHAT HAVE I DONE?!!
ARI?!

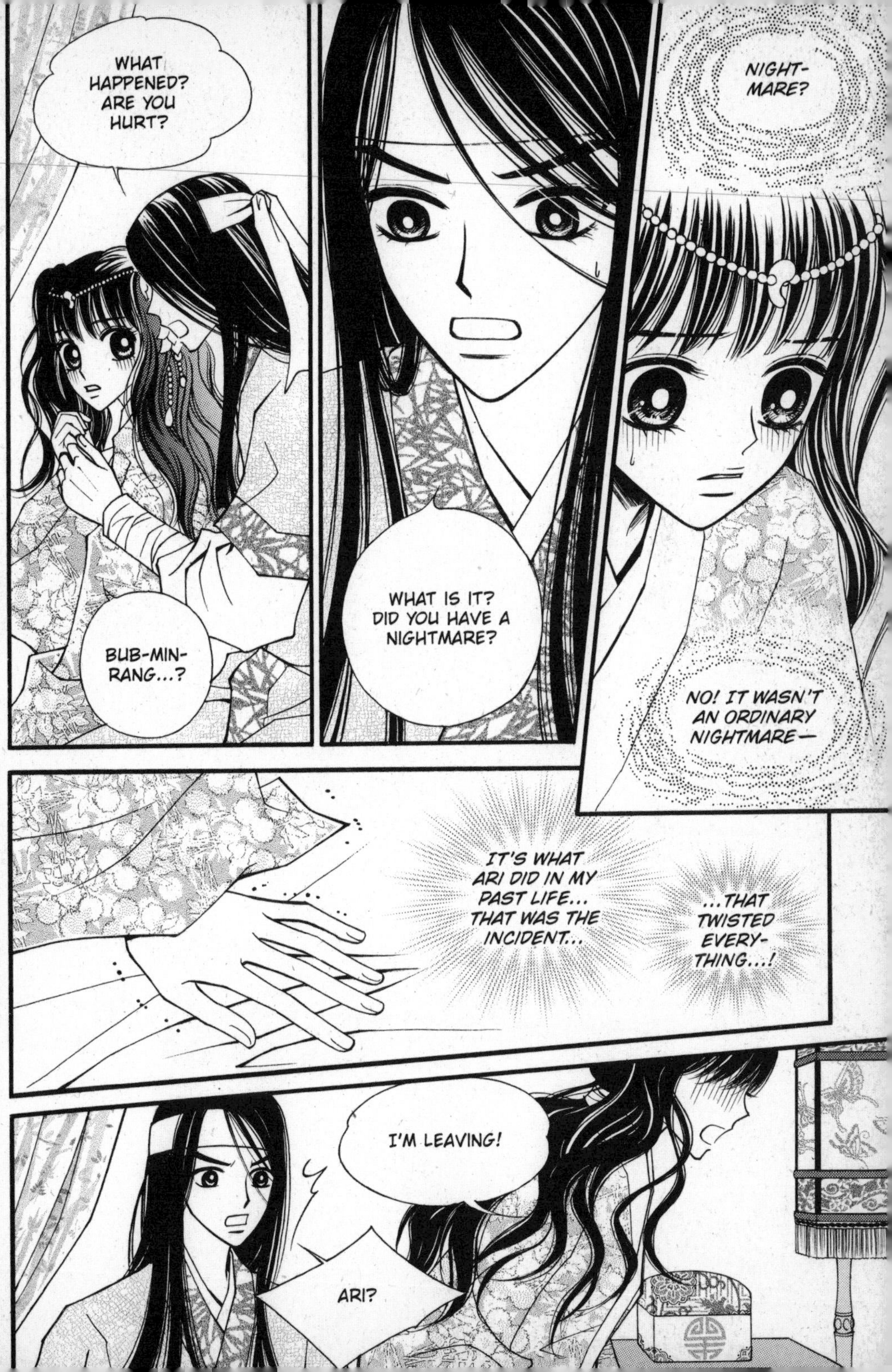
WHAT HAPPENED? ARE YOU HURT?
BUB-MIN-RANG...?
WHAT IS IT? DID YOU HAVE A NIGHTMARE?
NIGHT-MARE?
NO! IT WASN'T AN ORDINARY NIGHTMARE—
IT'S WHAT ARI DID IN MY PAST LIFE... THAT WAS THE INCIDENT...
...THAT TWISTED EVERY-THING...!
I'M LEAVING!
ARI?

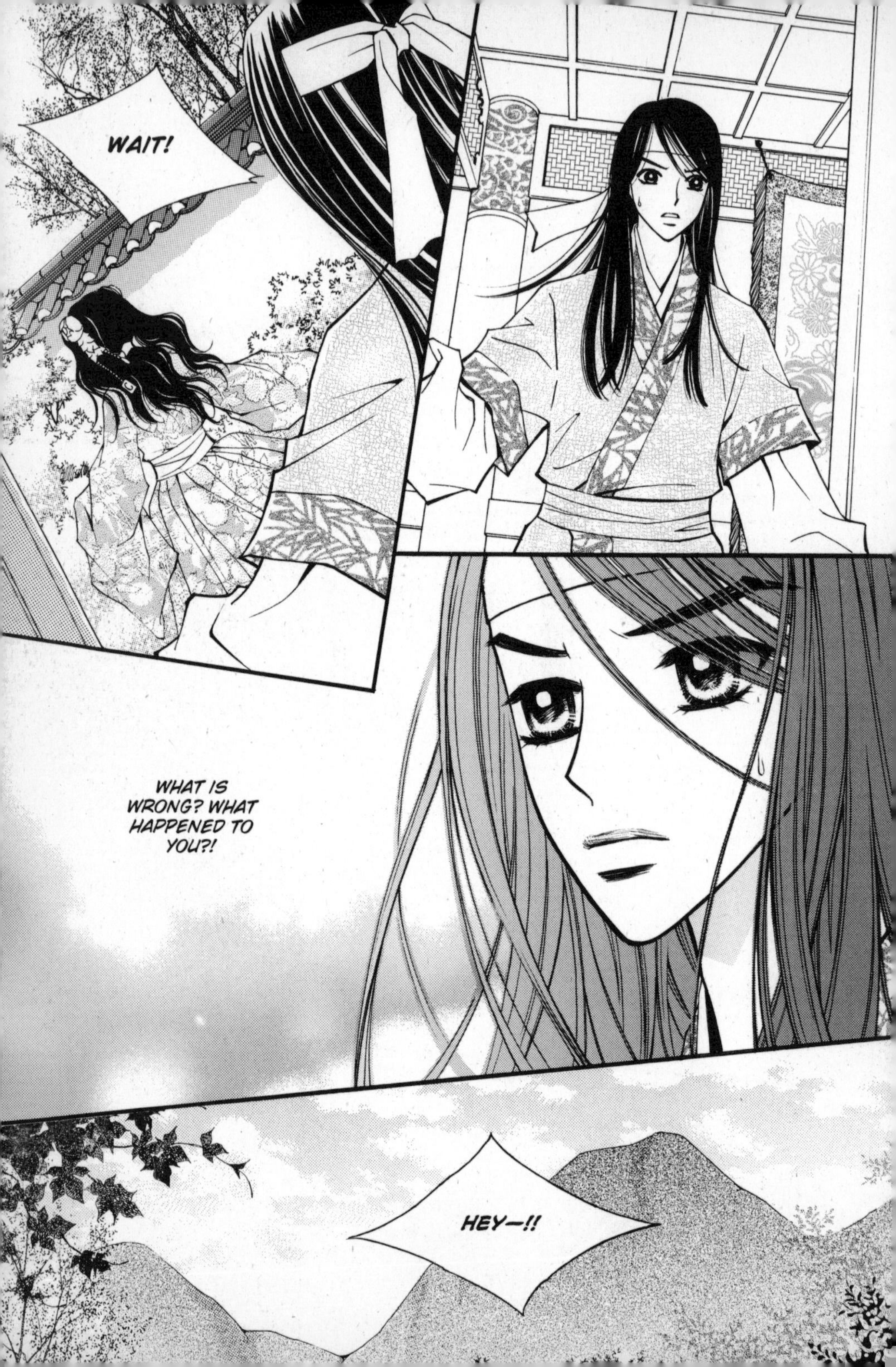
WAIT!
WHAT IS WRONG? WHAT HAPPENED TO YOU?!
HEY–!!

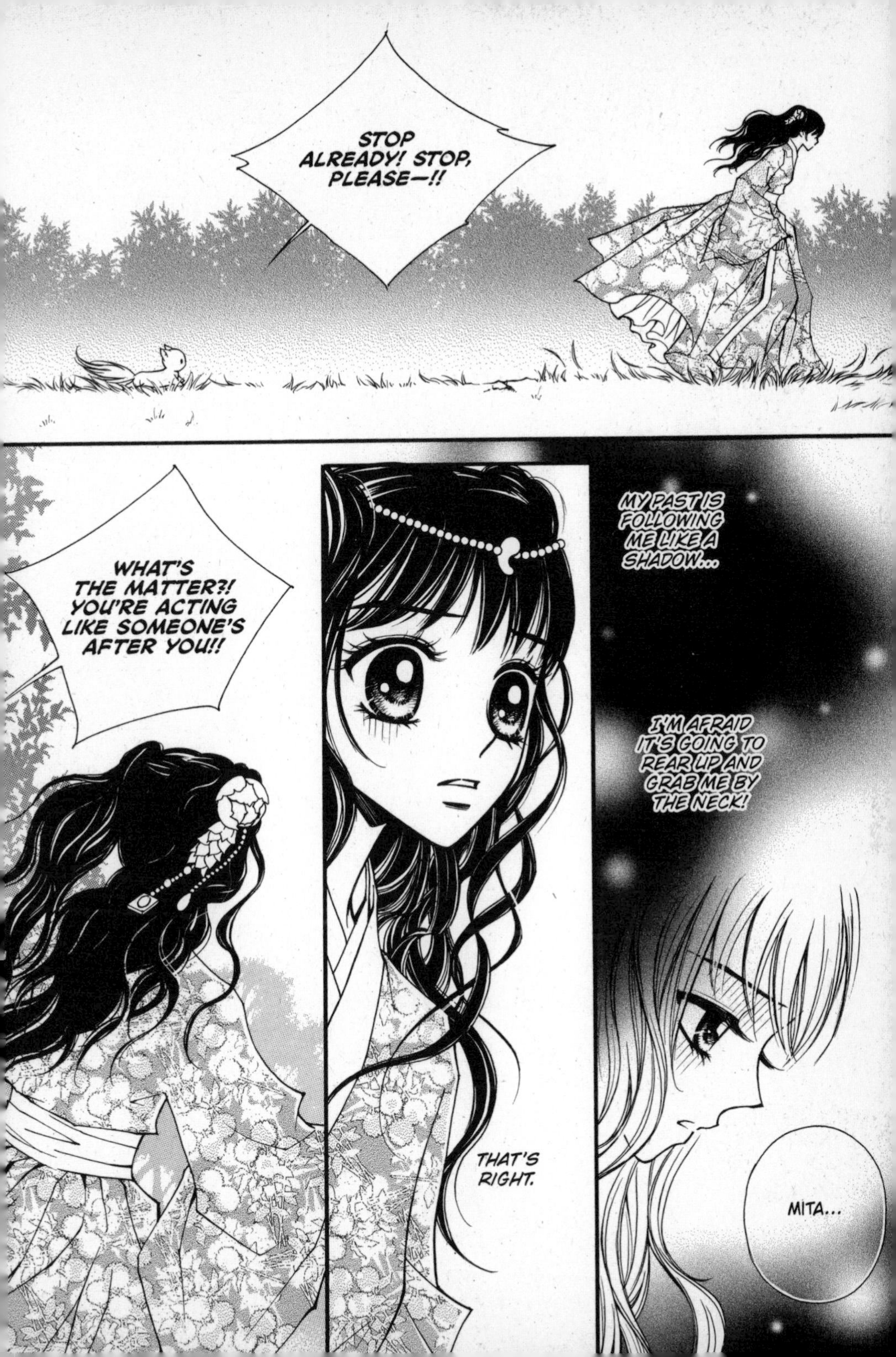

STOP ALREADY! STOP, PLEASE—!!
WHAT'S THE MATTER?! YOU'RE ACTING LIKE SOMEONE'S AFTER YOU!!
THAT'S RIGHT.
MY PAST IS FOLLOWING ME LIKE A SHADOW...
I'M AFRAID IT'S GOING TO REAR UP AND GRAB ME BY THE NECK!
MITA...

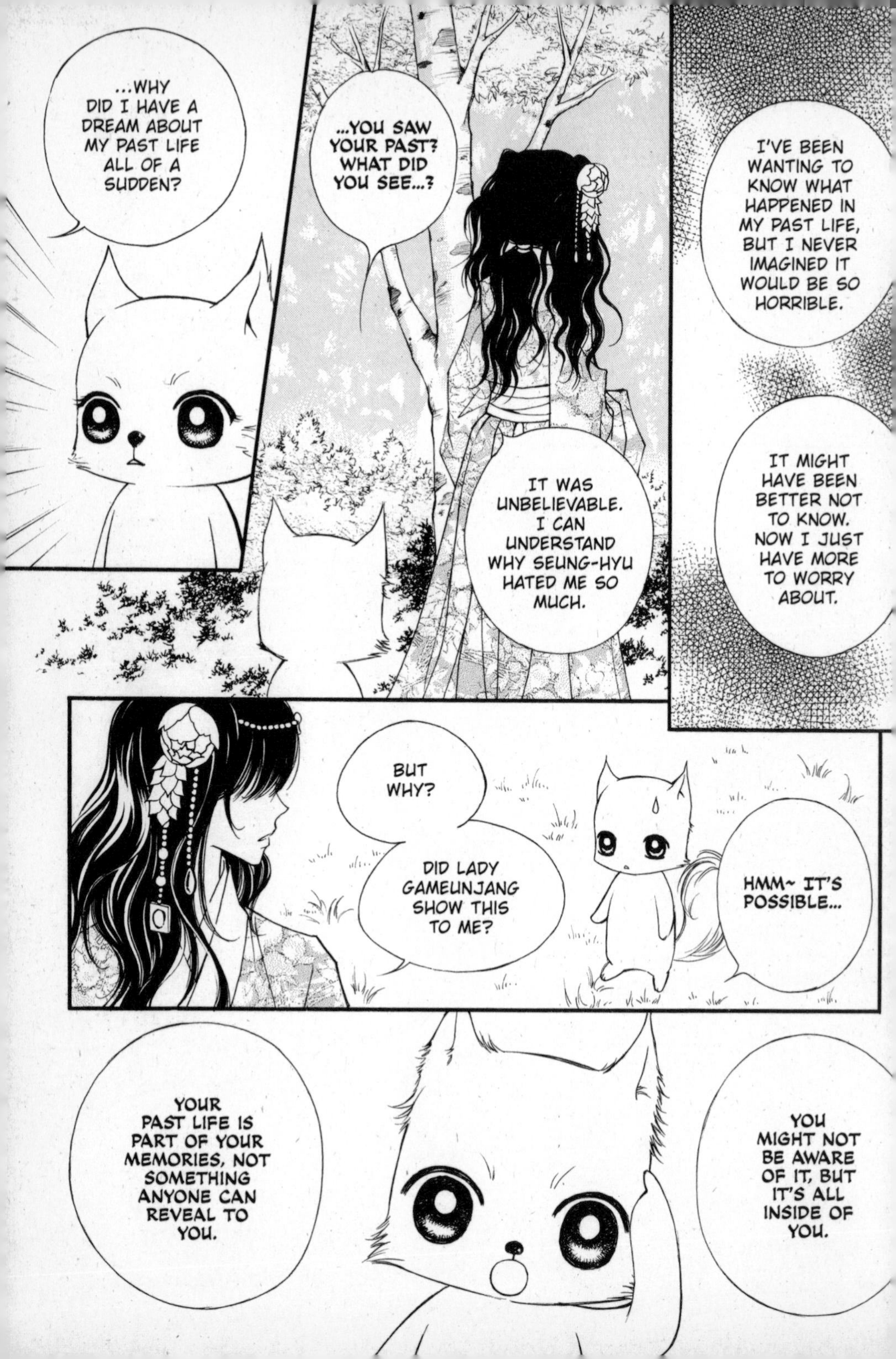
...WHY DID I HAVE A DREAM ABOUT MY PAST LIFE ALL OF A SUDDEN?
...YOU SAW YOUR PAST? WHAT DID YOU SEE...?
IT WAS UNBELIEVABLE. I CAN UNDERSTAND WHY SEUNG-HYU HATED ME SO MUCH.
I'VE BEEN WANTING TO KNOW WHAT HAPPENED IN MY PAST LIFE, BUT I NEVER IMAGINED IT WOULD BE SO HORRIBLE.
IT MIGHT HAVE BEEN BETTER NOT TO KNOW. NOW I JUST HAVE MORE TO WORRY ABOUT.
BUT WHY?
DID LADY GAMEUNJANG SHOW THIS TO ME?
HMM~ IT'S POSSIBLE...
YOUR PAST LIFE IS PART OF YOUR MEMORIES, NOT SOMETHING ANYONE CAN REVEAL TO YOU.
YOU MIGHT NOT BE AWARE OF IT, BUT IT'S ALL INSIDE OF YOU.

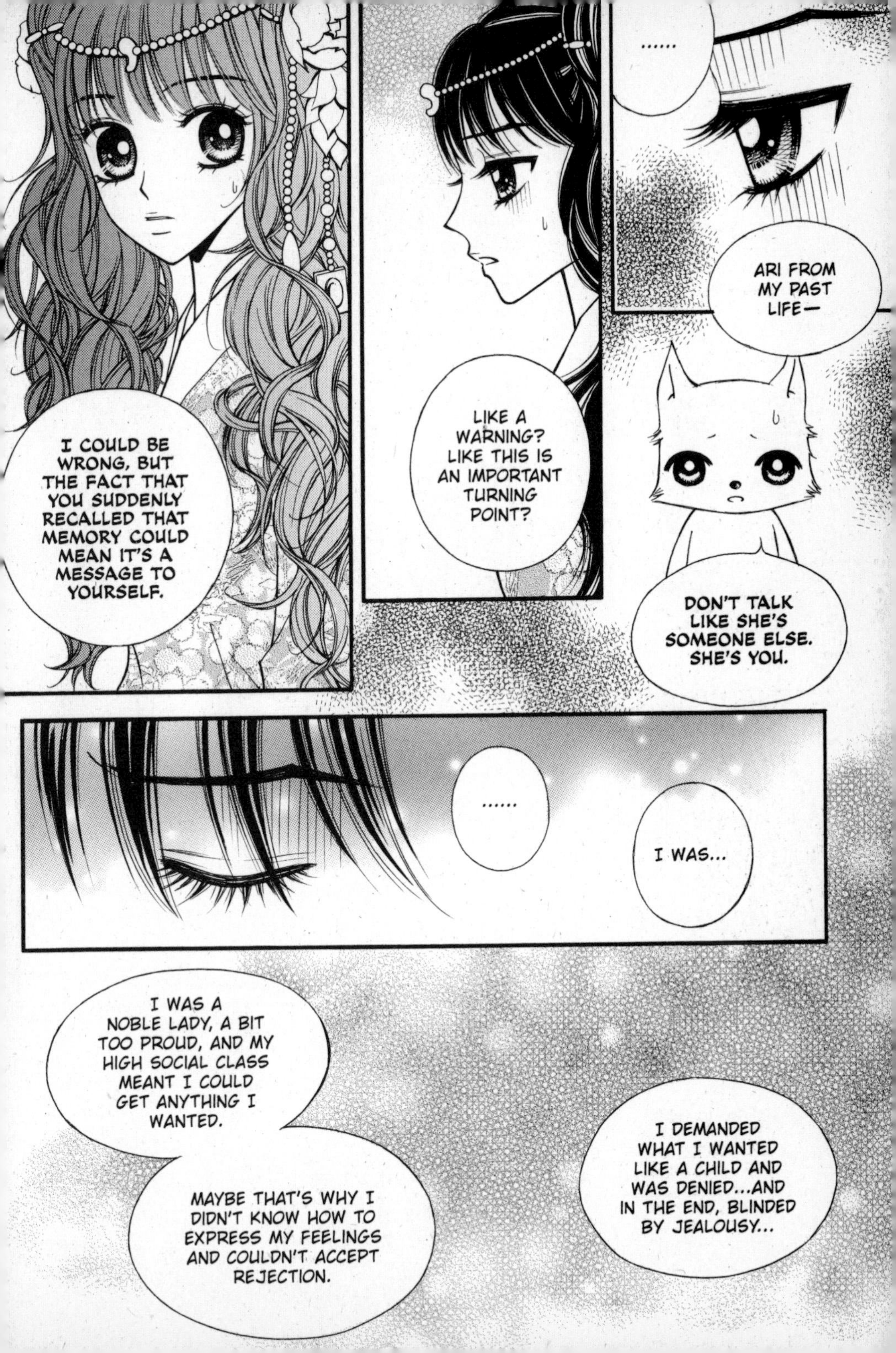
I COULD BE WRONG, BUT THE FACT THAT YOU SUDDENLY RECALLED THAT MEMORY COULD MEAN IT'S A MESSAGE TO YOURSELF.
LIKE A WARNING? LIKE THIS IS AN IMPORTANT TURNING POINT?
......
ARI FROM MY PAST LIFE—
DON'T TALK LIKE SHE'S SOMEONE ELSE. SHE'S YOU.
......
I WAS...
I WAS A NOBLE LADY, A BIT TOO PROUD, AND MY HIGH SOCIAL CLASS MEANT I COULD GET ANYTHING I WANTED.
MAYBE THAT'S WHY I DIDN'T KNOW HOW TO EXPRESS MY FEELINGS AND COULDN'T ACCEPT REJECTION.
I DEMANDED WHAT I WANTED LIKE A CHILD AND WAS DENIED...AND IN THE END, BLINDED BY JEALOUSY...

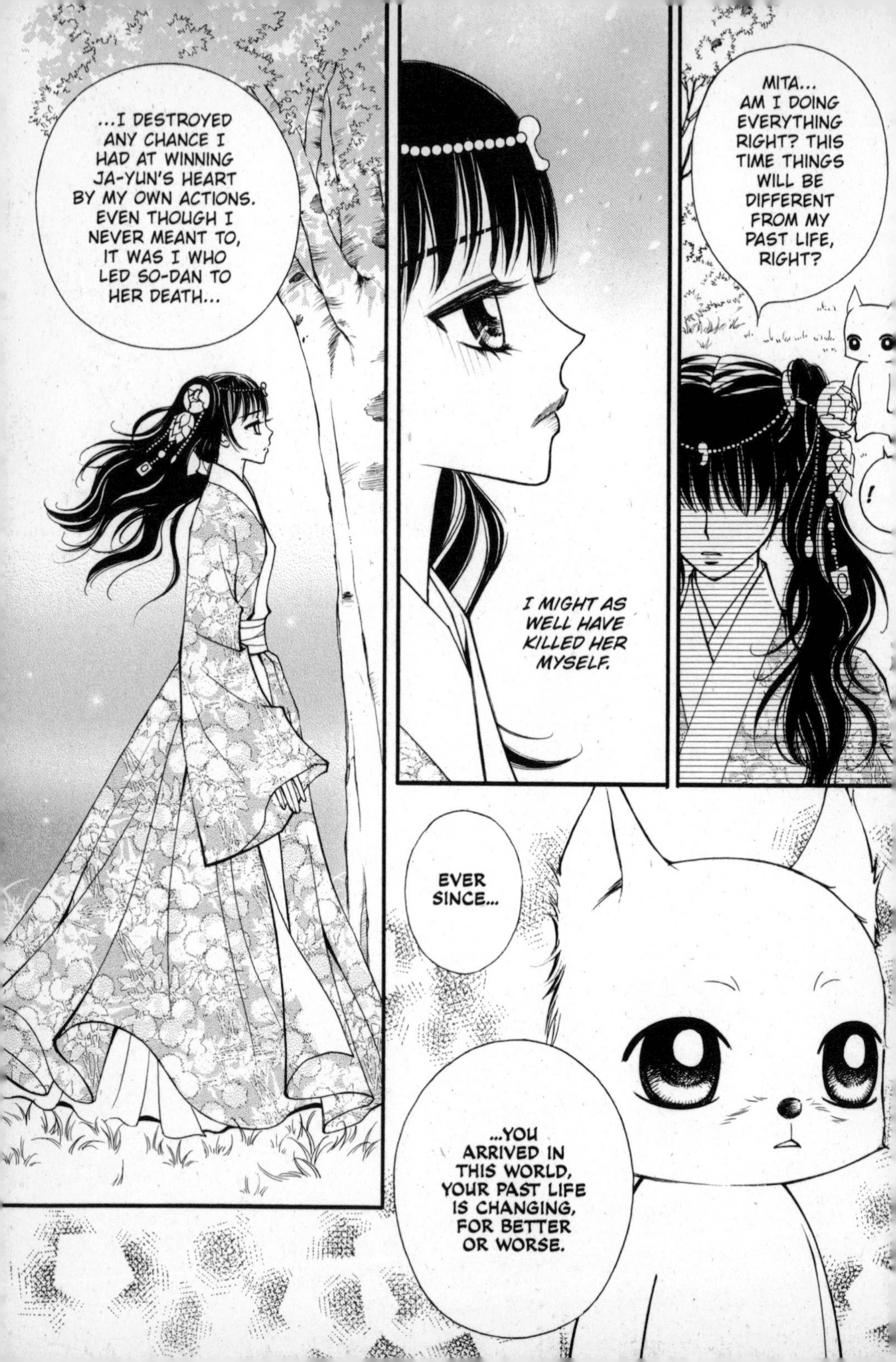
...I DESTROYED ANY CHANCE I HAD AT WINNING JA-YUN'S HEART BY MY OWN ACTIONS. EVEN THOUGH I NEVER MEANT TO, IT WAS I WHO LED SO-DAN TO HER DEATH...
I MIGHT AS WELL HAVE KILLED HER MYSELF.
MITA... AM I DOING EVERYTHING RIGHT? THIS TIME THINGS WILL BE DIFFERENT FROM MY PAST LIFE, RIGHT?
!
EVER SINCE...
...YOU ARRIVED IN THIS WORLD, YOUR PAST LIFE IS CHANGING, FOR BETTER OR WORSE.

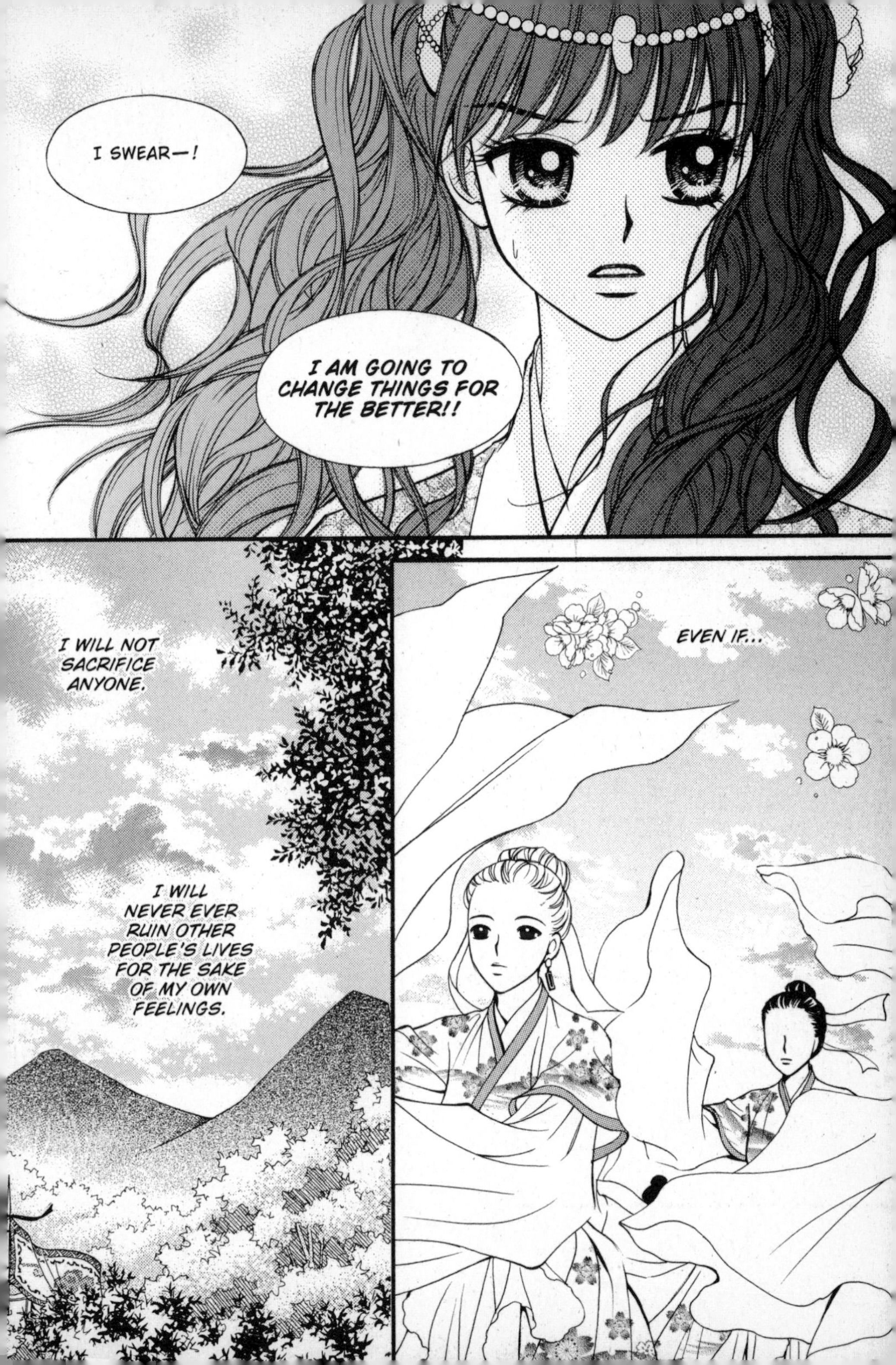
I SWEAR—!
I AM GOING TO CHANGE THINGS FOR THE BETTER!!
I WILL NOT SACRIFICE ANYONE.
I WILL NEVER EVER RUIN OTHER PEOPLE'S LIVES FOR THE SAKE OF MY OWN FEELINGS.
EVEN IF...

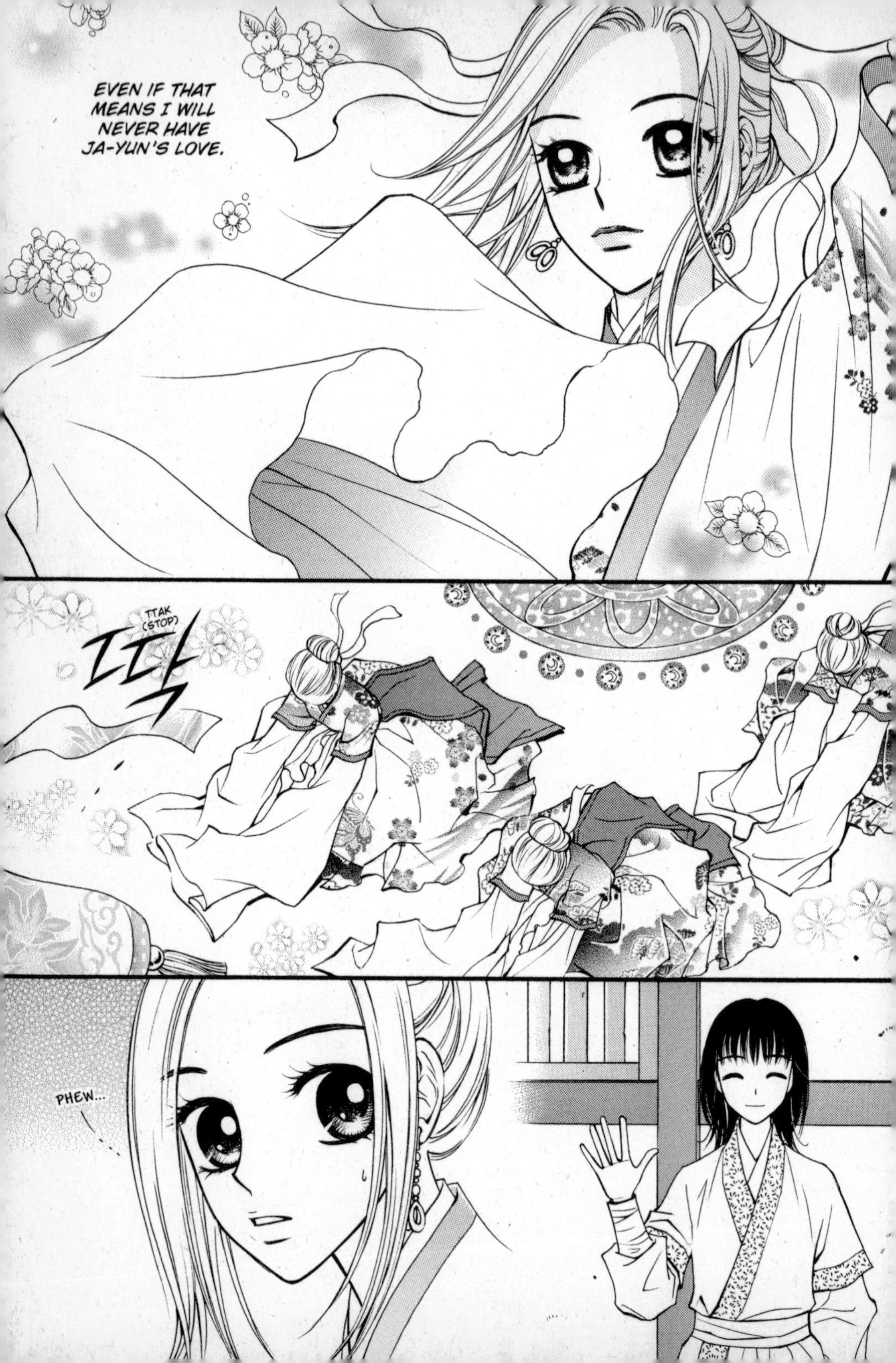
EVEN IF THAT MEANS I WILL NEVER HAVE JA-YUN'S LOVE.
TTAK (STOP)
PHEW...

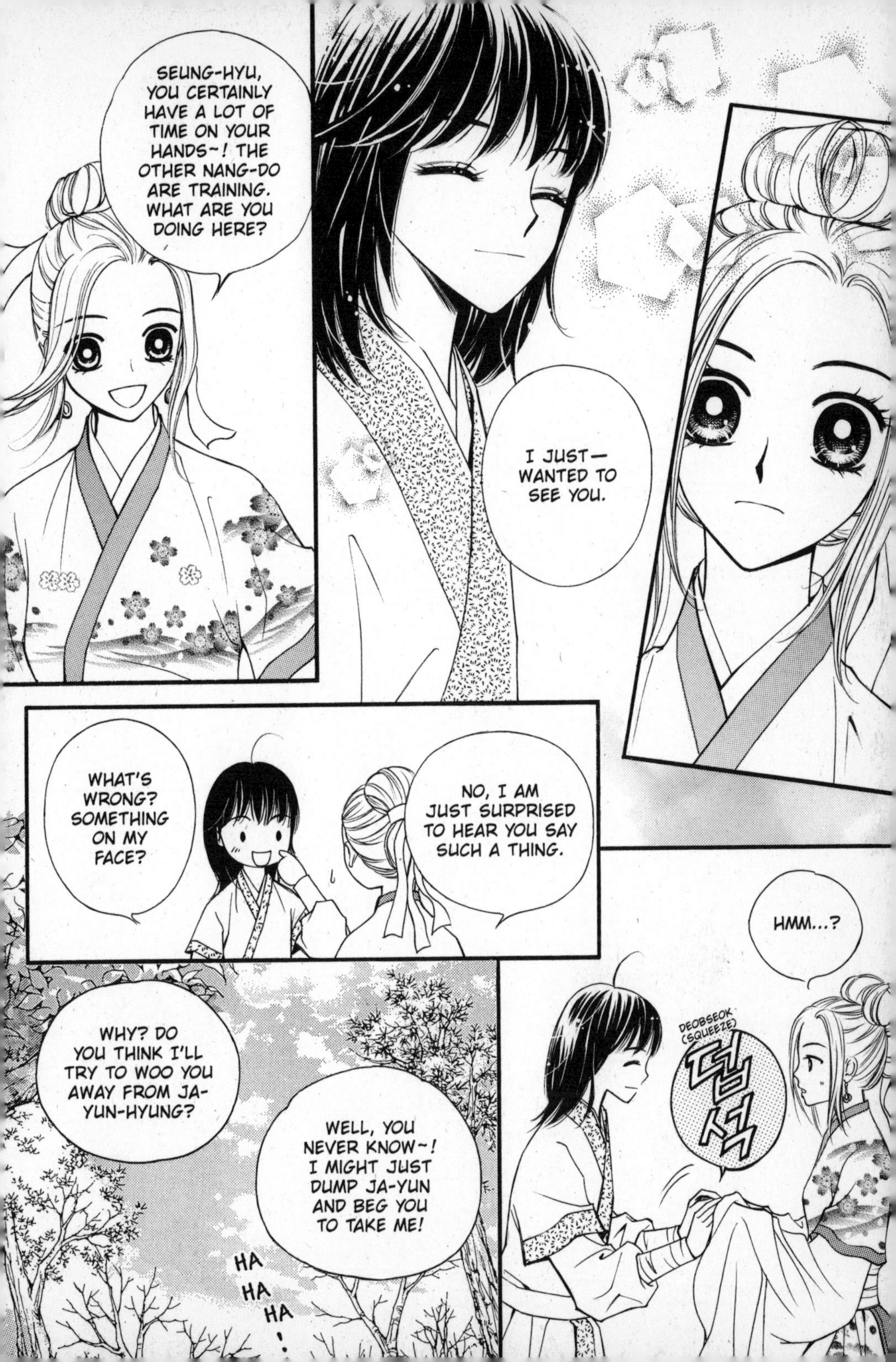
SEUNG-HYU, YOU CERTAINLY HAVE A LOT OF TIME ON YOUR HANDS~! THE OTHER NANG-DO ARE TRAINING. WHAT ARE YOU DOING HERE?
I JUST— WANTED TO SEE YOU.
WHAT'S WRONG? SOMETHING ON MY FACE?
NO, I AM JUST SURPRISED TO HEAR YOU SAY SUCH A THING.
WHY? DO YOU THINK I'LL TRY TO WOO YOU AWAY FROM JA-YUN-HYUNG?
WELL, YOU NEVER KNOW~! I MIGHT JUST DUMP JA-YUN AND BEG YOU TO TAKE ME!
HA HA HA!
HMM...?
DEOBSEOK (SQUEEZE)
덥석

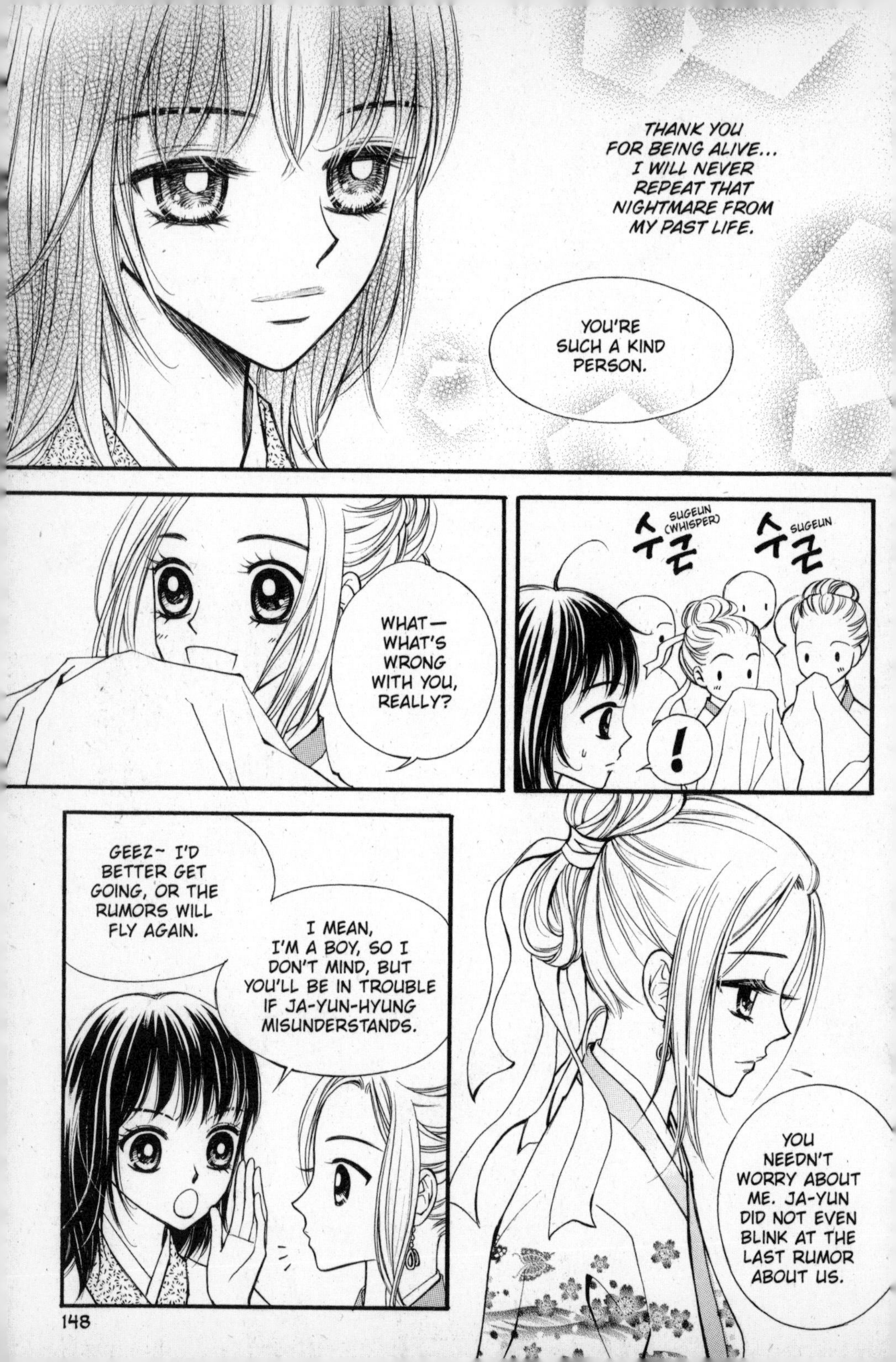
THANK YOU FOR BEING ALIVE... I WILL NEVER REPEAT THAT NIGHTMARE FROM MY PAST LIFE.
YOU'RE SUCH A KIND PERSON.
WHAT— WHAT'S WRONG WITH YOU, REALLY?
수군 SUGEUN (WHISPER)
수군 SUGEUN
!
GEEZ~ I'D BETTER GET GOING, OR THE RUMORS WILL FLY AGAIN.
I MEAN, I'M A BOY, SO I DON'T MIND, BUT YOU'LL BE IN TROUBLE IF JA-YUN-HYUNG MISUNDERSTANDS.
YOU NEEDN'T WORRY ABOUT ME. JA-YUN DID NOT EVEN BLINK AT THE LAST RUMOR ABOUT US.

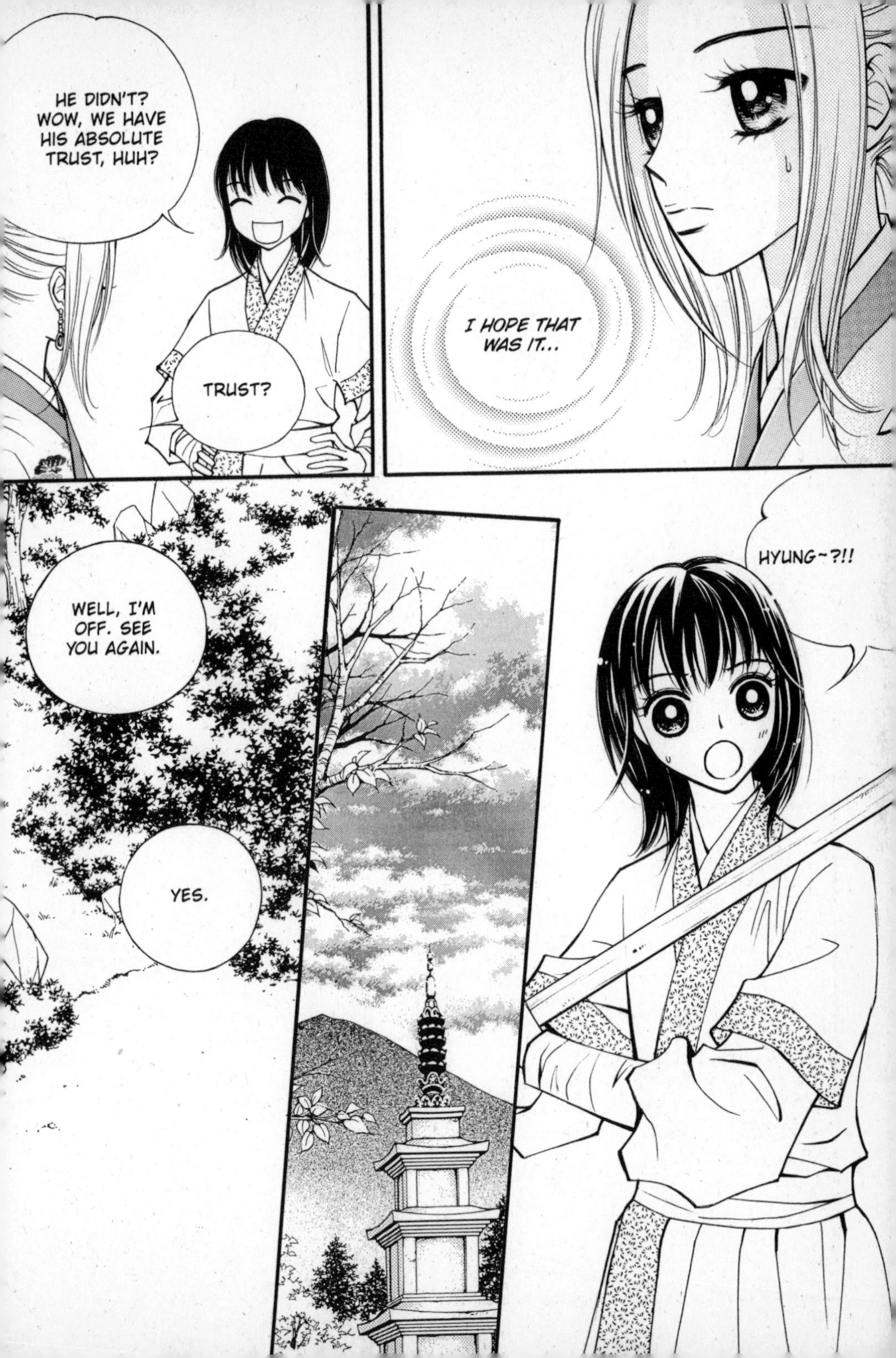
HE DIDN'T? WOW, WE HAVE HIS ABSOLUTE TRUST, HUH?
TRUST?
I HOPE THAT WAS IT...
WELL, I'M OFF. SEE YOU AGAIN.
YES.
HYUNG~?!!

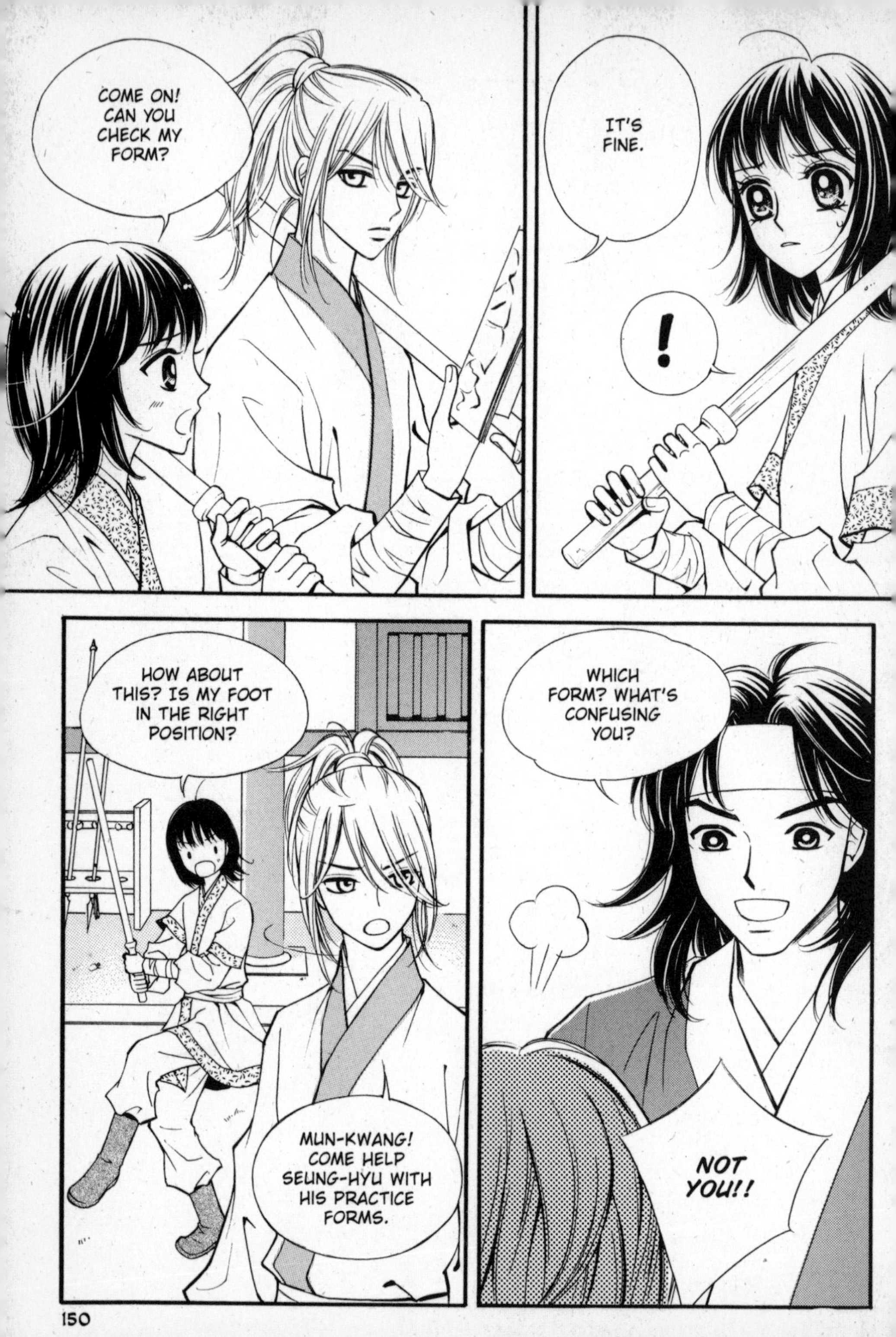
COME ON! CAN YOU CHECK MY FORM?
IT'S FINE.
!
HOW ABOUT THIS? IS MY FOOT IN THE RIGHT POSITION?
MUN-KWANG! COME HELP SEUNG-HYU WITH HIS PRACTICE FORMS.
WHICH FORM? WHAT'S CONFUSING YOU?
NOT YOU!!

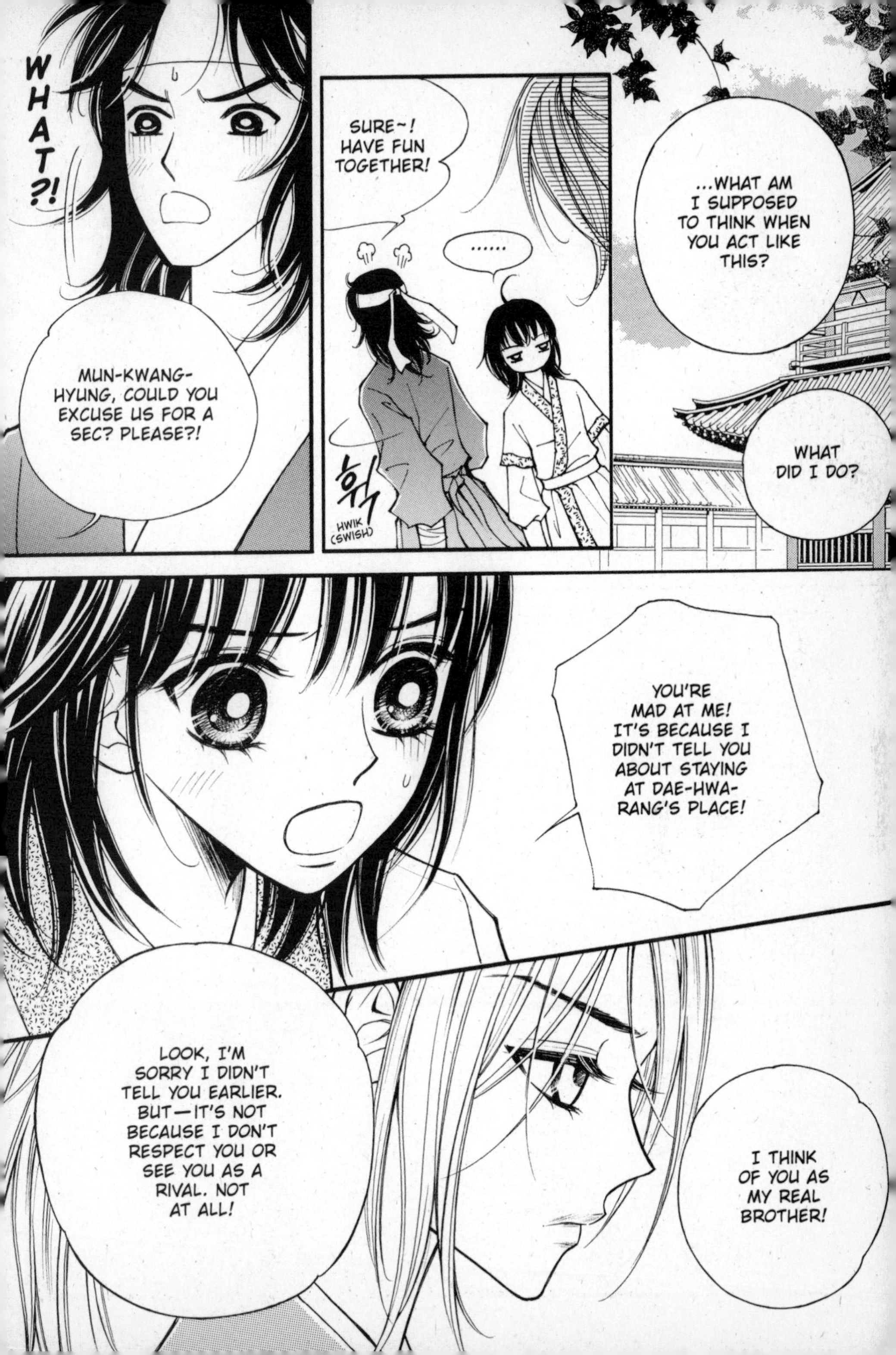
WHAT?!
MUN-KWANG-HYUNG, COULD YOU EXCUSE US FOR A SEC? PLEASE?!
SURE~! HAVE FUN TOGETHER!
......
휙
HWIK (SWISH)
...WHAT AM I SUPPOSED TO THINK WHEN YOU ACT LIKE THIS?
WHAT DID I DO?
YOU'RE MAD AT ME! IT'S BECAUSE I DIDN'T TELL YOU ABOUT STAYING AT DAE-HWA-RANG'S PLACE!
LOOK, I'M SORRY I DIDN'T TELL YOU EARLIER. BUT—IT'S NOT BECAUSE I DON'T RESPECT YOU OR SEE YOU AS A RIVAL. NOT AT ALL!
I THINK OF YOU AS MY REAL BROTHER!

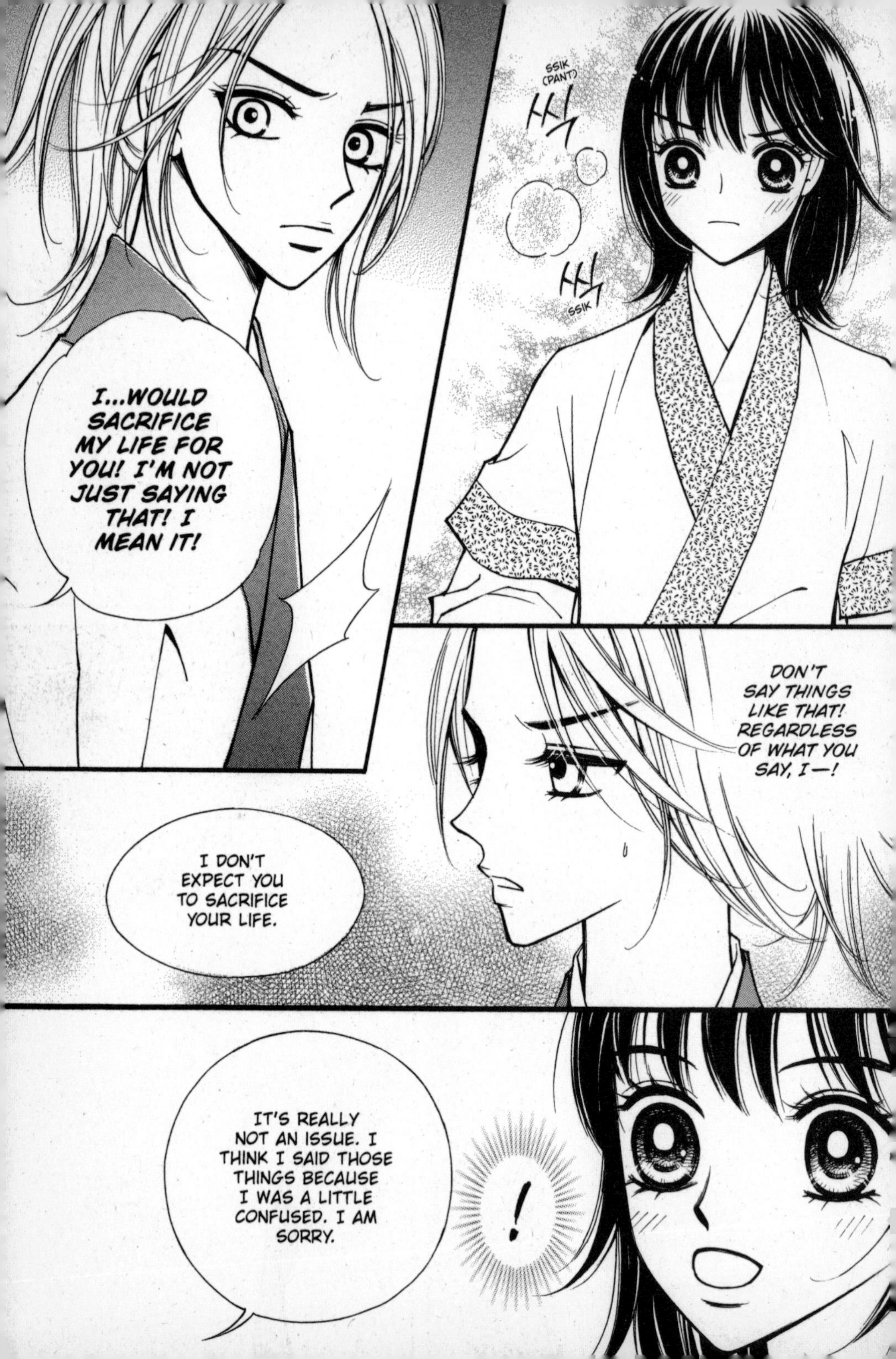
I...WOULD SACRIFICE MY LIFE FOR YOU! I'M NOT JUST SAYING THAT! I MEAN IT!
SSIK (PANT)
SSIK
DON'T SAY THINGS LIKE THAT! REGARDLESS OF WHAT YOU SAY, I—!
I DON'T EXPECT YOU TO SACRIFICE YOUR LIFE.
!
IT'S REALLY NOT AN ISSUE. I THINK I SAID THOSE THINGS BECAUSE I WAS A LITTLE CONFUSED. I AM SORRY.

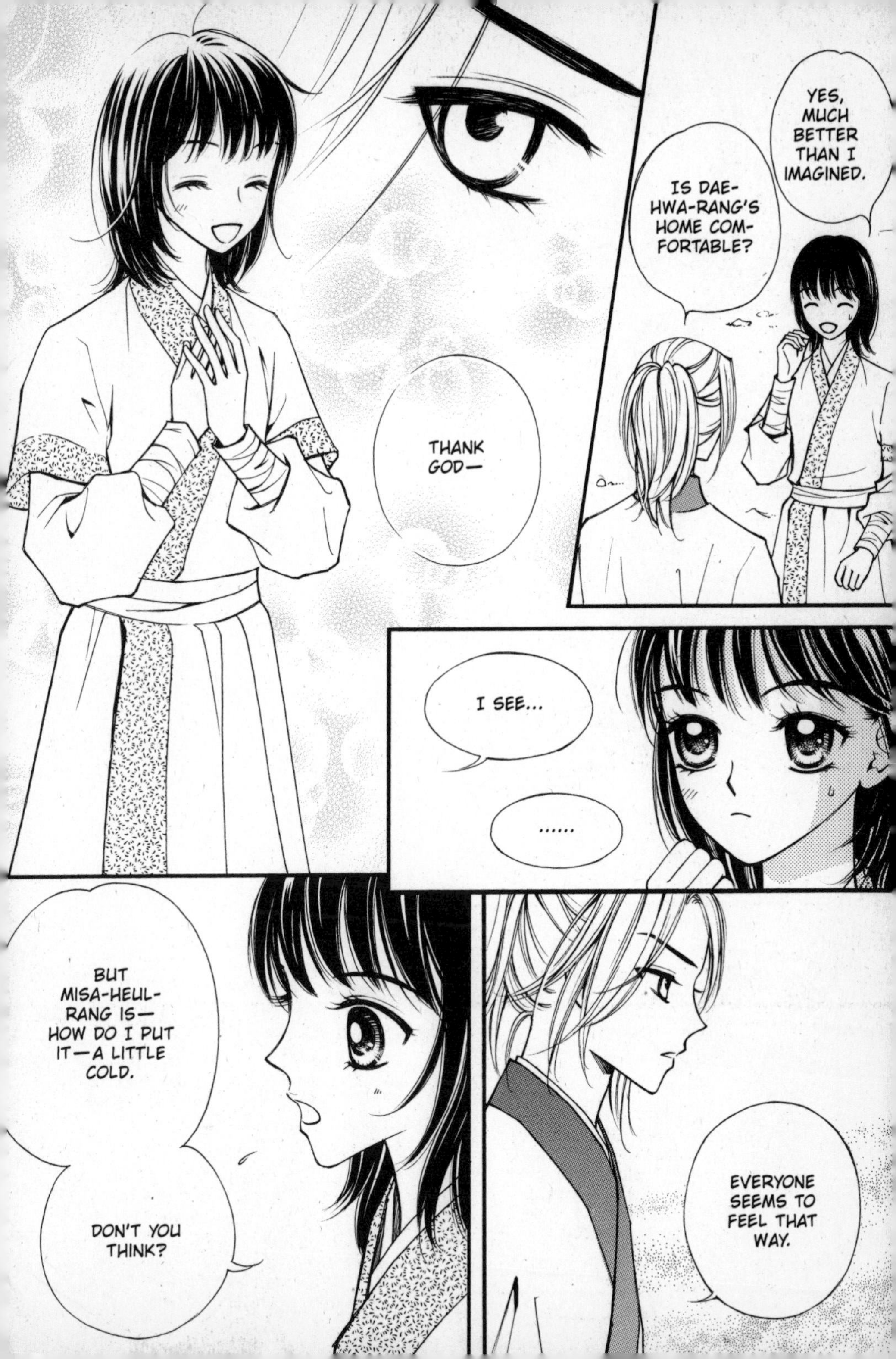
THANK GOD—
IS DAE-HWA-RANG'S HOME COMFORTABLE?
YES, MUCH BETTER THAN I IMAGINED.
I SEE...
......
BUT MISA-HEUL-RANG IS—HOW DO I PUT IT—A LITTLE COLD.
DON'T YOU THINK?
EVERYONE SEEMS TO FEEL THAT WAY.

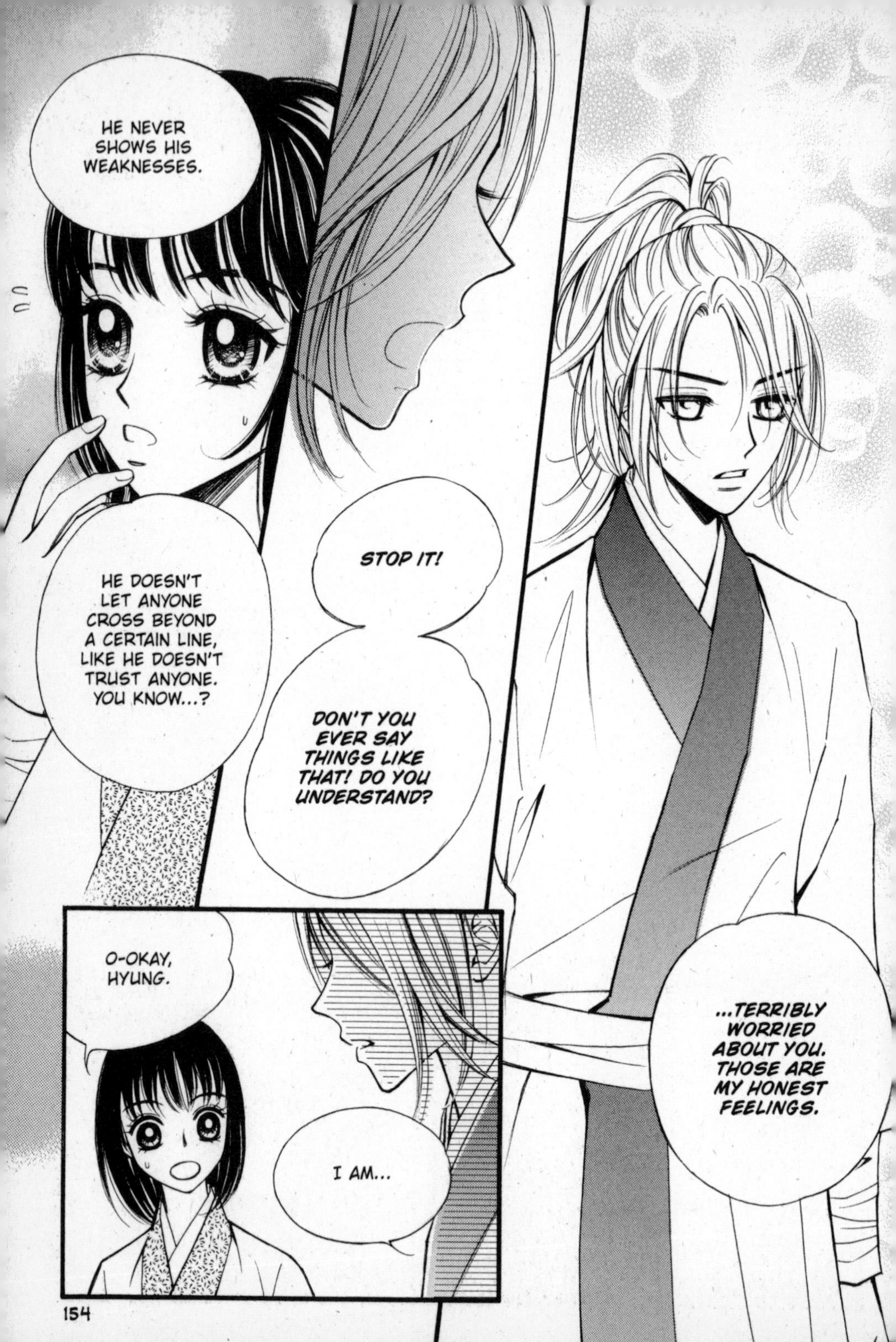
HE NEVER SHOWS HIS WEAKNESSES.
HE DOESN'T LET ANYONE CROSS BEYOND A CERTAIN LINE, LIKE HE DOESN'T TRUST ANYONE. YOU KNOW...?
STOP IT!
DON'T YOU EVER SAY THINGS LIKE THAT! DO YOU UNDERSTAND?
O-OKAY, HYUNG.
I AM...
...TERRIBLY WORRIED ABOUT YOU. THOSE ARE MY HONEST FEELINGS.

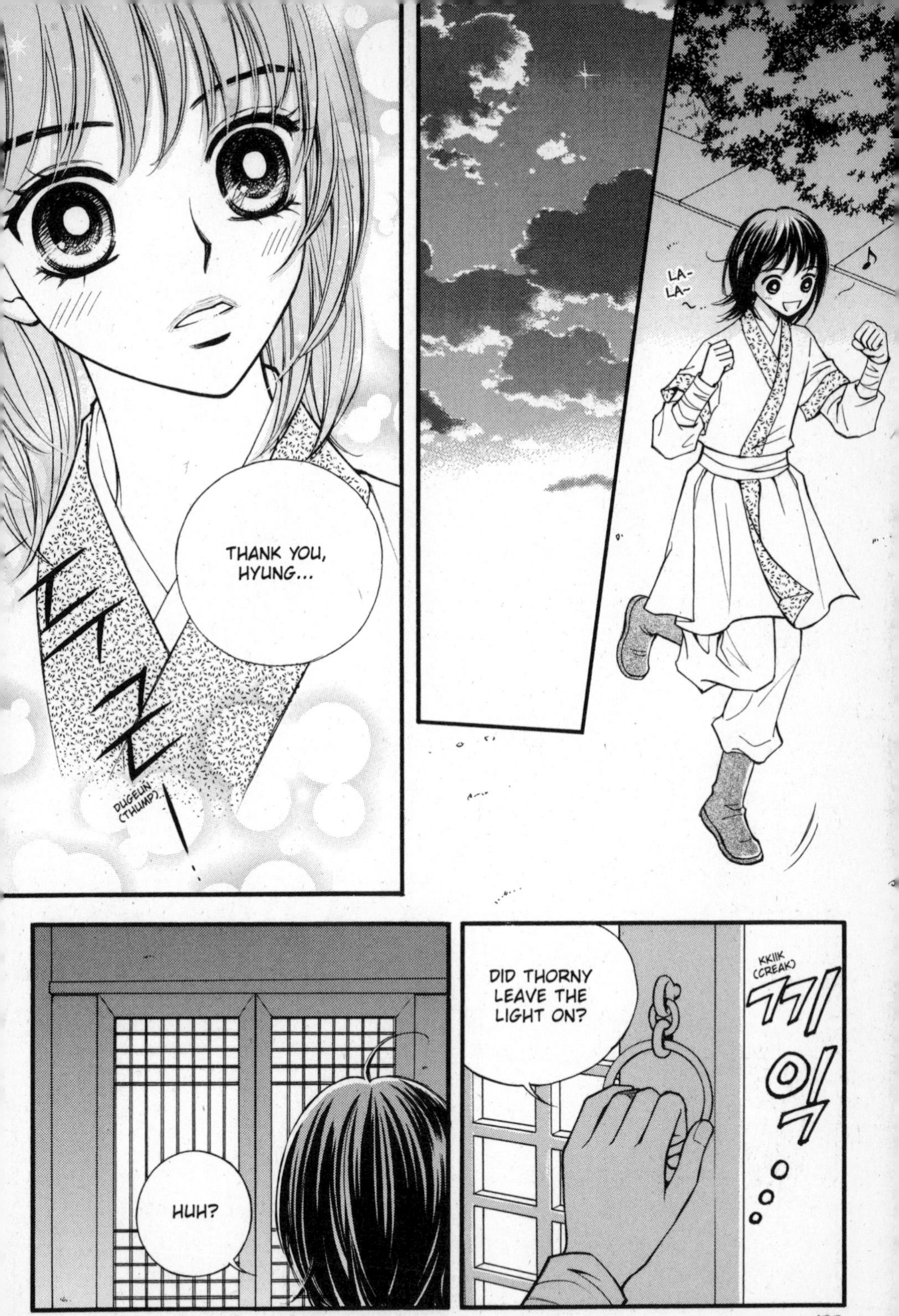
THANK YOU, HYUNG...
DUGEUN (THUMP)...
LA-LA~
HUH?
DID THORNY LEAVE THE LIGHT ON?
KKIIK (CREAK)

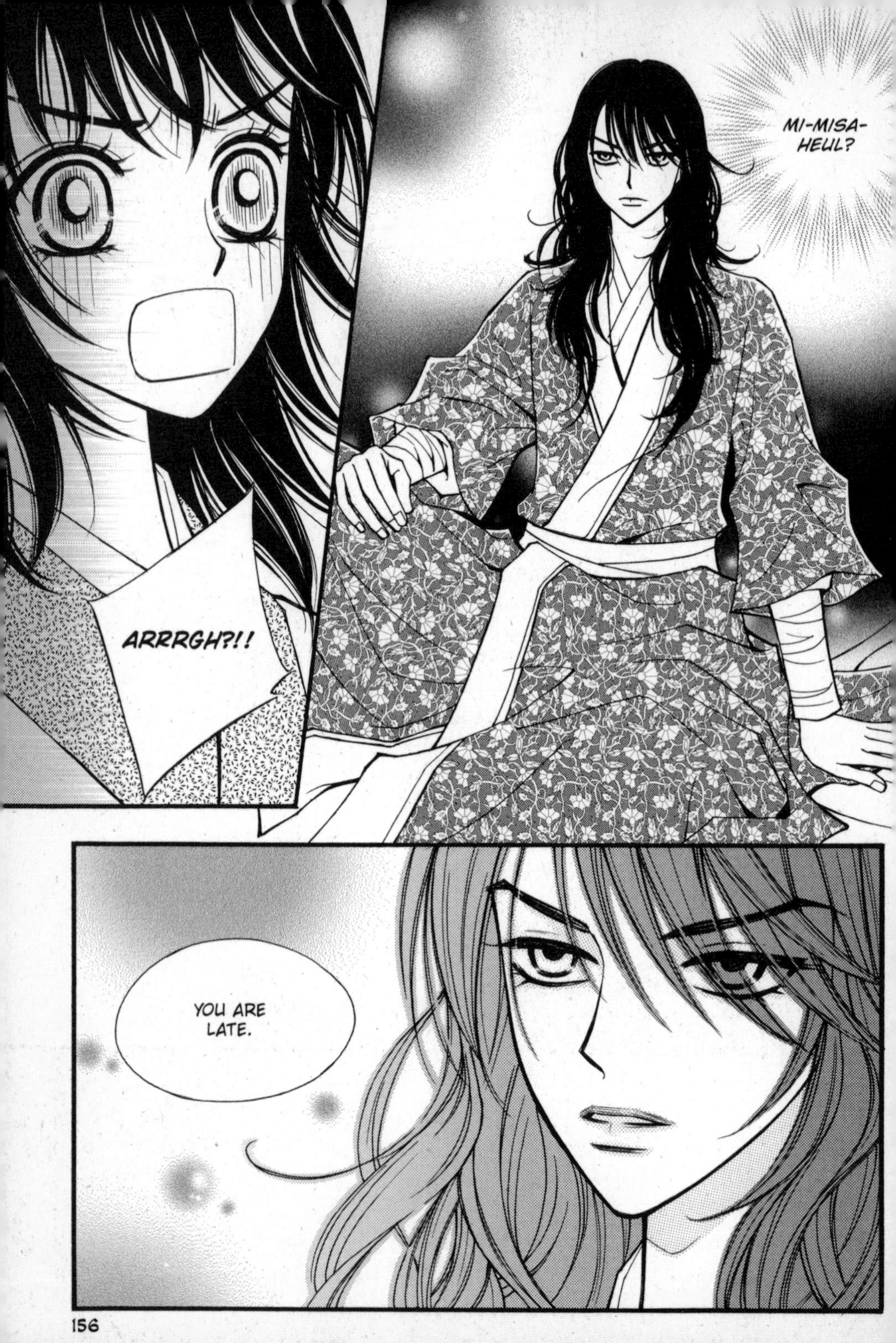
ARRRGH?!!
MI-MISA-HEUL?
YOU ARE LATE.

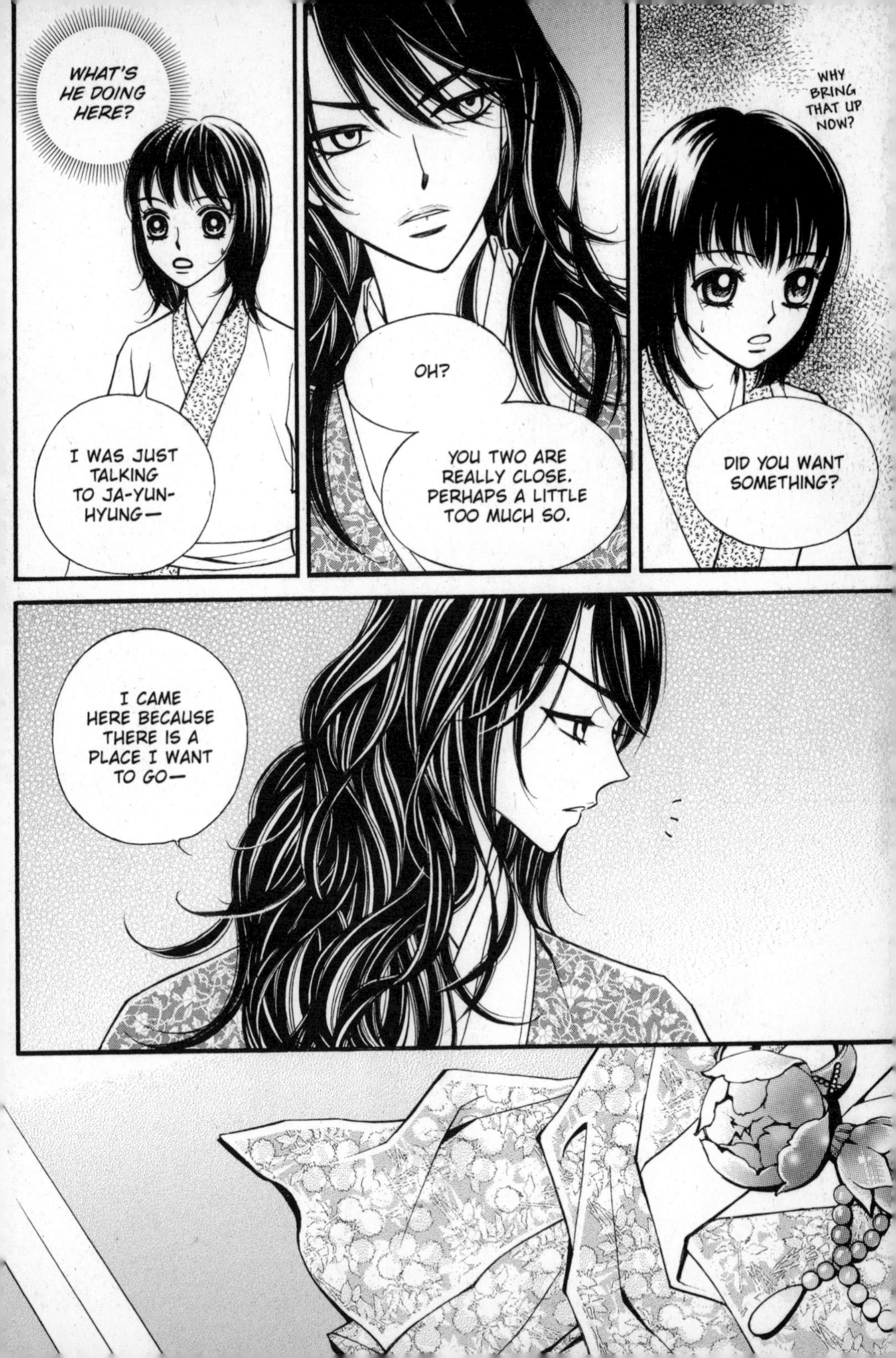
WHAT'S HE DOING HERE?
I WAS JUST TALKING TO JA-YUN-HYUNG—
OH?
YOU TWO ARE REALLY CLOSE. PERHAPS A LITTLE TOO MUCH SO.
WHY BRING THAT UP NOW?
DID YOU WANT SOMETHING?
I CAME HERE BECAUSE THERE IS A PLACE I WANT TO GO—

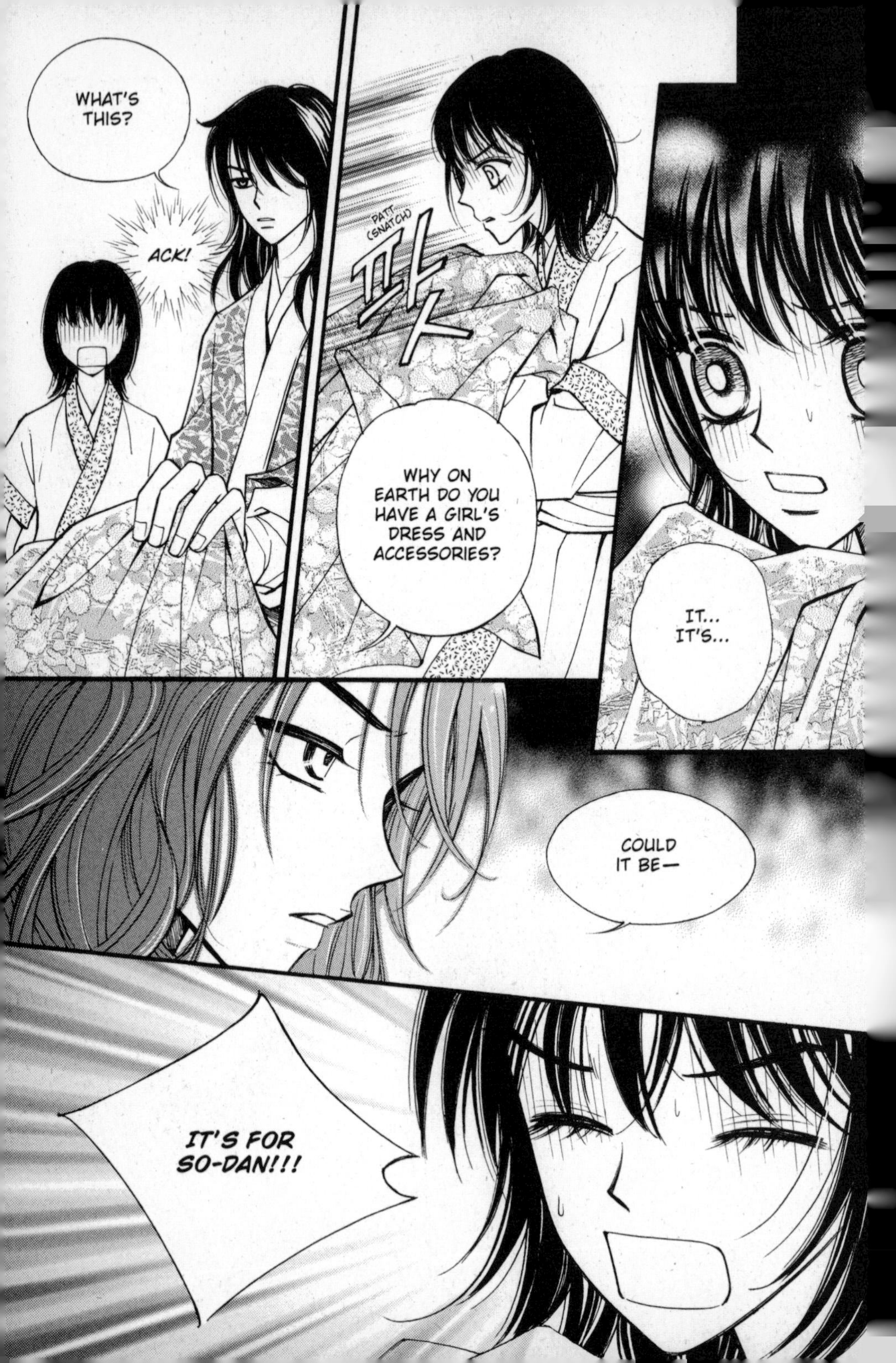
WHAT'S THIS?
ACK!
PATT (SNATCH)
WHY ON EARTH DO YOU HAVE A GIRL'S DRESS AND ACCESSORIES?
IT... IT'S...
COULD IT BE—
IT'S FOR SO-DAN!!!

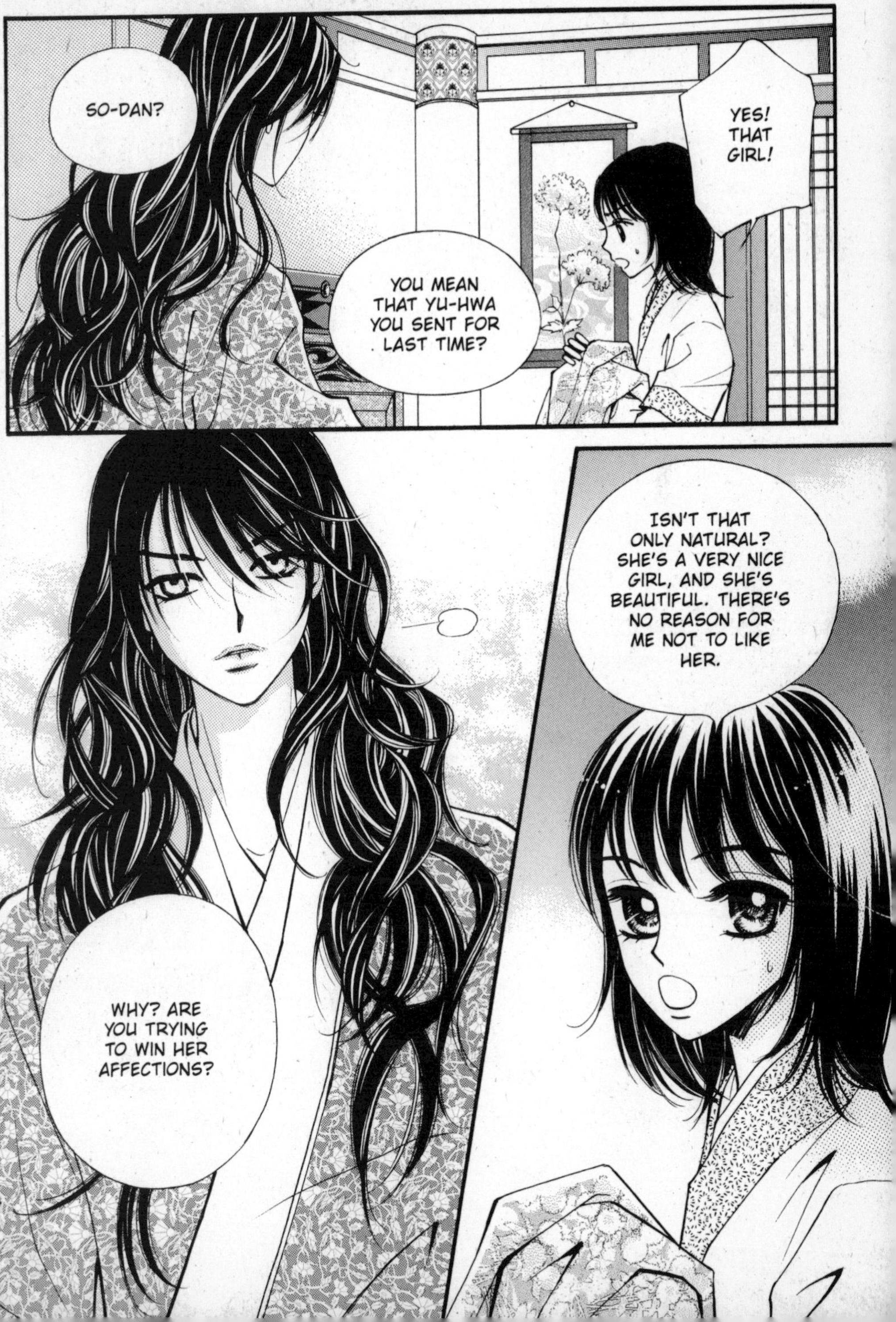
SO-DAN?
YOU MEAN THAT YU-HWA YOU SENT FOR LAST TIME?
YES! THAT GIRL!
WHY? ARE YOU TRYING TO WIN HER AFFECTIONS?
ISN'T THAT ONLY NATURAL? SHE'S A VERY NICE GIRL, AND SHE'S BEAUTIFUL. THERE'S NO REASON FOR ME NOT TO LIKE HER.

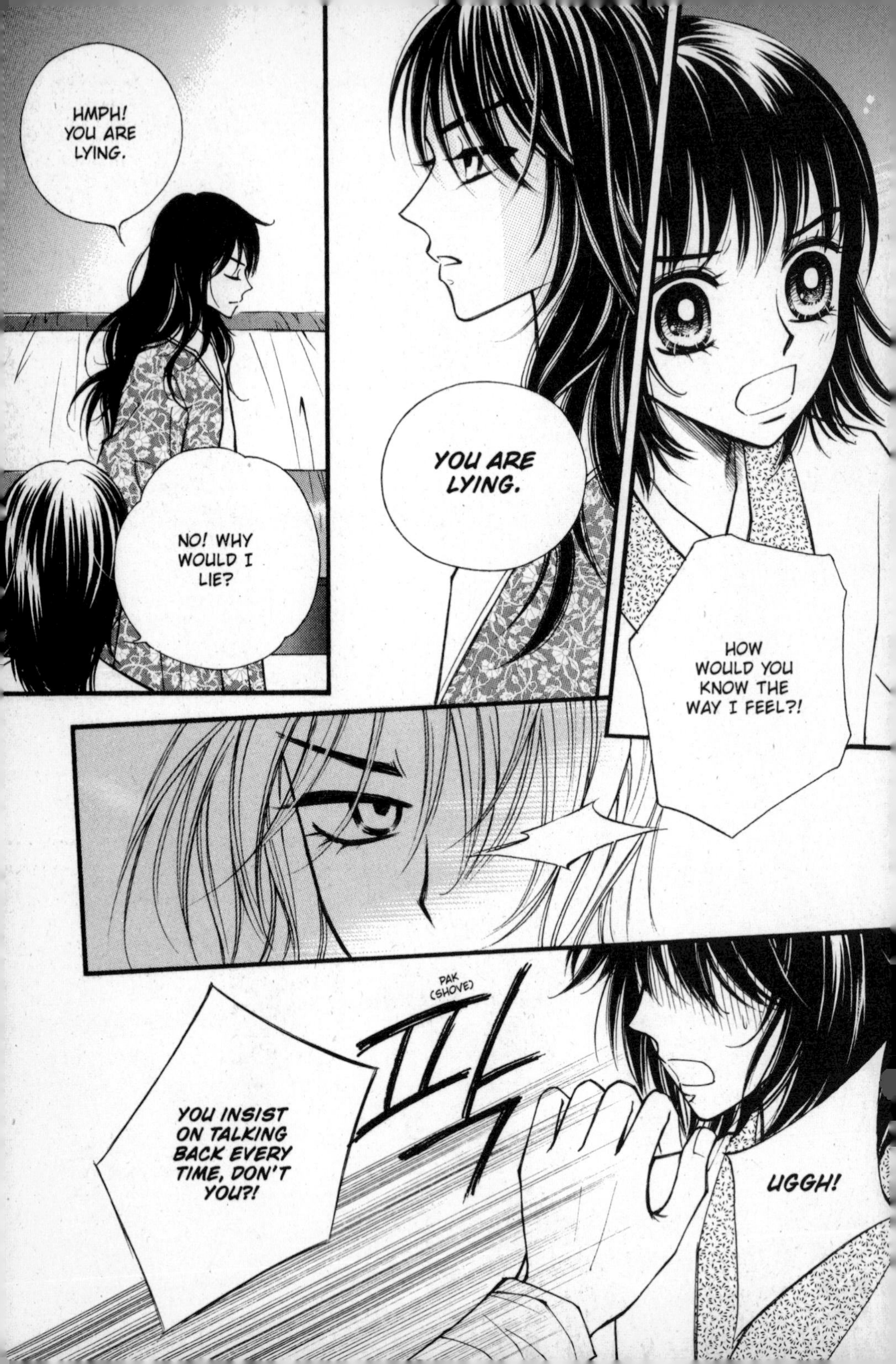
HMPH! YOU ARE LYING.
NO! WHY WOULD I LIE?
YOU ARE LYING.
HOW WOULD YOU KNOW THE WAY I FEEL?!
PAK (SHOVE)
YOU INSIST ON TALKING BACK EVERY TIME, DON'T YOU?!
UGGH!

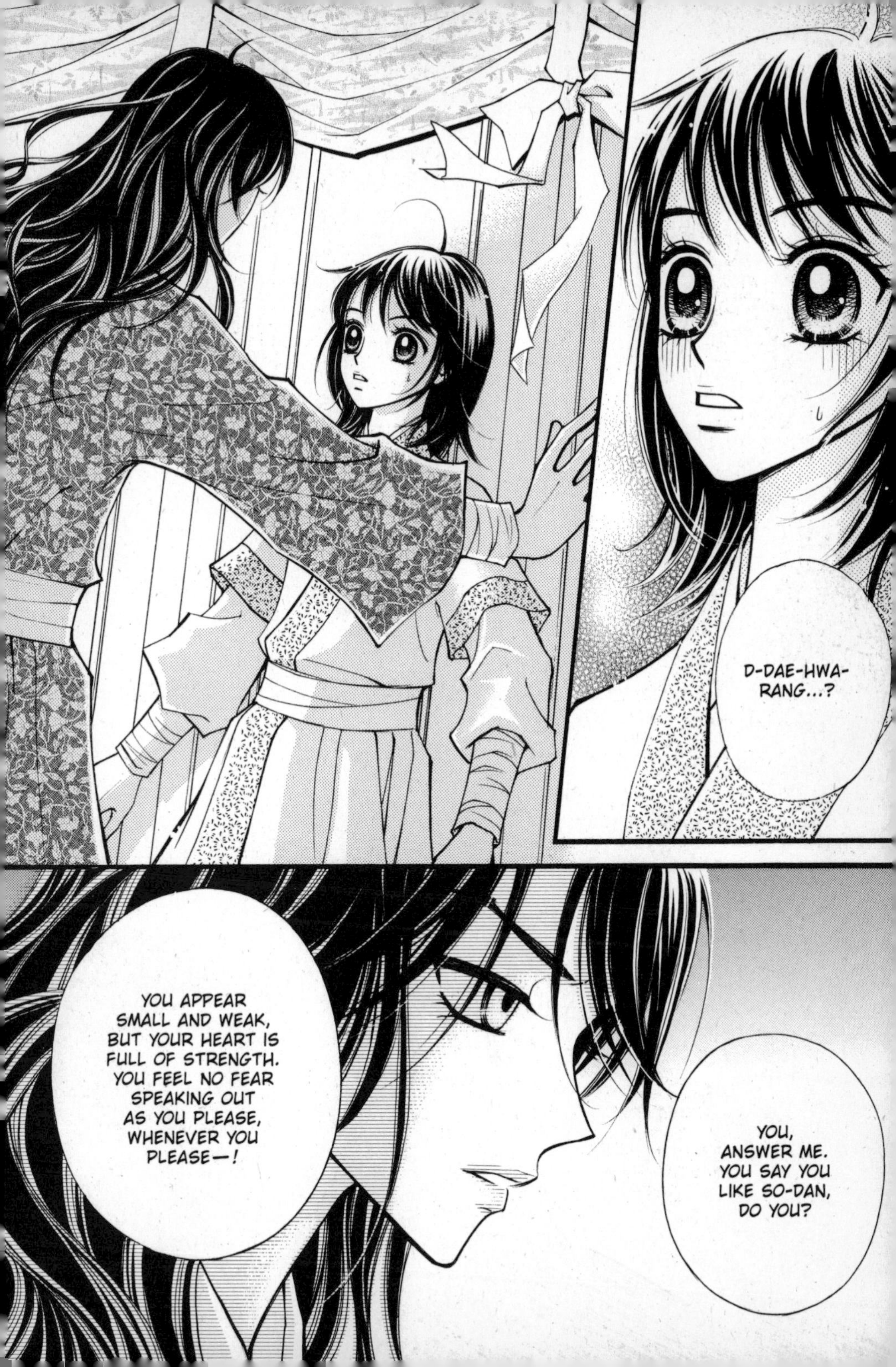
D-DAE-HWA-RANG...?
YOU APPEAR SMALL AND WEAK, BUT YOUR HEART IS FULL OF STRENGTH. YOU FEEL NO FEAR SPEAKING OUT AS YOU PLEASE, WHENEVER YOU PLEASE—!
YOU, ANSWER ME. YOU SAY YOU LIKE SO-DAN, DO YOU?

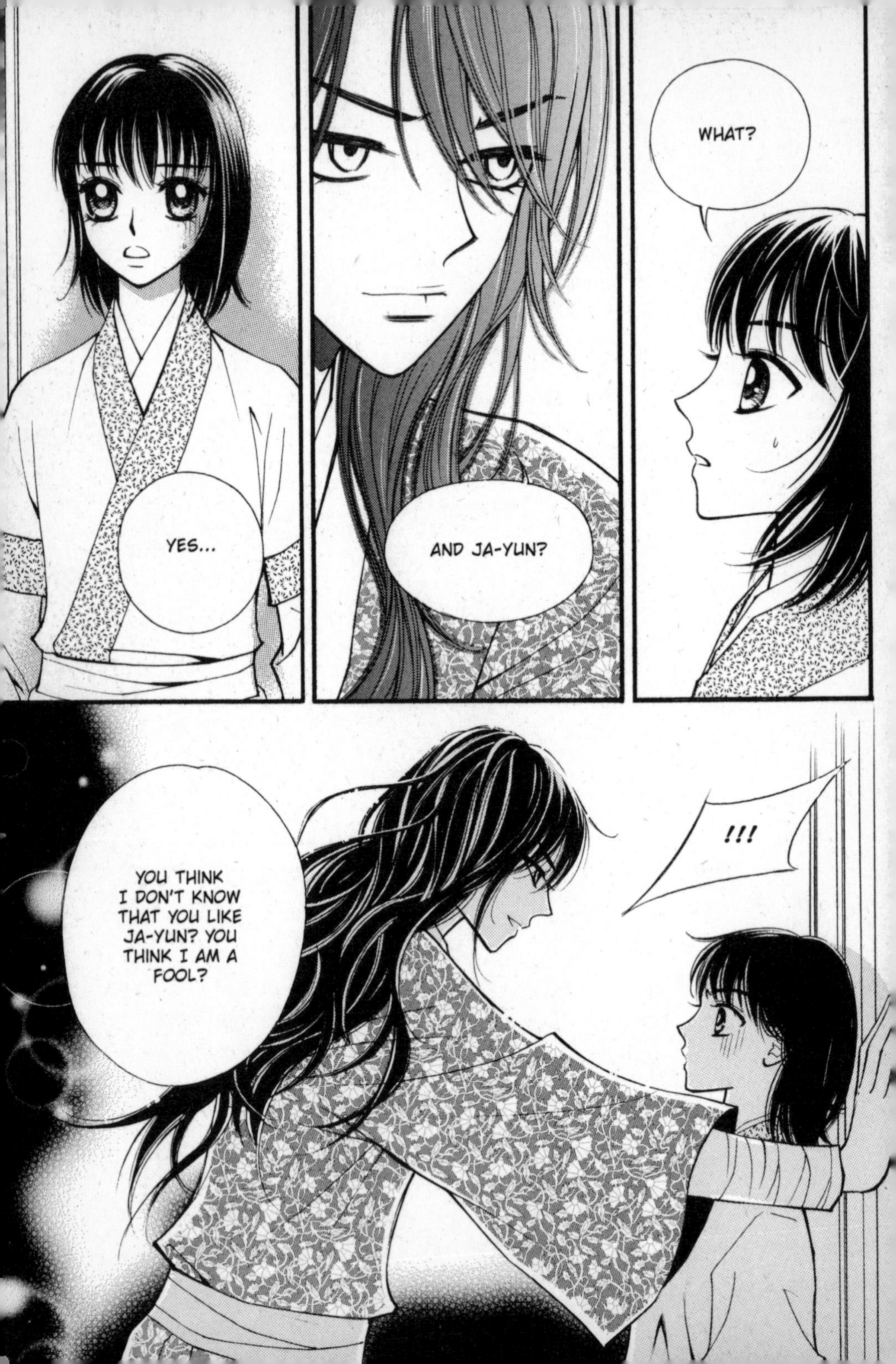
YES...
AND JA-YUN?
WHAT?
YOU THINK I DON'T KNOW THAT YOU LIKE JA-YUN? YOU THINK I AM A FOOL?
!!!

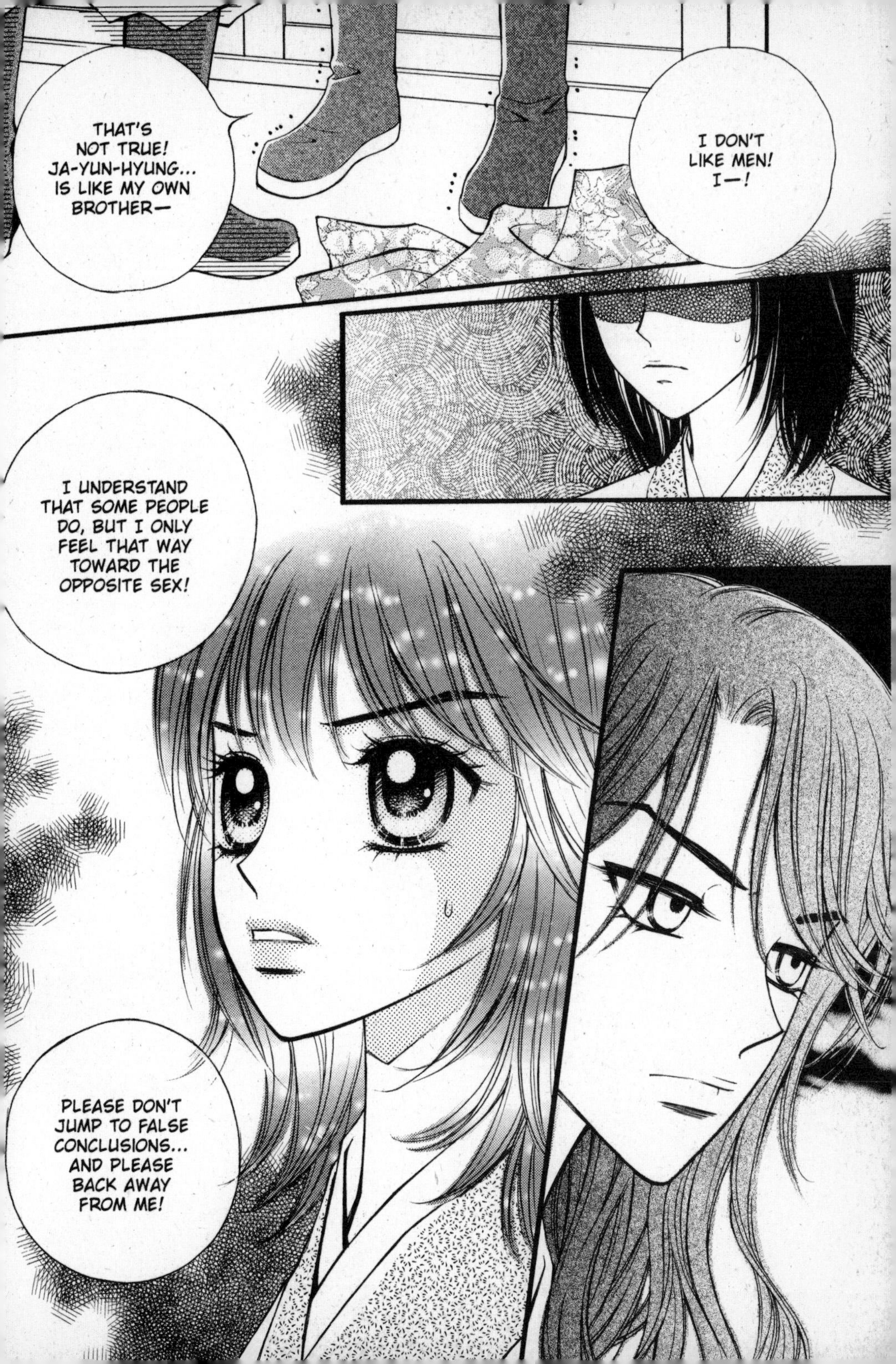
THAT'S NOT TRUE! JA-YUN-HYUNG... IS LIKE MY OWN BROTHER—
I DON'T LIKE MEN! I—!
I UNDERSTAND THAT SOME PEOPLE DO, BUT I ONLY FEEL THAT WAY TOWARD THE OPPOSITE SEX!
PLEASE DON'T JUMP TO FALSE CONCLUSIONS... AND PLEASE BACK AWAY FROM ME!

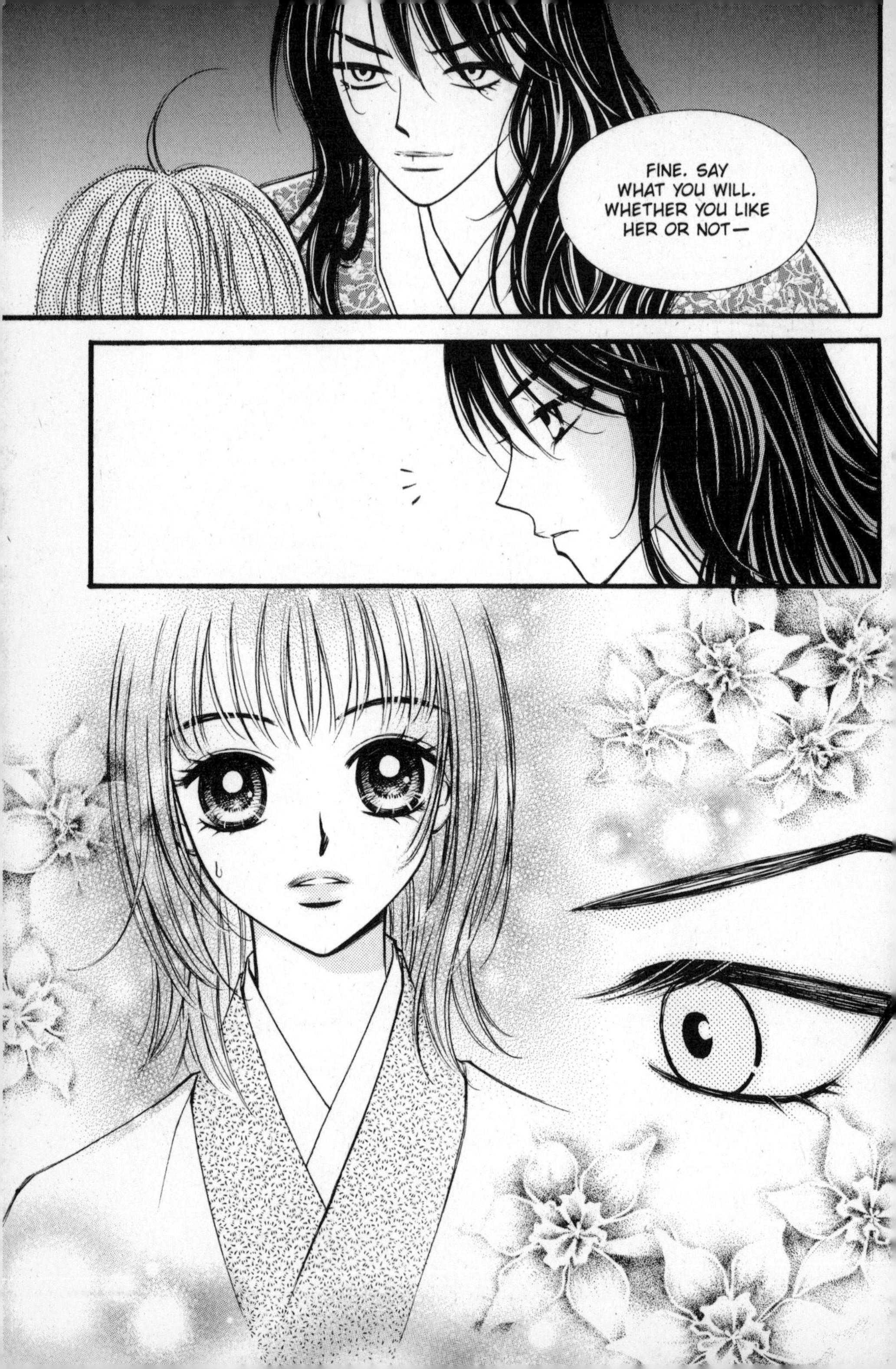
FINE. SAY WHAT YOU WILL. WHETHER YOU LIKE HER OR NOT—

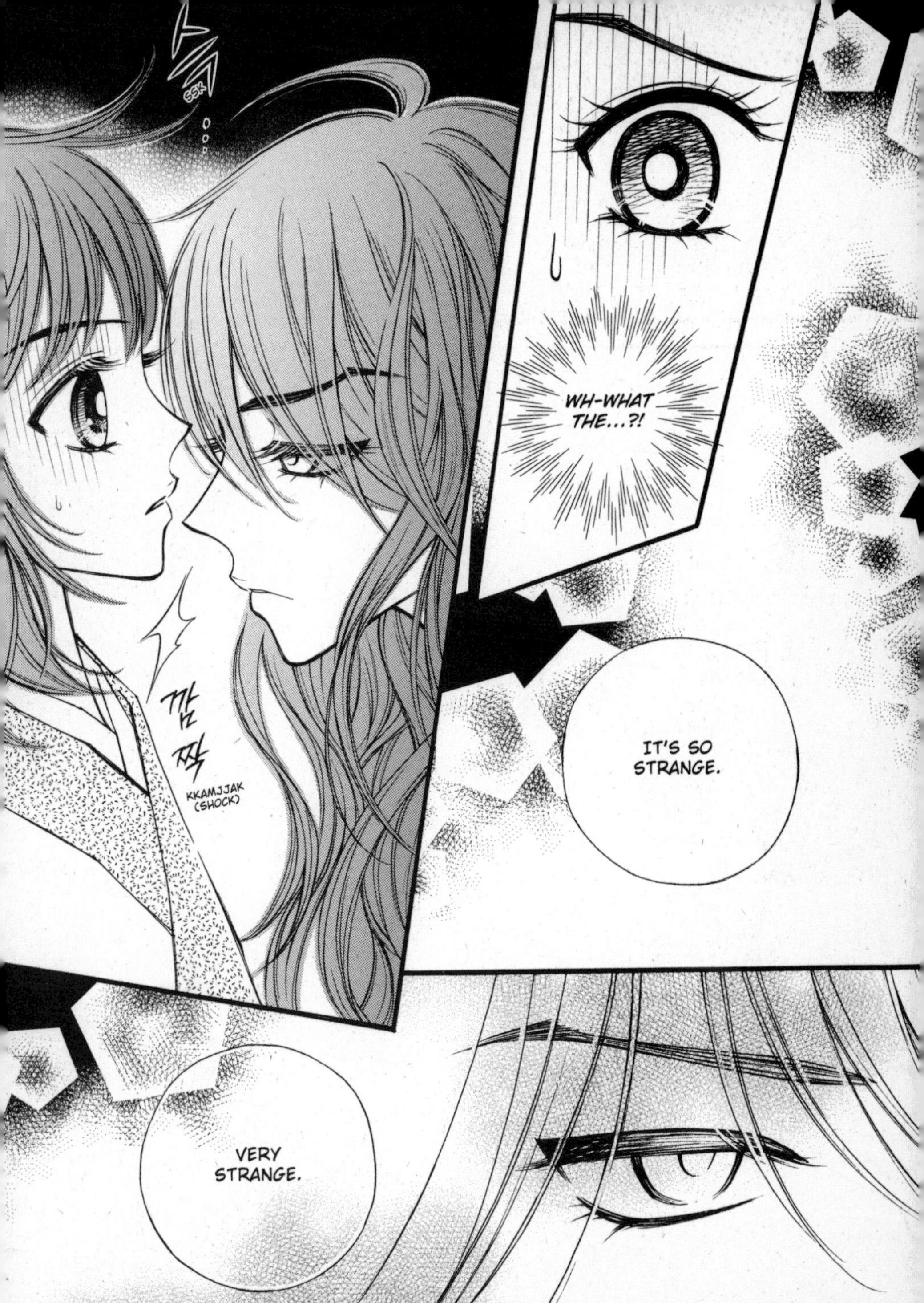
SSK
깜짝
KKAMJJAK (SHOCK)
WH-WHAT THE...?!
IT'S SO STRANGE.
VERY STRANGE.

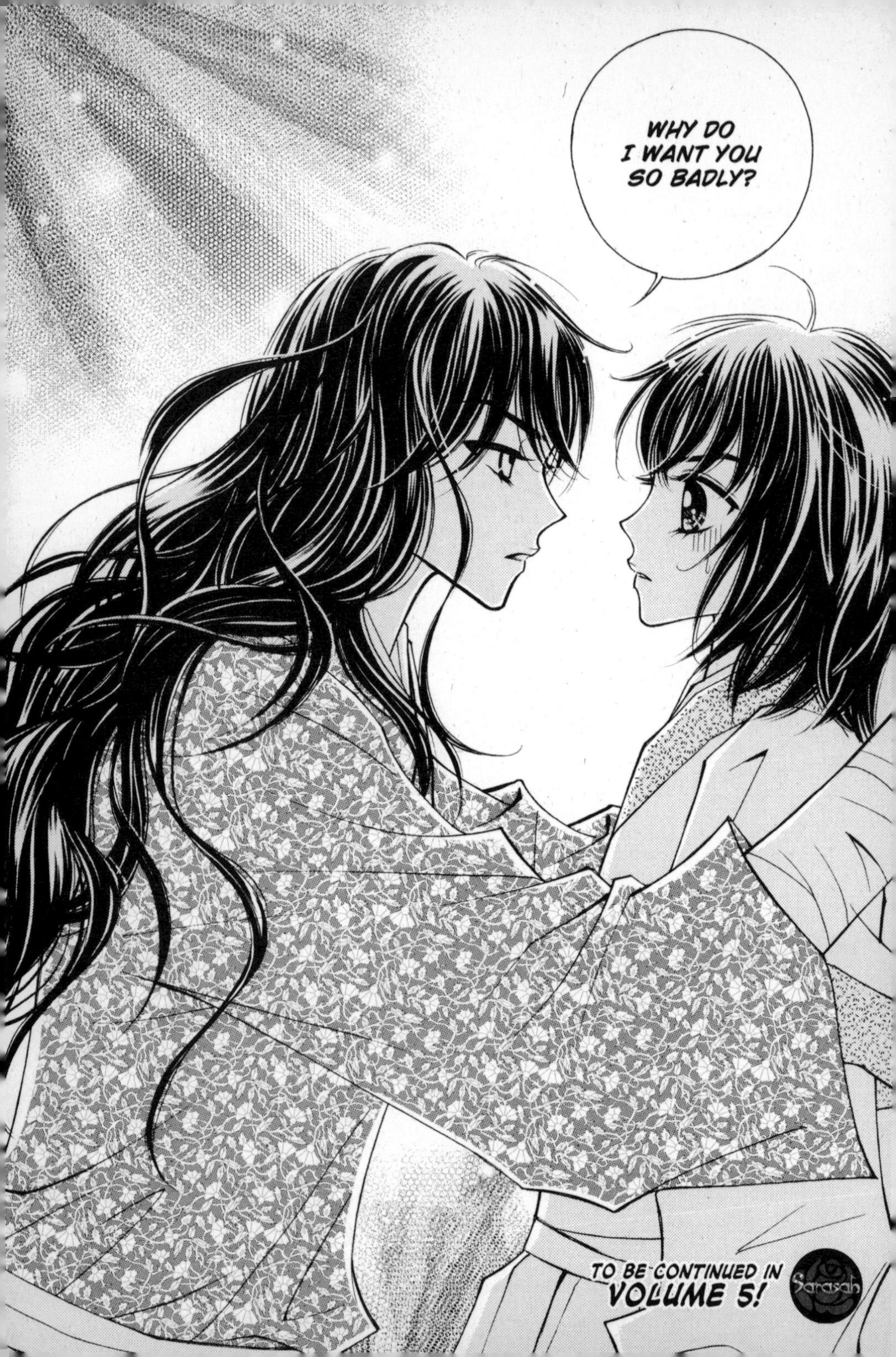
WHY DO I WANT YOU SO BADLY?
TO BE CONTINUED IN VOLUME 5!

TRANSLATION AND HISTORICAL NOTES

GENERAL NOTES

Three Kingdoms: Long ago, the Korean penninsula was made up of three major kingdoms: Goguryeo, Baekje, and Shilla, where *Sarasah* takes place. The Three Kingdoms Period lasted from 67 BC to 668 AD, when Shilla joined with China to conquer the other two kingdoms. As Shilla's power declined in the late 800s, the united kingdoms were claimed by Goryeo. The Goryeo dynasty ruled Korea until it was defeated by the Joseon dynasty in 1392. The Joseon Period lasted until 1910, when the Korean Empire was annexed by Japan.

Hwa-Rang-Do: An elite group of youths in Shilla. It was an educational institution as well as a social club where members, who were mostly sons and daughters of nobility, gathered for all aspects of study. This group developed into a more military organization and was most famous for its members' exceptional archery skills.

Pung-Wol-Ju: The head of Hwa-Rang-Do.

Hwa-Rang: A leader within Hwa-Rang-Do. (-Rang is added as a suffix to one's name, i.e. Bub-Min-Rang.) Each Hwa-Rang has many Nang-Do beneath him.

Nang-Do: A term referring to a member of the Hwa-Rang-Do.

Nang-Meun (or Seondo-Meun or Seon-Meun)*:* A training place for Hwa-Rang.

Page 38
Yu-Hwa: If a peasant girl was especially beautiful, she was allowed to join the Nang-Meun and become a Yu-Hwa. They provided entertainment and sexual favors for the Hwa-Rang.

Page 61
-hyung: A suffix used by boys to address an older brother or older brother figure.

Page 70
-nim: An honorific suffix used to convey respect to the recipient.

Big City Lights, Big City Romance

Jae-Gyu is overwhelmed when she moves from her home in the country to the city. Will she be able to survive in the unforgiving world of celebrities and millionaires?

Gong GooGoo

Sugarholic

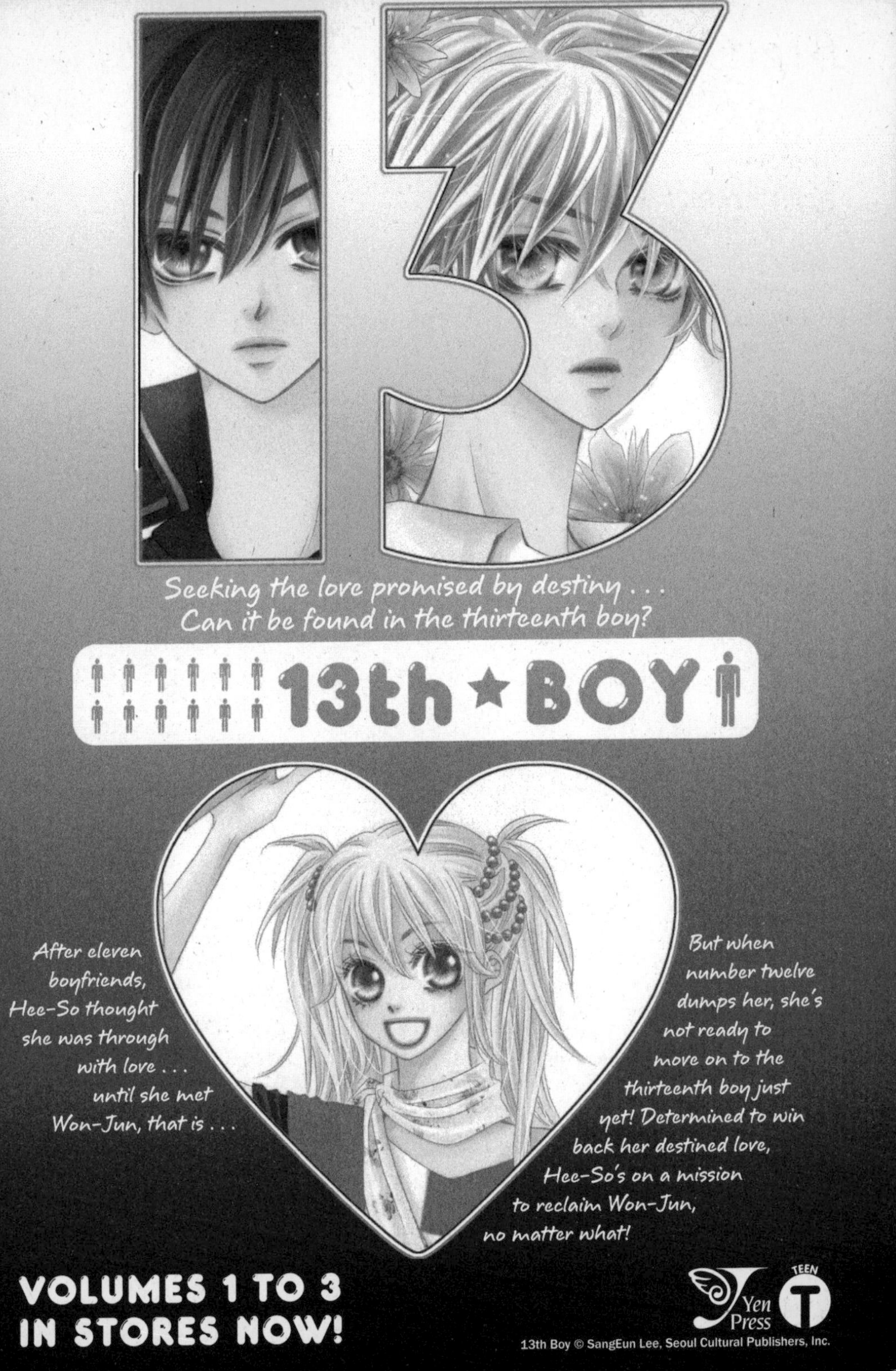

Seeking the love promised by destiny . . .
Can it be found in the thirteenth boy?
13th ★ BOY
After eleven boyfriends, Hee-So thought she was through with love . . . until she met Won-Jun, that is . . .
But when number twelve dumps her, she's not ready to move on to the thirteenth boy just yet! Determined to win back her destined love, Hee-So's on a mission to reclaim Won-Jun, no matter what!
VOLUMES 1 TO 3
IN STORES NOW!
Yen Press
TEEN
T
13th Boy © SangEun Lee, Seoul Cultural Publishers, Inc.

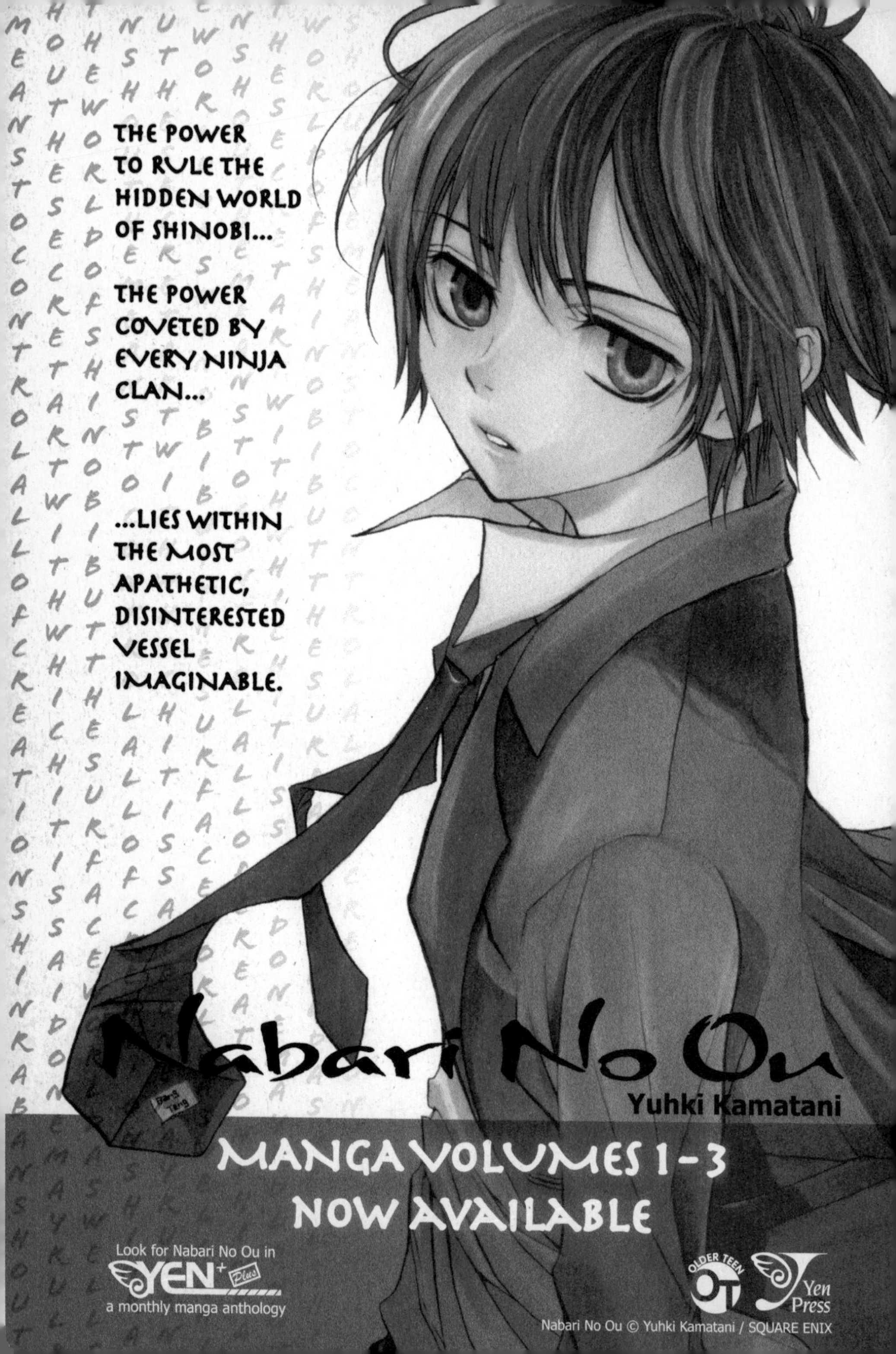
THE POWER TO RULE THE HIDDEN WORLD OF SHINOBI...
THE POWER COVETED BY EVERY NINJA CLAN...
...LIES WITHIN THE MOST APATHETIC, DISINTERESTED VESSEL IMAGINABLE.
Nabari No Ou
Yuhki Kamatani
MANGA VOLUMES 1-3
NOW AVAILABLE
Look for Nabari No Ou in
YEN+ Plus
a monthly manga anthology
OLDER TEEN OT
Yen Press
Nabari No Ou © Yuhki Kamatani / SQUARE ENIX

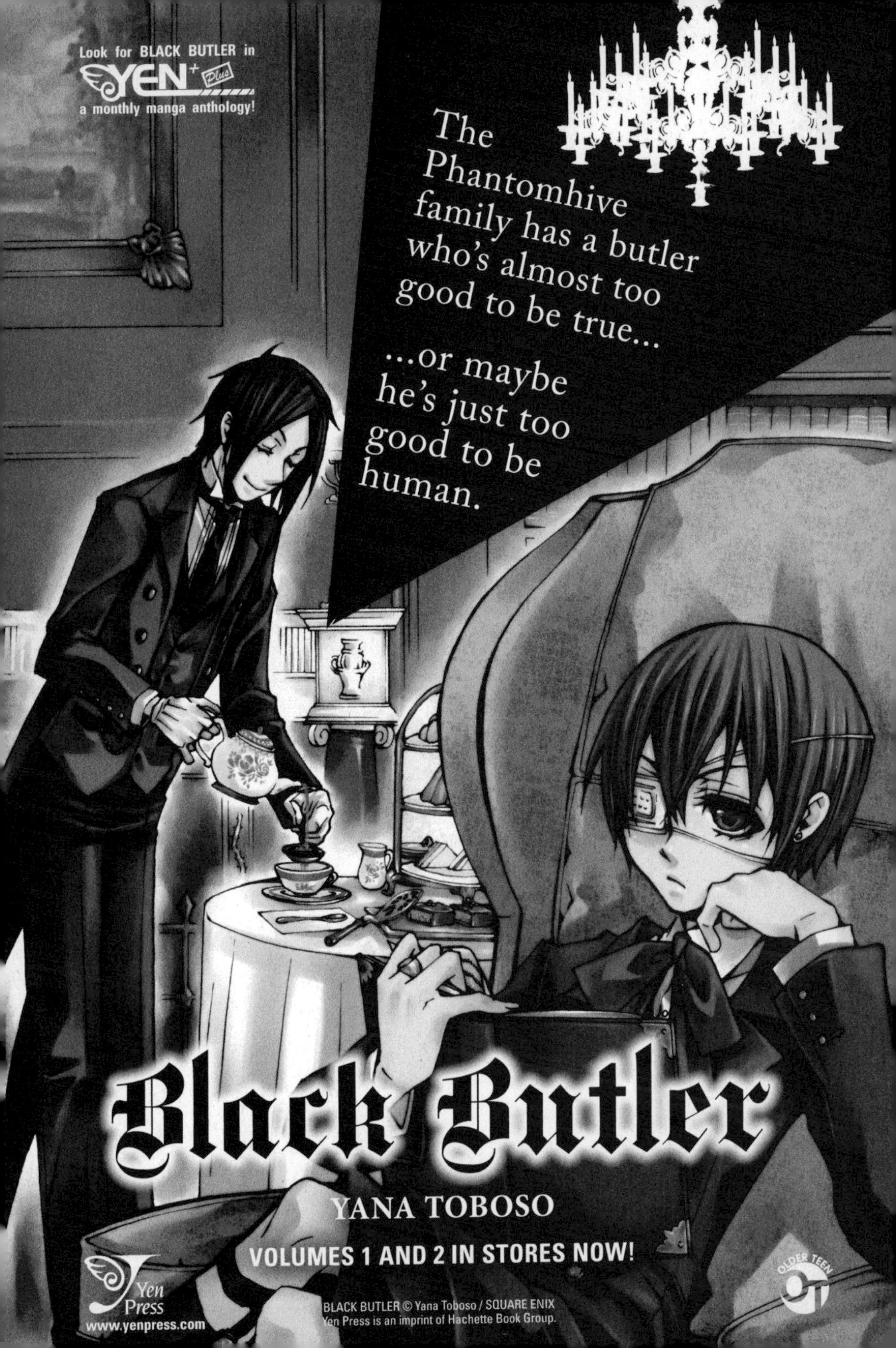
Look for BLACK BUTLER in
YEN+ Plus
a monthly manga anthology!
The Phantomhive family has a butler who's almost too good to be true...
...or maybe he's just too good to be human.
Black Butler
YANA TOBOSO
VOLUMES 1 AND 2 IN STORES NOW!
Yen Press
www.yenpress.com
BLACK BUTLER © Yana Toboso / SQUARE ENIX
Yen Press is an imprint of Hachette Book Group.
OLDER TEEN
OT

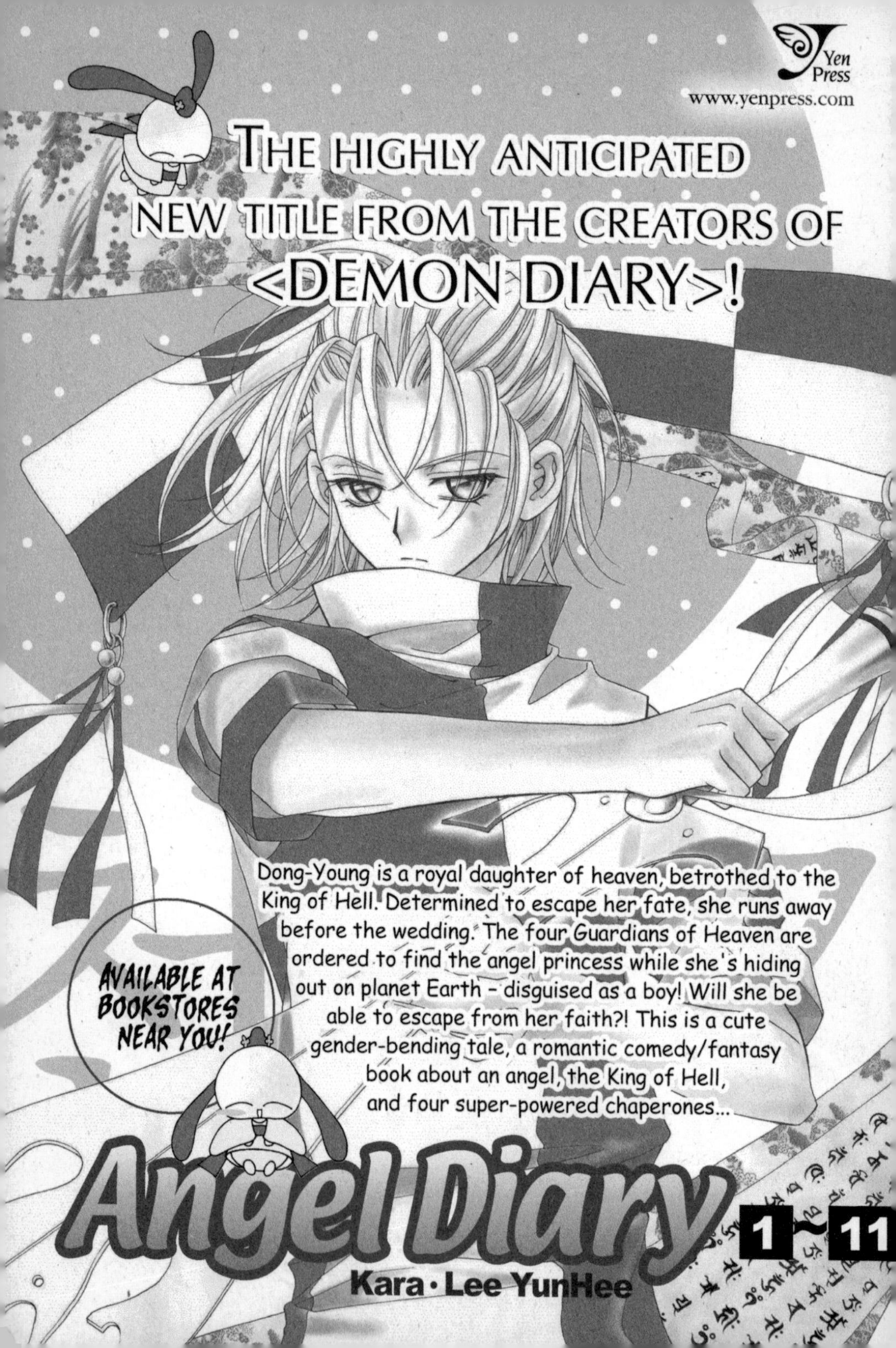
Yen Press
www.yenpress.com
THE HIGHLY ANTICIPATED
NEW TITLE FROM THE CREATORS OF
<DEMON DIARY>!
Dong-Young is a royal daughter of heaven, betrothed to the King of Hell. Determined to escape her fate, she runs away before the wedding. The four Guardians of Heaven are ordered to find the angel princess while she's hiding out on planet Earth - disguised as a boy! Will she be able to escape from her faith?! This is a cute gender-bending tale, a romantic comedy/fantasy book about an angel, the King of Hell, and four super-powered chaperones...
AVAILABLE AT BOOKSTORES NEAR YOU!
Angel Diary
1~11
Kara · Lee YunHee

Yen
Press
www.yenpress.com

Becoming the princess... Isn't that every girl's dream?!

Monarchy rule ended long ago in Korea, but there are still other countries with kings, queens, princes and princesses. What if Korea had continued monarchism? What if all the beautiful palaces, which are now only historical relics, were actually filled with people? What if the glamorous royal family still maintained the palace customs? Welcome to a world where Korea still has the royal family living in their everyday lives! Only for this one high school girl, Chae-Kyung, is this a tragedy, since she has to marry the prince — who apparently is a total bastard!

THE ROYAL PALACE
Goong
vol.1 ~ 8

Park SoHee

A totally new Arabian nights, where Scheherazade is a guy!

Everyone knows the story of Scheherazade and her wonderful tales from the Arabian Nights. For one thousand and one nights, the stories that she created entertained the mad Sultan and eventually saved her life. In this version, Scheherazade is a guy who disguises himself as a woman to save his sister from the mad Sultan. When he puts his life on the line, what kind of strange and unique stories will he tell? This new twist on one of the greatest classical tales might just keep you awake for another ONE THOUSAND AND ONE NIGHTS!

Yen Press
www.yenpress.com

Available at bookstores near you!

One thousand and one nights

1~10

Han SeungHee · Jeon JinSeok

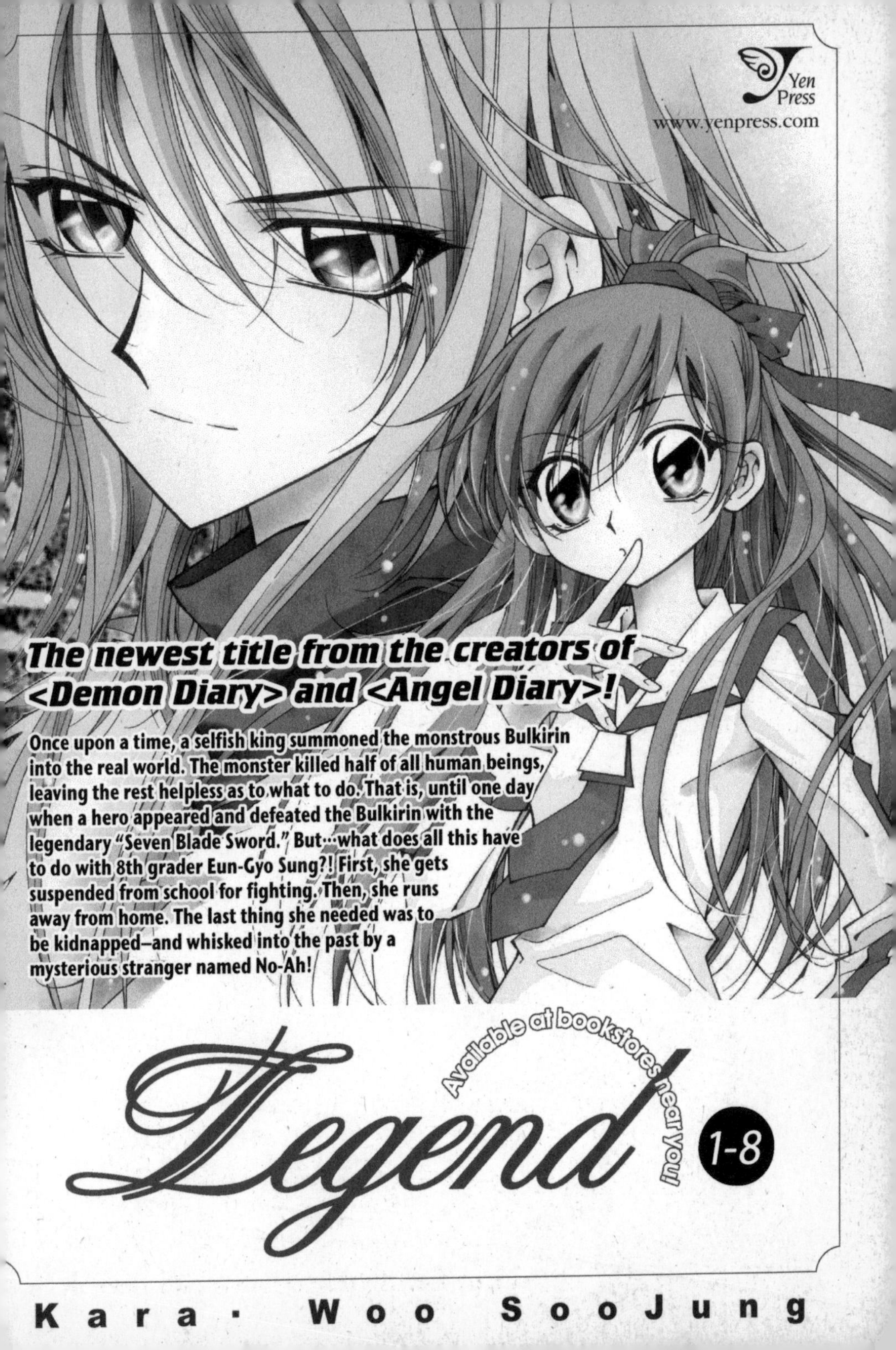
Yen Press
www.yenpress.com
The newest title from the creators of
<Demon Diary> and <Angel Diary>!
Once upon a time, a selfish king summoned the monstrous Bulkirin into the real world. The monster killed half of all human beings, leaving the rest helpless as to what to do. That is, until one day when a hero appeared and defeated the Bulkirin with the legendary "Seven Blade Sword." But…what does all this have to do with 8th grader Eun-Gyo Sung?! First, she gets suspended from school for fighting. Then, she runs away from home. The last thing she needed was to be kidnapped–and whisked into the past by a mysterious stranger named No-Ah!
Legend
1-8
Available at bookstores near you!
Kara · Woo SooJung

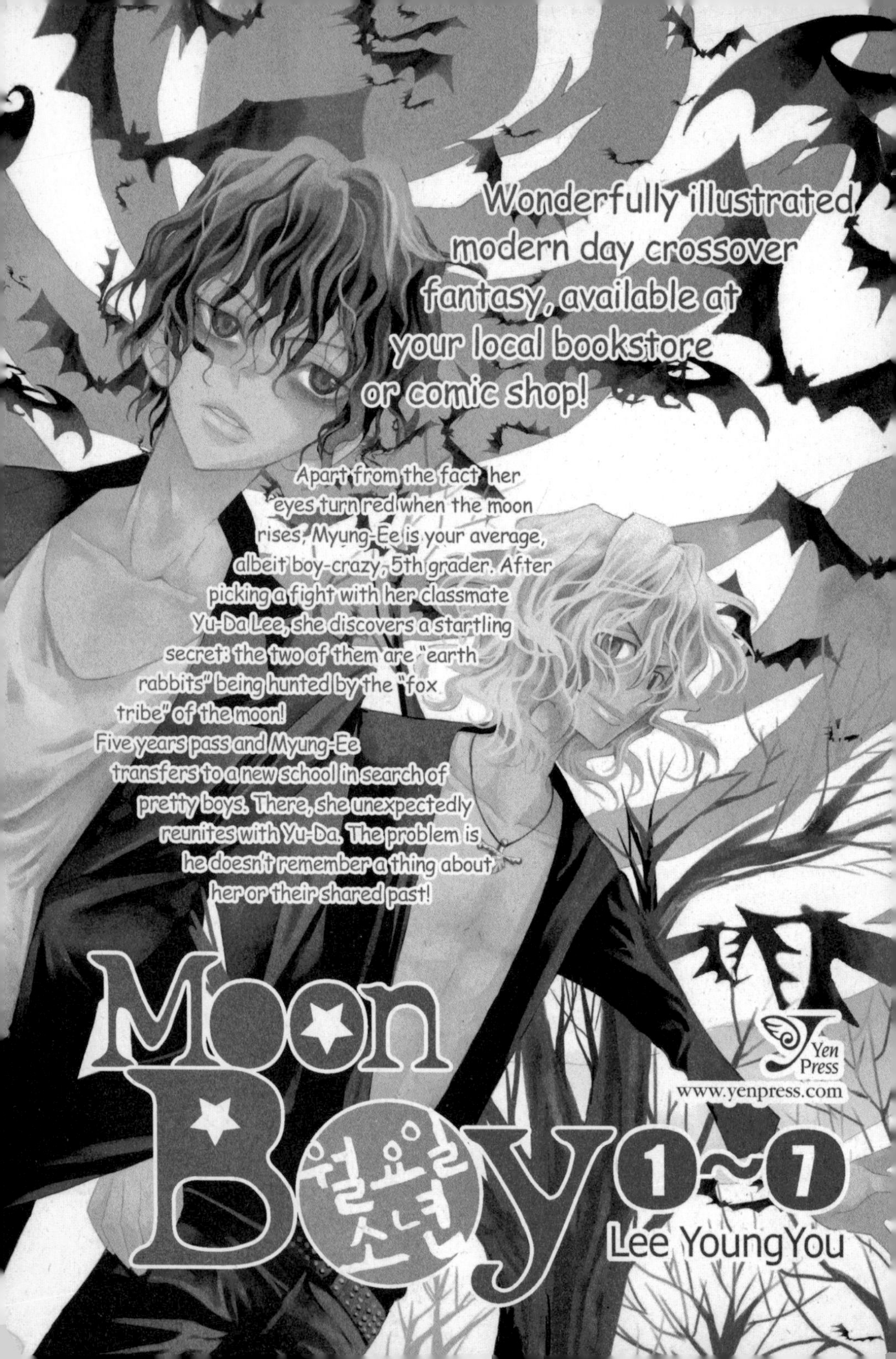
Wonderfully illustrated modern day crossover fantasy, available at your local bookstore or comic shop!
Apart from the fact her eyes turn red when the moon rises, Myung-Ee is your average, albeit boy-crazy, 5th grader. After picking a fight with her classmate Yu-Da Lee, she discovers a startling secret: the two of them are "earth rabbits" being hunted by the "fox tribe" of the moon!
Five years pass and Myung-Ee transfers to a new school in search of pretty boys. There, she unexpectedly reunites with Yu-Da. The problem is he doesn't remember a thing about her or their shared past!
Moon Boy
월요일 소년
1~7
Lee YoungYou
Yen Press
www.yenpress.com

Yen
Press

www.yenpress.com

THE MOST BEAUTIFUL FACE, THE PERFECT BODY,
AND A SINCERE PERSONALITY...THAT'S WHAT HYE-MIN HWANG HAS.
NATURALLY, SHE'S THE CENTER OF EVERYONE'S ATTENTION.
EVERY BOY IN SCHOOL LOVES HER, WHILE EVERY GIRL HATES HER OUT OF JEALOUSY.
EVERY SINGLE DAY, SHE HAS TO ENDURE TORTURES AND HARDSHIPS FROM THE GIRLS.

A PRETTY FACE COMES WITH A PRICE.

THERE IS NOTHING MORE SATISFYING THAN GETTING THEM BACK.
WELL, EXCEPT FOR ONE PROBLEM . . . HER SECRET CRUSH, JUNG-YUN.
BECAUSE OF HIM, SHE HAS TO HIDE HER CYNICAL AND DARK SIDE
AND DAILY PUT ON AN INNOCENT FACE. THEN ONE DAY, SHE FINDS OUT
THAT HE DISLIKES HER ANYWAY!! WHAT?! THAT'S IT! NO MORE NICE GIRL!
AND THE FIRST VICTIM OF HER RAGE IS A PLAYBOY SHE JUST MET, MA-HA.

vol.1~9

Cynical Orange

Yun JiUn

SARASAH ④

RYU RYANG

Translation: June Um

English Adaptation and Lettering: Abigail Blackman

SARASAH, Vol. 4 © 2008 Ryu Ryang. All rights reserved. First published in Korea in 2008 by Seoul Cultural Publishers, Inc. English translation rights arranged by Seoul Cultural Publishers, Inc.

English translation © 2010 Hachette Book Group, Inc.

Yen Press
Hachette Book Group
237 Park Avenue, New York, NY 10017

www.HachetteBookGroup.com
www.YenPress.com

Yen Press is an imprint of Hachette Book Group, Inc. The Yen Press name and logo are trademarks of Hachette Book Group, Inc.

First Yen Press Edition: May 2010

ISBN: 978-0-316-07784-2

10 9 8 7 6 5 4 3 2 1

BVG

Printed in the United States of America